# The Thomas Street Horror

Also by Raymond Paul

*Perception and Persuasion* (with P. W. Goione)
*Who Murdered Mary Rogers*

# The Thomas Street Horror

## An Historical Novel of Murder

*Raymond Paul*

The Viking Press   New York

First published in 1982 by The Viking Press
625 Madison Avenue, New York, N.Y. 10022
Published simultaneously in Canada by
Penguin Books Canada Limited

Grateful acknowledgment is made to the University of Michigan Press
for permission to reprint selections from *Hesiod,* translated by
Richmond Lattimore, 1959.

Library of Congress Cataloging in Publication Data
Paul, Raymond.
The Thomas Street horror.
I. Title.
PS3566.A8266T5      813'.54      81-51889
ISBN 0-670-70371-0                 AACR2

Printed in the United States of America
Set in Garamond

Map by Paul J. Pugliese, GCI

For Bill Paul
*my brother, the reporter*

Let the story be arranged like this: let the evidence not all be thrown at us in a lump, with comments beforehand; but let it grow up as a story unfolds, so that each new turn is a surprise to us as it was to those who saw it happen. Let there be no nods or elbow-joggings from the author, no hints, no speculations. But let the clues be scattered shrewdly, for the reader to find if he cares to do so. Let there be half a dozen persons, each suspected in turn, and each in turn proved innocent. Let there be a spice of terror, of dark skies and evil things. And at intervals, over our pipes and glasses, let us discuss the evidence.

John Dickson Carr

The events portrayed in the pages which follow are drawn from and based on documented fact.

The Author

# Contents

Book I   New-York Winter, 1835

Book II   Murder in Thomas Street

## Book III   The Trial

# BOOK I

## New-York Winter
## 1835

# 1  The Hoboken Ferry

I crossed to New York on a brisk November morning, the nineteenth. The coach had arrived in Hoboken the evening before in darkness, compelling the passengers to spend the night at the Phoenix Hotel, where the beds are too soft but the atmosphere in the taproom is tolerably congenial. I left my trunk in the care of the host until I could find suitable accommodations in the city and tipped him, too handsomely I suspect, judging from the manner in which he immediately began to slabber and scrape.

I rose early the next morning, having slept little, and shaved off my moustache. This was not a decision easily reached or executed, for it required the careful manipulation of razor and lighted candle for several minutes at great personal peril to be certain I had done for each of some two dozen hairs. I put on clean linen and my new clothes: the brown frock coat, black Valencia vest, fashionably cut black trousers, and brown boots. Surveying my appointments in the mirror, I laid to rest the question as to whether I was ready for New York.

I breakfasted and took leave of my landlord, who directed me to the ferry house. He bowed me out of his establishment. I had not gone three steps when I turned back on a sudden impulse and said, "Today, sir, is my twentieth birthday."

"Sir," he replied, bowing again and rubbing his bald head, "I would that it was mine."

Despite the bitter cold I stood at the ferry rail, feeling salt spray sting my face and gulping the wet air like a drowning man. Even in winter the North River is a floating city. Great trains of freight barges glide past, bursting with cargoes of grain, produce, or lumber for the shipyards of South Street.They are towed by powerful tugs and they trail in their wakes the tiny bumboats which are the general stores of the river. To the south you can see the sails of the packet ships bound for New Orleans, London, Liverpool, and Le Havre. They slip down the East River and anchor in the mouth of the Hudson off Castle Garden and the Battery, waiting for a favorable wind to carry them to Sandy Hook. When the flood tide slackens and the ship swings to the wind and the order is given to man the windlass and heave short, then the crew breaks into a pungent briny chanty that would stir the most land-locked heart.

For a time a Hudson River sloop, one of the few not yet driven from the river by steam, closed and ran alongside the ferry, her huge spread of canvas billowing from the single mast. As she passed, her crewmen sang out to me and waved. I removed my hat and bowed deeply, which brought another cheer. From upriver one of the great Albany night boats steamed toward us, her bright red and yellow pennants flying, black smoke belching from her stacks. "It's the *Champlain*," said a man beside me. "She's beaten the *Nimrod* again I see."

The voice was deep with a slight but distinct Irish brogue, so that I was surprised to find its owner dressed as a gentleman. His cloak, wrapped tightly around him with its collar turned up against the wind, hid the lower part of his face. I could make out a pair of shrewd brown eyes above a long, sloping nose and a close-cropped moustache lining his upper lip. He watched the steamboat bear down on us.

"Steam, speed, and profit," he said. "The cargo is a jumble and those passengers not lashed to their bunks have been swept overboard, but the *Champlain* has beaten the *Nimrod* to her berth. Have you been to Albany?"

The question surprised me. "No, sir."

"Well, go by schooner, if you can find one. With a little luck and a wicked head wind you'll have to lay over in Poughkeepsie. There is a girl named Peggie in Poughkeepsie . . ." His voice trailed off.

"Sir," I said, "if you are familar with the streets of the city, could you direct me to the offices of the New York *Sun?*"

"Do you have business with that journal?" my companion inquired mildly.

"I am a journalist. I carry a Letter of Introduction to Mr. Benjamin H. Day, the *Sun's* proprietor."

His eyes wrinkled slightly at the corners. "Well, then," he said, "when we dock, walk one block south to Vesey Street and east to Broadway. Cross Broadway and walk northeast on Park Row. The *Sun* will be on your right at Spruce and Nassau." He paused and then asked, "By the way, are you temperance?"

"No, sir!" The suggestion was appalling.

He nodded. "Good. The temperance movement has done almost as much mischief as Presbyterianism. But, be warned, Day is teetotal. He is certain to inquire as to your sentiments. My suggested reply is that you will drink milk only when you cannot get water. Are you Jackson man or Whig?"

"Truly neither. I don't—"

"Better and better," he interrupted. "Day despises both. Do you know Colonel James Watson Webb or Mr. James Gordon Bennett?"

I shook my head.

"Enough to know that the first is the devil incarnate and the second his only begotten son. That should prepare you for Day's inquisition. Incidentally, should you be asked your principal interest, answer murder."

"Barclay Street!" a voice sang out from above us. "All ashore! Barclay Street!"

I thought I had misunderstood him. I repeated, "Murder?"

"Oh, well . . ." He waved a gloved hand. "Pig stealing, wife beating, murder. They're hanging Manuel Fernandez this morning in the Bellevue yard, by the way." He shook my hand. "Good luck."

"Look here," I said, "I'm David Cordor. I have no quarters yet but as soon as I'm settled I'd like to repay your kindness."

"I accept," he said, drawing his hand away. The ferry grazed the slip, throwing me against the rail. Shouting men ran along the dock, catching and securing lines. When I looked again the Irishman was gone.

# 2  *A Hanging*

I had seen Philadelphia of course, and been to Boston once with my uncle when he was living, but no American with a soul can stand on Broadway at the juncture of Park Row and Vesey Street and not feel himself in the heart of the world's greatest city. The streets throb with activity. The very buildings seem to breathe. To be there on the morning of my twentieth birthday in a new suit of clothes with a Letter of Introduction in my pocket was just about as much as I could stand.

The sights and sounds of the living city washed over me. The cries and chants of the hawkers mixed with the shouts of the teamsters, the rattle of carts and wagons, and the clatter of the horses' hooves on the cobblestones. There are omnibuses everywhere, huge stages drawn by two matched teams which carry ten or twelve passengers inside and another two on the box. They lumber up and down Broadway, taking on riders at one corner, discharging others at the next. The rickety hansom cabs dash between them and dodge the drays.

The sun glints off the magnificent steeple and marble columns of St. Paul's. Stages and fine carriages draw up to the American Hotel, stand while the horses paw impatiently, and pull away up the avenue. Strollers linger at the bay windows of the shops, inspecting the merchandise through large rectangles of glass. "J. Lowe & Son. Carpeting." "Trapp's Fancy Store." "B. Rush. Tobacconist." Shouts and hammers ring from workmen putting the finishing touches on Mr. Astor's new hotel.

Great elms, beaches, and Lombardy poplars loom beside St. Paul's and wave above the gabled, three-story houses with their brightly painted shutters. Gray smoke rises from the brick chimneys. Boys whistle shrilly for the hansoms to earn a penny and then stand holding the horses while gentlemen mount to the cabs. Steam gusts from the animals' nostrils and rises from their heaving bodies in the cold November air. Old men promenade in sandwich boards and urchins hawk newspapers at the curbs. I called for a paper and was nearly trampled by three ragged boys, one waving the *Sun,* the second the *Herald,* and the third the *Transcript.* I managed to grab a copy of the *Sun* and thrust a penny at one child just as the teeth of one of his companions closed on his wrist and the whole trio tumbled over one another into the gutter in a torrent of shrill, blackguard oaths.

I went into the American Hotel, ordered coffee and crullers, and scanned the paper. I tend to read a journal backward, beginning with the liners and advertisements and concluding at the news and editorial columns. The *Sun* carried a number of liners, each set off by the tiny cut of a ship, shoe, cow, or clock.

A CARD—TO HIGBIES—Mr. Stamler, having retired to private life, would be glad to see his friends, the Higbies, at his house, No. 5 Rivington Street, this afternoon, between the hours of 2 and 5 p.m., to partake of a collation.

Hearty appetite to the Higbies.

SIX CENTS REWARD—Run away from the subscriber, on the 15th of November, Charles Eldridge, an indentured apprentice to the Seegar-Making business, about 16 years of age, 4 feet high, broken back. Had on, when he left, a round jacket and blue pantaloons. The above reward and no charges will be paid for his delivery to
JOHN DIBBEN, No. 354 Bowery.

Silently I wished Charles Eldridge well. What manner of man would betray a fellow creature, made, like him, in the image of his Creator, for a paltry six coppers?

The advertising was dull reading, consisting principally of those ridiculous patent-medicine notices with their dreary letters attesting to countless cures and penned, as always, by "Unsolicited Anonymous." Here and there, however, an ad seemed worth attention.

TRY THEM: And You Will Be Sure to Recommend Your Friends to Buy Them—DR. GOODMAN'S ANTI-GONORRHEAL PILLS!

An item on the second page caught my eye: "Manuel Fernandez, otherwise Richard C. Jackson, convicted of the murder of John Roberts, is to be executed at 10 a.m. this morning, the 19th instant, at the Bellevue Prison, New York." The name of the murderer recalled my nameless Irish friend on the ferry.

Fernandez, according to the story, had killed a fellow sailor for becoming enamored of Fernandez's mistress, one Mrs. Schultz. The culprit was apparently something of a Sinbad, and the *Sun* was serializing his "Life and Adventures." Page 1 headlined installment 6, in which Fernandez was wrecked in a storm off the coast of Wales, and promised further escapades among the African savages. The author was Richard Adams Locke, and I immediately suspected the truthfulness of the article. Like everyone else, I connect Locke's name chiefly with the "Moon Hoax."

It was only three months since the *Sun* had astounded New York, and then the whole country, with the news that Sir John Frederick William Herschel, the most famous astronomer of our time, in his South African observatory, by means of an immense telescope of an entirely new principle, had discovered *life on the moon.* Day after day for weeks the *Sun* published reports, supposedly reprinted from the *Edinburgh Journal of Science,* describing in wonderful detail the lunar vegetation and animal life. Of chief interest were the *vespertiliohomo,* or man-bats, simian creatures with batlike wings which, with carefree abandon, fluttered and fornicated among the flora and fauna.

Even after the hoax was exposed, the *Sun,* with mock solemnity, refused to retract the man-bats without an official denial from Edinburgh or Capetown. It was an open secret, however, that the entire affair was Locke's invention, and I suspect many readers shared my doubts about some of Manuel Fernandez's more romantic exploits, seeing that Locke was the reporter. Had it not been for the notice of his hanging, I might have questioned the reality of Fernandez himself.

A curiosity of which I am not particularly proud impelled me to take a hansom to Bellevue yard, where a massive crowd of perhaps as many as two thousand had gathered to witness Manuel Fernandez breathe his last. The mob pressed around the elevated scaffold in the middle of the yard, so that it was with difficulty that the high constable and his officers were able to clear a path from the bleak prison to the place of execution. When the condemned man was led out, the spectators surged forward, particularly the ladies, who were admitted to executions although barred from attendance at trials. Fathers hoisted snuffling children onto their shoulders—one young man near me urging his offspring to "remember this always," as a tale he could tell his own grandchildren. Hawkers moved through the crowd peddling oranges and chestnuts.

Fernandez was a tall, strapping, swarthy man with dark moustachios, "very neatly dressed [reported an evening newspaper] in a dark cloth frock coat, blue pantaloons, light vest, boots, etc." The clothes looked ill-fitting and borrowed to me. Somehow I doubted he would be buried in them.

The United States having never accepted the humane methods of M. Guillotin, Fernandez was to be hung, but by a gallows of recent design which owed something to the Frenchman's genius. The rope around his throat passed up and through a groove in the top beam to where it was attached to a three-hundred-pound weight suspended near the top of one of the side beams, also by ropes. When these ropes were severed by a hatchet wielded by the executioner, who was dressed even more fashionably than Fernandez, the weight dropped rapidly and Fernandez ascended with corresponding swiftness.

The virtues of this new method of execution were applauded, at least by gentlemen standing in my vicinity. One noted that this device was clearly superior to the old technique of dropping the criminal through a trapdoor, particularly as it elevated rather than lowered the body and thus afforded a better view. A second, who wore a clerical collar, expressed the point that this new contraption appeared to reduce almost to half the number of minutes required to strangle the condemned man, comparing Fernandez's death to a hanging he had witnessed in the same prison yard only three years before. A third gentleman contented himself with the notion that Fernandez had "died well," an opinion shared by all the newspaper accounts of the execution which I read, and with which I, myself, certainly agree.

# 3  *The* Sun *Newspaper*

At ten-forty-five I was walking up Park Row toward the *Sun's* offices. In warm weather the lawns of City Hall Park, to my left, and called by New Yorkers *the* Park, would have been green, with strollers wandering among the flower beds or admiring the fountain. Now the grounds beyond the painted wooden fence stretched brown and barren up to the pillared portico of the City Hall. Behind the City Hall stands the recently completed Hall of Records, which has been built literally around the old New Jail, where debtors used to be housed. It was modeled on the temple of Diana of Ephesus, no less, and is quarters for the Recorder, the Surrogate, the Comptroller, and the Street Commissioners. Here also felons are held during their trials in City Hall under the unblinking eye of the elephantine jailor, Pappy Lowends, and here are the grisly dissecting rooms of the morgue, which, despite its renown as a prodigy of classical architecture, have already earned for the new structure the name of the Dead House.

At the northeast corner of the Park, fronting on Centre Street, stands the Hall of Justice, more commonly called the Police Office, where, assisted by the aldermen, the special justices preside from dawn to sundown over the Court of Special Sessions. Except in the bitterest weather, several roundsmen from the police force may always be found lounging about on the steps while a steady parade of pickpockets, prostitutes, and pig stealers are marched through its doors. For a reporter with a penny newspaper the Police Office is easily the most fertile news source in the city.

One unusual event marked my brief journey up Park Row. Opposite the corner of Beekman Street I heard loud, angry shouting. The crowd of pedestrians parted suddenly and two men came rushing toward me, one pursuing the other and brandishing a leather strap. His quarry, an angular, squinting fellow of about forty with an outrageous gaff of a nose, stumbled and fell almost at my feet. The other set about him with the strap, applying it with great vigor but, so far as I could tell, little effect. A circle of cheering spectators gathered around the combatants of which I found myself part of the innermost ring. As no one else seemed disposed to intervene and the contest appeared to be clearly decided, I stepped forward and took hold of the assailant's arm.

"Enough, sir," I said. "You have carried the day."

He glared at me beneath ferocious eyebrows but, as his arm was useless in my grip, he recovered his dignity rapidly. "Quite right, young man," he said. "This yapping Scotch terrier owes you his gratitude, and most probably the opportunity to continue engaging in his vile habits of inhaling and exhaling."

His victim had wasted no time in scrambling to his feet and sprinting toward Broadway, shouting over his shoulder something about satisfaction. The crowd laughed raucously and the remaining warrior brushed the dust from his cloak, nodded to me curtly, and set off at a brisk pace for City Hall. The crowd moved on and the fracas was over in no more time than it takes to tell it.


"My name is David Tobias Cordor," I said. "I have a Letter of Introduction to Mr. Benjamin H. Day from Mr. Arunah S. Abell, whom I believe is his former associate."

The boy took the letter and indicated a long wooden bench where I was to wait. The *Sun*'s offices were in a three-story building at Spruce and Nassau facing the Park. It was impossible not to remark the contrast with the sleepy little office of the *Gazette* in Smithville. Our old flatbed press took days to print our weekly circulation of six hundred. The *Sun* had two double-cylinder Napier presses, which threw off copies at an hourly rate of four thousand and circulated thirty thousand papers daily. The *Gazette* was essentially a one-man operation, but here scores of employees rushed back and forth and dozens lined up before the wooden railings to insert advertisements and liners or to purchase copies. Ink-stained printer's devils trailed behind their aproned masters and grimy newsboys ran in empty-handed and out moments later with new stacks of copies.

My confidence might have wavered had I not had my Letter of Introduction from Mr. Arunah S. Abell. A Letter of Introduction, my uncle often said, will open all doors to an ambitious young man. I congratulated myself on my prospects. I rejoiced in my good fortune at having so influential a sponsor as Mr. Arunah S. Abell. It was only when I saw the boy who had taken the letter approaching that I remembered Mr. Abell and I had never met, and that he'd consented to write the letter only on condition that we postpone that pleasure indefinitely.

"Mr. Day will see you now," the boy said. "This way, please." He led me up a narrow, dusty staircase to a landing overlooking the ground floor, rapped on a door, and ushered me in.

Mr. Benjamin H. Day, printer, editor, publisher, and sole proprietor, sat behind a massive, cluttered, mahogany desk. Another man, who I later learned was his bookkeeper and brother-in-law, Moses Yale Beach, stood beside him with a ledger open in his hands. Day, surprisingly, was only six or seven years my senior, but no less formidable for that. He was a thickset bulldog of a man, solid Puritan stock, oozing all the virtues of Poor Richard. His coat and cravat were black, as his trousers and boots proved to be when he stood. He had a great shock of jet-black hair and, though his upper lip was clean shaven, he wore a black beard (to hide, his employees believed, a receding chin). His eyes were dark and sought to hold mine through the entire interview—part of Day's method of making intruders as uncomfortable as possible.

Beach, by contrast, is a tall, mild-looking man, at least ten years older than his brother-in-law. He has a high forehead and quizzical eyebrows, pale-blue eyes, and a bulbous nose from which, however, he draws attention with magnificent side whiskers. His overall impression is one of placid intelligence; that of Day, indefatigable tenacity. When I entered Beach began to withdraw, but Day held up his hand and spoke in ? New England twang.

"This will only take a minute, Moses."

He fixed his eyes on mine. "Good morning, Mr. Cordor. How is our mutual friend, Arunah Abell?"

I twisted my hat and felt like a fool. Not one plausible lie entered my mind. "Mr. Abell and I have never really met, sir."

"So he says in this letter you've brought me. He further states that you are an unprincipled stripling who has hounded him mercilessly for his recommendation on the strength of a fabricated acquaintance you claim between him and your uncle, now deceased." He glanced down at the paper and back up at me. "On the ground of what little he knows of you, sir, he concludes with a somewhat unpleasant charge against the chastity of your late mother."

His lips hardened into a taut, humorless line. Beach, to my great annoyance, was suppressing a smile. I drew a deep breath, found a chair, sat down, crossed my legs, put my hat in my lap, put my hands on my hat. "My late uncle," I said, as calmly as I could, "often told me, sir, that Arunah Abell was as excellent a fellow as was ever born, provided one could become accustomed to his pestilential breath and abominable belching. He always insisted that the vicious rumors of Mr. Abell's lecherous connections with pavement princesses were greatly exaggerated and maintained stoutly, to his dying day, that if one could overlook his moral leprosy and habitual lying, Mr. Abell was as boon a companion as a gentleman could wish. I leave it to you, Mr. Day, whether my uncle knew Arunah S. Abell."

Beach was grinning like a jester and fairly dancing up and down. Day's expression never changed, but he leaned forward across the desk.

"Mr. Cordor, my annual outlay for material and wages exceeds ninety-three thousand dollars. That is very nearly two thousand a week. More than three hundred a day for the six working days. I circulate daily thirty thousand papers. Allowing the other nine morning papers an average of three thousand circulation, it will appear that the circulation of the *Sun* is daily more than all of the others united. Every individual from the rich aristocrat who lolls in his carriage to the humble laborer who wields a broom in the streets reads the *Sun.* Already we can perceive a change in the mass of the people. They think, talk, and act in concert. They understand their own interest, and feel that they have numbers and strength to pursue it with success. I have assembled the finest staff of reporters, editors, and compositors in history. The *Sun* has done more to benefit the community by enlightening the minds of the common people than all the other papers combined. Mr. Cordor, in what conceivable manner could the addition of you to my payroll possibly improve my newspaper?"

"Mr. Day, I am an excellent reporter."

"Mr. Cordor, do you imbibe intoxicating spirits?"

"Mr. Day, I do not," I lied.

"Mr. Cordor, you are hired. I am busy. Please get out."

On the landing, Beach, still grinning, introduced himself. "It's a pleasure to meet the nephew of so splendid a judge of character. That's the first time I've heard Ben say 'please' in three years. I'm going to let Prall give you the tour."

This last was a reference to a young man who had just rushed in from the street and was taking the stairs two at a time. He came toward us at a trot, puffing and laughing and trying not to laugh, so that the laughter burst out of him in sporadic hoots and wheezes. He was gesturing wildly, and when he reached us he jerked his head toward the office we had just left and managed to say, "He in?"

"He's busy," Beach said.

"He's not too busy for this," Prall said, and the laughter exploded inside him so that he shook violently while Beach and I began to laugh out loud without the slightest idea of the joke.

At last, when Prall caught his breath, he gasped out, "The colonel has attacked Bennett!"

"What?" Beach said, wiping his eyes. "Is that all?"

"No, no! Not in his paper! In the street!"

"Good Lord! Where?"

"Right outside!" Prall cried. "Right in Park Row, I tell you! The colonel spots Bennett skulking about and, 'What ho!' shouts he. 'My Christian eyes have been offended by that blasphemous monstrosity, the infamous Bennett!' Just then Bennett stops and raises his magnificent nose to sniff the air, almost impaling a passing pigeon. 'Gadzooks!' cries Bennett. 'Either the villainous Colonel Webb is abroad or there is rancid meat in the immediate neighborhood!' "

Prall hopped about the landing like St. Vitus, playing all the parts.

"The belligerents close! Webb lets fly with a stinging anti-Jackson editorial and Bennett counters with a learned lecture on political economy. The colonel thrusts with his cane and Bennett parries with his nose, and thrust! and parry! and thrust! Until at last Bennett is driven from the field!"

Grasping at his throat, Prall staggered and reeled in mock defeat while Beach, helpless with laughter, collapsed against the wall. The crowd in the office below broke into spontaneous applause. The door to Day's office was yanked open suddenly, and the publisher and sole proprietor loomed on the landing.

"Mr. Day," Prall cried, "Webb has assaulted Bennett in the public street!"

The corners of Day's mouth twisted slightly. It was the closest thing to a smile I ever saw on his face. He said, "Did you see it?"

Prall shook his head. "They were talking about it at the Police Office. Webb chased him up Beekman into Park Row and knocked the rascal silly with his cane."

"His belt," I amended.

Immediately I was the center of their gaping attention.

"Good Lord," Beach gasped. "Did you see it, Cordor?"

"See it? It happened right at my feet."

"An eyewitness!" Prall shouted. "By God, a veritable eyewitness!"

"Foolscap!" Day ordered. "Pens! Ink! Mr. Cordor, you are going to write that story at once!"

Beach let me use his office and sent in Prall to fill in the background for me. William H. Prall was a plump, red-haired youth of twenty-four, gregarious and unfailingly good-humored. His face, though pock-marked and freckled, was open and guileless, and he had a ready smile and an infectious laugh which made him popular with the entire staff. From the beginning he was my closest friend at the *Sun*.

"You must understand, Davy," Prall said, "that Day, Webb, and Bennett waste about as much love on one another as three cats in a sack. Webb owns the *Courier and Enquirer,* the most powerful of all the six-cent journals. He's a feisty little pepper pot, thick as thieves with old man Hone and the whole Whig gang, and living proof that gentlemen are made, not born. That is, if a gentleman is someone who swears in seven syllables and fights a duel a month."

"And Bennett?" I asked.

Will Prall grinned. "There's a piece of work! He used to work for Webb until they broke over Biddle and the Bank. He came here begging for a job and Day pitched him out on his ear. I hear he's tried to start three papers and gone under each time. Since May he's run the *Herald* singlehanded out of a basement on Nassau Street and he's still in business, though he's been burned out once and beaten up twice now. The boys in the compositors' room have a pool on how long he's going to stick it. If you want in, it'll cost you fifty cents."

He was rummaging through Beach's files. "Moses keeps clippings of Bennett's most outrageous items. Here we go." He tossed a folder on the desk in front of me. I began to read.

The *Herald's* location is quite remarkable—a very religious and theological neighborhood, with the Bible Society on my left, the Tract Society on my right, and, directly across the street, Dr. Spring's venerable brick church. I regret to state that a few doors on my left is Mr. Tappan's Anti-Slavery concern; and, what is worse, a few doors on the right, just across Spruce Street is the office of a thing generally called the *Sun* newspaper. I mean to take a few spots out of the *Sun* as fast as I can, and I pledge myself thus far—that with the aid of the Bible Society, and the Tract Society, the Missionary Society and Dr. Spring, we shall be able to emasculate the whole of them in nine or twelve months at farthest.

"Here's another," Prall said.

I don't think much of Moses. A man who would take forty years to get a party of young women through a desert is only a loafer. Moses himself, according to the best biblical critics, was the first white man who married a Negro woman, and thus gave a sanction to amalgamation and abolition.

"Are you Catholic?" Will asked. I said I was not. He said, "Read this one anyway."

If we must have a Pope, let us have a Pope of our own—an American Pope, an intellectual, intelligent, and moral Pope—not such a decrepit, licentious, stupid, Italian blockhead as the College of Cardinals at Rome condescends to give the Christian world of Europe.

"Bennett's French," Will said, tossing down another clipping, "but he was born and raised in Scotland."

The Scotch are a damned scaly set, from top to bottom, and when I pass them in the street, I always take the windward side, and avoid shaking hands as I would the itch.

I whistled softly. Will stood grinning down at me. "It's Bennett's theory, apparently, that a paper which is universally denounced will also be universally read. He claims a circulation of ten thousand already."
"Has he got it?"
"No," Will answered, "but he will if somebody doesn't kill him first. He loves to attack the other journals. Calls the *Sun* 'our highly re- spected, dirty, sneaking, driveling, contemporary nigger paper.' He's been accusing Webb of some crooked stock deals lately. I expect that's what brought the colonel's blood to a boil. You ready, Davy?"
I waved my pen above the foolscap.

"Try this," Will said, beginning to pace. " 'Low as he had fallen (comma) both in the public estimation and his own (comma) we are astonished to learn . . .' "

" '. . . to learn,' " I continued, " 'that Colonel Webb has stooped so far beneath anything of which we had ever conceived it possible for him to be guilty (comma) as publicly (comma) and before the eyes of hundreds (comma) to descend to a public personal chastisement of that villainous libel on humanity (comma) . . .' "

" '. . . the notorious vagabond Bennett (period),' " finished Will.

I shook my head. " '. . . notorious vagabond Bennett (comma) whose only chance of dying an upright man will be that of hanging perpendicularly from a rope (period).' "

"Excellent!" Will cried, clapping his hands.

I went on. " 'As witnessed by one of us, the Colonel met the brawling coward yesterday in Park Row, took him by the throat, and with a cowhide striped the human parody from head to foot. For the space of nearly five minutes . . .' "

"Twenty," Will suggested.

"Will, it couldn't have been more than two."

"So?"

I scratched out "five." " 'For the space of nearly twenty minutes did the right arm of the Colonel ply his weapon with unremitted activity, at which time the bystanders, who evidently enjoyed the scene mightily, interceded in behalf of the suffering, supplicating wretch, and Webb suffered him to run.' "

"Good, good," Will muttered.

I paused for inspiration. " 'Had it been a dog, or any other decent animal, or had the Colonel himself with a pair of good long tongs removed a polecat from his office, we would not have been so much surprised; but that he could have so far descended from himself as to come in public contact with the veriest reptile that ever defiled the paths of decency, we could not have believed.' "

I read my paragraph aloud, with Will nodding vigorously. "We need," he said, "a *coup de grâce*." I dipped my pen.

" 'That miserable scribbler, Bennett, has become a public flogging property, and Webb has announced his intention to cowskin him every Monday morning until the Fourth of July, when he will offer him a holiday. We understand that Webb has offered to remit the flogging upon the condition that Bennett will allow him to shoot him; but Bennett says: 'No; skin for skin. Behold, all that man hath will he give for his life!' "

"Magnificent!" Will shouted. "Davy, Day will make you a partner for this."

And thus did I write my first story for the *Sun.*

# 4 *The Theater*

In my first weeks in New York Will Prall made me his personal
responsibility. He arranged lodgings for me at the same house in Ann
Street where he boarded, just three blocks from the *Sun* building. He
introduced me to the rest of the paper's staff, to Wisner, the police court
reporter, and Lucius Robinson, who covered Wall Street and the Merchants' Exchange, and finally to the famous inventor of the celebrated
Moon Hoax, Richard Adams Locke, a fastidious, self-important fellow
whose habit of addressing me as "youngster" did nothing to endear him
to me.

Locke, when I met him, was rejoicing over the autopsy report on
Manuel Fernandez, which, it seems, verified the various serious injuries
the late Spaniard had claimed and Locke had reported in his "Life and
Adventures."

"Even the fractured vertebrae from that affair in Leghorn!" he proclaimed to Prall. "Now let them say this is another hoax!" He glanced
in my direction. "Have you treated the youngster to a night or two of
pub crawling, Prall?"

"We've crawled out of a couple," Will said.

"And the Five Points?" This was a reference to New York's most
notorious section. "Has he been initiated into our Aspasian Society as
presided over by the gross Mother Gallagher and the fair Rosina
Townsend?"

"Not yet," Will answered.

"Time enough, youngster, when you've got your growth," Locke said, tousling my hair before I could duck his hand. "I fear you'd make too tender an hors d'oeuvre for the fair Rosina."

James Gordon Bennett, to do him justice, had the brass to report his own beating by Webb as an eyewitness:

> My damage is a scratch about three-quarters of an inch in length, on the third finger of the left hand, which I received from the railing I was forced against, and three buttons torn from my vest, which any tailor will reinstate for a sixpence. Webb's loss is a rent from top to bottom of a very beautiful black coat, which cost the ruffian $40, and a blow in the face, which may have knocked down his throat some of his infernal teeth for anything I know. Balance in my favor, $39.94.
>
> As to intimidating me, or changing my course, the thing cannot be done. Neither Webb nor any other man shall, or can, intimidate me. I tell the honest truth in my paper, and leave the consequences to God. Could I leave them in better hands? I may be attacked, I may be assailed. I may be killed, I may be murdered, but I will never succumb. Conscious of virtue, I will never abandon the cause of truth and morals!

"He's absolutely correct, you know," said Prall when he had read this article. "He may very well be murdered."

It was Prall, too, who introduced me to the theater. My first Monday in the city he and I were part of the full house which jammed the Bowery Theater to see *Othello* with the Bowery's manager, Thomas S. Hamblin, as Iago, and the brilliant Junius Brutus Booth in the title role. Not a sound could be heard in the huge house when the curtain rose on a street in Venice and Iago, accompanied by the lovesick Roderigo, roused the household of Brabantio to warn him that his daughter and the Moor were "now making the beast with two backs." The distraught father and his servants rushed off and in a moment Iago re-entered with the attendants of Othello bearing blazing torches. Prall's elbow dug into my ribs. "Booth's coming," he whispered.

Iago stepped stage front, looking a bit unnerved, I thought, considering that his plot was going so well.

> *Though in the trade of war I have slain men,*
> *Yet do I hold it very stuff o' th' conscience*
> *To do no contriv'd murther. I lack iniquity*
> *Sometimes to do me service. Nine or ten times*
> *I had thought t' have yerked him here under the ribs.*

Iago paused. He waited. He peered offstage. The attendants peered offstage. One or two of the torches waved dangerously close to Brabantio's house. Iago coughed. "I had thought t' have yerked him here under the ribs!" he bellowed, somewhat unnecessarily. I, for one, had heard him the first time and my seat was certainly not the best.

The audience began to murmur. We shifted in our seats. All at once a roar went up from every corner of the house, followed by thundering applause, as Othello peeped out from behind the curtain. He waved at the pit and stalked across the stage until he was breathing directly into Iago's face. Iago turned away abruptly. The applause died in an instant and the theater was as silent as a tomb. Othello stared out at us and then, with sudden determination, strode to the rear and attempted to enter Brabantio's house. The door proving stubborn, he redoubled his efforts until the entire wall came down, scattering the attendants and their flambeaux, and revealing another wall of brick in which was yet another door. Othello turned and bowed from the waist. Then he went through the door and vanished for three days.

"Poor Booth," Prall said a week later. "He's taken a liner in the *Sun* by way of apology. He suffered, he says, 'a serious visitation, affecting and enfeebling my nerves, and a long deprivation of sleep, acting on a body debilitated by a previous illness, and a mind disordered by domestic affliction, occasioning a partial derangement.'"

Beach grunted. "Drunk as a fiddler," he muttered.

———

Our second trip to the theater proved more successful. We went to the Park on Broadway to see James Sheridan Knowles in his own play *The Hunchback*. The Park Theater, Prall informed me, is known to "true" New Yorkers simply as *the* Theater, and has recently been completely remodeled. There are three tiers of boxes, the first decorated by medallion portraits of celebrated British actors, the second by painted scenes from Shakespeare, and the third by pictures of Stratford and the Globe Theatre. The truth is that the third tier, where we sat, is ornamented even more beautifully by a score of lovely young ladies who grace its boxes, assuming the most charming postures and smiling behind their fans in a quite fascinating fashion.

One girl in particular, with long, blond curls and a scarlet dress, smiled at us as we took our seats and continued to smile long after we had settled in them.

"Will," I said, "do you see that girl in red?"

Prall's nose was buried in his program.

"She's smiling at one of us, I think," I said. "I'm certain I don't know her. Do you know, Will, I'm sure she's smiling at you. She's waving now. For God's sake, Will, why don't you look up and see if you recognize her?"

"Damn you for an ass, of course I know her, you bumpkin!" He had slumped down until he was practically sitting on the floor. "Will you shut up," he hissed.

He slid right off the edge of the seat. I bent over. "What the devil is the matter with you?" I demanded. "Crawling around on all fours!"

A melodious voice said, "Why, Sweet William, it *is* you." The lady in red stood directly over us. Prall's round face was the color of a boiled beet. The lady's lips pursed into a pout. "Am I to think you are avoiding your little Maria?"

"My friend seems to have lost . . ."

"I seem to have lost . . ." Will echoed feebly.

". . . his program."

". . . my program."

The lady smiled sweetly. "But, *chéri,* here is your program on your seat."

"Why," I said, "no wonder you couldn't find it . . ."

"No wonder I couldn't find it . . ."

". . . on the floor."

". . . on the floor," Prall concluded, glowering at me murderously.

"And now, *chéri*," purred the lady, "are you going to introduce me to your handsome friend?"

I attempted to get to my feet. Prall struggled to get off the floor. "My name—" I began. Prall pushed my seat down, catching me at the back of my knees, and I flopped backward into it.

"Miss Maria Stevens," he said, "allow me to present Mr. Felton Hockenberry."

"Charmed," said the lady prettily. "Sweet William, we have missed you in Thomas Street. You must come and visit us, and you *must* bring Mr. Hockenberry with you. There now . . ." She pressed her finger to her crimson lips and touched it to Prall's mouth. "That's a promise to your little Maria. You won't be naughty and disappoint me, will you?"

Without waiting for an answer she glided away. Prall was fidgeting furiously. I said, "Felton Hockenberry?"

"Damn it, Davy! What a puling infant you are! Don't you know with that sort of woman one always uses an alias?"

"I beg your pardon, Sweet William."

He glared at me. "If that gets out at the *Sun!*"

"My lips are sealed," I said, pressing my finger against them.

It took Prall two acts to cool down. At the second intermission he agreed to go down to the lobby with me for a pipe. We did not quite make it to the lobby, however.

At the head of the staircase leading down from the second tier I was astonished to find ascending toward me the most beautiful girl I had ever seen.

Her hair was rich and jet black. She parted it in the middle and it hung in long, graceful curls to her milk-white shoulders. She wore a jeweled tiara with a single droplet pearl at the center of her forehead. Her eyes were green, deep, and lustrous; her lips were moist and full and red. The whole expression of her face bespoke intelligence and, above all, a wonderful gentleness. Her figure was magnificent. She wore a gown of rich green silk and she moved as though she were set to soft music. "Good Lord, Prall," I whispered, only half joking, "I think I'm in love!"

I was immediately horrified that she might have heard me, for she looked up and smiled gently. As she did so a piece of paper slipped from her hand and fluttered to the carpeted stair and, at the same moment, two young rowdies jostled past us arm in arm on their way to the lobby. One of them, a flushed, foolish-looking character, picked up the paper, which proved to be a ten-dollar bill, and extended it toward her, but when she reached for it he let it go so that it again fell to the stair. As the lady bent to retrieve it, assuming, so it seemed to me, a completely charming attitude, the ruffian hauled back his boot and sent her sprawling (but gracefully, gracefully).

What happened next can only be attributed to the fact that I was then but two weeks in New York and had not yet learned the customs of the natives. I leaped down the stairs, seized the hooligan by his collar with one hand, assisted the lady to her feet with the other, had the pleasure of hearing her assailant apologize with great sincerity, and then placed my heel against the seat of his pantaloons and aided his descent to the lobby.

As I handed the lady the banknote she smiled again, as if she and I shared some secret which no one else would ever know.

"I don't know what you're sulking about," I said to Prall when we had resumed our seats for the final act. "I was simply defending a lady's honor."

He rolled his eyes toward the ceiling. "The boy hero!" he muttered. "Defending the 'honor' of Miss Helen Jewett, alias Helen Mar, alias Marie Benson, alias Dorcas Doyan–'The Girl in Green'–'The Comet of the Sidewalk'–the undisputed 'Queen of the Pave'!"

I heard him telling the story to Locke the next morning at the *Sun* office. "Helen of Jewett," Locke said. "Ah, I know her. 'Was this the ass that launched a thousand ships?' "

"And true to every man in the fleet in her fashion," Prall added.

Locke laughed unpleasantly.

# 5  *The Great Fire*

O ne more event in 1835 remains to be recorded, though the grief and ruin it brought to so many lives might render it better forgotten. Between eight and nine o'clock on the night of Wednesday, December 16, a sound was heard throughout the city which strikes more terror in the heart of urbanized man than any other. The fire alarm was rung, the signal indicating a blaze in the business district. Minutes later the bell sounded a second alarm, and suddenly every bell in New York seemed to take up the fearful clanging.

I was preparing to leave the office, and I ran out into Spruce Street toward the Park. It was a frigid night and the wind gusted in arctic blasts. The sky above the lower city glowed the color of blood. Dense clouds of black smoke gathered over the downtown streets. The din of the alarm bells increased, mixing with the shriller ringing of the engine bells as the horse-drawn fire engines thundered past me on the stone pavement. The streets were beginning to fill with the curious and the terrified, in various stages of dress and undress, huddled together against the biting wind. The same horrible word was whispered and shouted again and again: Fire! We were two hundred thousand souls in a wooden city.

I rushed back into the *Sun* building. Day was beside himself, hopping up and down, yelling orders to Beach. "Wisner! Get me Wisner!"

"Not here," Beach said. "At the Police Office, I think."

"Where is Locke?" Day demanded. When Beach shrugged, Day cried, "All right, God help us, get me Prall!"

Again Beach shrugged, and I wondered if he knew where Sweet William was spending the evening. Day looked about desperately and his eyes fell on me.

"Cordor! You're covering the fire. Get down there as fast as you can. Take a cab. I want dispatches, as many as you can write. Keep moving, *keep moving,* do you understand?" I nodded rapidly. He gripped me by the shoulders. "Good lad! Don't come back till it's over, understand? I don't want to see your face until the last spark is quenched!" He released me and flung his arms upward. "Oh!" he implored the heavens, "give us one of your real Moscow fires!"

I hailed a hansom and raced down Nassau toward Wall Street. Fire engines clanged and clattered beside us, grazing our wheels. Wagons and carriages rumbled behind us. Wild-eyed men sprinted along the sidewalks. Ahead of me tongues of flame leaped up against the sky and showers of sparks, hundreds of times larger than fireworks, exploded as buildings collapsed. The city, from Wall Street to the upper bay, was a seething furnace.

The fire began in the store of Comstock & Adams in Merchant Street, a crooked little lane of recently built, four-story dry-goods stores jammed to the rafters with flammable merchandise. Merchant Street went up like a tinder box, and the sparks and flames spread on the high northwest wind in all directions, kindling blazes a half mile away. Gangs of merchants in Pearl Street formed human chains into their burning stores to save their valuable stock, heaping it in the center of Hanover Square. Within an hour flaming tinders had fallen on their mountain of goods and reduced it to ashes.

The great banks on Wall and Exchange were burning. The bursting warehouses on Broad Street caught fire and were destroyed in minutes, toppling with great roars into the street one after the other like dominoes. I joined a crowd manning one of the pumps, trying to save the Merchants' Exchange building. Men in silk hats and evening clothes worked beside men in corduroy and overalls. The water froze as it fell. It seemed hopeless.

At one-thirty I scribbled a hasty dispatch and sent the hackman up Nassau to the *Sun* with orders to deliver it and meet me again at the corner of Exchange Place:

HALF PAST ONE O'CLOCK — A TREMENDOUS CONFLAGRATION is now raging in the lower part of the city. The Merchants' Exchange is in flames. Nearly all the blocks in the triangle bounded by William and Wall Streets and the East River are consumed! Several hundred buildings are already down, and the firemen have given out. God only knows when the fire will be arrested.

Shortly after two the Merchants' Exchange crumbled. Five young sailors who had tried desperately to rescue the statue of Hamilton standing in the rotunda barely escaped with their lives seconds before the huge dome came crashing down in a sea of flame. Both the Exchange and Dr. Mathews' church nearby had been thought beyond danger, and hundreds of thousands of dollars in merchants' stock had been brought there for safety. The church survived until almost three, when its bright-gold ball and star, which had gleamed in splendor above the flames, gave a surge and fell, in all their glory, into the chaos beneath them.

Near dawn I sent Day another dispatch:

The entire downtown area is a terrifying inferno. The sky over the Battery glows brilliant orange, and as building after building falls, the district bounded by Wall and William Streets belches flames and vomits smoke. Fire engines are brought from the upper city and landed here on ferries from Jersey City and Brooklyn, all to no avail. The hydrants are frozen or exhausted. The water turns to ice in the hoses, while the furious wind fans the flames and carries the burning embers for blocks. We are told that a thousand men, sent with horses and equipment from Baltimore and Philadelphia, are stranded at Perth Amboy. The Broad Street warehouses are destroyed; the Merchants' Exchange has fallen. It is now thought only the deliberate destruction of buildings in the fire's path by explosives can control the holocaust. To that end a boat has been launched to secure the necessary explosives from the Navy Yard in Brooklyn, manned by volunteers under Captain Mix and Mr. Quinncannon.

Mix I knew as one of the best of that robust and superior breed of men, the packet captains. Of Quinncannon I knew nothing except that he was directing the placement and strategy of the explosives. Their crew were said to be picked men, but they had launched their boat in dangerous waters at night in the teeth of a howling wind, and little hope was held for them.

By midmorning of the seventeenth the destruction had begun to engulf the waterfront along South Street. The piers and most of the great shipbuilding yards were on fire, and the air hung heavy with the odor of burning piny wood and fragrant spices. The scents seemed oddly festive in the midst of that dreadful catastrophe. As if directed by a conscious power, the flames systematically devoured the rigging lofts, sail lofts, the shops of the pump makers, gilders, ship chandlers. They spread to the international bordellos of Water Street, where each house flew the flag of the sailors it serviced and a man could be robbed, drugged, and shanghaied in his native tongue.

By afternoon, looting was rampant in the burned-out sections. Where valuable merchandise had miraculously escaped the fire it did not escape the sharp eyes of the scavengers who rooted through the charred rubble and took to their heels with stolen goods on their backs, or loaded their plunder into horse carts and wheelbarrows. Other wretches prowled along the wharfs, becoming violently drunk on the wine and liquor left strewn in the gutters, and forming into riotous gangs. Companies of uniformed militia had to be called out, and eventually orders were issued to shoot to kill.

There was no relief from the brutal cold or the winds which still whipped across the city from the East River. The flames continued to spread to the north and west, and the fire companies were at the end of their resources. One fire captain frankly told me there was no hope that any of the city could be saved.

Near evening the rumor spread that Captain Mix's boat had been sighted off the Liberty Street pier. I directed my hackman past the smoking wreckage of the Exchange, whose façade and marble columns now seemed the ruins of some ancient pagan temple. We picked our way up Pearl and down Liberty to the river.

The boat had docked and the explosives were already being unloaded into horse carts. Captain Mix, a huge, weather-beaten man, stood on the bridge bellowing alternately cheering encouragement and terrible threats. His crew, a motley mix of navy regulars in pea jackets and merchant sailors in thick, coarse wool and dungarees, unloaded their cargo with mechanical precision. No heroics could overmatch the icy calm with which these men carried about the kegs and barrels of gunpowder amid a steady shower of sparks and tinders, any one of which might at any moment have blown the entire wharf out of the water.

But the figure that most arrested my attention was a man incongruously dressed in a silk hat and flowing cape who moved up and down the pier, here assisting in heaving a powder keg into a cart, there shouting orders to a sailor or giving directions to a teamster just before he whipped up his horses. In that gale and general din I could not hear his voice, nor could I see his face with his collar up against the wind, but as he turned I had a fleeting impression of a black moustache lining his upper lip. In that instant I recognized my Irish companion on the Hoboken ferry just a few weeks before.

It was evident that, though Mix had commanded the boat, once ashore the party was in the Irishman's charge. He moved slowly, yet seemed to be everywhere at once, dispatching single horsemen, supervising the transfer of his lethal cargo. I handed the last of my dispatches to the hackman and directed him to Ben Day for his fare. Jumping down from the cab, I ran toward the wharf.

A wagon pulled by a team of grays rumbled onto the cobblestones of South Street. I shouted, "Need an extra hand?"

The driver grinned toothlessly. "Climb aboard, lad!"

I scrambled up over the tailgate and found myself between a grizzled merchant seaman and a hawk-faced city fireman, each seated with his arms wrapped around a powder keg. The fireman motioned me to a third keg. "Don't let it roll around," he ordered. "Keep the blanket covering it and keep the blanket wet!" He doused his own blanket with sea water from a large jar and passed the jar to me. Dutifully I soaked both the blanket and myself. Icicles began to form on the collar of my coat. I wondered what frostbite felt like.

The wagon rolled up Liberty, swung north of the fire area through Maiden Lane, and doubled back down Nassau to Cedar. The old driver reined in before a stable and carriage house of a height of three stories. Behind it, a block away on Pine, a wall of solid flame moved nearer with each minute that passed. A few of the elms in the field beside the stable were already burning.

The fireman swung down from the wagon. "Unload the kegs quickly," he barked. "We've got to be certain the building's deserted." He ran for the stable. The seaman and I dragged the barrels to the tailgate and set each of them down gently on the ground. In spite of the frigid cold I found I was sweating. Then I heard the shot.

I spun around to face the stable and saw the fireman returning to our wagon. He wore an expression of astonishment. There was a small red spot just above the bridge of his nose. As I watched, the spot increased in size. The red started to run down his nose and drip onto his shirt. His knees buckled and he fell forward into the muck of the stableyard.

From the stable door two brawny louts lurched toward us, neither very steady on his feet. We had surprised a pair of looters in the act of dividing the spoils and celebrating their windfall with contraband booze. They thought we were the police. Both of them carried guns.

Half a dozen impossible plans of action occurred to me in the space of five seconds, the most ridiculous of which was to dive behind the kegs of explosives for cover. I hate situations where my only recourse is to the truth.

"Listen," I shouted. "These kegs are full of gunpowder! If you shoot and hit one we'll all be blown up! ALL of us—do you understand?"

One of the drunken fools raised his gun and deliberately pointed it at us, trying to steady his aim. For an instant I had the insane idea of throwing myself in front of the kegs. Then he squeezed the trigger and the bullet whined past my ear and I got angry.

I found myself charging at him. He shot again wildly and then I was on top of him and we were rolling in the mud and manure. I groped for the gun with my left hand and struck him repeatedly in the face with my right. I heard another shot and caught a glimpse of the merchant sailor dropping to his knees, blood spurting from his thigh. I wrestled the gun away from my man, brought it down as hard as I could on his head, and he lay still. I kicked free of him and rolled over on my back. I was staring up into the barrel of his partner's pistol.

I aimed my gun up at him and pulled the trigger. The weapon clicked harmlessly. I closed my eyes, heard a shot, and felt a tremendous weight smash against my chest.

For a few seconds I could neither open my eyes nor understand exactly what had just happened. I was not completely sure that I was still alive. Then a voice with a distinct Irish brogue said, "Well, Mr. Cordor, how are you enjoying New York?"

The Irishman was putting his gun in his pocket and pulling the dead man off my chest. "Get up," he said. "The stable is already on fire."

At his order I helped the wounded seaman into the wagon. Flames were licking at the stable roof. "This man is losing blood rapidly," the Irishman said. "Can you apply a tourniquet?" I nodded. To the driver he said, "Do you know the hospital on Church Street? Get him there quickly."

I began to protest. "The explosives! You'll need help." He slapped one of the horses and the wagon surged forward. I removed my scarf and wrapped it tightly around the sailor's leg. The driver whipped up the team. We careened out of Cedar into Broadway. To the south the sky still glowed orange, but the smoke had thinned out and the flames were no longer visible. From every direction the city rocked with explosions.

# 6  The Case of Ephraim Avery

My curiosity as to this mysterious Irishman, who had entered so opportunely into my affairs and abruptly vanished, now became insatiable. Strangely, there was no one at the *Sun,* with the possible exception of Moses Beach, to whom I cared to broach the subject. During the long tours of duty we had served together at the Police Office I had formed a friendship with Bill Attree, the crime reporter for the *Transcript.* Attree was nearly ten years my senior, a man with a ready wit and a dry sense of humor and, moreover, a man of some experience and mature judgment. More and more, after the Great Fire, I felt myself drawn to his company. One evening early in January 1836, in a John Street tavern, I raised the topic with him.

"Quinncannon?" he repeated. "Ah, you're referring to the gentleman who singlehandedly saved the city from the flames. You see, I *do* read your stuff in that rag you labor for." He raised his glass and observed me closely over the rim. "But I see, Davy, you are serious, and so I shall be, too. Though there's damn little I can tell you about Lon Quinncannon. He has money—that much is certain, though where he gets it is a mystery. Some say he's the bastard son of an Irish nobleman. Others will tell you he's been banished from the British Empire for some unspeakable crime. The nature of the crime depends on who's telling the story. Few believe Quinncannon is his real name. The man himself appears to court this air of mystery. There is, perhaps, one story about him I can tell you. Have you ever heard of the murder of Sarah Maria Cornell?"

I shook my head. Attree ordered another round of drinks and began:

"Sarah Maria Cornell was a factory girl, thirty years old, unmarried, pregnant, and a Methodist. Those facts are not necessarily listed in order of importance, but they are all significant. In 1832 she was boarding in a house in Fall River, Massachusetts, and working in the mills of Tiverton, Rhode Island, about a half mile distant. At five-thirty on the afternoon of December 20, before the mill closed, she left her job and went to her rooming house, where she had an early supper and announced to the landlady that she had a rendezvous on the lands of a Tiverton farmer named Durfee—that she might return immediately but in any case before nine. In fact, she never returned at all.

"The following morning farmer Durfee found the corpse of Miss Cornell hanging by a length of rope from a stake in the fence of one of his stackyards. The rope was tied to the stake six inches from the top and the distance from that knot to the knot at her throat was slightly less than six inches. She wore a cloak and bonnet, but her shoes had been removed and placed side by side about eighteen inches to her right. Her handkerchief lay the same distance to her left. Her feet were close together, the toes touching the ground, and her legs carried back so that her knees came within a few inches of the ground. Her clothes were folded back smoothly under her legs.

"Durfee summoned help, cut down the body, and sent for the coroner, who charged his jury at the scene. Letters were found in her trunk at the boardinghouse, postmarked from Rhode Island, obviously from a man and establishing a meeting between them on the twentieth. A bandbox was also found containing a slip of paper, but this was not immediately examined.

"Although there were marks and bruises on the body indicating the girl had been beaten shortly before her death, the inquest verdict was suicide. Then the authorities learned that the woman had been pregnant. On Christmas Eve, Sarah was dug up again and an autopsy performed. Her uterus contained a female fœtus eight inches long. The paper in the bandbox was now examined. It read, as I recall: 'If I should be missing, inquire of the Rev. Mr. Avery, of Bristol. He will know where I am.' It was signed by Sarah Cornell and *dated the day of her death!*"

Attree paused, for dramatic effect I suppose. "All right," I said finally, "who was the Reverend Mr. Avery? And how does Quinncannon fit in?"

He raised his hand. "Patience, Davy, patience. Ephraim K. Avery was a Methodist minister, formerly from Lowell, Massachusetts, who had a church in Bristol, Rhode Island, at the time of the murder. It developed that the victim had been one of his parish in Lowell and that she had written him some compromising letters which he refused to destroy. He met her at a camp meeting in Thompson, Connecticut, the summer before her death and promised to burn the letters on condition she submit to him. When the girl resisted his advances, he dragged her into the woods and forced himself on her.

"All this was confessed by Sarah Cornell to her sister and brother-in-law, who testified to it at the trial."

"Then there was a trial," I said.

"Yes, in Newport in May 1833. I covered it. The case against Avery was airtight. The prosecution had the letters and the girl's death note naming Avery. Her sister testified that the girl had her 'monthly indisposition' in August, before the camp meeting, but failed to have it in September. She had named Avery as the father. The evidence of the appearance of the body proved she had been beaten and strangled *before* she was hung on the fence. They had a witness who heard screams from Durfee's stackyard. They had three witnesses who placed Avery in the area of the murder on the night she was killed. They even had the goddamn *fœtus!*"

"And Avery was convicted."

Attree looked at me grimly across the table.

"My God," I said. "With all that against him, do you mean to say he got off?"

"He did indeed," said Attree, "and *that* is where your friend Lon Quinncannon fits in."

"Was Quinncannon the defense attorney?" I asked.

"Yes, Davy."

He swirled the remaining gin and water in his glass, staring moodily at the candle which flickered bravely between us. I waited for what I thought was a reasonable interval. "Have you any intention of telling me the rest of it?" I asked at last.

Attree glanced up as if surprised to find me still sitting there. "Sorry," he said. "I was recalling it—the trial. You know, Davy, when you've been in this business for a few years, sitting in the Police Office six days a week, watching the steady parade of flotsam dragged before the bar—drunkards, drifters, brawlers, whores, thieves—they begin to look like so much livestock. You forget they're human. I think you must forget it, if you're going to do your job well. To us each one of them is just a paragraph, a punch line to amuse the penny readers. They're merely freaks and we exhibit them in the press the way Barnum does in his museum."

I was sensing the symptoms in him of one too many gin-and-waters.

"You're smiling, Davy [I'm certain I was not], but you're still so young. No, no, you *are,* my friend. You're bright and clever, but you have no real experience. You are here this cold evening to sit at my feet and imbibe my wisdom—I, to sit at your table and imbibe your gin. I'm about to say something incredibly wise. Let us both pay close attention."

He drained his glass and leaned forward, eyeing me intensely. "We see them, this sludge of society, these orphans of those creative hedonists, the gods—we see them as comical freaks because we are privy only to the brief moments of absurd public exposure which punctuate their long, pathetic, desperate lives. We charge them as enemies of society and we fine them their pittance to pour into the bottomless coffers of the state, or inter them prematurely in the Tombs until our righteous indignation has been satisfied. Then the state performs a necromantic miracle and magnanimously restores them to their miserable, worthless lives."

He put his hand on my arm. "Davy, you're barely twenty. Believe me. I'm almost twenty-nine and I know what I'm talking about."

He removed his hand and leaned back in his chair. "It's at a pro-tracted public trial like the one at Newport that you can plumb these truths to their depths. One good trial will do more for your education than a thousand brief hearings in the Police Office. The picture that emerged of the victim was so clear in its dismal pathos. Born in abject poverty, given little schooling beyond her letters, orphaned and cast adrift in a brutal, predatory society without a single defense—turning for her only consolation to the church and finding her religion in the bushes at a camp meeting!

"Sarah Cornell was more than the victim of a murder, Davy. She was almost the archetypal victim of society: poor, ignorant, and, worst of all, a woman, subject in her frailty to the lusts of men and afterward to the sneers and insults of the respectable. And Avery, the man! He was the very symbol of respectable society. Married, a family man, a college graduate, a man of the cloth, and never a whisper to soil his good name. He wasn't a Congregationalist, of course, or even a Presbyterian, but he was a Methodist and that was enough. A jury of his peers—*his* peers, mind you, not hers—found him not guilty. The contemptible, respect-able hypocrites!"

"And Quinncannon?" I said.

"I need another gin for that," he answered.

When the drinks came Attree tossed off half of his and then sat rolling the glass between his palms. "Quinncannon, at that time, was living in Boston, I believe. At least it was rumored he was employed by the Methodist bishop in Boston to investigate the case and defend the Reverend accused. For weeks before the trial he prowled through New England from Providence to Portland, poking into the dead girl's life from the age of sixteen and dredging up every vicious rumor and dirty lie he could sniff out. Not content with smearing her reputation, he rooted through the physical evidence of her death, so twisting and manipulating the facts that the jury became convinced she had taken her own life. There's no doubt at all that Quinncannon masterminded that tragic abortion of justice from beginning to end."

He finished his drink and stood. "You asked what I knew of Lon

Quinncannon, Davy. It is this. That he is a parasite of the aristocracy whose talents are for sale to the highest bidder. That he is a despoiler of dead girls and a dealer in faked evidence and perjured witnesses!" He clapped his hat on his head. Then he said in a much milder tone, "Beyond that, my dear fellow, I'm afraid there's very little I can tell you."

I found Attree's characterization of Quinncannon extremely disturbing. It was so completely at odds with what I believed about him, or at least with what I wanted to believe. It was true I had seen Quinncannon only twice, very briefly, but I could not shake off the impression of that caped figure moving with quiet authority through stacked kegs of gunpowder amid showers of sparks. Nor could I reconcile that image with the cynical manipulator painted by Attree. After all, Quinncannon had very probably saved my life, not, I reflected, that that was likely to entitle him to special consideration at the last assizes. I took the first opportunity to question Beach about the trial of Ephraim Avery.

"Yes, I remember it," Beach said. "Up in Rhode Island about three years ago. Clergyman killed his mistress. Strung her up on a fence post."

I reminded him that Avery had been acquitted.

"Was he? Oh, well, by the jury perhaps."

I suggested that their opinion was probably of primary interest to the accused.

He did not look up from his books. "Yes," he said absently, "I suppose so."

A few days later Locke buttonholed me. "I hear you're interested in the Cornell murder, youngster. Terrible affair. A man of God, no less, got some tart heavy with child, as the good book says, and dispatched her with a length of rope." He screwed up his face. "Messy," he said. "Messy."

"The jury found Avery not guilty," I said.

"*Mais naturellement, mon enfant.* Nevertheless, he lost his church and was driven out of the state. All the way, I hear, to Ohio. You see, he was found guilty by the most important tribunal."

"Are you talking about public opinion or the press?"

"There's no difference, youngster," Locke said. "No difference."

## 7 Helen before the Bar

In mid-January I saw Helen Jewett for the second time. It was early on a snowy morning at the Police Office. Attree and I were preparing to go out for a late breakfast when a loud commotion erupted at the outside door and a crowd of screaming women came tumbling into the small courtroom followed by two men in the uniform of British officers escorted none too gently by a potbellied, slack-jawed plainclothesman named Brink.

The justice on the bench was Robert Taylor, a dignified and even-handed man who had impressed me as a veritable solon among his fellows. With a look of grim resignation on his long face he pounded his gavel laconically while Brink attempted to bring some order to his charges. Four of the women continued shrieking at the officers, particularly the younger of the two, a weakly handsome fellow in the uniform of a British captain. Certain words, which had not been learned at their mothers' knees, rose shrilly above the din. The oldest of them, by at least twenty years, several times indicated an interest in digging her claws into the captain's face, terrifying that worthy into cringing retreat and requiring vigorous restraint from the burly Brink. I recognized her as the Duchesse de Berri, known to the unromantic police as Mrs. Berry, keeper of the finest house in Theater Alley.

"The ladies of the evening in the morning," Attree muttered dryly.

It was the fifth woman who caught my eye. She stood quietly to one side. Even with her hair disarrayed and her cloak disheveled and hastily thrown on, she seemed out of place in a police court beside those banshees. When she saw me staring at her she blushed modestly and smiled shyly. Modestly and shyly—I'll swear it!

The justice continued to hammer his gavel even while he asked, "What are the charges against these women?"

The girls howled as if wounded mortally, "Here now, Judge," squawked the Duchesse, "we're here to *bring* charges, I'll have you know. We're here as native Americans who've been cruelly victimized by conniving foreigners! That's the fact of it!"

"All right," Taylor said. "Mr. Brink, just exactly who is charged with just exactly what?"

Brink shoved the captain forward. "This bird, your honor. One . . ." He consulted a grimy note pad. "James L. Burke, captain, Her Majesty's Royal Guard."

"The charges?" Taylor asked wearily.

"Oh," said Brink, "the captain's been a busy boy, haven't you, Captain? Possession of counterfeit money, attempting to pass counterfeit money (as the bona fide, your honor), assault and battery upon the person of Miss Helen Jewett (that's this tart here, your honor), a willful destruction of property belonging to said Helen Jewett to the amount of one hundred dollars, drunk and disorderly, public nuisance, and inciting to riot."

"I was not!" said the captain indignantly.

"Not what?" snapped the justice.

"Uh, well, disorderly, your honor," stammered the captain.

The older officer, paunchy and balding, stepped forward and coughed. "Your honor, I am Colonel Steven McGovern . . ."

Taylor tapped his gavel. "In your turn, Colonel. Now, Duchesse, you know the routine here."

The Duchesse put one manicured paw on the Bible and swore to tell nothing but the truth. "This wretched villain, this miserable swine, this rascally swindler of honest women, in a word, your honor, this *gentleman,* came to my door last evening seeking respite and refreshment, which I consented to grant him notwithstanding that it was a most unseemly hour, your honor, and him stinking to the gills; nevertheless, I proffered him the hospitality of my house, your honor, and conveyed him to the door of Miss Jewett, one of my boarders, from whose room there shortly issued such a riotous noise that, by Jesus! your honor, I thought the house would come down on our heads, whereupon I hastened to the second floor and was astonished to see this vile varlet brawling with Miss Jewett over a monetary matter, your honor, at which I demanded he remove his arse from the premises upon making restitution for some champagne he had ordered, not to mention assorted broken bric-a-brac, which he endeavored to pay for with a bill which I ascertained to be of a questionable character or, in a word, bogus, your honor, and summoned the watch forthwith!"

The justice was gasping for air. The Duchesse wasn't even breathing hard.

"It's all true, your worship, every word," squealed one of the "boarders." "He got hold of Helen's scissors and threatened to cut off her hair. Then he sliced up her beautiful dresses, carved 'em to ribbons, he did!"

"Your honor," intoned the colonel, "if I may be allowed to speak."

Taylor raised his eyebrows. "And again, who are you, sir?"

"Colonel Steven W. McGovern, sir. I am this unfortunate young man's commanding officer. I can assure the court of the excellence of his family and the respectability of his character. His father, your honor, is a particular friend of mine in England. I would take the liberty of asking the court's leniency in view of the captain's tender years. Your honor is obviously a man of the world and realizes that boys will sometimes be boys."

The colonel chortled unctuously. I could hear Attree grinding his teeth.

"May I ask," Taylor said mildly, "were you a witness, Colonel, to these events?"

The colonel's mouth opened and closed several times. His collar seemed suddenly to be too tight. Attree leaned forward in his chair, smiling demonically.

"G'wan, Cuddles!" thundered the Duchesse. "Tell 'em you was with me!"

" 'Boys will be boys,' " Attree growled later over coffee. "And old goats will be old goats, that's certain."

I dropped my spoon in the saucer. "At long last, will you climb down off that?"

"And that nonsense about the 'captain's tender years'! The fool was at least as old as I am." He sat brooding, tapping on the table with a butter knife. "I'm surprised at Taylor. I'm really surprised at Taylor, dropping all the charges like that. And please don't remind me again that our tender little captain had to cough up a hundred dollars to pay for his merry romp through his paramour's wardrobe. And that lecherous old colonel, swearing to his soldier boy's *respectability!* The goat vouching for the kid. Did you see him, Davy, drooling on his beard and leering at that pretty little whore?"

"She is pretty, isn't she?"

"Yes," Attree said. "She is pretty."

## 8 *Two Nights in Theater Alley*

The following night I went to Theater Alley. I had decided that when I went it would be alone. The house was dark, as it always is, the shutters tightly closed and no light outside the door. The snow had been falling since before dawn, and although occasional sleigh bells could be heard from Fulton Street, the alley was deserted.

I crossed the narrow street and rapped at the door. I had pulled the collar of my cloak up to cover as much of my face as possible. I tugged the peak of my cap down and rapped again. From inside came the sound of bolts being slowly drawn open, and then the door clicked and opened to the length of a still-fastened chain. A candle flickered against the wind, casting its eerie light up into the peering, bloated face which blinked out at me. I raised my collar still higher.

"Miss Jewett, please," I said.

"That you, Frank?" came the unmistakable squawk of the Duchesse de Berri.

"I've come to see Miss Jewett," I repeated.

"Who the hell *is* that?" the Duchesse demanded.

For one long horrible moment the only name I could think of was Felton Hockenberry. Damn Prall! "It's . . . Robin," I managed at last. "Tell her it's Robin."

She held the candle higher. "Hood or Redbreast?"

The door began to close. In an absolute panic, inexplicable to me ever since, I feared above all things it might be shut against me. Forgetting to cover my face, I braced my weight against it. "Wait! Tell her it's the young man who did her a small service in the Park Theater."

Again the door swung back. "Are you expected?" she asked.

"Perhaps," I said, "not unexpected."

She loosened the chain, admitted me, and rechained and bolted the door. From the owlish manner in which she continued to squint at me I gathered she had not seen my features. At last she said, "This way."

The old bawd padded up a staircase and down a darkened hallway, and I followed, stamping the snow from my boots and shaking it from my cloak. She paused and knocked softly. "Helen, dear," she rasped, "here's one of your friends come to see you, claiming to be theater folk and some manner of bird."

Helen Jewett opened her door. She held a small lamp in one hand and something in the other which at first I could not see. Her magnificent black hair was drawn back and tied with a yellow ribbon, and her shoulders and bosom were as white as the newly fallen snow outside her window. Her green eyes brightened, I was pleased to see, when she recognized me.

"You want champagne?" A commercial note sounded by the Duchesse. She waddled off without waiting for an answer.

It came to me suddenly that I was still standing in the hall, where one of the other doors might open at any second. "May I come in?" I asked foolishly, and she stepped back with the same gentle smile on her lips. I suffered from the strange conceit, ludicrous under the circumstances, that she was the younger daughter of some country squire whom I'd come to court and that in a moment I would be meeting her father. I would shake the old reprobate's hand and "sir" him to death and laugh at his jokes and exchange shy, secret glances with his daughter, and later I would take her for a long ride in a rented sleigh.

A knock at the door. A fat arm extended through the opening from the hall holding a tray with a wine bottle and two glasses. The Duchesse was the soul of discretion. The door clicked shut.

Helen helped me with my wet cloak and spread it near the fire. I removed my cap and tossed it by the cloak. She brushed some snow-flakes from my hair and smoothed it back across my forehead. Her eyes never left mine.

"You are awfully beautiful," I said. I felt as stupidly awkward as a schoolboy in a haystack. She laughed and held up a book. It was this she had been holding when she admitted me, a slender volume of sonnets by Shakespeare, marked with a thin red ribbon at number 130.

*My mistress' eyes are nothing like the sun;*
*Coral is far more red than her lips' red . . .*

"You see," I said. "Even the Bard must surrender his similes rather than face the impossible task of describing your beauty, Miss Helen. It would have cost him all his art and half his gospel in the attempt."

She was very, very close to me. Her fingers touched my face tenderly as if she were blind and must use this method to discern my features. My face felt on fire. I bent down and kissed her, clasping my hands behind my back, deliberately postponing the pleasure of holding her.

She reached back and undid her yellow ribbon. Her raven hair tumbled richly down to her shoulders. She yielded to the pressure of my arms and I held her tightly. Her face was upturned, her eyes closed, her moist lips partially open. She ran her tongue around them. I kissed her again, covering her mouth with my own, touching my tongue to hers, pressing her soft body to mine. Her breath was sweet and I fancied the taste of honey in her kiss.

Along with my excitement I felt a growing tenderness toward her, a feeling almost of brotherly protectiveness, which was strangely, in fact ridiculously, at odds with my every other sensation. My hands moved gradually down along her back, the tips of my fingers touching briefly while they held her narrow waist. Then her buttocks rested against my palms while she leaned back, smiling, unfastening my coat and vest, loosening my cravat, one by one by one undoing the buttons of my shirt. I began to speak but she pressed her finger against my lips. Her warm hands slipped inside my shirt, encircling my waist and drawing me again near her, pressing her hips gently against mine, undulating them as if to soft, unheard music.

Oh, my God, thought I, removing my coat and vest. I do not recall another coherent thought. One boot slid off easily. The other gave me no end of trouble.

Her skin was incredibly beautiful, white and smooth, without a blemish. Her hair was warm and silky against my cheek, and her breasts were firm. I turned over upon her and plunged my tongue between them. I could feel her fingers descend tremblingly from my ribs and touch gently along the inside of my thigh.

I put a fresh log on her fire before I left. With something like a shudder I placed a bank note, payable by Mr. Biddle himself, on a small table beside her bed. She lay partially on her side, deeply asleep, the bedclothes rising and falling with her rhythmic breathing. I bent down and kissed her closed eyes tenderly. Then I groped my way down the unlighted stairs and, wrapping my cloak around me, let myself out into the street. The snow was still falling softly. As I walked toward Fulton, it filled my tracks behind me.

Five nights later I went again to Theater Alley, but Helen Jewett had gone. "Fancied herself too good for the like of us," coughed the Duchesse.

"Please tell me, where has she gone?"

"Uptown," the Duchesse answered, opening the door wider to spit into the snow. "Won't do you no good to follow her, Master Robin, as she has already set her cap for another, a puling, puking infant, ten o' which, to judge from looks, ain't worth one like you, young sir, but then there's no predicting the ways a woman's foolish heart will lead her, and us o' the gentler sex, by Jesus, was always slaves to the whimsies and tuggings of our hearts, poor helpless creatures that we are."

I started to go and she quickly reached out a fat hand and seized my arm. "Come inside for a second or two, young sir," she said. "No need for suspicion. No interior motive intended." I pulled up the collar of my cloak and she, I suppose to demonstrate good will, blew out her candle. She closed the door against the cold and we stood together in total darkness.

"Meaning you well, and speaking only for your own good, young sir"—her hoarse voice seemed to rasp up at me out of a bottomless Tartarus—"and talking as a woman of some experience in matters of this peculiar nature, which, God knows, I am that, I want only to say, sir, that whatever your feelings of the moment, at which I might be so bold as to guess, it would be the height of wisdom for you to give no further thought to her, since if you hope to save her, Master Robin, it may be that you are ten years behind times, and if you wish to see what she will become, then I am my own crystal and can tell the future in no longer than it takes to strike a match."

She scratched a locofoco against the wall. It flared beneath her stubbled chin, hollow, rouged cheeks, and sunken, haunted eyes. My own face must have appeared quite as ghastly in that phosphoric light, for she quickly extinguished the flame with a blast of her pestilent breath.

I yielded, that night, less to the logic of the old bawd's words than to the logic of the old bawd herself. Perhaps I was jealous of the "puling, puking infant" whom Helen supposedly preferred to all her other suitors, fawning on him as her "dear Frank," though, according to the Duchesse, he was "a mere pantywaist, for whom 'stripling' is too manly a description." Perhaps, also, I was unduly affected by tiny Dolly, an auburn-haired little seamstress that afternoon misdirected into the Duchesse's household, who greeted me with wide-eyed terror and bade me good night with a pledge of eternal love and devotion.

And perhaps it was only the result of the spell into which the old Duchesse had cast me, that each time I looked at little Dolly's sweet, frightened face it seemed to dissolve into Helen's, and then into the hideous mask of the Duchesse herself. I have since had cause to wonder many times what might have been the result had I turned my back on the Duchesse that evening and gone in search of Helen Jewett. For, today, as I write this, the Duchesse is still doing business at her old stand and little Dolly is the respected wife of a state senator.

As for Helen Jewett, I was never to see her again, alive.

# 9   The Horse-Expressman

Late in January, quite by accident, I rose another step in Day's estimation. It was always a matter of fierce competition among the papers as to which printed first the latest news from the national government in Washington City. The six-penny press, at Colonel Webb's instigation, formed a combination and ran a horse-express up from Philadelphia which brought the news faster than the penny papers could get it by mail. Day was furious, and determined to establish his own horse-express, but Beach argued that the costs would be prohibitive unless the *Sun* combined with the other penny papers. Gradually he talked Day into broaching the scheme to Stanley, Lynde, and Hayward, the triumvirate who owned the *Transcript,* though Ben refused absolutely to deal with the hated *Herald* and Bennett.

There had been a long-standing bitterness between Washington City and Paris over American claims for reparations stemming from France's seizure of our neutral shipping during the Napoleonic Wars. This dispute threatened periodically to explode into war. When France reneged on the first payment in 1835, President Jackson threatened reprisals on French property, and Henry Clay, as always, leaped into the fray seeking compromise. Clay notwithstanding, rumors of war were everywhere in December and January.

On Tuesday, January 19, toward evening I went to the taproom of the American Hotel, ordered a Scotch, and took a table. Shortly a man of about thirty-five in the costume of a horseman with the mud of the street thick on his boots approached me.

"Excuse me," he said breathlessly. "I trust I'm not disturbing you, sir. You were pointed out to me as a gentleman who works for the newspapers." He reeked of horse sweat and conspiracy. I nodded.

"May I sit down? I've ridden hard, up from New Brunswick to get here." I motioned him to take a chair and he sank into it, exhaling hugely. His eyes darted around the room and he leaned forward, speaking in harsh whispers. "Do you know," he asked, "Colonel James Watson Webb?"

Again I nodded. He looked immensely relieved.

"Would you be so kind, sir, as to tell me where I can find Colonel Webb? I have here"—and he tapped his breast pocket—"a message for the colonel of the utmost urgency and importance." He again looked quickly around and then added under his breath, "From Washington."

I determined to be casual at all costs. "Washington?"

"Ay," he said. "A copy of a special message sent to Congress by the President."

"Oh, yes," I said. "The message concerning . . ."

"France!"

I reached across the table and took his hand. "Thank God you've come at last!" I exclaimed. "We feared you were lost."

"Why, I was. I am!" He lowered his voice again. "Can you direct me to the office of the *Courier and Enquirer?*"

"Of course, sir. Nothing easier." I watched his face closely. "You've met the colonel, of course."

He shook his head. "I'm told that he's a man of about thirty-five of a military bearing."

I signaled the waiter. "What will you drink, sir?"

"Nothing!" He looked alarmed. "I must first deliver this packet into Colonel Webb's hands."

"You shall, sir, you shall." I patted his arm to reassure him. "Colonel Webb will meet you here, sir. We can't risk you wandering about the city with such an important dispatch. There is always the danger, sir, that you might fall into the hands of the enemy."

He seemed confused. "The enemy?"

"The penny newspapers," I said, and he nodded solemnly.

I left him with a drink and went into Broadway, where a crowd of urchins were trying to earn pennies by holding the heads of the horses when carriages drew up to the hotel. I pulled the dirtiest of them aside. "How would you like to earn a quarter?"

"You bet I would!"

"Do you know the *Sun* office near the Park?"

"Yes, sir!"

"Go there and find a man named Mr. Beach. Bring him back in ten minutes and it's worth two bits."

"Yes, *sir!*" He started to run and I hauled him back by his collar. "Bring him back in five minutes and it's worth a dollar."

"He'll be here in two," yelled the greedy little ragamuffin.

Beach was there in four, puffing and looking as if he couldn't decide whether to be puzzled or angry. I stood and motioned him to our table. He saw me and decided to be angry.

"Cordor, what in hell . . . ?"

"Good evening, Colonel," I almost shouted. "Colonel Webb, I'd like you to meet Mr., uh . . ."

"Bridges," said the messenger.

"Bridges. Mr. Bridges, this is Colonel Webb. Colonel Webb, Mr. Bridges is one of the men in our horse-express. He's just arrived, Colonel *Webb,* with an important dispatch from Washington City. Do you understand me, sir? It concerns France, *Colonel Webb.* War has broken out . . ."

"No, no," said the messenger. "Peace . . ."

"*Peace* has broken out, sir," I said. I was standing behind Bridges, gesturing and pointing. At last a slow dawn of comprehension broke on Beach's face.

Bridges removed a packet from his coat. "I'm to deliver these papers to you personally, Colonel."

"Quite right," said Beach, accepting the envelope. "One cannot be too careful. I shall see to it you are amply rewarded, my good fellow."

Bridges yawned. "Frankly, Colonel, I'd be satisfied at the moment with a hot bath and a soft bed."

"I took the liberty of arranging for a room for Mr. Bridges here in the hotel," I said. "Your key is at the desk, sir. The staff is instructed to provide for your every comfort. Naturally," I added with an eye on Beach, "everything is to be charged to Colonel Webb's personal account."

"Naturally," said Beach generously.

The messenger rose wearily. "Most kind," he said. "Then, gentlemen, if you will forgive my early departure, I am anxious to take advantage of your hospitality. I will hear from you tomorrow, Colonel?"

"I can guarantee," I said, "that you will hear from Colonel Webb tomorrow."

I saw Bridges safely to his room. On the way down I stopped at the desk and signaled the clerk. I placed a five-dollar note on the counter and covered half with my hand. His palm slid over the other half. "Mr. Bridges in 314 is the guest of Colonel James Watson Webb," I said quietly. "The colonel does not wish him disturbed under any circumstances. We have reason to suspect—" I looked about cautiously and motioned him closer. "We have reason to suspect that there is a man in this city posing as Colonel Webb."

The clerk was shocked.

"This man may attempt to contact Mr. Bridges. It is imperative that they be prevented from meeting. It is a matter of national security."

"You may rely on me, sir," said the clerk, his fingers busily inching their way up the note.

"I trust I may, sir." I released the bill and it vanished into his vest pocket.

Beach was rummaging through the papers and fairly giggling when I rejoined him. "This is marvelous, Davy. William IV of England has acted as mediator in the French reparations matter. The upshot is that Paris will pay twenty-five million francs in a lump sum and Jackson will accept it. War is averted. There's the fine hand of Clay in this business, you may be certain. How on earth did you get on to this man of Webb's?"

"Would you believe he just walked in and sat down at my table?"

Beach squinted at me. "Not for a single minute," he said.

"Nevertheless," I said, "that is my story and I'm sticking to it."

"Hum," said Beach, studying me narrowly. Then his eyes began to widen until I thought they would pop out of his head. "Good God!" he murmured.

I turned. In the doorway leading from the taproom to the lobby loomed the solid figure of James Watson Webb. Like Zeus searching out Hermes he glared from beneath his ferocious brows into every corner of the room. The little desk clerk quaked beside him. At last the colonel spun angrily on his heel and stormed away. When he was safely out of sight Beach peered cautiously from behind his papers and the clerk sprinted toward our table.

"That was *him,* Mr. Cordor!" the clerk announced frantically. "A terrible man, truly, sir! Oh, it *is* fortunate you warned me about him."

Beach raised his eyebrows, completely baffled.

"He didn't see Bridges?" I asked.

"Oh, *no,* sir!" cried the clerk. "I told him there was no one registered by that name."

"It's all right, sir," I said to Beach. "Merely that impostor again, pretending to be you, Colonel."

The clerk jerked a thumb toward Beach. "Then, *this* is—"

I raised my hand. "No names, please," I said quickly.

"Of course, of course." The little man edged away, bowing. "You may depend on my discretion, gentlemen." He sidled back to the lobby.

Beach stared after him and then focused on me once again. "I'm remembering," he said at last, "the day you applied for a job in Ben's office. Tell me the truth, Davy. Your uncle never knew Arunah Abell at all, did he?"

"The truth, Mr. Beach," I said. "My uncle and Arunah Abell were raised as brothers from infancy in the Jersey woods by a she-wolf."

"Finally," said Beach, "a story I can believe." He stuffed the precious papers back into the envelope. "I'd better get this packet to the office." He consulted a large gold pocket watch. "There's just time to set it up for the morning edition. This should singe Webb's side-whiskers!" He laughed, then in a second turned serious and regarded me again. "Hum," he said, "hum. Good evening, Davy." He turned and walked out.

I picked up my long-neglected Scotch and drained it. The waiter was immediately at my elbow with a fresh drink. "Ralph," I said, "I didn't order this."

"Compliments of the gentleman sitting behind you, Mr. Cordor," replied the waiter.

I looked around into a pair of shrewd brown eyes above a sloping nose and a close-cropped black moustache.

"Mr. Quinncannon would like you to join him, sir," the waiter concluded.

## 10　Mr. Lon Quinncannon

Mr. Lon Quinncannon, now that I had a close, unhurried look at him, appeared a pleasant-enough sort of fellow, not nearly the man of mystery he was reported to be. He seemed to be about thirty, though he might have been as young as twenty-five or as old as thirty-five. He was one of those fortunate men whose physical appearance does not change markedly between the ages of twenty and forty-five. It is a quality envied by men like myself who, at twenty, are still sometimes mistaken for striplings of sixteen.

His eyes were not only his most expressive feature but virtually his only expressive one. When they were closed it was quite impossible to guess what he was thinking. Though he smiled readily and pleasantly enough, his mouth, unlike that of most men, revealed little of what was in his mind. He had a habit of raising one eyebrow slightly when he was skeptical of a statement or an opinion, which was often. His natural manner was cordial, even genial when among friends, yet there was a reserve, a privacy about the man which even I never fully succeeded in penetrating, though I came to know him, I believe, better than any man living.

When I had seated myself at Quinncannon's table I protested his having bought me a drink when it was clearly I who was already too much in his debt. He waved away my concern.

"You've given me considerable entertainment with my dinner, Mr.

Cordor," he said in his slight Irish brogue. "The expression on Colonel Webb's face alone would have brought a charge of admission." He broke into a laugh. "You see, I have eavesdropped on the entire episode. If you ever tire of journalism, Mr. Cordor, you have a brilliant future as a confidence man. Come and see me. I have connections." He laughed again, as if at a private joke.

"Nevertheless, sir, you place me even deeper in your debt."

He raised one eyebrow slightly. "Were you in so very deep before this evening?"

"There is an ugly rumor," I said lightly, "that you saved my life in Cedar Street."

"There is an uglier rumor," he replied, "that I lost a man in Cedar Street." The image of the hawk-faced fireman flashed into my mind. I saw again the look of astonishment on his dying face. "His name was Ralston," Quinncannon said. "He was twenty-nine. He left a widow and two youngsters. He played good banjo and bad whist."

"Did you know him well?"

"Never met him," Quïnncannon said. He took out a pouch of tobacco and began to fill his pipe.

"The fact remains," I said earnestly, "were it not for you and men like Ralston we would be sitting here on a mound of ashes."

"So I read in your newspaper." He smiled slightly. "You've even made the blasphemous suggestion that I am a fit subject for a Sunday sermon. Fortunately, no decent clergyman in the city would have Ben Day's rag in his privy."

I picked up my Scotch. "You gave me, by the way, some excellent advice on how to approach Mr. Day."

He was holding a locofoco over the bowl of his pipe. Between puffs he said, "Did I?"

"You told me to study temperance and murder."

A smile slowly creased his face. "I can see how far you've progressed with the first," he said. "How are you coming with the second?"

At that moment, the murder of Sarah Maria Cornell crowded all other thoughts out of my mind. I both longed and feared to raise the subject. Remembering Attree's bitter comments on the Avery trial, I imagined, I suppose, that Quinncannon might be ashamed of the role he had played in the Cornell investigation. Still, I had made up my mind to introduce the topic, when we were interrupted by a stout, bearded man in his fifties who separated himself from a group just entering and made his way rapidly to our table. He and Quinncannon greeted each other vigorously and the Irishman introduced us.

"Ogden, this is Mr. David Cordor. Cordor, meet Ogden Hoffman of Hoffman and Maxwell, the second-best trial lawyer in the city of New York."

"I'm pleased to meet you, sir," I said.

"Cordor is a reporter for Ben Day," Quinncannon said.

"Well, you're a young fellow," Hoffman boomed, pumping my hand. "You still have time to find honest work."

"Now, what was it Decatur said about you when you left the navy?" Quinncannon asked dryly.

"That his one regret was that such a fine young man should exchange an honorable profession for that of a lawyer!" Hoffman threw his massive head back and laughed. "Great old salt, Decatur! And what's this about the 'second-best attorney'?"

Quinncannon's eyes rolled in mock astonishment. "Why, Ogden, is Aaron Burr dead?"

Ogden Hoffman laughed again. Despite his lack of stature he was an imposing man, with the voice and bearing of a great actor and a presence that seemed to fill even that large room. "Don't listen to this Irish son of a bitch, Mr. Cordor. I was the finest district attorney this town ever saw."

"Excepting Cadwallader Colden," Quinncannon said quietly.

"Colden was an ass! He let Burr tie his witnesses in knots."

"Not to mention Hamilton."

"Precisely my point!" Hoffman roared. He invited us to sit down (as if we had invaded his table) and looked around for a waiter. "What the hell do you have to do to get a drink around here? Ralph!" He leaned toward me and said genially, "Don't mind us, son. Some men refight old military engagements or political campaigns. The Irishman and I battle over old murder trials." He glared at Quinncannon. "The hell with Hamilton! Without Burr, Weeks would have been convicted and you know it."

"After they fished the corpse out of Burr's own well," Quinncannon said, smiling, "defending Weeks was the least he could do."

"Excuse me, gentlemen—" I began.

The waiter arrived. Hoffman took command. "Ralph, a Scotch for me and another of whatever these gentlemen are drinking. And, Ralph—" His voice grew confidential. "I don't want to alarm you but there's an Irishman loose in your establishment. Have you counted the silverware?"

"Yes, sir, Mr. Hoffman," said the waiter, grinning at Quinncannon.

"Good boy," said Hoffman. "Now count the chambermaids."

"Yes, sir." The waiter left, still grinning.

I said, "May I ask you a question?"

"Of course, lad," Hoffman said.

"I should have mentioned," Quinncannon explained, "Cordor also has a professional interest in murder."

"The Hamilton you mentioned, sir," I said to Hoffman. "Was that Alexander Hamilton?"

"The very same."

"Then, do you mean that Hamilton and Burr were associated in a murder case?"

"Why, yes, lad. Just four years before Burr killed him." Hoffman slapped his palm down on the table. "Lon, you and I are being extremely rude. Mr. Cordor is unfamiliar with the Weeks trial. Will you explain it or shall I?"

"By all means, you," Quinncannon replied. "I'll be here to correct the most ridiculous of your assertions." He leaned back, smoking his pipe, watching Hoffman out of the corner of his eye with a smile of indulgence and affection.

"Well, then, lad, the murder happened thirty-six years ago. Neither one of you fellows was even born, and I was only a boy myself, a year or two younger than you, Mr. Cordor. It was just the turn of the century, December 1799. I remember that General Washington had just died. Now, lad, it's important to know that New York had only two banks back then."

"Not crucial," said Quinncannon.

"Interesting," Hoffman insisted. "Both banks were controlled by the Federalists, who had carefully arranged that the legislature charter no Republican banks. That is where Aaron Burr first makes his appearance, you see, for he tricked Albany into chartering the Manhattan Company, ostensibly for the purpose of developing a water source untainted by the yellow fever. What he buried in the bill was a provision permitting him to put the company's surplus capital into any other venture, and the venture he had in mind was a Republican bank. Still, he had to make some effort to find water, so he sank a well in Lispenard's Meadow, as the swampland along the river north of Reade Street was called in those days. Then he boarded the well over and abandoned it. And thus, Mr. Cordor, had Burr not wished for a banking career there would have been no well for Levi Weeks to throw the body of his lover into after he strangled her."

"Objection," said Quinncannon. "Incompetent, irrelevant, immaterial, and assuming facts not in evidence. There was no proof that it was Weeks who killed her."

Hoffman cleared his throat. "Well, if you're going to break in every fifteen seconds, Lon, perhaps you should tell the story."

Quinncannon rested his chin in his hand. "You see, Cordor—tell me, what do your friends call you?"

"Davy."

"Mine call me Lon and Hoffman has no friends. You see, Davy, you must understand at the outset that Hoffman believes Levi Weeks was guilty while I am convinced of his innocence." He waved his hand. "Now go ahead with your narrative, Ogden. I won't interrupt again."

He did, of course, several times, but gradually the story emerged. The victim's name was Elma Sands, a pretty little thing of twenty-two who lived on Greenwich Street near Lispenard's Meadow in a boardinghouse owned by her Quaker cousin Kate Ring and her husband, Elias. Among the boarders were Hope Sands, Kate Ring's younger sister; an attractive Englishwoman named Margaret Clark; and Levi Weeks, the nephew of a prosperous builder. The young man was employed by his uncle, had plenty of ready money, a handsome fellow who considered himself the local Casanova.

Hope Sands was plain and pudgy, in her late twenties, an age when, even now, a woman is considered an old maid. She set her cap for the elusive Weeks, but that worthy was romancing Margaret Clark. To clear a path for Hope, Kate Ring, as Quinncannon said, "lobbed Miss Clark's lovely body out into the slush," but the sisters had not counted on the charms of the recently arrived cousin, Elma.

"I recall the usual yellow-fever epidemic in the summer of '99," Hoffman said. "Those who could afford it, including Kate Ring, headed for the countryside to Greenwich Village to wait out the plague. The rest of us protected ourselves as best we could with bags of camphor around our necks and garlic cloves in our shoes and our heads doused with the Vinegar of the Four Thieves. That summer Weeks began a rather shabby affair with Elma Sands. To this day I don't know how they stood each other. By August most of us couldn't bear to be in the same room with someone else for *any* purpose."

Keeping tabs on the lovers became the favorite sport of the other boarders, particularly Hope. Her room faced Elma's and during the height of the passionate intrigue Hope moved her bed so that, by keeping her own door ajar, she could monitor the traffic in and out of Elma's chamber.

This sordid romance continued until December 22, when Elma vanished. At Weeks' trial Hope Sands swore that, a few days before her disappearance, Elma had confided that she and Levi were planning to elope on the twenty-second, pledging her cousin to secrecy. Kate Ring testified to hearing the same story from Elma on the day she disappeared, but neither sister had mentioned the impending marriage to anyone and Weeks hotly denied it.

Early in the evening of the twenty-second Elma borrowed a muff from a neighbor girl but said nothing about a wedding. That night Hope went out. Kate and her husband sat with some of the boarders in the parlor, where Levi joined them shortly after eight. About eight-twenty, Weeks went into the hall. A few minutes later Elma came downstairs, and the folks in the parlor heard whispering and the front door open and close. Between eight-thirty and ten, no one entered or left the house.

At ten Weeks returned and went into the parlor, where the Rings were now sitting alone. He asked if Hope had gotten home yet and was told she had not. He then asked if Elma had gone to bed. Kate testified she was surprised at the question and replied that Elma had gone out. At this Weeks seemed amazed and said it was odd for the girl to be out at that hour alone. Mrs. Ring answered that she had no reason to think Elma had gone alone. Weeks made no reply and shortly after went to bed. Kate found Elma's room empty and waited up until midnight, when she decided the girl was spending the night with friends.

It snowed heavily that night and, had an alarm been raised at once, Elma's tracks might have been easily traced, but there was no discussion of the girl's disappearance for two days, until the boarders began to notice it. On Christmas Eve the borrowed muff was found in Lispenard's Meadow, but no one followed up this clue until January 2, when Elias Ring led a search party which discovered Elma at the bottom of Aaron Burr's well. She was fully dressed, with marks on her throat suggesting strangulation, but no autopsy was performed to determine the amount of water in the lungs and the doctors had to admit she might have drowned.

"But drowned or garroted," Quinncannon said, "it was murder, Davy, because the well was boarded over. She could not have committed suicide or fallen in accidentally because, once in the well, she could not have covered it again."

"I remember her body was laid out on a table in front of the Ring house for a full day," Hoffman said. "Believe it or not, I stood in line for three hours in a biting wind to get a glimpse of her. Four days later they arrested Levi Weeks."

It had been the prosecution's contention, and was now Hoffman's, that Elma had demanded marriage and respectability, and Weeks, the dashing young blade, valued his freedom and murdered the girl to be rid of her. There had been no autopsy, and therefore no proof of pregnancy, but the district attorney had hinted darkly at this possibility. Quinncannon argued that even Kate Ring, "who surely must have been watching for signs and who did everything in her power to get Weeks convicted," had never suggested the girl was pregnant. Hoffman countered with six eyewitnesses to the movements of Elma and Levi on the fatal night.

"Levi's uncle Ezra lived just a short distance away, Davy," Hoffman said, "and nearby was the stable where Ezra kept his horse and sleigh. A neighbor, Susanna Broad, saw Ezra's sleigh leaving the stable at about eight-thirty. A witness, Maggie Freeman, saw the sleigh driving up Greenwich Street toward Lispenard's Meadow with a man and a woman whom she identified as Elma Sands. Another witness, Buthrong Anderson, also saw the sleigh and recognized the horse as belonging to Ezra Weeks. Lawrence and Arnetta Van Norden, who lived near the well, heard a girl's voice crying 'Murder!' Catherine Lyon, who also lived near the well, not only heard the cries, but saw Elma running across the meadow. Of course, tight as this chain of evidence is, it is only circumstantial—"

Quinncannon here gave such a groan that I feared for a moment he was actually ill. "Shyster," he muttered, "reprobate! You should have been disbarred twenty years ago. How dare you dignify that ridiculous claptrap as 'circumstantial evidence'? Even Cadwallader Colden never sank that far."

"You've wounded me now, Lon," Hoffman said, reaching for his drink. "A palpable thrust, so help me. I bleed."

"Ersine defecation!" said Lon Quinncannon. "Observe this aging mountebank, Davy, shamelessly parading the most elderly flimflam in his ancient bag of tricks. For centuries these pettifoggers have promoted the fiction that direct, eyewitness testimony is more to be relied on than circumstantial evidence. Ogden has provided the perfect example to prove my point. Not one shred of evidence in the state's case against Weeks was circumstantial. It was all direct testimony, and what, in the end, was it worth? Susanna Broad wasn't certain which evening she had seen Ezra Weeks's sleigh, was she? It could have been a week before the murder, or a week later, or any time at all, couldn't it? Buthrong Anderson—you remember good old Buthrong, don't you, Ogden? He's the fellow who made the positive identification of the *horse?* Well, good old Buthrong, on second thought, recalled he might have seen that horse back on Thanksgiving, didn't he? And good old Buthrong had a couple of friends who swore he was so drunk he couldn't have seen anything so small as a horse.

"And Maggie Freeman, who saw Elma in the sleigh? She eventually decided it had been snowing so hard that night she couldn't have identified her own mother. The Van Nordens, who heard cries of 'Murder,' concluded that it could have been the wind. Old Mrs. Lyon, who heard the murder and saw Elma fleeing, turned out to be so deaf she couldn't hear the prosecutor's questions and so blind she couldn't find one hand with the help of the other."

Quinncannon lit his pipe. "You see, Davy, that nonsense and the vicious gossip of a few boarders was the state's whole case. Not a circumstance in the batch. Nothing but eyewitnesses, and I'm going to let you in on a shocking fact about witnesses." He leaned forward in conspiratorial fashion. "Witnesses," he said, "sometimes tell lies."

He reclined in his chair, smoking, smiling at each of us in turn I asked, "How did Levi Weeks get off?"

"Alibi was airtight for one thing," the Irishman answered. "The boy was at his uncle's home until eight, left briefly for his rooming house, and returned about eight-thirty. He stayed until ten and went home. Both Ezra and his wife so swore and they withstood cross-examination a lot better than good old Buthrong. As for the sleigh, one Demas Meed, who kept the stable, testified there was no evidence that either the sleigh or the horse had been taken out that night.

"And the state couldn't prove a motive. There was no evidence that Elma was pregnant, no evidence she was hounding Weeks into marriage, no evidence she ever intended to elope with him except the statements of Hope and her sister, who didn't remember the elopement until after the body was found."

"Then," I said, "who *did* murder the girl?"

"Hope Sands," he said simply.

Hoffman raised his glass in a mock toast. "Comes now the pet theory."

Quinncannon lifted both his glass and his eyebrow. "Hope had young Weeks to herself briefly between Margaret Clark's eviction and Elma's arrival. She was violently jealous of her pretty little cousin, and on the night of December 22, she lured the girl to the meadow on some pretext, attempted to strangle her, and ended by shoving her in the well and stupidly boarding it over again, probably to prevent discovery.

"Her sister waited up until midnight, not for Elma, but for Hope. Possibly Kate expected the worst. At any rate, Hope confessed. They must have thought it would all blow over. Even when the boarders got curious, even when the muff was found, they made no search, no inquiry, no effort to contact the authorities. Finally, ten days later, when the snow had obliterated all trace of the crime, Elias Ring led a party straight to the well.

"Only then do the sisters concoct the elopement story. The boards over the well prove murder and Weeks, whom Hope planned to ensnare once Elma was gone, must now be sacrificed.

"Kate Ring is clearly lying about the elopement. If the young couple were really going to put an end to the family scandal she'd have been bursting with the news, yet she didn't even tell her husband. She certainly would have questioned Weeks when he arrived at ten claiming to know nothing of Elma's whereabouts. As it was, Kate saw no alternative to protecting her little sister. She went along with the elopement story."

He paused to refill his glass. "The strength of a good circumstantial case, as you well know, Ogden, is that it's much like a Chinese puzzle. There is only one way to fit the pieces together, and all the pieces must fit or the whole thing collapses into a rubble of reasonable doubt."

"Odd how everyone connected with the Weeks case came to a bad end," Hoffman said. "Kate Ring died within a year. Hope Sands lived out her days a lonely, bitter old maid. Burr shot Hamilton and destroyed his own political career. Even the judge . . ."

I asked what had happened to the judge.

"Chief Justice John Lansing." Hoffman shuddered. "Terrifying character. Some years later he left the City Hotel to catch the night boat for Albany and evaporated into thin air. Never heard from again."

"Cadwallader Colden was elected mayor," Quinncannon said dryly.

Hoffman laughed. "Just my point. Everyone a bad end."

"Levi Weeks, too?" I said.

Hoffman nodded his shaggy head. "In the eyes of the public Weeks was guilty. The jury took only four minutes to acquit, yet there was an angry outcry even as he walked from the courtroom. In less than a year he was forced to leave the city."

I turned to Quinncannon. "Was the trial of Ephraim K. Avery a good circumstantial case, Lon?"

"Yes, Davy, it was."

"And you got him acquitted, but public opinion drove him away, too."

The Irishman smiled. "I suppose the reason I've remained in your country longer than I intended, gentlemen, is that I find you, as a nation, such an interesting study in attitudes. You are so young, so vigorous, so noble, so certain of your destiny, so—what is that word you're fond of using, Ogden?—so 'right-minded.' Understand, Davy, that 'right-mindedness' is merely conscious virtue and to be 'right-minded' in 1800 was to know that respectable Christian ladies like Hope Sands and Kate Ring would not lie under oath, and to *know* that Ezra Weeks would lie, and his nephew would commit murder. Levi and Ezra Weeks, Davy, were Jews."

Hoffman growled, "Damn it, Lon."

"In your country," Quinncannon went on, "where the human race has set higher moral goals for itself than ever before, you have developed a greater capacity than any nation in history for hyprocrisy."

"You snide, slanderous Irishman!" Hoffman snapped. "Be thankful you're among friends and curb your insults. No other nation on earth would endure the barbaric ignorance of so many of your—"

He stopped suddenly.

"Countrymen?" Quinncannon offered quietly.

Hoffman glowered at him.

Quinncannon shook his head. "Entrapment. That wasn't fair. I'm sorry, old friend. Truly sorry." He turned to me and began to fill his pipe. "I should make it clear, Davy, that Ogden Hoffman is as decent and honest a man as I, and probably you, shall ever meet. That is because, instead of devoting himself to the good of all his fellowmen at once, he has given his skill and energy to helping them one at a time and therefore accomplished a great deal—far too much, in fact, to be likely of mention in the history books."

"I still don't understand Avery," I said. "If he symbolized anything it was the conservative establishment. His acquittal should have been welcomed by the righteous and respectable."

"Avery was a basically weak man who strayed too far from his wife's side. He committed the unpardonable sin. He created a scandal. Sarah Cornell, the murdered girl, was a cheat, a thief, a liar, and a slut. The liberal press loved her. They created a martyr-saint, a symbol of the poor, the weak, the frail, and the halt. Symbolic thinking is slovenly. The trial was a great morality play. They divided the characters into heroes and villains and prejudged on the sole ground of rooting interest." He looked at me narrowly. "Did you think the establishment held a monopoly on conscious virtue?"

The Irishman finished his drink and reached for his hat. "Poor Avery. The press turned him into a pariah. The church paid his legal fees and let him be kicked out of his pulpit. His neighbors pointed their fingers and crossed the street when they saw him coming."

Hoffman clucked his tongue softly. " 'They helped every one his neighbor; and every one said to his brother, Be of good comfort.' " He looked up. "Isaiah, gentlemen."

"Ogden." Quinncannon's lips compressed into a taut smile. "Conscious virtue is bad enough from a clergyman or a penny-press editor. From a lawyer it's merely embarrassing." He threw on his cloak. "Remember what heathen Hesiod said: 'When you deal with your brother, be pleasant, but get a witness.' "

## 11 Mr. Cordor before the Bar

The following morning I was rudely aroused from a deep sleep by someone shaking me vigorously and shouting my name. At last I blinked up into the pockmarked faces of Will Prall and his watch, both of which immediately informed me it was past ten o'clock.

It had been our custom, since we roomed in the same house, to breakfast and walk together each morning to the *Sun* offices. Being the lighter sleeper, it was normally my problem to drag Prall out of bed and render him, after a fashion, ambulatory. "Damn you, Will," I growled, "why didn't you wake me? Now we'll both be late."

"Not I, Davy." Prall grinned. "I'm already at work. I'm covering an important story."

Still half asleep, I pulled on my shirt. "What important story?"

"Your arrest."

He was smirking in a most infuriating manner. "There are three officers downstairs waiting with a warrant. You seem to be quite a dangerous character. If there's a reward, I'm to share in it."

I finished dressing quickly. "This is ridiculous. What in hell are the charges?"

"Oh," he said, "something about kidnapping, breaking a seal, and impersonating some colonel or other. By the way, have you seen this morning's paper?"

The *Sun*'s front page carried the full text of Jackson's message to

Congress under the head: WAR WITH FRANCE AVERTED. I smiled. "So that's it. And Webb has brought charges against me. Will, do Day and Beach know I'm being arrested?"

"I would imagine so," he replied, following me down the stairs. "It's rumored the three of you are going to share a cell."

The commotion in Justice Robert Taylor's court was such that he was later reported to have said he would take on the Duchesse de Berri's ladies-in-waiting and six more hen coops of the same rather than have two journalists before his bench. The colonel was storming in apoplectic fashion, periodically calmed by a harsh warning from the judge, constantly soothed by the fussy attentions of Mr. Hoskin, his commercial and foreign editor. Ben Day was not present, but Beach was, looking scholarly and befuddled, surrounded by attorneys. The benches reserved for the press—the "pews," as Attree called them—were packed with the cream of New York journalism and the atmosphere was Saturnalia. In a quick glance I could make out Major Mordecai Manuel Noah of the *Evening Star,* Charles King of the *American,* William Leggett of the *Evening Post.* Gerard Hallock, the editor of the *Journal of Commerce,* who shared the expense of Webb's hijacked horse-express, sat nervously on a front bench near the rail. Representing the *Transcript,* Attree leered and winked at me madly from the moment I entered. I noticed William Leete Stone, editor of the *Commercial Advertiser,* and at least a half dozen others.

At the extreme end of the hindmost bench, like the leper sponging at the feast, sat an angular, squinting man of about forty, smiling malevolently beneath a huge, hooked nose. The *Herald* also was represented.

The judge gaveled wearily for order while Colonel Webb shouted his charges that a "diabolical plot" had been rigged against his *Courier and Enquirer* by three "nefarious denizens" of "that kennel on Spruce Street known as the *Sun* newspaper." With "outrageous guile and deliberate malice" the "bulldog, the hound, and the puppy" had lured the *Courier*'s messenger into their "kennel" and duped him out of a packet intended only for the eyes of the colonel himself. Day apparently was the "bulldog" and Beach the "hound." The "puppy," I imagined, was a reference to me.

In a state of stark terror, the little room clerk from the American Hotel was brought in to testify. He spoke tremblingly of arranging accommodations for a guest named Bridges at the request of Mr. Cordor and of being warned by Mr. Cordor that there was a man about passing himself off as Colonel Webb. It was for this reason, he stuttered, that when the real Colonel Webb inquired he lied and stated that there was no Mr. Bridges in the hotel.

"Aha!" thundered the colonel. "And will you identify this man named Cordor for the court?"

The clerk pointed a shivering finger at me.

Justice Taylor pounded his gavel. "If you please, Colonel Webb, this is my court and I will put the questions to the witness."

"In that case," said the colonel, "will you ask the witness," and he wheeled and thundered at the clerk: "Is this man, Mr. Moses Yale Beach, the man who masqueraded as myself last evening in your hotel?"

"Yes, sir," the clerk murmured.

"Thank you, Colonel, for allowing me to put the question," said Taylor with a sigh.

"The proofs are clear, Bob," Webb shouted.

"This is a court of law, Jim," Taylor said. "Try to remember to call me 'your honor.' "

"All right, damnation, but the case is transparent! This Cordor fellow works for the *Sun.* The whole thing was a vicious scheme to kidnap my horse-express man!"

"Excuse me," I said. "Justice Taylor, may I ask some questions of this witness?"

One of the *Sun*'s lawyers groaned. Another said sharply, "Mr. Cordor!" I felt Beach's grip on my wrist. "Davy," he whispered, "dear boy, shut up!"

Taylor shrugged his assent. I turned to the clerk. "Did I warn you last night that there was someone about impersonating Colonel Webb?"

"Yes, sir, you did."

"And is it now your understanding that someone was, in fact, impersonating Colonel Webb?"

"Yes, sir. But—"

"So I did not lie to you, did I?"

"No, sir, but—"

I pointed to Beach. "Do you know this man's name?"

"It's Beach, sir, as I come to find out this morning, but—"

"Have you ever seen Mr. Beach before this morning?"

"Only last night, sir, when I went over to your table, but—"

"Did you—" I began.

"BUT!" the clerk howled. The room was silent. He looked around sheepishly. "Sorry, your honor, but I have to get my but in here someplace!"

The crowd laughed and Taylor gaveled. "You may get your but in here," he said kindly.

"Thank you, your honor." The clerk turned toward the bench and almost rested his chin on the judge's desk top. "But, you see, your honor, last night I thought Mr. Beach was Colonel Webb."

"Did I say so?" I asked. No answer.

"Did Mr. Cordor say so?" Taylor asked.

"Well, no, your honor. Not exactly."

"What did Mr. Cordor tell you about Mr. Beach?" asked the justice.

"He said no names was to be used," the clerk answered at last.

Taylor looked at Webb helplessly. "Well, Colonel, if this is your only witness . . ."

"He is not!" the colonel fumed. "Damnation, there's Bridges, the horse-express man."

The justice waited expectantly. Finally he said, "All right, where is the witness?"

Hoskin stepped up in some embarrassment. "At the present moment, your honor," he said in a clipped English accent, "we are unable to ascertain the whereabouts of Mr. Bridges."

"But *they've* got him," Webb exploded with a gesture that took in Beach and myself and the entire "kennel" on Spruce Street. "They've got him hidden somewhere, kidnapped or murdered for all we know!"

One of the *Sun's* attorneys now, at last, sprang into action. "I must warn you, Colonel Webb, that you have already overstepped the bounds of slander!"

Webb shouted back something about going to the grand jury. Hoskin tried to quiet Webb. Taylor pounded his gavel and shouted, "Case dismissed!" Beach stared about him and I seized his arm and steered him out of the courtroom. In the general uproar behind us I caught sight of one face towering above the rest, the narrow eyes wrinkled in high amusement, the thin lips still smiling beneath the hooked nose.

Beach and I scrambled through the Park and across Park Row to the relatively ordered din of the *Sun* building. When I'd caught my breath I turned on Beach. "All right, where *is* he?"

"He?" Beach echoed, and then his face relaxed into a grin. "Oh, he's safe enough. Come on, Davy, I'll show you."

He led the way across the main floor and up the narrow stairs to the landing. "You've got him here?" I whispered hoarsely. "Right in the building?"

"Naturally. Where else?"

"But, for godsake, it's the first place the police will look for him."

"It was indeed," Beach said. "This building was full of roundsmen this morning." He paused at the door to Day's office and opened it. The room was cluttered as usual, but empty. Beach went inside and I followed and closed the door.

"Now, Davy," Beach began, "I want you to appreciate what an honor this is for you. I have Ben's permission to show you this, and aside from Ben, Wisner, and myself, you're the only member of the staff who will know. Normally we wouldn't have let you in on it, to be frank, but we agreed last night that you were as much responsible for what happened with Bridges as anyone."

"Look," I said, "just tell me. He is . . . all right, isn't he?"

Beach looked puzzled. "Of course he is. Look here. No, Davy, you've got to come over here and look. Do you see the lever concealed behind this portrait of Ben? It's attached to a spring lock. Pull it. Well, go ahead, lad, pull it."

I pulled the lever. A panel in the office wall to the left of the desk swung back immediately. "Step through," Beach said.

"How long has he been in there?" I asked.

"Only since early this morning." Beach laughed. "But we could keep him there indefinitely if it became necessary. Go on. Step through."

I stepped through into an office which was almost an exact replica of the one I had just left. Behind a desk nearly as large and twice as cluttered sat Benjamin Day.

"But where is . . . ?" I stopped short. I was not going to admit that I had expected to find the kidnapped and possibly lifeless form of the *Courier and Enquirer*'s missing horse-express man.

Day gazed up at me and fixed his dark eyes on mine. "This office adjoined my own when the *Sun* took over this building, Cordor. I merely had the hall door bricked up and that spring-lock panel substituted for the interoffice door. There are an infinite variety of people in an average day whom the publisher of a successful penny newspaper might wish to avoid."

"Such as police," I suggested, "and process servers?"

"Exactly so. This arrangement is convenient for the purpose. If that devious derelict who edits the *Herald* had such an arrangement, his skull might have been spared a dozen or so of the numerous lumps which have rendered it a phrenologist's nightmare."

He rose and passed a paper to Beach. "Here is an editorial for tomorrow's edition, Moses. Read it aloud for Cordor's benefit."

Beach put on his spectacles and read:

We propose to expend little time or effort in answering the libelous charges flung at us by the publisher of the *Courier and Enquirer*. The space in our columns (though we have just increased our pages in size to fourteen by twenty inches, our third enlargement in less than a year) is precious and must be reserved to provide our readers with the most important news of the day published with greater speed than any of our competitors (as our recent report of the president's message to congress on France proves).

The insinuation of Webb that we violated the sanctity of a seal we hurl back in proud defiance to his own brow. We remind him (though well he knows it) that no daily newspaper in the world enjoys so extensive a circulation as the *Sun*.


"Well, gentlemen?" Day demanded.

"Incisive," Beach said. Apparently because he liked the word he repeated it.

The sole proprietor turned to me. "Your opinion, Cordor?"

"I don't think the colonel will like it," I said.

Day sighed contentedly. "Exactly so," he said.

I left Beach in the office and found Will Prall waiting in ambush on the landing. "Been in with the old man, eh?"

Remembering my oath of secrecy, I said, "Day's not in the office."

"Not that office, the secret one." I must have shown my surprise, because he said quickly, "There are no secrets in this asylum. You should know that by now. Everybody knows about the sanctum sanctorum, but no one's ever been there except Wisner and Beach."

I continued past him and started down the stairs. Behind me he said, "And you?" I kept walking.

Prall scrambled down after me. "No fooling," he kept saying, "no fooling. Boy, Davy, they must have big plans for you. No fooling." At the bottom of the stairs he caught up with me. "Listen," he said earnestly. "You and I are good friends and I've got some excellent advice I've been hoarding up to give you, but–"

I started to pull away from him. "Will you listen?" he hissed, grabbing my arm. "I'm not going to give it to you till we're both drunk, so relax. All I'm going to say is don't tell anybody you were invited to the Inner Temple. I mean it, Davy. I'm the only one in the building who wouldn't try to knife you if he knew."

"All right, Will," I assured him. "Not a word."

Prall smiled. "That's all I wanted to say. Except to tell you you handled yourself well in court this morning. Hey, what are you going to do if that horse-express man turns up?"

"Will," I said, "I wish I knew."

The mysterious disappearance of Bridges was my first concern. I left the office intending to go to the American Hotel and almost ran into one of the *Sun*'s newsboys.

"You're Mr. Cordor, ain't you?"

I confessed.

"I got a message for you," he announced with importance, "which was sent by a gentleman."

"Well, let me see it," I said.

"The gentleman said it would be worth four bits to you," said the little bandit.

"What sort of gentleman was it?"

"A proper one with a dark moustache and a funny way of talking," he answered. "He had another man with him and they got in a hansom early this morning where I was hawking the papers."

"Was that near the American Hotel?"

"It was."

"Then," I said, "it's worth six bits."

The little heir scampered off to spend his fortune while I quickly unfolded the note. It was handwritten on hotel stationery:

*Davy: Mr. Bridges will be unable to attend Special Sessions this morning as he is stricken with a sudden impulse to travel and is off to join Sam Houston in Texas. Kindly convey his regrets to the Colonel.*

*Q.*

# 12  A Conversation in a Taproom

In the weeks that followed I came to know Lon Quinncannon as well as he permitted any man to know him. His most striking quality was the sharpness of his mind and occasionally, it must be admitted, of his tongue. He seemed to enjoy deliberately shocking people in a manner which was no less barbed for being subtle. From this humor not even his friends were always spared.

Politically he considered himself a moderate, a posture from which he attacked all sides with equal ferocity. He disparaged all institutionalized religion, yet appeared to take seriously the most outrageous and discredited superstitions, extending even to lycanthropy and vampirism. Though I came to supect his iconoclasm was expressed as much for effect as from conviction, I willingly acknowledge that Quinncannon was as free of prejudices and of settled, *a priori* convictions as any man I have ever met. This was the more remarkable at a time, and in a country, when the thoughts of the vast majority of people were fixed and circumscribed by the most impregnable moral, social, and political presumptions.

If I, to a degree, was also uninhibited by firmly rooted notions, it was because, as Attree often and with some justice contended, I pointedly avoided serious thought and resisted any faint temptation to pursue premises to their logical conclusions. Two years spent at Princeton College had furnished me with a semblance of learning and a veneer of sophistication which I had discovered I could combine to my advantage with a natural glibness.

My college studies having been cut short by an unfortunate incident in which an elderly cow was found in the rooms of one of the less popular tutors, shot dead and a bit gamy, and this event coinciding with the death of a bachelor uncle, the last of my relations, I had tried my hand for a time at running the country newspaper he had willed me. The *Gazette,* of Smithville, New Jersey, never more than a struggling weekly in my uncle's time, moved rapidly toward bankruptcy under my direction, until at last I sold it—lock, stock, presses, and type—and struck out for New York at the age of nineteen.

No doubt I was, as Attree said, "as green as grass," and "as shallow as a bird bath," although Attree's gift for hyperbole was always most acute when he was criticizing me. On occasion I even worried over his charge that I lacked what he called "awareness," and a true social concern for the less fortunate, without which, he maintained, a journalist, even while writing for the penny press, was merely a tool of the artistocracy.

My problem, as Attree diagnosed it, was a result of my age. I bristled when reminded of how young I still was (an accurate observation, I confess). Yet, to his view, I used my youth as a defense, an excuse for my "essential callowness" and "lack of commitment." In short, I was a man in my own mind, but quite willing to play the boy when it might save me the trouble of adult responsibility. "We all go through it at your age, Davy," Attree would say. "I'm almost twenty-nine and I know."

My reaction to Attree normally was to assume that he was right and occasionally even to resolve that I would do something about myself. I was bursting with self-reliance, he said, but had absolutely no concept of true "individualism." I recall being particularly impressed with his distinction between self-reliance, "a belief in one's own ability and prospects," and individualism, which he defined as "a fervid conviction of the individual dignity and sanctity of every human being."

Through March and into April of 1836 my life took on an increasingly settled character. My days were spent at the Police Office with Attree, where the conversation concentrated on the necessity for social reform or on my own shortcomings. My free evenings were often passed in Quinncannon's company, discussing witchcraft and demonology in his rooms or debating old crimes with Ogden Hoffman at the table which, I soon discovered, was referred to by the staff of the American Hotel as "Mr. Quinncannon's table." There we were often joined by Hoffman's partner, Hugh Maxwell; Jacob Hays, New York's gruff, shrewd high constable; William Leete Stone, the great "investigative editor" of the *Commercial Advertiser,* who had exposed such religious frauds as Maria Monk and Matthias the Prophet; and Moses Beach, whom I had myself introduced into the circle. In such a distinguished band I made it a point to keep my mouth shut unless addressed directly.

The conversation on these occasions, accompanied by excellent Scotches, Irishes, and brandies, and savoring of the finest tobacco, wove a rich, oral tapestry of premeditated mayhem. I could close my eyes and witness the Reverend Francis Riembauer, tall and of mild countenance, whose enthusiastic piety had gained him a saintly reputation, draw near to his pregnant mistress with expressions of endearment and suddenly plunge his razor into her throat.

I heard the tale of the widow Anna Schonleben, whose sentimental heart had wept over the *Sorrows of Werther* and bled for the sufferings of Pamela and Emilia Galotti, and who, in her capacity of nurse and housekeeper, had systematically poisoned countless victims who fell under her maternal care. I heard, too, of the brutal murder of Captain Joseph White at the instigation of his nephews just six years before, at Salem, Massachusetts. I could visualize the hired killer, Richard Crowninshield, creeping up a plank and through a window into the old merchant's room, raising his bludgeon over the sleeping man's head, and coolly, deliberately, bringing it crashing down again and again.

"There must be men who are simply born evil," I observed one evening to Quinncannon when the others had left the table for their homes and he and I lingered for a final pipe.

The Irishman leaned back and closed his eyes. "What brings you," he asked through a puff of smoke, "to that conclusion?"

"How else do you explain a man like Richard Crowninshield? He was daring, subtle, adroit, circumspect, yet he turned all his talents to theft and murder. In all his life he never did one decent act."

"He had the decency to hang himself in prison and spare the general population the expense of an execution," Quinncannon remarked dryly.

"Oh, well, if you choose to be sardonic . . ."

"I choose," he said, "to be ironic."

"I am attempting," I said, "to make a moral point."

"I'm aware of that."

"And what do you make of Francis Riembauer?" I asked. "A clergyman with the highest character for intelligence and unction, who coldbloodedly poisoned two women and slit the throat of a third. I tell you, it's an argument for natural depravity."

"Poor Riembauer. His flock thought him the personification of Christian humility. He walked always with his head sunk down and his eyelids drooping, and his hands, when they weren't folded reverently on his breast, were pawing the ladies. He impregnated the carpenter's daughter at Fürth, and when she and their unborn child pursued him to Lauterbach, he panicked and murdered her with a razor. Then he had to poison the other two women."

"Had to?" I repeated incredulously.

"From his point of view. They had seen him commit the first murder, and the younger, Magdalena, was already pregnant by him. He had dug the hole himself, you see, and every fresh crime required still another to cover it. Yet, for all the blood he spilled, he would never have been caught except for the umbrella. Anna Eichstadter, his first victim, had borrowed an umbrella from her employer on the day she died. It was green, with a monogram, a good umbrella, and Riembauer kept it for a rainy day. It was the only piece of evidence he couldn't explain." He paused and opened one eye. "Don't you find that ironic?"

"I find it," I replied, "a bit seamy, to be honest."

"The Greeks might have found it tragic," he said. "Has it occurred to you that the major difference between Riembauer and Oedipus might be that Riembauer had no Sophocles to tell his story?"

"Are you saying there is something noble or tragic about Riembauer?"

He closed his eye again. "Perhaps I'm saying there was something about Oedipus which was a bit seamy."

We sat smoking for a few minutes in silence. Except for a few loiterers like ourselves the taproom was empty. A new sound, familiar but unexpected, abruptly broke the quiet. The huge drops of a sudden spring shower splashed noisily against the panes of the window near our table. I could see the late strollers on Broadway scurrying for cover.

"You have a remarkable way of changing the subject of a conversation," I said.

"Oh? I thought we were sticking to the subject rather well."

"My fault," I said. "I seem to be in a theological mood tonight, Lon. I was suggesting that the origin of evil might be sought in human depravity."

"Then you would agree with the American Puritan, Thomas Shepard, that the only route to salvation lies in learning to loathe yourself as God loathes you."

"Of course not," I answered. "But where does the guilt lie, if not in man? We buried Satan in the last century. That leaves only society to blame, or God."

Quinncannon straightened up slowly. He rested his elbows on the table and his chin on his folded hands. "Forgive me, Davy, if I observe that you share your countrymen's obsession with guilt, and their resultant, compulsive need for scapegoats. To deal with any issue in this country one must be either smugly self-righteous or abjectly guilt-ridden. Not only is there no middle ground, but more often than not the two extremes are compatible—simultaneously present. It is the most damnably incredible phenomenon, a heritage, no doubt, from your Puritan ancestors. Evil exists. Very well. Why must you seek to fix blame for it?"

"A murder occurs. Very well. Why must *you* seek to fix guilt for it?"

"That," he said, "is an intellectual exercise, not a moral judgment."

"I see," I said coldly. "There is something wrong, I gather, with moral judgment."

"You see, Davy," he said in his damn, easy Irish manner, "you wish me to express a moral judgment on the subject of moral judgment."

The rain had stopped as quickly as it began. Outside, the strollers were venturing forth, with cautious eyes on the darkened skies. The bartender sang out, "Time, gentlemen," and wound his watch.

I said, "Perhaps you would give me your definition of moralism."

"Certainly," Quinncannon replied. He finished his drink and dropped some coins on the table. "Moralism is the opposite of irony— the total absence of irony—just as melodrama is the absence of tragedy, and sentiment the absence of satire."

We walked out to the street together. The rain had washed the air clean of smoke and left it fresh and brisk. A light breeze was blowing east from the river. It seemed a beautiful evening for a walk and I passed up the cab which stood at the door. Quinncannon touched the handle of his folded umbrella to the brim of his hat with a smile and crossed the street. I watched him go, then thrust my hands into my pockets and sauntered down Broadway toward Ann Street.

When I reached the corner of the Park the skies opened up again. By the time I got to my rooming house I was drenched to the skin.

## 13  The Five Points

Away from the *Sun* I had spent very little time with Will Prall; in fact, for weeks I had avoided him. Therefore, on the evening of April 1, a Friday, when he bluntly proposed a night at the Five Points, I found myself out of excuses. It was not that I had a grudge against Prall, though I'm afraid the poor fellow suspected I was still angry over his behavior on the morning of my arrest. The problem rather, as I then saw it, was simply that I had rapidly outgrown him. His good-natured clowning, which at first I had treated as amusing, now seemed merely childish. The petty office gossip in which he delighted bored me, and I found it increasingly tedious to feign interest. Worst of all, he had developed an admiration for me which I considered both embarrassing and absurd, in light of his being almost five years my senior. Though I tried to evade him I had no wish to hurt him, and thus, on the evening of All Fools' Day, Prall and I walked north on Centre Street toward the Five Points.

Three blocks north of the Dead House, where Cross Street runs into the intersection of Centre and Duane, lies the area known as the Five Points, the most fashionable of New York's most unfashionable sections. Young gentlemen who would not be caught dead on South Street, and who would be dead if caught on Water Street, promenade its sidewalks and seek repose and refreshment in its saloons. There is nothing—absolutely nothing—that cannot be bought there.

In a sense the district is well located. Walk three blocks west—you are at the hospital. Four blocks to the south stands the Police Office, and four blocks to the north, the House of Detention. Walk to the east and you are on your own.

The Five Points never closes. From sundown to dawn its streets are the most brightly lit, and its alleys the darkest in the city. The watchmen, whose leather helmets mark them as irresistible targets for the packs of butcher boys and soap locks prowling the district, steer a safe course around the Points, and even the regular police will not enter unless in force.

The sidewalks are crammed with beggars, amputees, dwarfs, blind venerealees. Pickpockets brush through the crowds, and pimpled prostitutes lure their victims, not to the pleasure palaces of Thomas Street, but to the dismal haunts of Duane and Cross. The black curtains are drawn tightly over the windows of the opium dens. The drunk and the dead lie where they fell, their pockets yanked inside out.

The barrooms are all alike: sawdust floors, raucous clamor, reeking of stale beer, vomit, and cheap seegars. After the first saloon I took charge of Prall's wallet. After the second I took charge of Prall. When an hour had passed in the third I dragged him to his feet.

"Where're we going, Davy?"

"To the canal for a swim."

"No—no—too many fish," he said. "You know how I *hate* . . . what're we talkin' about?"

"Fish." I gave him a shove toward the door.

"Right!" he shouted. He stumbled into a table, knocking a full stein of beer into the lap of one of two young men sitting there.

"Here now, you lummox!" cried the damp young man, leaping to his feet. His companion remained seated and quite as calm as he was dry. "Give him hell, Jimmy," he said.

To the extent that Prall could realize what he had done, he was profoundly sorry for it. He tugged a soiled handkerchief out of his pocket and attempted, in a clumsy fashion, to make amends, but his intention was apparently misunderstood by the damp young man, who immediately let fly his right fist, or at least the closest approximation of a fist he could manage. As this blow was launched somewhat unsteadily at a moving target, it merely grazed Prall's cheek, but Will recoiled as if he'd been shot.

"A challenge, Davy! A veritable challenge! The puppy struck me with his glove!"

"He did not, Will," I said. "He took a swing at you."

"The worst kind of insult," he ranted. "He stuck me with his glove with his fist still in it!"

"And I'll do it again, if I can find you," cried Jimmy, who had been spun completely around by the force of his swing.

"Gentlemen, gentlemen," said the second youth, rising from his chair. "This is most unseemly behavior for men of good breeding in a public establishment. May I suggest we retire to the street?"

He guided his friend in the direction of the door and I followed with Prall, endeavoring to hold him back and up at the same time. On the sidewalk the calm youth propped his companion against the saloon wall and lectured him gently but firmly.

"Now you stand there, Jimmy, do you understand?"

"Yes, Richie," said the other meekly.

"Not a move till I come back."

"Yes, Richie."

I wedged Prall between a horse trough and the pump. "You twitch once and I'll brain you," I said under my breath.

"Awww, Davy."

He twitched, but I let it pass. The one called Richie motioned me to a corner of the building. By the street lamp I made him out to be a boy of perhaps seventeen, about my own height, remarkably slender but athletic in appearance. He wore his brown hair curled over his forehead in the classical fashion, and his features were as soft and boyish as a ten-year-old's, though there was a devilish gleam in his eye such as the wickedest ten-year-old cannot muster.

"May I ask your name, sir?" he said.

"David Cordor."

"Mine, sir, is Robinson, Richard P." He pronounced it in a ringing tone. "It appears, Mr. Cordor, sir, that there is an affair of honor to be settled, and that it falls to you and me, as the representatives of the involved parties, to agree upon the arrangements. I believe the choice of weapons is yours, sir."

Smart, insufferable little college boy! I should have recognized the type. I had been one recently enough.

"Your choice of weapons, Mr. Cordor, sir?" he prodded.

He spoke without slurring and stood, God knows, straighter than I, but I had the sudden sense that I was by far the soberest of the quartet.

"The only weapons available seem to be walking sticks, Mr. Robinson, but . . ." I glanced back at the slim youth, who was commencing to turn slightly green, and at the now furiously twitching Prall, who had six years and sixty pounds on his rival. "Since it is obvious that my man will kick the hell out of yours," I continued, "wouldn't it be prudent simply to apologize?"

"Prudent perhaps, sir," he replied, "but hardly honorable. I suggest that we fight to their deaths, sir, if need be."

I shrugged. "In that case, Mr. Robinson, a small side wager would appear to be in order. Shall we say—"

A harsh shout from Prall interrupted me. He had stepped into the street and stood with his feet braced and his back to us, holding his stick over his head as a club. Advancing down the street toward him were ten or twelve youths between the ages of fifteen and eighteen, all carrying clubs. They wore jackets marked with painted insignia and their shirts were open to the waist. Another half dozen were moving from the opposite direction. It came to me that the street was otherwise deserted, that Will and I had wandered too far from the crowds at the hub of the Five Points. I could see that Will was suddenly cold sober, but Jimmy had slumped into a sitting position, helpless and perhaps unconscious. I turned toward the door of the saloon just as the bartender slammed it shut. Bastard!

I grasped my own walking stick in both hands like a staff and took a position beside Prall, facing the other end of the street. Robinson was not standing with us. I looked back and saw him leaning casually against a streetlight, his hands resting on the head of his cane. From there he might dash down the street or into an alley when the fighting started.

I tried to calculate our position. Prall had courage but his gut was soft and he had swallowed enough beer to float the *Champlain*. Even if he chose to fight, the slender Robinson looked as though he'd snap like a dry reed. We were outnumbered by better than five to one, and most depressing of all, I was our best man. Aside from the skirmish in Cedar Street during the great fire, I hadn't been in a real scrape since the sixth form. It occurred to me abruptly—I had lost that one.

Had they rushed us we would have been engulfed in minutes. Fortunately all young men, even street gangs, fight by a code of sorts. There was a ritual which had first to be performed. They stopped within ten yards of us on either side and the leader, a tow-headed youth of eighteen or so whom the others called Michael, stepped forward. His features were handsome, but dirty.

"Well, well, well. Will ye have a look, boys, at these foine dandies, come to pay us their respects." He spoke in a thick brogue, and strutted to the center of the street with his thumbs hooked under his braces. He smiled, showing his teeth unpleasantly.

"Here's a pretty nursery now," he said. "One flabby, though he looks fearsome, boys, he looks fearsome."

Prall tensed. I said quietly, "Take it easy, Will."

"A second so drunk he can't even stand," said Michael, strolling to the fallen Jimmy. "Or is it possum you're playing, lad?" He fetched the boy a savage slap on the side of his head and Jimmy rolled over. If he wasn't unconscious before, he was now.

Michael stepped over Jimmy and sauntered toward Richie Robinson. The street boy stood, feet spread apart, thumbs still in his braces, eyeing Robinson from sole to crown, while a malicious grin widened until he burst into strident howls of laughter in which the others soon joined. Robinson regarded him coldly with a slight, aristocratic curl of his lip, as though he anticipated being infected with some dread, communicable disease, and perhaps with justification. The two boys now were close enough to each other for the lice to make the leap.

The gang leader stopped laughing and the rest of the hooligans followed suit. Michael took hold of Robinson's small nose between the tips of his fingers and used it as a handle to turn Robinson's head while he inspected both profiles. With his other hand he knocked Robinson's cap off, grabbed a fistful of brown curls, and yanked the boy's face into the light of the street lamp. "Glory be to God, lad," Michael cried. "You're as pretty as a girl!"

"I must warn you, sir," said Robinson. "I have a violent temper which is quite beyond my control when I am aroused." He said this with a dignity which was admirable under the circumstances.

"I'll be sure to watch my step, young master," said the thug with a smirk. He pulled Robinson's face within inches of his own and continued tweaking his nose savagely. "Be certain to tell me when you're getting mad, young master, so I'll know."

"Wait a minute!" I said. I handed my walking stick to Prall and started toward them. The gang formed a semicircle around us. Prall gave ground slowly, staying at my back, waving both his cane and mine. "You great, hulking lout," I said. "Get your paw away from his nose."

"Ain't none of your business," Michael growled. "It's between me and the young master here."

"Not when you tweak a nose like that," I said. "Nose tweaking is an ancient and honorable practice. When an ignorant buffoon like you tweaks a nose in that ridiculous, inept fashion, it becomes the concern of every right-minded man."

I had no idea what I was going to do next. Keep talking. Keep talking.

"And what's wrong with the way I tweak a nose?" Michael demanded.

"Finger tweaking!" I snorted. "Finger tweaking went out with powdered wigs, damn it! No real man would finger tweak today. Knuckle tweaking—that's the style! All your great tweakers were knuckle tweakers. Look. I'll show you."

I put my hand on his shoulder. With an angry murmur the gang surged forward. I stepped back, holding my hands up, palms out. "I'm not going to hurt him, boys," I said. "You're not afraid I'm going to hurt you, are you, Michael?"

"I ain't afraid of nothing!"

"There you go, boys. He ain't afraid of nothing." I replaced my hand on his shoulder. "Well, Michael, you're going to have to let go."

I believe he'd forgotten he still had Robinson's nose pinched in his fingers. He grunted and released it. There were tears in the boy's eyes but he wasn't crying. His knees, which had begun to buckle, now locked, while his shoulders gave a convulsive shake. His hands remained, as they had throughout, resting lightly on the handle of his walking stick. His mouth was slack, half open, and he breathed tentatively through one nostril, then the other, to be certain both were in working order. No other human being could have endured almost three minutes of nose tweaking and carried it off with more aplomb.

I faced Michael, with my left hand still on his shoulder, and took his nose gently between the thumb and index finger of my right. "Now this is finger tweaking," I explained. I tightened my grip and began to twist his nose slowly. "As you can plainly see, Michael, this is totally ineffective. Come in closer, boys, so you can see better. No, no, boys, come right up close. Let the smaller fellows stand in front. You'll notice that even when I . . . twist . . . as . . . hard . . . as . . . I . . . can, Michael can feel almost nothing. Of course a weaker man might be in pain, but not a stalwart lad like Michael. Tell them, Michael. No worse than a mosquito bite, is it?"

His eyes were watering, and his hands opened and clenched spasmodically at his sides. "Can't feel a . . . thing," he managed to say.

There was an admiring hum from the group. I spotted Prall watching with great interest. I let go of Michael's nose and, forming my hand into a kind of claw, seized it again between the knuckles of my first and second fingers. "Here is the basic grip of knuckle tweaking," I said. "There are variations, naturally, but this is the preferred technique. Can everybody see? Turn a little to your left, Michael, so your head is more in the light. Now, the secret of knuckle tweaking, gentlemen, does not lie in the grip, as many have claimed, but in the action of the wrist while tweaking—thus!"

The circle of ruffians drew in even tighter, their mouths gaping, their eyes staring with rapt attention. "You will please observe, gentlemen, the reactions of the tweakee during this process. For the purposes of this demonstration, gentlemen, I am the tweak-er, and Michael, here, is the tweak-ee. Notice the popping of the eyes and the muscle spasms in the cheeks. In a few moments you will find that the entire face has turned quite scarlet. Observe also how the thighs and knees are drawn together and the toes point inward as the body rises upon them. For the most successful tweaking the arm should be held at a right angle to the body, with the elbow slightly bent and rigid. This allows for maximum leverage. Now, gentlemen, you see how the tongue of the tweakee begins to protrude from the corner of the mouth?"

With an angry snarl Michael shoved my hand away. I couldn't imagine what had taken him so long. "You bastard!" he shouted. "I'll kill you for this!"

"Just you and me, Michael."

"I don't need no help." He was taking off his jacket. His sleeves were rolled up to his armpits and the muscles rippled in his arms. One of the gang handed him a club.

This was what I'd been waiting for. I wasn't sure I could beat him, but the odds were much better than taking on the whole mob at once. I began to remove my own coat and felt a hand on my arm. It was Robinson.

"I beg your pardon, Mr. Cordor, sir," he said in the polite tone one reserves for maneuvering through a crowded theater lobby. "I believe the right of combat is mine."

I imagine my disdain must have been evident. "Please, sir," he insisted. His lips twisted into a strange smile. "It is what we might perhaps term an affair of dishonor."

He thrust his cane into my hand and removed his jacket—then gave it and his cap to me and folded his sleeves up. I looked in vain for his shoulders. It occurred to me they might have been left in his coat. I could feel my better judgment utter a terminal gasp and fall over into its grave.

"Where," I asked under my breath, "would you like me to ship the body?"

"Oh," he replied softly, "I suppose the lad has a mother."

Afterward Will Prall, that master of cliché, kept on repeating that "if he hadn't seen it with his own eyes he would never have believed it."

The sight of that lithe stripling dancing nimbly just out of reach of the street thug's frantic, flailing blows, any one of which might have crippled him, remained with me for a long time. With daring and athletic grace Robinson had forced his furious adversary to carry the fight to him, darting within inches of the murderous club to poke his walking stick into Michael's stomach or trip him up at the heels until the Irish boy dropped to his knees in wheezing exhaustion. With cool deliberateness Robinson had grasped Michael's mop of hair and, bending the youth over the rim of the horse trough, pushed his face down into the filthy water.

Michael came up dripping and gagging out of the trough. "Help!" he shouted. "For God's sake, lads!"

Prall stiffened, but I restrained him. "Look to the other one," I said, jerking my head toward the fallen Jimmy. "Master Robinson will handle them." I relaxed against a lamp post with my arms folded.

The pack of toughs moved forward uncertainly. Robinson calmly shoved Michael's head under the water again. "I shall not let him up, gentlemen, until I can no longer see any of you on the street." All sixteen of them stood in hesitant confusion. A gurgling noise emanated from the trough. The gang broke ranks and began to run. One of the youngest ran up to me.

"Don't let him drown me brother, mister," he pleaded. "If Michael gets drowned, Ma will kill him."

"Go home, boy," I said. "Your brother won't drown." The child took to his heels.

When all the gang had vanished Robinson released Michael. The Irish youth lay across the trough, choking and heaving for air. "How is Jimmy, sir?" Robinson called.

"Beginning to sit up and take notice," Prall said.

Robinson nodded with satisfaction, stood, stretched, propped one boot on the edge of the trough. "I am greatly indebted to you, Mr. Cordor," he said.

"I think," I replied, "it is my friend and I who are indebted to you, Mr. Robinson."

"No, sir," the boy said earnestly. "I wonder if you could understand. Tonight, for the first time in my life, I believe my father would not have been ashamed of me." He pushed Michael's head back into the trough.

"Do me a favor, Robinson," I said, "and don't kill him. I sort of promised his mother."

# 14　*February–April 1836*

In retrospect, the events of the late winter and early spring of 1836 strike me especially for our general failure to anticipate their consequences. For example, the *Sun,* along with the city's other papers, printed all dispatches on the Texicans' war for independence as they arrived, but without editorial foresight or even comment. When the Alamo fell on March 6, the story did not reach New York for over a week, and then the papers treated it as incidental to the obituary of ex-congressman Crockett, the war being listed as "cause of death." There was little speculation over the effect of the Alamo on the rebellion in general, nor did any paper foresee that, only forty-six days later, Houston's Texicans, though outnumbered almost two to one, would rout Santa Anna at San Jacinto.

Texas, of course, was very far away, and it lay to the west. Lead most New Yorkers to the Jersey bank of the Hudson and they become instantaneously myopic. They tend to acknowledge the existence of nothing beyond the boundaries of Manhattan Island, including Brooklyn, except Washington City, which they regard as a necessary suburb, and Albany, which they consider a foreign power.

Lead a New Yorker, especially an editor, to the bank of the East River, however, and he can see the skyline of Paris clearly on the foggiest day. Thus the satisfactory settlement of what was called the "French question" was in large part responsible for the fact that burned-out lots in the fire district were being knocked down to speculators for more than they were thought to be worth when covered with valuable buildings.

The fact was that President Jackson had at last triumphed over Mr. Biddle and the National Bank, releasing a deluge of paper money from state and wildcat banks and setting off the inflation which would culminate in the panic of 1837. A major result was increasing labor agitation. The problem was simple: living costs went up–wages did not. Walkouts, strikes, and riots ensued. A riot among the stevedores in late February on the wharves ended with one of the police officers, Dennis Brink, hospitalized with a fractured skull. A month later, as one Haliban, the stevedore who had split Brink's crown, was receiving a sentence of seven years, leaders of the tailors' union were being indicted for striking, or "conspiracy," as the Whig press called it.

By the middle of March it was apparent that rents would rise by 50 percent in the next twelve months. Beef soared to twenty-five cents a pound, veal to eighteen cents a pound. Small turkeys went for $1.50. The price of liquor was so outrageous that Prall was predicting the presidential election would turn on that issue.

"If only men could accurately predict the consequences of their actions," I remarked one evening to Quinncannon in his rooms, "think how the crimes and suffering of this life would be reduced. Poor Haliban."

Quinncannon nodded. "Seven years for cracking Brink's skull," he said.

"If he could have predicted the future when he kissed his wife and children goodbye a month ago, Haliban would never have gone to the piers."

"If the courts could predict the future," Quinncannon said, "when Haliban broke Brink's pate they'd have built a monument in his honor."

I lowered my newspaper. "What is it that you and Brink have against each other?"

"Nothing a small bribe couldn't cure," he answered.

"At all events," I said, "Hesiod was right."

"Hesiod?"

"I've been reading your copy," I said. "It was Hesiod who said that the wise man is one who works out every problem and solves it by knowing what will be best in the end."

He glanced up at me.

"I'm sure I'm right."

"Oh," he said, "that's what the philosopher wrote." There was a long pause. "Do you know how Hesiod died?"

I shook my head.

"He was warned by the Delphic oracle that a visit to the groves of Zeus would prove fatal, which he took to mean the famous groves in the Peloponnese. Instead, he visited the sacred groves in Locris and there seduced the sister of his host."

I waited. "Well," I said finally, "what happened to him?"

Intent on his paper, Quinncannon replied, "His host had him murdered."

Between February 1 and April 9 there were three big stories, aside from the union agitation, in New York. In mid-February two men crossed Long Island Sound on foot from Hempstead Harbor to Rye Point and returned—a round trip of fifteen miles. We printed the story to demonstrate to our faithful readers that it was cold.

In late February a black woman named Joice Heth died. That, of itself, was not remarkable, since she was thought to be 165 years old at the time. For some years P. T. Barnum had exhibited her as the nurse of General Washington. A few skeptical physicians, whom Barnum had successfully barred from examining her while living, got possession of her corpse, performed a postmortem, and announced that Nurse Heth could not have been over seventy-five at her death. The doctors declared Mr. Barnum a fraud—Mr. Barnum declared the doctors to be frauds. The press declared the public to be divided in its opinion, but it is not recorded that Mr. Barnum has as yet refunded any admissions, or been requested to.

The third story was as simple as it was tragic. On March 15 the stables of John Murphy, who owns one of the lines of Broadway omnibuses, caught fire, and thirty-two horses and three hostlers were burned alive. This sad event was duly reported in the papers, but it is the sequel, for which I am indebted to Ogden Hoffman, that I find fascinating.

Nine days after the fire the Reading Club, of which Hoffman was a member, held a dinner at the Washington Hotel, to which Hoffman dragged Quinncannon. Present among a similarly distinguished company were Washington Irving, Fitz-Greene Halleck, President William Duer of Columbia College, Charles King, and former mayor Philip Hone. The conversation turned to the stable fire and Mr. Hone averred that "Irishmen and horses are plenty enough in New York, but means should be adopted to prevent such awful sacrifice of their lives."

There was a lethal silence around the table. Quinncannon raised one eyebrow and puffed at his pipe. "It is not surprising there are so many Irishmen in New York," Mr. Hone continued. "There are stables enough."

"It is somewhat surprising to find so many politicians in New York," Quinncannon said mildly. "There are gallows enough."

"Uh, gentlemen . . ." said Dr. Duer.

"Actually," said Hone, "the horse has always reminded me of the Irishman. One may observe how each species senses the presence of a fellow by noting when one of them sniffs."

"The politician has always reminded me of the dog for the same reason," Quinncannon responded. "Of course, in that case, it is less a matter of when one sniffs than where."

"I must say," said Mr. Hone, "that I find it most distressing to break bread with someone whose manners properly belong to a sty."

"My sainted grandfather used to say," observed Quinncannon, "that the manners of the sty are best understood by the pig."

Mayor Hone left the party early with a headache. Mr. Quinncannon is said to have remained exchanging courteous pleasantries until the last.

"I will *never* take that Irishman to another meeting of the Reading Club," Hoffman stormed to me later.

"That sounds to me like a safe prophecy," I answered.

Saturday, April 9. Will Prall and I were assigned to hold down the fort at the *Sun*. Absolutely no news was breaking, and we killed the time by discussing the battle which continued to rage between Mr. Bennett of the *Herald* and Colonel Webb of the *Courier and Enquirer*. Prall, for a change, was in a terribly serious mood, and feeling expansive.

"I tell you, Davy, the entire community is heartily sick of and disgusted with this continued character assassination in the public press, and with every editor who indulges in the practice." He put his feet on his desk and swiveled back and forth in his chair, waving a fat cigar in his hand. "One might expect this sort of behavior from pugilists or actors, but from gentlemen of the press—professors of letters, leaders of public opinion, directors of public taste, guardians of public morals—it is simply ridiculous. At a time when the public *must* consider the press as so many Caesar's wives, what do Webb and Bennett do? They accuse each other of being swindlers, liars, extortionists, and worse. What other result can this have than the degradation of our profession and the erosion of our impact upon the community?"

Behind Will I saw Ben Day loom out of the shadows into the doorway. I attempted to signal a warning to Prall, but it was hopeless.

"Bill Attree is absolutely right," Prall declared. "Have you read his editorial in today's *Transcript?*"

I shook my head grimly. Day slipped silently into the office and read over Prall's shoulder with considerable interest.

"Attree details the accusations Bennett and Webb have made against each other and then says: 'For respected gentlemen of the Press to descend to the expression of opinions which are unbecoming even to the most ignorant and brutal of the race, is to set an example to the rising generation that must terminate in creating a condition of society which will make every worthy man consider the freedom of the Press as painful a curse as can be inflicted upon a country.' "

Day drew down both corners of his mouth in mock accord. I said, "Uh, Will—"

"Wait," he said. "There's more. 'There are those in high places in this country who fear the Press, fear our curiosity, fear our courage, fear our credibility. For the credit of the Press, for the elevation of journalists as a class, for the hopes which exist for a more glorious future for professional writers, in the name of Humanity, in the name of Decency, in the name of Truth, let us do away with the practice of throwing such heedless and disgusting slanders at one another.' "

"If you can't write, Mr. Prall," Day said, "at least you can read."

Poor Prall rose a foot out of his chair and, to my amazement, came down at attention.

"Let me tell you both something, gentlemen," Day intoned. "In my view James Gordon Bennett is scum, but if his accusations against Colonel Webb are correct, I salute him. Journalism, Mr. Prall, is a trade, not a profession—an honest trade! Would you have us behave like a profession, concealing our incompetents and coddling our corrupt? Are you suggesting that the public place no more trust in its newspapers than it places in its *professional* men?"

Prall's mouth was working like a fish's against the wall of a tank.

"I'll tell you something else," Day snapped. "The minute we journalists forget, in the business of being watchdogs on everyone else, that before all we are watchdogs on each other—*that* is the minute that freedom of the press *will* become a curse on this country!"

I spent the hours between midnight and three a.m. on April 10 at a tavern in Ann Street. When finally even it closed, I found myself still wide awake, and strolled up to the Police Office. Dennis Brink, now fully recovered from his fractured skull, was the police officer on duty. George Noble was the captain of the watch.

Nothing was happening of any consequence. Near four I found myself yawning and decided to walk back to my rooming house and get some sleep. A watchman entered breathlessly as I went out into the street. I turned around and followed him back inside.

I didn't see Brink, but Noble was standing near his desk. "What is it?" he asked.

"Murder," gasped the watchman. "Murder in Thomas Street."

# BOOK II

## Murder in Thomas Street

## 15  Murder in Thomas Street

The hansom cab raced down Chambers Street and careened south into Broadway, the horse's hooves striking sparks from the cobblestones. Opposite Quinncannon's rooms we reined in and I leaped to the ground, running toward the street door. I began to pound heavily with both fists. After a few minutes lights began to be seen and shutters creaked open on the upper floors of the house, and then the bolts were withdrawn and the door pulled gradually back, revealing a tousled, bleary-eyed houseboy who peered drowsily out at me, holding a flickering candle in one hand and rubbing the sleep from his eyes with the other.

"Quinncannon!" I rasped out under my breath. After making that infernal racket, God knows why I was whispering. "I must see him at once!"

The boy gave me a long, barely tolerant look while grasping the sleeve of his nightshirt and wiping it slowly across his nose and upper lip. With an enormous sigh he turned and plodded up the staircase. A minute or so later he was back.

"Mr. Cordor, I have a message for you from himself. He wishes merely to observe that you are a quadrilateral, astronomical, incandescent son of a bitch." He gasped with the effort of the speech, which he had delivered in a single breath. "He also begs you to take notice of the hour as one when only the spawn of the devil should properly be abroad, and requests, therefore, that you pay your respects to your father, who, he doubts not, has been ready and anxious to receive you for twenty years."

I seized the boy's shoulders and shook him so that he nearly dropped the candle. "Tell him that there is murder and arson in Thomas Street! Tell him that one of the women at Rosina Townsend's has been killed with an ax and her body set afire, and tell him that I shall only hold the cab for two more minutes."

The lad took the stairs two at a time. Quinncannon appeared shortly, completely unruffled and dressed as if he were just returning from the theater instead of having been dragged from his bed. He pulled on his gloves, drew his cloak around him against the damp chill of the early morning, and swung casually up into the hansom.

I sprang up beside him and shouted to the hackman, "Number 41 Thomas Street! Hurry!"

The cab swerved around, the driver cracked his whip, and we thundered up Broadway past the Park and the sullen façade of the Dead House. "One of Rosina's tarts," Quinncannon said grimly, "foully slain in her working clothes. Did you get a name?"

"Helen Jewett," I said.

The rattle of the hansom and clatter of the hooves echoed hollowly in the deserted streets as we dashed into Duane toward Hudson. "Sorry, Davy," he said. "You knew her well, didn't you?"

"Not well," I replied quietly. "Intimately, but not well."

He may have glanced up to see if I was smiling. If so, he discovered that I was not.

"Who's investigating? Hays?"

"Hays is chasing those three forgers who sawed their way out of Bellevue last week. Brink's got the case."

A derisive snort of a laugh popgunned out of the darkness. "Brink!" He spat out the name. "That's a nice, ironic touch."


Thomas Street begins at the river, near the pier of the Newburgh steamboat, and runs northeast for five short blocks to Hudson, where it veers due east for two more cross streets, Chapel and Church, and terminates directly before the gates of the city hospital. On the south side of Thomas, between Hudson and Chapel, stands a row of pale-yellow, four-story buildings, unseparated by alleys. First built as single houses, many of them, including number 41, have been joined together to form single, "double-house" dwellings.

Rosina Townsend's house stood last, at the west end of the row, near the intersection with Hudson Street. On its west side it was originally divided from the rear of a house fronting on Hudson by an alley which ran from its rear yard to Thomas Street. Sometime prior to 1836 a piazza was built onto number 41 which covers the rear two-thirds of the alley and abuts the adjoining house. The alley leading from the street thus became a dead-end, and the rear yard can now be reached only through the house itself.

Expense was spared in the construction of these buildings. Though the houses have brick fronts, the side walls which separated them were paper-thin, and the workmen engaged in joining the houses together found these walls easily demolished. At number 41 the entire center wall has been removed on the first floor, and all on the second save the partition which divides the two bedrooms at the front of the house and two others at the rear. The latter rooms are reserved for the premier attractions of the establishment. Helen Jewett, at the time of her death, occupied the rear bedroom on the west side. The other room belonged to Miss Maria Stevens.

Normally the shades and shutters of number 41 are drawn as tightly as those of a nunnery, and like a nunnery there is little or no evidence to be seen of the female denizens. But as our hansom reined in and Quinn-cannon handed a bill up to the hackman, we could see the gaping windows of the murder house ablaze with light. A carriage stood at the curb, its team of matched black horses stamping nervously. A small knot of silent neighbors, grouped near the door like professional mourners, turned and watched our progress up the short walk to the front steps, where a bearded watchman was posted.

"Here now, sorry, gentlemen. No one admitted but officials of the city. This is police business."

My friend lowered his collar and the watchman's dour face brightened.

"Oh, it's you, Mr. Quinncannon. Do you remember me, sir? McCraw, sir. I was with you on the Fernandez murder. I was wondering when you was going to show. Damn me, sir, if you ain't got a nose like a bird dog when it comes to murder, meaning no offense." He stepped aside and winked his eye broadly. "Mr. Brink will be tickled to see you, sir."

"No doubt, McCraw," the Irishman said. "Have you your smelling salts about?"

"Don't need 'em, sir. Just a bucket for him to stick his head in."

Quinncannon smiled and stepped through the door, and I prepared to follow. "Here now," the watchman said sternly. "This ain't no parade!"

"It's all right, McCraw," Quinncannon said.

"Is this lad with you, sir?"

"My bird dog," Quinncannon said confidentially.

"Oh," replied McCraw, removing his bulk from the doorway. "No offense meant, lad, and, one may hope, no offense taken."

The front doors opened on a long entrance hall at the end of which could be seen the door of the main parlor, which stretched the full width of the house. Being a "double house," it had a double set of stairs, each flight rising halfway up one side wall of the entry and then turning to meet the other at the center of the upstairs landing. A burning lamp hung from the ceiling to the right, as one entered, of the door, but there was no other light in the hall, in sharp contrast with the brilliantly illuminated interior rooms.

As we entered, two other watchmen emerged from the rear parlor, and the shorter of the two, a clean-shaven man with a bulldog jaw who appeared to be in his mid-forties, came forward at once to shake Quinncannon's hand.

"Glad to see you, sir. You remember me from the Erskine murders?"

"Of course," Quinncannon said. "Davy, this is Peter Collyer, one of the finest watchmen and charcoal inspectors in the city. Peter, Mr. David Cordor."

Beaming, Collyer nodded at me and gestured toward his taller companion. "This is Bill Lane. Bill, Mr. Lon Quinncannon and . . . ?"

"Cordor," I said.

Stoop-shouldered, with a drooping gray moustache, Bill Lane pumped the Irishman's hand. "An honor," he kept muttering. "An honor."

"There's something queer about this one, Mr. Quinncannon," Collyer said in a hoarse whisper. "I wish Old Hays, beg pardon, High Constable Hays was here. Not intending to say nothing against Officer Brink, sir."

Quinncannon's mouth tugged up slightly at one corner. "Nothing?" he repeated.

Collyer grinned. "Well, maybe *some*thing. Still, I'm happy to see you, sir. Who you working for this time, sir? The one that killed her?"

"Do you mean," I asked, "that they already know who killed her?"

"They got a name, anyway," Collyer said. "Frank Rivers. Ain't that right, Bill?"

Lane nodded. "That's the name Mrs. Townsend says. Only, of course, it ain't his real moniker."

"Yeah, but I got a hunch Brink knows his real moniker, too." Collyer looked at Quinncannon. "Rosina Townsend's holding court in the back parlor, sir. Do you want to talk to her?"

My friend shook his head. "The body first, Peter." He said to me, "You can stay down here if you'd rather."

I had steeled myself to it. "No," I said. "I'm coming."

We began climbing the steps to the second floor. Collyer walked ahead with Quinncannon, and Lane and I trailed. "Near as I can tell," the square-jawed watchman said, "it was Rosina who found her. Sometime after three this morning she went upstairs and found smoke coming out of the bedroom. The door was unlocked and the girl was lying on the bed with her head bashed in and the bedclothes on fire. No weapon found yet, but it looks to most of us like an ax or hatchet."

The door to the murder room burst open suddenly and Dennis Brink loomed on the landing. The excitement in his little eyes turned to smoldering resentment when he saw Quinncannon. He stopped short in his tracks and his potbelly quivered slightly above his belt buckle.

"The magnificent Mr. Quinncannon!" the policeman sneered. "I thought your time was much too important to waste investigating the murder of a mere whore."

The Irishman reached the landing and smiled pleasantly at the officer. "Now, now, speak well of the whores, Brink," he said in a thick brogue. "They always speak well of you."

Brink glowered at him and then rushed past us down the stairs.

"This is the way she was found," Collyer said, leading the way into the bedroom. "She ain't been moved." Quinncannon and Lane followed him. I could hear the voices of other watchmen greeting the Irishman in hushed tones. "You remember me, sir . . . The Harvey murder . . . The Breedlaw case . . . The Romley killing . . ."

I had seen dead bodies before. I had buried my uncle. I had been the one to find my older brother where the horse threw him, with his neck all twisted. When I was only fifteen I was part of the search party that discovered Zach Prouty in the Jersey woods after thirty-one days with his legs crushed and the maggots crawling in the sockets that had been his eyes.

But Helen Jewett's eyes were not eaten away. They were closed, as if in sleep. They appeared exactly as they had on that snowy morning when I bent down and kissed them tenderly before I left her room. Helen Jewett's hair was still smooth and soft, as soft as the low-cut, chiffon nightdress she wore with the puffed sleeves and the delicate lacework.

Death should be ugly. One is revolted by maggots, but one expects them, requires them. There *ought* to be maggots, damn it! A man feels cheated without a maggot or two.

"Three wounds on the right side of the head," Quinncannon said aloud, but more to himself than to anyone present. "Two with the blunt edge of the head of a hatchet—the third with the sharp edge of the blade. That's the blow that killed her. Murdered in her sleep from the look on her face."

Helen lay on her back, partially on her left side, her body rigid.

Quinncannon bent over her. "The death wound is only three to four inches long," he said thoughtfully. "That's odd." He rolled her over on her right side and examined the burns on her body. "Severe, but not enough to kill her," he said. "The fire was set after she was dead." He rolled the corpse back onto its left side. "Stiff as a board." He scratched pensively at the corner of his moustache. "Blood splattered on the floor beside the bed."

I felt the gorge beginning to rise. Turning away, I went quickly down the stairs and out through the front door, gasping for air. McCraw glanced at me but had the decency not to comment. I leaned back against the jamb and inhaled and exhaled until I was certain I had regained my self-control.

While I stood there Dennis Brink emerged onto the stoop, with George Noble at his heels. "Order my carriage!" Brink snapped at Noble.

"Order Mr. Brink's carriage!" Noble snapped at McCraw.

"Captain," said McCraw, "the carriage is right there at the curb. It don't need to be ordered."

"Your carriage is ordered," said Noble with a flourish.

"Thank you, Captain," Brink called, descending the steps.

Noble turned to McCraw. "If Officer Welsh arrives," he said, "tell him we have gone to arrest Frank Rivers."

Noble marched toward the carriage and I bounded after him. "Captain Noble, do you mind if I ride along with you? My name is Cordor, sir. I'm with the *Sun.*"

His foot poised to enter the carriage, Brink looked back at Noble. "The *Sun.* Is that Ben Day's newspaper?"

"Yes, sir!" I shouted, and then in hushed tones, "yes, sir, it is."

"I think it would be all right, Mr. Cordor," Brink said, not to me, but to Noble. The latter eyed me and then looked at Brink and shrugged. While the captain of the watch gave orders to the driver, I climbed in behind Brink and took a seat opposite him.

# 16　The Arrest

"**I**'ve never had a newspaperman along on an arrest before," said Dennis Brink. Though we sat in darkness, the curtains of the coach being drawn, I fancied I could still see Officer Brink, the stout body wrapped in his surtout, the heavy jowls, the clean-shaven lip and chin protruding between massive side-whiskers. Noble stepped up nimbly and closed the door behind him. I estimated Noble's age at about forty-three, five to seven years older than Brink. The captain of the watch was far more wiry than his younger companion. He wore a thick handlebar moustache, and his leather helmet, set back on his head, revealed a receding hairline and a perpetually furrowed brow. He sat down beside Brink as the carriage lurched forward, and touched my hand in a mildly restraining fashion with his stick when I attempted to lift the curtain covering one of the windows.

The three of us rode in silence, the pitch blackness of the coach relieved only by the occasional glow of Brink's stogie. Several times I attempted to begin a conversation in the hope of getting a line on our destination, or the real identity of the mysterious "Frank Rivers," or the evidence which had led to his being under suspicion. The Law was not feeling communicative. My questions were answered with inarticulate grunts. At last I gave up and began to fill my pipe.

The coach rumbled slowly through the narrow, twisting back streets of the city. With the curtains drawn it was impossible for me to tell where we were, which I gathered was the point of keeping the curtains drawn. When the horses stopped we had ridden for about thirty minutes and had covered perhaps three or four miles. There appeared to me an unseemly lack of haste, considering that we were on the trail of a heinous ax murderer.

Noble pushed the door open and descended, followed by a heaving, bulky Brink. When I prepared to alight, Noble held up his hand, the one with the stick in it. "We'd rather you stayed in the carriage, sir, just at present."

In the act of pushing up from my seat I shrugged and dropped back into it. Noble closed the door. I heard their footsteps moving away, and with the stem of my pipe, I pushed up one corner of the window curtain nearest me. By the dim glow of a gas lamp I recognized our location, the intersection of Pearl Street and Maiden Lane in the heart of a district dominated by small retail businesses. The streets were lined with apothecary shops, hardware and dry-goods stores, tobacconists, and greengrocers. We were in the second ward on the East Side of the city below the Park, less than one mile from Thomas Street as the crow flies, but no crow would have followed our rambling, random route. My curiosity was becoming intolerable. I opened the door and began to step down.

"Beg pardon, sir, you're to remain in the coach. Captain Noble's orders." The driver, also a watchman, had been posted to keep an eye on me.

"Just wanted to stretch my legs," I said.

"Nevertheless, sir." There was a quiet, almost menacing quality in his manner, but perhaps that was only my imagination. Still, I reflected, returning to my seat, there was something decidedly furtive in the behavior of these minions of the law, and something damned odd about the whole business.

The little I knew of the youth who called himself Frank Rivers I had learned from the Duchesse, who considered him callow and weak, possibly cowardly—she had called him a pantywaist. Certainly to murder a sleeping girl with so vicious a weapon as a hatchet, and then set fire to the corpse in an attempt to cover the crime, was a cowardly act. I felt the corners of my mouth tighten and my face grow warm. I wished for nothing more at that instant than the throat of Frank Rivers within the grasp of my fingers and a few minutes of leisure.

The coach door opened suddenly and Brink lumbered up. At his back Noble shouted to the driver, "Dey Street! Number 42!" The whip cracked and the team surged forward. Now we were moving at a rapid clip and the officers were rolling up the curtains to admit the dawning light of the grim, gray morning. We trotted up Maiden Lane and swung into Broadway, and with every roll of the carriage Dennis Brink became more expansive.

"The man we are going to charge with the murder, Mr. Cordor, is a clerk in a dry-goods store owned by Mr. Joseph Hoxie at Number 101 Maiden Lane. For some time he has visited the dead girl at various houses in the city under the name of Frank Rivers. He was her favorite, in a manner of speaking. He visited her last night, and we have a witness who places him with Helen Jewett in her room the last time she was seen alive."

"That witness would be Rosina Townsend?" I prodded.

A slight hesitation? "Rosina Townsend," he affirmed.

We halted before Number 42 Dey Street, a small, drab rooming house catering to retail clerks and bookkeepers in a sleepy, respectable neighborhood on the lower West Side near Greenwich Street. This time there was no question of my remaining in the coach. Brink motioned me down with a sweeping gesture. Noble preceded us and rapped sharply at the door with his stick. The door was opened by a drowsy housemaid in her late teens, and Noble touched his stick to his helmet and bowed slightly.

"Beg pardon, miss, for the early hour. Police business, miss. Is there a Mr. Robinson here?"

"Minnie," came a young man's voice from the darkness of the passageway, "if someone wants to see Robinson, he's still asleep in bed."

Noble's tall figure brushed past the maid and strode down the hall to the first door on the left. Just inside the entry Brink turned to me. "You stand here," he said, and then added, "in case there's trouble."

The young man who had spoken had gone back into the room. The bedroom door remained open. From where I stood I could hear Noble's brisk, official voice clearly, though the responses were barely audible.

"Are you Mr. Robinson?" the watch captain asked. "Then I must ask you to step out into the hallway for a moment, sir." A moment or two later a slender, rumpled youth emerged from the room, tucking his nightshirt into his trousers and running one hand through tangled, curly hair. In that second I recognized my acquaintance from the Five Points.

The boy and Noble conducted a hushed conversation in which they were joined by Brink. It was held, or such was my impression, deliberately out of my earshot, and the only word I could clearly distinguish was "cloak," which was used by each of them several times. From the lack of agitation exhibited by Robinson I could only assume that, as yet, he had no idea of the crime with which he was to be charged. This was confirmed by Brink when Robinson had returned to his room to finish dressing under the watchful eye of George Noble.

"I haven't mentioned the murder to the young man as yet, Mr. Cordor. I have my particular reasons for this. Ain't no one's business what they are, but I'd appreciate it if you keep quiet."

"Mr. Brink!" Noble poked his head out of the bedroom. "Any objection to the other lad coming with us?"

Brink shook his heavy head. Robinson came into the hall, dressed in drab mixed pantaloons and a dark, double-breasted frock coat. He walked toward us beside Noble, and his soft, boyish face brightened when he recognized me.

"Good morning, Mr. Cordor, sir," he said in the same polite, deferential tone I remembered.

"Good morning, Mr. Robinson."

He smiled cordially. "I don't believe my father will be too proud of me when he hears of this," he said.

When his roommate joined us I recalled him as "Jimmy," Robinson's drunken companion in the Five Points. His name was James Teer;

he was a slim youth of about my own age with dark hair, olive skin, flaring nostrils, and heavy eyebrows, who showed no sign of recollection when he saw me. If he wondered who I was, no one took the trouble to enlighten him.

It was pouring rain and we had to run for the coach. Teer and I shared one seat, while Robinson sat opposite, wedged between the erect, military Noble and the slouching, seegar-smoking Brink. Yet Robinson appeared as calm and contented as if nestled between two beautiful virgins on his way to a country picnic. Jimmy Teer was nervous and babbled constantly. The Law sat in silence, Noble looking as though he'd swallowed a ramrod, Brink as though he'd swallowed a canary.

I watched Robinson's face carefully, waiting for a sign of trepidation, or at least of concern. It seemed incredible that he had placidly surrendered himself into police custody after being dragged out of bed before seven on a Sunday morning and had not once inquired as to the charge.

We turned up Broadway, and when we were opposite the Park I saw the first change in Robinson's countenance. It was, however, no more than a slight tremble of the lower lip. "I thought," he said, "that we were going to the Police Office."

There was no reply, and after a moment the boy settled back and said nothing. The carriage continued up Broadway and then left into Duane, rolling toward Chapel. Near the corner of Thomas, Jimmy Teer broke the silence.

"See here, you know, gentlemen, what's this all about?"

Brink leaned forward, addressing himself to Teer. "A dreadful crime has been committed—a woman was murdered tonight in a house in Thomas Street." He paused, keeping his eyes on Teer and licking his fat lips unpleasantly. "Her name was Helen Jewett," he went on slowly, "and we intend to charge Mr. Robinson with her murder."

Robinson's cherubic face went pale, briefly. He closed his eyes and one corner of his sensitive mouth twisted up. The coach stopped before the murder house.

The rain had softened into a light drizzle. A large but subdued crowd now filled the front yard of Number 41 Thomas Street, and the watchmen quickly cleared a path for us to the door. A murmur spread through the crowd, becoming increasingly angry as we sprinted up the walk. A line of watchmen closed behind us as we entered the house.

A number of lamps had now been brought into the entry, brightening the area considerably. Several watchmen milled about, and two or three of Mrs. Townsend's girls clustered near a door at the left of the hallway. One of them gave a shriek of surprise when she saw Robinson, rushed up to him, and planted a kiss on his cheek. He walked past her toward two men who stood whispering together near the foot of the right-hand staircase. I stuck to Robinson like flypaper.

One of the two men was Joseph Hoxie, Robinson's employer. He was a spindly, fragile man in his mid-sixties, completely bald except for a few wisps of snowy hair combed carefully across his pate. His face was heavily lined, yet it seemed to me that twenty years ago it had probably resembled nothing so much as a clenched fist.

The other man was tall and exceptionally well dressed, clean-shaven and graying slightly at the temples. He had an aquiline nose and a small, rounded chin, and a bit of a bulge in the vicinity of his waistcoat, which he appeared perpetually at pains to suck in. He was introduced to Robinson by Hoxie.

"Richie, this is Mr. Whitlaw Price, one of the best young attorneys in New York. I've retained him to represent you in this ridiculous matter. The police, as usual, have made an absurd blunder. I've explained to Mr. Price that you are unquestionably innocent."

Robinson smiled sadly. "I'm pleased to meet you, Mr. Price, sir, though I could wish it were under more pleasant circumstances." He turned to Hoxie. "Sir," he said, "my family . . ."

"I shall take care of notifying your father," the old man replied in a tremulous tenor. "We shall do our best to keep this from your mother, my boy. Considering the state of her health, I'm afraid . . ."

"It would kill her," Robinson finished.

Whitlaw Price sucked in his stomach and exhaled his words in stentorian tones. "I have been associated in the past with Mr. Ogden Hoffman of Hoffman and Maxwell, Mr. Robinson, and I believe he will be willing to associate himself with me again in your behalf."

"And, Richie," Hoxie said excitedly, "Lon Quinncannon is here. I've already spoken to him, and he may be interested in your case. He wants to talk with you, son. Another man's handkerchief has already been found under the girl's pillow with his name embroidered on it in full. There is excellent reason for hope."

Robinson's expression did not change, but his hands took a tight hold on one of Hoxie's own. "You are too good to me, sir," he said. "Too good, sir, too good." A tear rolled down his smooth cheek, to be matched by one from the old man's eye which dripped slowly from furrow to furrow.

I was born with a suspicion of sentimental scenes. There were too many Richard Robinsons already to suit me. This new one, squeezing out tears over an old man's generosity, was supplanted immediately by yet another, who asked Price coolly, "When will they let me see her?"

"Not yet, lad," Price responded. "I understand that decision is Mr. Brink's. If you wish, I'll speak to him now."

"Please, sir," Robinson said.

As Price moved away, I searched through the crowd for Quinncannon. At the end of the hall, between the staircases, stood the double doors which led into the main parlor. From these portals there suddenly erupted one of the most amazing phenomena I have ever seen.

Mary Gallagher, known affectionately as "Mother" to hundreds of the city's young libertines, and their fathers, and their grandfathers, swept into the entry in a magnificent flurry of orange feather boas, resplendent in a silk evening dress of purple and scarlet which clung to her body as if it were glued on, notwithstanding that Mother Gallagher stood barely five foot four, and weighed, when soaking wet, something over two hundred pounds.

Out of the corner of one yellow eye she espied Robinson and pounced on him like a massive grimalkin lunging at a tame white rat.

"My dear boy," she cried, in a voice remarkably high and sweet. She reached up a fat, hairy arm around his neck and pulled his head down until his downy cheek almost rested against her stubbled one. "Whatever in the world could have persuaded you to commit so horrid a deed?" she purred.

"Why," Robinson replied in some heat, "what do you *suppose* could have induced me to commit so ridiculous an act and blast my brilliant prospects? I am a young man, only nineteen yesterday, and I have the most brilliant prospects."

"My dear boy," she said unctuously, "may you prove innocent."

She held him ever more tightly and began to salivate while he struggled gently to extricate himself. "There's another man's handkerchief under the pillow with his name on it," he said. "I am not afraid but what I shall be acquitted."

"My dear, dear boy, your cloak has been discovered in a rear yard on the other side of the fence. Still, God grant you may prove innocent for the sake of your dear mother." She pulled his face around into hers. "Have you seen Miss Jewett?"

Robinson paled discernibly, but whether from the mention of the victim's name or the painfully contorted position of his neck or the blast of Mother Gallagher's breath, I could not determine. "No," he said, "they won't let me see her."

"She's a horrible sight," Gallagher assured him, "what with her poor head split open and her all burnt to a crisp. When you see her, if you did the awful deed, my dear boy, I'm sure your heart will break."

Poor Robinson looked as though he was about to faint when he was rescued by Dennis Brink. "No one is allowed to talk to the prisoner," said the burly detective, prying Mother Gallagher's arm from the boy's neck by main force. "I don't want nobody speaking to him so as to influence him to commit himself."

Whitlaw Price was standing at Brink's elbow and I could not help but wonder if this last speech was primarily for the lawyer's benefit. It had, however, the desired effect on Mother Gallagher, who apologized contritely and flung herself down on a divan beside Jimmy Teer, laying her hand carelessly on his thigh.

Brink turned to Robinson. "You wanted to see the body," he said.

"Come with me." He took the youth's arm and led him up the stairs. Old Hoxie followed, assisted by Price, with George Noble serving as a rearguard to guarantee that no one else joined the party, especially, so it appeared to me, a certain eager young reporter. I wandered into the main parlor in search of Quinncannon.

# 17  Mr. Quinncannon Accepts a Client

It is the rule for the finer bawdy houses of the city to be furnished in the most elegant manner, but the main parlor of Madam Rosina outdid for sheer opulence any room I had ever seen. By contrast with the plush but shabby sitting rooms of the Duchesse de Berri, or even with the rich but sparse appointments of the entrance hall I had just left, I felt as if I had stepped into the palace at Versailles.

The walls were lined with ornate mirrors and magnificent oil paintings in gilded frames, and the floor was covered with Oriental rugs, woven into luxuriant patterns of dark maroon and black, and fringed with tassels of golden thread. Posh divans and ottomans and deep-cushioned sofas were stationed about, attended by delicate little tables of mahogany decorated with beautiful figures of china and porcelain. The furniture was upholstered with fine fabrics in ebony and blood-red hues. A marble mantel stood at either end of the long room, a chiming clock in the center of each, flanked by silver plate. A small gaming table was placed at the right side of the room and a spinet with its tiny bench at the left. The total impression was one of the most splendid decadence.

Directly facing the double doors entering the parlor was another double door of French design which led into the gardens behind the house. A little marble-top table stood beside these doors, which were ajar. The only other exit lay through a portal in the right-hand wall beside the chimney which opened, I later learned, into a smaller parlor built onto the original building as part of the piazza. At this moment it was closed.

Seated on one of the sofas with his boots resting on an ottoman and his pipe dangling from one corner of his mouth was Quinncannon, intently studying a sketch pad he had propped against his knee and on which he occasionally jotted a note. Without looking up he said, "Come in, Davy. In a minute I'm going to need your help with an experiment in stupidity."

"Whose stupidity?" I asked.

He tapped his pipe stem against his teeth. "Now, that's what I can't quite understand as yet." I observed a bottle of champagne and a long-stemmed glass on the table beside him. "Want some wine?" he inquired. "Moët & Chandon, 1828. Rosina's cellar yields treasures quite as interesting as those of her upper floors."

I shook my head, and still without glancing up from his notes, he said, "Take a look at those French doors, will you, and tell me what you notice about them."

"No key—no lock," I said. "They're fastened by a bar placed across them from inside. Provides easy access for the inmates to the privy at night, I suppose."

"That's the idea. It also makes it possible for anyone standing in the entry door to tell whether someone has gone out into the yard simply by whether the bar is up or down."

I came back and sat down opposite him. "I gather you've been talking to some of the witnesses."

"No," he responded absently, "listening to them." He thumbed rapidly through the pages of his pad. "Now, between nine and nine-thirty last evening Rosina Townsend says she admitted a young man known to her only as Frank Rivers. He asked to see Helen Jewett, and Rosina went to fetch her from the rear parlor—from this room. The young man went up the right stairs and Helen followed him."

I was taking my own notes as he spoke. "Does Rosina identify Richard Robinson as Frank Rivers?"

He arched an eyebrow. "It is my information that she does—now."

"She didn't earlier?"

"There's some confusion on that point," he said. "Let's skip for the moment the question of whether Robinson was here last night; *some* young man was here and spent time with Helen Jewett in her room. Several people saw him come in. Nobody seems to have seen him leave. Are you with me so far?"

"So far," I said.

"All right. Nothing was seen of either Helen or her young man between nine-thirty and about eleven, when Helen came to the head of the stairs in her nightgown and called for champagne. Rosina Townsend took up the wine on a tray and handed it in. At that time Rosina saw a young man lying on the bed. That places him in the house with the victim as late as eleven-fifteen.

"At five after twelve Rosina went to bed, making certain the street door was bolted and locked. The street door is kept locked at all times, and each night, between eight and midnight, Rosina posts herself at the door to keep track of her girls' visitors. Each of the girls has her own key, however, and the house rules are that, after midnight, the girls are responsible for letting their own visitors out and relocking the door so that Madam Rosina's slumbers, or whatever, are not disturbed.

"Last night, some time after twelve and before three, Rosina was awakened by someone knocking at her bedroom door, asking to be let out. She told him to get his woman to unlock the door and went back to sleep. She has no idea who the man was or what time he woke her. Then, at about three, she was awakened again, this time by a man knocking at the street door to be let in. She got up and admitted him— he was a regular customer. It was at that point that she saw a lamp burning in this room. She came down here to the parlor to investigate and found that the lamp was one of a matched pair, one of which was normally kept in the room of Maria Stevens and the other in Helen Jewett's room. She also discovered that the bar was down and the French doors were open. She then returned to her own room."

"Assuming that either Helen or Stevens was using the privy," I said, and he nodded. "Which room is Rosina's?"

"Ground floor," he answered. "First door to your right as you enter from the street."

"One other question," I said. "Was Rosina alone in bed last night?"

His eyes met mine. "No," he said simply. He offered no additional information and I didn't press him. "Go on," I said.

"After five or ten minutes," he continued, "Rosina realized that she hadn't heard anyone come back in, and she returned to the parlor, called into the yard, and getting no response, she closed and barred the doors. Then, apparently puzzled by the lamp, she went upstairs, checked Maria Stevens' door, found it locked, checked Jewett's door and discovered the smoke. The girl was dead."

"And the boy was gone," I said. I got to my feet and began to pace. "Problem: how did little Frankie Rivers get out of the bawdy house? Presumption: he used Helen Jewett's lamp to light his way to the parlor and went out the French doors into the yard. Simple, eh?"

Quinncannon smiled. "Next problem: how did little Frankie Rivers get out of the yard?"

"Is that a problem?"

He led the way into the garden. "Come out and see," he said, waving a full champagne glass.

At the threshold I cried, "Wait!"

"What's the matter?"

"Tracks!" I said. "It's been raining or drizzling most of the morning. If the killer went out through the yard he must have left tracks. Are there any footprints in the gardens?"

His eyes narrowed. "You want footprints?" he inquired grimly, and swept his hand out in a gesture that included the entire district. "I give you footprints!"

The muddy yard looked as if an army had marched over it. "The watch?" I asked.

"And the regular police. The officious nincompoops swarmed all over the area looking for 'clues' and destroyed all chance of finding any."

"But they did find a cloak, didn't they? I heard they found Robinson's cloak in one of the adjacent yards."

"That's all part of our experiment in stupidity," Quinncannon replied. "Take a look at the yard."

Perhaps at the height of the summer season Rosina Townsend's gardens were, as the *Herald* later said, "an Eden of delights, of lovely, shaded arbors and retreats, where grew the gayest of flowers and all the beauties of the vegetable world." To my eye, on that misty April morning, they rather resembled a small swamp with a few skeletal trees writhing up out of the mire.

The entire yard is surrounded by a board fence which is at least nine feet high all around, and twelve feet in some places. No alley or passageway leads from the yard to the street, so that to escape from the yard requires that the fence be scaled at some point. Emerging from the French doors, one finds the yard is bordered on the left, or east, by the yard of the next house in Thomas Street—at the rear, or south, by the yard of a house in Duane Street—and at the right, or west, by the yard of a house which fronts on Hudson Street.

"The cloak was found in the Hudson Street yard," Quinncannon explained, "approximately fifteen feet from the fence, and spread out on the ground rather than bunched or rolled up. The hatchet was found over here."

"Hatchet?" I said quickly. "What hatchet?"

"The police think they have the murder weapon. A watchman named Eldridge found a hatchet in the southwest corner of this yard, about six inches from the base of the fence. The official theory is that the killer ran from the parlor into the yard and dropped the hatchet while he was climbing the west fence. Then he supposedly lost the cloak while fleeing across the Hudson Street yard."

I examined the west fence. It was between nine and ten feet high, white in color, with pickets set on top at irregular intervals of a foot to eighteen inches. The privy stood against it, but at some distance from the southwest corner, so that it could not have been used to assist the climber.

"It wouldn't be easy," I said finally, "but it certainly could have happened that way."

"Could it?" There was a dry tone in his voice that should have warned me what he was leading up to, but I didn't hear it. Intent on my own theory, I walked right into the trap.

"Of course it could," I insisted. "We're talking about a young man, nimble and reasonably athletic. He shouldn't have any serious difficulty scaling that fence."

"Well, why don't you prove it?" he said mildly, taking a sip of champagne. I eyed him narrowly. "After all"—he smiled—"here we have a fence, and here you are, a young man, nimble and reasonably athletic. You're wearing a cloak, so all we need is a hatchet." He picked up a dead branch from the ground and handed it to me. "This will do. It's much lighter than an ax, but it wouldn't have been the weight that bothered him but the encumbrance of having only one free hand."

"Damn it, Lon! Is this your experiment in stupidity?"

"Yes, Davy, it is."

"*My* stupidity," I growled.

"No," he said. "I rather think the murderer's stupidity. Are you game?"

I sighed hugely. "All right, damnation, what am I supposed to do?"

"Go back to the parlor. When you come out again, remember you're the murderer. You're frightened. All you can think of is escape. Run over here and scale the fence."

I went to the house feeling extremely foolish, but I composed myself and tried to imagine myself the killer. I burst out the doors, stared about me wildly, and sprinted for the southwest corner of the yard. As I ran I realized that my only hope of getting over the fence was to leap for the top on a dead run, pulling myself up with the strength of my arms. I would need both hands—I certainly wasn't going to carry an ax blade in my teeth—and yet . . .

"Lon!" I skidded to a halt in that damn mud. "Why would he drop the hatchet *here*—on this side? He's gone to the trouble of bringing it with him this far. Why wouldn't he *throw* it into the next yard before he climbed over?"

Quinncannon nodded, puffing on his pipe. "Good, good, exactly the same conclusion I came to. Ask yourself this, Davy. Why is he so anxious to carry that hatchet away with him? Where did he get it?"

"Why, from the house here, I suppose."

"Then he would have left it here, in the house. No, the only reason to carry it away would be if he'd brought it with him in the first place—if there were some way in which it could be traced to him. And if that were the case, why would he leave it here? Why wouldn't he simply lob it over that fence? Or, if he *did* drop it, why not reach under the fence from the next yard and retrieve it? There's room for a man's arm to reach under the fence, and the damn ax was only *six inches* away."

"He must have been panicky," I said. "Not in his right mind. He couldn't think or function rationally."

Quinncannon's lips were taut as he shook his head. "Perhaps . . . perhaps . . ."

"Look, aside from the hatchet, how are you going to explain the cloak? It was found, spread out on the ground, fifteen feet the other side of a ten-foot fence. There isn't any way it could have been thrown over from this side, Lon. The only possible explanation is that the killer wore it over the fence and then dropped it in flight."

The Irishman eyed me through a white cloud of tobacco smoke. "Let's see if you're right. Do you mind playing the murderer again?"

"Without the hatchet?"

"I think we've learned all we're going to about the hatchet for the moment."

I tossed the branch into the next yard and again went back to the house. A couple of deep breaths and I felt as much like a murderer as I figured was necessary to scale a fence. Again I rushed into the yard and dashed for the southwest corner. I pushed off a few feet from the base of the fence, lunging for the top, and hung on, scrambling and clawing until I managed to hook my right boot over one of the pickets, and heaving and puffing and promising myself to get more exercise, I dragged myself up over the top, narrowly escaping being impaled on the pickets, and dropped, at last, exhausted, into the Hudson Street yard beside Quinncannon.

"Very nicely done," he said.

"Thanks," I gasped. "I must be getting out of shape. That isn't as easy to do as it looks."

"Nevertheless," he said, taking a sip of champagne, "I thought you managed it with grace and finesse."

"Thanks, Lon."

"No need for thanks, Davy. You've certainly proven that it was possible for the killer to have scaled that fence, and I must say that . . ."

But I was scowling at him lethally.

"*Why* am I thanking you? Why in hell am I even *talking* to you? Did I climb that fence or dream it? Which side of the fence is this, anyway?"

"The Hudson Street side."

"Then you couldn't be here and I am obviously hallucinating you. I examined that fence thoroughly and the boards are solid, and they are ten feet high, and you couldn't possibly have climbed it, especially with a glass of champagne in your hand, unless you had spilled at *least* a drop or two, which I know is far too great a risk for you to take! Blood? Yes. But champagne?"

I stopped short because I was staring at a place in the fence so broken down and demolished that a person could step easily through it from one yard to the other. "But I *did* check that fence," I blurted out. "Don't tell me the damn fence is only rotted on one side?"

He only stood quietly, smoking and watching me.

I snapped my fingers. "The privy! The goddamned privy!" I ran to where the boards were broken in and found I was looking at the rear of Rosina's privy shed. "I never thought to examine behind it," I said.

"Don't feel bad," Quinncannon said. "The police haven't noticed it either."

I wheeled around. "Then this explains how the killer got into this yard!"

"Then why did he drop his hatchet?"

I glared at him furiously for a few seconds, and then lowered my hands to my sides. "I don't know," I said helplessly.

"If it's any comfort," he said, "neither do I."

I looked around the Hudson Street yard. Like the one behind Rosina Townsend's house, it was completely enclosed by a high board fence, and no alleys led to the street. "If the killer did come in here," I said, "he did himself no favors. There's no way out of this yard except to climb another fence. Unless there's a break in this fence somewhere else?"

Quinncannon shook his head. "None, in either yard. I've been over every inch. The only escape from here is through the house itself, and the residents are ready to swear the doors were locked all night."

We returned to Rosina's yard, and as we emerged from behind the privy I caught sight of the piazza which abutted the house on the west side. "Lon!" I cried. "The roof of the piazza!"

He smiled and I knew the irritating Celt had already thought of it, but I finished the idea anyway. "The piazza roof lies just outside the window of Helen Jewett's room. All the killer had to do was step out of the window, walk along the roof, and drop down into the alley that leads to Thomas Street."

Quinncannon finished his wine. "Simple, isn't it?"

We walked toward the house. "It seems to me as though you're right. We may be dealing with a very stupid killer," I said.

"Unfortunately," he replied, "that is usually the first prerequisite of a perfect murder."


Dennis Brink was waiting for us in the parlor. "Beginning to think you two would never finish your game of blindman's buff out there," he said, smirking and licking his lips. "I've been waiting to tell you personally that the coroner's jury has finished holding the inquest upstairs and the verdict is willful murder against young Robinson. Hoxie and Price are hovering out in the hall, Quinncannon, waiting to waylay you, and I figured, in the interests of fair play, I'd give you decent warning we've got the little bastard cold. Just what we've got is none of your damn business, but I'm only saying this is one case you don't want to get mixed up in."

"You're a liar, Brink," Quinncannon snapped. "What could you have on Robinson in only a few hours?"

Brink lounged back on a divan and sucked on his cigar. "All we got is motive, weapon, and opportunity. We got an eyewitness who puts him in this house last night. We got the cloak he dropped and we can tie him to it. We got the hatchet he used and we can prove it came from Hoxie's store. And we can *tie* the hatchet to the cloak." He laughed at his joke. "That's the way he brought the blade in, tied with a piece of string to a tassel on his cloak. Get it? There's a piece of string still tied to the cloak and one still tied to the hatchet, and we can prove they were once one piece."

"I don't hear anything about motive," Quinncannon said.

"And you don't need to. You've heard enough. You know the one about giving the man enough rope? Well, this is the one where we give the boy enough string. We're going to hang Robinson with that string, Quinncannon. You can make book on it!"

Hoxie and Price did ambush Quinncannon in the hall. Since it was clearly a private conversation, I went on into Thomas Street and hailed a hansom. McCraw, the watchman, was still on duty at the door, and a long line of people, stretching out of sight around the block, was waiting for a promised chance to file past and gawk at the murdered girl.

At length Quinncannon came down the steps and swung up into the cab. I gave his address to the driver. The Irishman appeared both puzzled and troubled.

"I assume you are now working for the defense of Richard Robinson," I said.

"Not for publication?"

I nodded.

"You assume correctly," he said.

It had begun to drizzle again.

"Out of curiosity," I said, "does Robinson admit coming to see Helen Jewett last night?"

"No, he doesn't."

"And Rosina has made a positive identification?"

"Yes, Davy, she has."

"Well," I said, "obviously somebody is lying."

Quinncannon sat gnawing on the stem of a cold pipe. "No," he said finally, "everybody is lying. That's the trouble with this damn case. Absolutely everybody is lying."

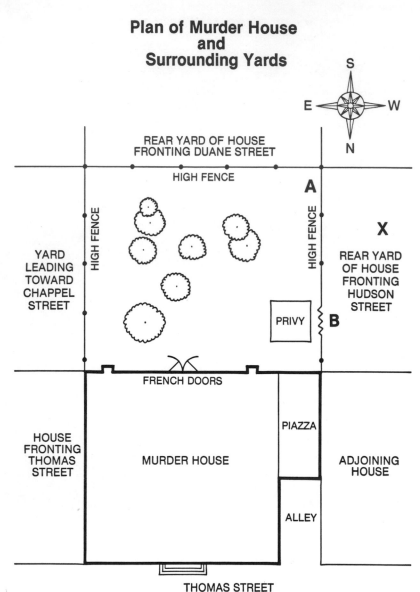

# Plan of Murder House
## and
## Surrounding Yards

S

E — W

N

REAR YARD OF HOUSE
FRONTING DUANE STREET

HIGH FENCE

**A**

**X**

HIGH FENCE

HIGH FENCE

YARD
LEADING
TOWARD
CHAPPEL
STREET

REAR YARD
OF HOUSE
FRONTING
HUDSON
STREET

PRIVY **B**

FRENCH DOORS

PIAZZA

HOUSE
FRONTING
THOMAS
STREET

MURDER HOUSE

ADJOINING
HOUSE

ALLEY

THOMAS STREET

**X** indicates where cloak was found
**A** indicates where hatchet was found
**B** indicates where fence broken down behind privy

# First Floor, Thomas Street House

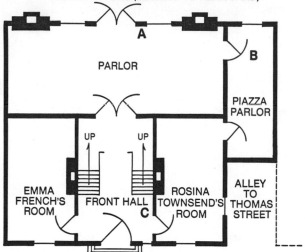

FRENCH DOORS (LEADING TO REAR YARD)

**A** indicates table where oil lamp was found burning
**B** indicates where cloak and hatchet were originally placed after being found
**C** entry lamp suspended from ceiling

# Second Floor, Thomas Street House

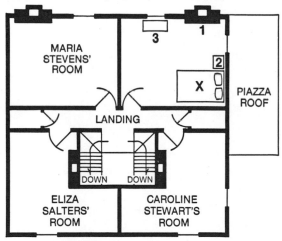

**X** indicates where body was found
**1** Fireplace
**2** Table on which candle stood
**3** Desk

# 18  *The* Herald *Reports a Murder*

I spent Sunday afternoon talking with various watchmen who had been called to the murder house and learning what testimony had been offered at the inquest. Toward midafternoon Dennis Brink came in and huddled excitedly for about thirty minutes with one of the justices. On his way out he took me aside.

"A word in your ear, Mr. Cordor," he said smugly. "Robinson had a miniature painted of himself which he presented as a gift to Helen Jewett. It was in her possession last night, but this afternoon I found it in Robinson's room. He carried it away with him after he killed her. Oh, we've got him nailed, Mr. Cordor, we've got him hung!" He grinned, showing brown teeth. "You might mention the miniature to your friend Quinncannon."

Near five o'clock I left the Police Office to walk down to the *Sun,* just as a cab thundered up and a tall, homely man with a huge nose bounded to the sidewalk. Bennett recognized me immediately. With a snort he rushed into the building.

At the *Sun* Moses Beach greeted me frantically. "Where the devil have you been?"

"In a whorehouse."

*"All night?"*

"No," I said, "only since the saloons closed."

*"Mr. Cordor!"* Ben Day bellowed from the landing. "I'm not a man to mince words. You're fired!"

"Fine!" I shouted up to him. "I'll just take my story of the Helen Jewett murder down the street to the *Herald*. I'll come in tomorrow to clean out my desk. In the meantime, gentlemen, maybe one of you will be kind enough to water my nasturtium."

Beach stared at me. "You've got the Jewett story?"

"Not too much water, Moses," I said. "And put the pot on the windowsill, will you? Nasturtiums need plenty of light."

"*Mr. Cordor!*" Day roared. "I'm not a man to mince words. You're hired again!"

I wrote my story for the Monday edition, the first to be published after the crime.

Bennett's Monday account of the murder was brief and filled with errors. It concluded:

> Robinson is a native of one of the Eastern States, aged 19 and remarkably handsome, and has been, for some time past, in the employ of Joseph Hoxie, 101 Maiden Lane. *But his conduct upon this occasion must stamp him as a villain of too black a dye for mortal. Of this there can be no doubt,* for he took the hatchet with him, with which the murder was committed, and the deed done, he attempted to destroy all evidence of his guilt, by firing the house, and thus induce the public to believe that she had perished in the flames.

"Of all the outrageous, unscrupulous, libelous, poisonous pen pushers in history!" Quinncannon cried. "Is there anything to compare with this Bennett and his rag?"

It was such an unusual occurrence to see him express deep emotion that I was astonished.

"Apparently we may now retire all the justices and tear up all the jury rolls," he continued between clenched teeth. "No need for prosecutors and defenders—send the witnesses home—fire the court clerk and pension off the sheriff. All we need is Mr. Bennett and the hangman!"

He stood up and flung the wadded *Herald* into the chair he had just vacated. "How many readers has this moron got?"

"About ten thousand circulation," I answered. "That's thirty, maybe forty thousand readers."

"Three-fourths of whom are potential jurors for Robinson's trial," he growled. "What the hell kind of society is it that licenses dogs and lets journalists run free?"

"You might try to be civil," I said.

He wheeled on me. "David, it is a simple matter of the potential danger that each species poses to the common welfare. A journalist can poison forty thousand minds before breakfast. The worst a dog can do is become rabid and bite a baby."

He picked up the newspaper again and thrust it toward me. "Have you read this drivel? How many facts does this idiot have right? He's wrong about the wounds on the body. He's wrong about the cloak. He's wrong about the circumstances under which the body was found. The only fact he's got straight is Robinson's address! Yet he presumes to invent a fictional account of what passed between Robinson and the girl when it has not even been established that Robinson was near the house on Saturday night. And he states that Robinson is guilty *beyond doubt* when the man has not yet been indicted! Doesn't this clod know the difference between an inquest and a court of oyer and terminer."

He dropped into his chair and began filling his pipe, glaring moodily into the fire. I said quietly, "You know, Lon, I also think Robinson is guilty."

"I know you do," he answered. "You had the decency not to state his guilt in your newspaper as if it were a fact."

We sat for several minutes in lethal silence. At last I broke it. "The difficulty is that Bennett's readers believe everything he writes."

I saw, in the corner of his eye, the natal gleam of an idea which, as it slowly took shape, transformed his whole face into a sly, grinning fox's mask, until he burst out in what I can only describe as a very dirty laugh.

I said, "What are you plotting?"

Quinncannon smiled. "My sainted grandfather used to say," he remarked, "that if you're going to eat with the pigs, you've got to get in the trough."

That was the only clue I could pry out of him. But it didn't matter. I guessed what he was up to soon enough.

Before visiting the Police Office on Sunday afternoon, Bennett had gone to the house in Thomas Street. Most of the mob of ghoulishly curious which had gathered in the hope of being permitted a view of the corpse had been scattered by the watch. This seems to have inspired Bennett with the notion that the entire city might wish a glimpse of the dead girl. The slightest wish of his public is the veriest command of an editor of the penny press:

VISIT TO THE SCENE.—Yesterday afternoon, about 4 o'clock, I started on a visit to the scene at 41 Thomas Street. A large crowd of young men stood around the door. The excitement among the youth of this city was beginning to spread in all directions.

I knocked at the door. A Police officer opened it, stealthily. I told him who I was. "Mr. B. you can enter," said he, with great politeness. The crowds rushed from behind seeking also an entrance.

"No more comes in," said the Police officer.

"Why do you let that man in?" asked one of the crowd.

"He is an editor—he is on public duty."

I entered—I pressed forward to the sitting room or parlor. There I found another Police officer in charge of that apartment. The old lady of the house, Mrs. Townsend, was sitting on a sofa, talking to several young men in a great state of excitement. The Police officer when he saw me said—"Mr. B. would you like to see the *place?*"

"I would," replied I.

He immediately rose—I followed him. We mounted an elegant stair case, dark and gloomy. On reaching the second story, the Police officer took a key from his pocket, and opened the door. What a sight burst upon me! There stood an elegant double mahogany bed, all covered with burnt linen, blankets, pillows, black as cinders. I looked around for the object of my curiosity. On the carpet, I saw a piece of linen sheet covering something as if carelessly flung over it.

"Here," said the Police officer, "here is the poor creature."

He half uncovered the ghastly corpse. I could scarcely look at it for a second or two. Slowly I began to discover the lineaments of the corpse as one would the beauties of a statue of marble. It was the most remarkable sight I ever beheld—I never have, and never expect to see such another. "My God," exclaimed I, "how like a statue! I can scarcely conceive that form to be a corpse!" Not a vein was to be seen. The body looked as white, as full, as polished as the purest Parian marble. The perfect figure, the exquisite limbs, the fine face, the full arms, the beautiful bust, all, all surpassed in every respect the Venus de Medici. I was recalled to her horrid destiny by seeing the dreadful bloody gashes on the right temple, which must have caused instantaneous dissolution.

It is said that she threatened to expose Robinson, when she lived, having discovered that he was paying attention to a respectable young lady. This threat drove him to madness. On Saturday she walked up and down Broadway half the day, nodding to her acquaintances among the dissipated young men.

In what a horrible moral condition is a portion of the young men of this devoted city?!

As far as the "devoted city's" newspapers were concerned, Bennett's Visit to the Scene created as great a sensation as the murder itself. A general denunciation of the *Herald*'s editor, as a ghoul and worse, immediately ensued. Colonel Webb led the onslaught. Bennett's "Visit" was the action "of a vampire returning to a newly found graveyard—like the carrion bird to the rotting carcass—like any vile thing to its congenial element."

"For once I agree with Webb," Moses Beach said in the office on Tuesday morning. "Bennett has finally sounded bottom. What do you think, Davy?"

"If you mean, how do I react to the image of that dirty old man salivating over the remains of Helen Jewett, I consider it to be in very poor taste."

"Adjectives such as 'disgusting' and 'loathsome' come to mind," Beach said firmly. "The entire affair is scandalous!"

"Yes," I said slowly. "I expect the vast majority of the mob swarming around Bennett's office this morning, clamoring for his latest edition, would probably agree with you."

I paused, and then added, "It was all I could do to get hold of a copy."
I watched him. He fidgeted uncomfortably, drumming his fingers on his desk top. When eventually he met my gaze, he did not return my smile.

"All right, damn it," he grumbled, "what does Bennett have to say today?"

Helen Jewett was well known to every pedestrian on Broadway. Last summer she was famous for parading Wall Street in an elegant green dress, and generally with a letter in her hand. She used to look at the brokers with great boldness of demeanor—had a peculiar walk—something in the style of an Englishwoman. From those that have known her, we have been informed that she was a fascinating woman in conversation, full of intellect and refinement, but at the same time possessed of a very devil, and a species of mortal antipathy to the male race. Her great passion was to seduce young men, and particularly those who most resisted her charms. She seems to have declared war against the sex. "Oh!" she would say, "how I despise you all—you are a heartless, unprincipled lot—you have ruined me—I'll ruin you—I delight in your ruin!"

With a happier destiny—and a steady moral principle, this young woman had talents calculated for the highest sphere in life. We know no private circumstance that has caused such a sensation in our city as the recent transaction. It is the whole topic of conversation wherever one goes. It is horrid. It creates melancholy. It produces horror. Will it work a reform? Will it make the licentious pause?

"Sort of makes you want to weep, applaud, and sing a hymn, all at the same time, doesn't it?" said Will Prall, who had wandered up while I was reading the story aloud to Beach. "I wonder how much of it is true."

"About one word in a thousand," Beach muttered.

"Oh, I don't know," Prall said. "The part about her promenading on Wall Street is true. I remember her. We called her the Comet of the Sidewalk."

"Well, parts of it are pure fiction," I said. "This nonsense about her 'mortal antipathy' to all men, for example. Bennett makes her out a combination Circe, Medea, and Lucrezia Borgia. 'You have ruined me—I'll ruin you—I delight in your ruin!' Now, gentlemen, there's a man who could write dialogue for Susannah Haswell Rowson."

"I expect we're in for a good bit of preaching from old Bennett now," Prall said. "What else can you expect from an aging bachelor virgin, surrounded as he is by the Bible Society, the Tract Society, and the Missionary Society? Eh? Some uplifting *Herald*-style sermonizing on the inevitable fate of fallen women and promiscuous youths in the wind?"

"I don't know about the fallen women," Beach grunted, "but a few sermons on promiscuous youth wouldn't do either one of you the least harm."

# 19   The Victim's Private History

Robinson's attorneys had lost no time digging into Helen Jewett's past. Over dinner I got some particulars from Quinncannon. "The lady's career was brief but busy," he said. "Her mother died while Helen, or, to give her right name, Dorcas Dorrance, was still an infant, and she was raised in Augusta, Maine, by her father, a poor but honest souse. The girl matured rapidly. When she was about twelve she became enamored of a local boy named Sumner who would live, and die, to regret the connection. After a short acquaintance with him, as the penny press would say, 'all was gone that constitutes the honor and ornament of the female character.' "

I glanced up. "Rape?" I asked.

"Probably. The poor lad never had a chance."

He took a sip of champagne. "At all events, her father, dismayed that he had sired a child prodigy, could no longer hold his head up at the local pub. He fell into deep depression and shortly died of shame and gin. Dorcas was taken into the home of a Judge Cyrus Weston, whose daughters pampered and petted her. Eventually she was packed off to what is called a Female Academy on the Kennebeck River, where she appears to have distinguished herself. In the summer of 1829, when she was sixteen, Dorcas went to spend her vacation with a distant relative in Norridgewock and caught the eye of a young cashier named Horace Splenny. Unfortunately, Sumner rematerialized simultaneously and a series of surreptitious midnight rendezvous were held until Splenny surprised the lovers and beat Sumner into a very dead pulp. Dorcas fled back to Augusta and threw herself on Judge Weston's mercy, and he behaved as any respectable gentleman would."

I smiled. "Don't tell me the judge died of shame."

"No, Davy. The luxury of dying of shame is reserved for the deserving poor. The deserving rich prefer the gout. The judge had as much practical common sense as the villain of any melodrama. He threw Dorcas, bag and baggage, out of the house, and went to his club the next day with his honor unsullied."

"And the girl?"

"Ah, Dorcas." He leaned back and began filling his pipe. "With her few pitiful possessions clutched under one arm and her copy of Byron under the other, she groped her way to Portland and took the alias of Marie Benson. In Boston she was known as Helen Mar, after the heroine of some young lady's novel. In this town she moved about remarkably often considering her popularity. She began at Madam Post's in Howard Street, then the Laurence House in Chapel, then Elizabeth Stewart, Mother Gallagher, and the Duchesse before Rosina's. And at each house the same story."

"Friction among the girls?"

He nodded. "That, and trouble with a man. Sumner was murdered. Splenny was hung. She broke up three marriages in Portland. In Boston her extravagance drove a young man to embezzle from his own father. And here we have . . ."

"Robinson," I finished.

"Robinson," he echoed grimly.

## 20 Mr. Cordor Reflects

Robinson was scheduled to be examined before Justice Oliver Lowends, the jailor's cousin, on Tuesday at two, and along with half the reporters in the city, I was at the Dead House to see the prisoner taken from his cell to the Police Office. A dense crowd of curious bystanders had gathered in the Park behind the City Hall by noon, surrounding the prison completely. Their mood was not dangerous, but it was hostile enough to raise serious official doubts over the wisdom of attempting to move Robinson. At one point a carriage was brought to the Chambers Street doors of the building with the apparent intent of rushing the prisoner behind a wedge of police into the coach, driving a few hundred yards around the corner, and rushing him into the Police Office behind another phalanx. When the carriage had remained standing for almost an hour, the rumor spread through the crowd that it was a decoy, and that Robinson had been meanwhile smuggled out of the bridewell on the Park side. Another rumor held that Lowends and other officials had been brought into the prison in disguise and were conducting the inquiry in Robinson's cell. Still a third rumor circulated that the examination had been postponed at the request of the prisoner's attorneys, which is precisely what had happened, but the crowd, which had swelled to over two thousand, some of them waiting since before dawn, refused to believe it. Out of fear of a riot, no announcement was made to them, and they were left to drift away or mill around on into the evening, still hoping for a glimpse of the notorious ax murderer.

During the long afternoon I wandered through the crowd, listening to their conversations. I noted with some satisfaction that quite as many were carrying the *Sun,* with my discourse concerning the rear yards and fences of Thomas and Hudson Streets and reflecting on the killer's possible escape routes, as were carrying Bennett's paper. Moreover, I became aware that, where arguments were being waged over the guilt or innocence of Robinson, those dogmatically insisting on the youth's guilt invariably toted, and quoted, the *Herald,* while more measured and moderate viewpoints seemed to cite my articles for support.

At seven I went back to my desk and wrote my story for the Wednesday edition. There being no new facts of any significance to report, I speculated instead on the vast amount of information still unknown. The inmates of the murder house, for instance, were being held incommunicado by the authorities. Rumors seeped out of their testimony. One of them, Elizabeth Salters, was said to have identified the cloak by a broken tassel which she had sewn on for Robinson when he was paying court to her, and it was whispered that she was violently jealous of Helen's attraction for the boy. Another, Emma French, was reported to have backed up Rosina's identification of Robinson, which was vitally important if true, because otherwise the prosecution was left with only one witness to place him at the scene on the murder night.

A third, Maria Stevens, who had the room adjoining Helen's, had supposedly stated that she heard no word or groan, or any sound during the night except a shutter slamming in the wind, which she had risen to fasten. Then, too, there were a large number of witnesses from whom absolutely nothing had yet been heard—the men patronizing the house on that evening. True, all of them had managed to escape in the initial confusion, but it was thought the police knew their names. Had they been questioned, and had any of them revealed any facts of importance?

More rumors. There were questions being raised about the circumstantial evidence linking Robinson to the crime. It was said that no blood had been found on the hatchet, and that the watchman who originally found and handled the weapon could not remember seeing any twine on it. There were reports that Robinson could prove an alibi for the time of the murder, by Jimmy Teer, or by someone else.

Confusion reigned over the supposed motive for the crime. Was Robinson jealous of Helen's attentions to another youth, who called himself "Bill Easy," and who had been frequenting her boudoir? The grapevine at the Police Office murmured that Bill Easy had been identified and that a handkerchief found under the dead girl's pillow was his. Or was Helen threatening to expose Robinson to a respectable young lady to whom he was theoretically paying respectable court? Or did Robinson have a motive at all? And who else might wish to murder Helen? Elizabeth Salters? Bill Easy? Might there not be a dozen jealous tarts and ex-boyfriends with lethal ambitions?

Why had the room been ransacked? Again, the official explanation was that the murderer, Robinson, was searching for his miniature lest it be found at the scene to incriminate him. Yet to be found in his room, as it was, was far more incriminating. And if he took the miniature, why didn't he take the letters he had written to her, which were rumored to have been found in her bureau? Was it possible the killer had only pretended to search the room? Was it possible the room had been searched, or the fire started, or both, by someone other than the murderer?

There were, I concluded, simply too many unanswered questions.

I read the article over when I had finished it, and reflected with a smile that I was proving an apt pupil of Lon Quinncannon. A few months before, perhaps none of these questions would have occurred to me. Now they seemed to pour out of the inkwell in a torrent across the pages of foolscap. I sent the story down to composing, grabbed a quick supper in Ann Street, and went home to bed, eagerly anticipating the impact my article would have on the investigation, on the whole city, when it hit the streets the next morning.

There were two things I didn't count on. One of them was that Quinncannon had himself a new pupil.

# 21  The Polluter of the Press

Wednesday, April 13. I rose early, left a note for Prall, bought copies of the *Sun* and *Herald* from hawkers, and strolled over to Broadway to have a leisurely breakfast at the American Hotel.

When I began to read the *Herald* I almost choked on my coffee.

STILL FURTHER OF THE TRAGEDY

REFLECTIONS—WHO IS THE MURDERER?—It is rapidly becoming a doubtful point, notwithstanding the startling circumstances, whether the poor, unfortunate girl was destroyed by the young man now in the custody of the public authorities. It is asked—is it possible for a youth, hitherto unimpeached and unimpeachable in his character, to have engendered and perpetrated so diabolical an act as the death of Helen Jewett was? Is it the character of crime to jump at once from the height of virtue to the depths of vice?

The various circumstances indicating the probable guilt of Robinson—can they be explained? Can they not be shown to be naturally growing out of other person's guilt—of a deep laid conspiracy of female rivals—of the vengeance of female wickedness—of the burnings of female revenge?

I read Bennett's long article to the bitter end to win a wager with myself that it would not contain a single fact or cogent argument. He had simply and brazenly reversed his original position on the murder.

When I put the *Herald* down, I turned to the *Sun,* and my own piece, with a sense of positive relief.

But my story was not in the *Sun.*

There was a brief article stating that the examination of Robinson had been postponed, that no new facts had been uncovered since the last edition, and that was it. Not a trace of my story. Not a trace.

I cannot remember ever being so angry before—or so calm. I left the hotel under a full head of steam and strode toward the office at a precise and deliberate pace, neither too hurried nor too slow. I reached the building in exactly four minutes and fifty seconds by my pocket watch. Moses Beach was waiting for me just inside the rail.

"Davy, I want to talk to you."

I threw the swing gate open and pushed past him toward the stairs. He ran around me in circles as I walked. To an observer it must have appeared comical.

"Davy, I want you to cool down."

I began to climb the stairs, one step at a time. At the top I saw Prall waiting for me. Beach was following me. They must have had it planned. At the landing Prall gave way, as I knew he would, and I continued to Ben Day's office and entered without bothering to knock.

Day was seated behind his desk. In a chair at one side of the desk, facing the door, sat Richard Adams Locke. Prall and Beach had trailed me to the door. I looked around the circle—Prall quaking, Beach worrying, Locke smirking, Day scowling—everybody right in character.

"I want to know what this young idiot is doing in here," Day snapped at Beach.

"What happened to my story?" I demanded.

"I killed it!" Day barked.

"Why, damn it?"

"I'm going to give you an explanation," he said, "and I want you to understand that I don't owe you one. I own this newspaper and I set the editorial policy of this newspaper. Your article violated the editorial policy of this newspaper. It criticized the authorities who are investigating the Jewett murder. It is the editorial policy of this newspaper that the authorities are doing everything humanly possible, and more, in their investigation of the Jewett murder."

"But that's not true," I growled. "My story told the truth!"

"The truth? You presumptuous, posturing little peacock! *What is truth?*" He brought his fist down on the desk.

I waved the *Herald* almost under his nose. "I can tell you what truth is not! Truth is not the sensational, obscene, hypocritical rot that Bennett is grinding out. My articles are researched, reasoned, balanced!" I glanced at each of them. "Which one of you says they're not?"

With a groan Day leaned back in his chair and flipped his pen up so that it ricocheted off the ceiling. Locke crossed his legs and smiled. "You see, youngster, with that obscene rot, Mr. Bennett is tripling his circulation."

"Ye gods!" Day hissed. "That has nothing to do with it, you simpleton! Do you have the temerity to suggest, Mr. Locke, that I run my paper for the purpose of personal profit, or that I would subordinate the welfare of my readers to any consideration of my own financial gain?"

It was the only time I ever saw Locke at a loss for words. He squirmed nervously. "Of course not, Ben."

The sole proprietor turned back to me. His voice was measured but his eyes smoldered. "I want to make my position clear to you, Mr. Cordor. I once told you, in this office, that the function of the *Sun,* the *calling* of the *Sun,* is to benefit the community by enlightening the minds of the common people. That is the essential role of a free press in a democratic society, Mr. Cordor. It was not until the advent of the penny-press system, Mr. Cordor, not until the advent and success of the *Sun,* that the masses began to be informed, to act in concert, to comprehend their own interests. My newspaper is responsible for that, Mr. Cordor. Do you understand?"

"How do you enlighten the minds of the people by suppressing the truth, Mr. Day?" I asked. "How are the masses to understand their interests if they are denied the facts?"

"Your story contained no facts. Your story contained speculation, speculation calculated to cast doubt on both the motives and the competence of the authorities."

"But . . ." I searched for words, feeling my frustration growing. "What if the authorities *are* corrupt or incompetent? Surely the public has the right to know."

He fixed his eyes on mine. "Have you proof of those allegations?"

"Damn it, I made no allegations! I raised questions—legitimate, unanswered questions—to which the police and the magistrates ought to be forced to respond."

"In other words, you have no proof." Day got to his feet and walked to the window. He stood with his back to me, looking out at the boisterous city below. "This is a young country, Mr. Cordor, conceived and born in violence and revolution. We remain basically a violent, even a lawless people, and perhaps we always shall be. You have spent enough time in the police court to know what I'm speaking of." He turned around and came back to his desk. "It is not in the best interests of such a people to have their faith and trust in authority and the forces of order undermined. I will not, do you hear, I *will* not see my newspaper used for such a purpose."

We stood now on opposite sides of that huge desk, facing each other. "I thought I once heard you say, sir, that the common people understood their own interests because your newspaper informed them of the facts on which they could base such judgments."

"I said, Mr. Cordor, that the masses understand their best interests because my newspaper understands their best interests and informs them of what they are."

"Then suppose, Mr. Day, that Richard Robinson is innocent?"

"It is the editorial policy of this newspaper that Richard Robinson is guilty of the willful murder of Helen Jewett," he responded evenly.

"But— For God's sake, *why?*"

Day placed both palms on his desk top and leaned forward. "Because, Mr. Cordor," he said venomously, "that venal heretic, that polluter of the press, *Bennett,* has declared him innocent!"

# 22 Uncle Colum

I took a cab to Theater Alley and rapped loudly on the Duchesse's door. After several minutes I could hear the numerous bolts being withdrawn. The Duchesse peered out.

"By Jesus, but you gave me a start, young sir, at this unholy hour, when only the police ever come to call, and me certain that the house was afire at the very least."

The Duchesse by daylight was a memorable sight. Resplendent in a ragged robe and tattered mules, she squinted up in toadlike fashion. Her face, without the accustomed cosmetic mask, had an honest ugliness which I found almost appealing. All that was needed to complete the picture was a caldron.

She shuffled ahead of me to the parlor. In the glare of the sun, the room's cheap tastelessness lost all vestige of the tawdry witchery it seemed to secrete by candlelight. Like its mistress, the room showed cracks and its paint was peeling.

"You want to see Dolly, I suppose," the Duchesse squawked, "but she had a busy night and is still abed; however, I'll rouse her if you'll be so kind as to take a glass or two of libation while you're waiting."

No, not Dolly, with the auburn hair and the fawn's eyes. Not gentle little Dolly, with the musical voice and the tender, warm body that pressed softly against yours. Dolly had the room where Helen Jewett had once shyly held out her hand and let her hair fall to her white shoulders.

"Edna," I said.

Edna was forty and fat and laughed constantly and never talked and loved to listen and took nothing seriously, especially herself, or you.

"Edna?" echoed the Duchesse.

Edna had a wart on her cheek and her hands were always too cold, but she made you feel like a man, she reminded you that you were alive, and afterward, you never dreamed about Edna.

"I'll fetch a bottle of champagne and two glasses," the Duchesse said.

"One glass," I said. "Edna's not thirsty."


Prall found me, early that evening, at the Bull and Bear tavern in Ann Street. It was my own fault. We had been there often enough together and it was the first place he looked. If there was anyone I didn't want to discuss the matter of the *Sun* and the Jewett murder with, it was Will Prall. He started several times, and each time I turned him off. I was pretty drunk when he arrived and he was cold sober, but by nine o'clock, as always, I had sobered up and Prall was boiled. God knows what it is about Prall. I simply cannot get the least bit crocked in his vicinity.

"I admired the way you stood up to the old man this morning," Prall said, taking infinite care with his pronunciation. "No, no, don't change the subject, Davy. I got something I gotta say to you. Moses is afraid you're gonna resign." He reached out unsteadily and put his hand on my arm. "Just you stick to it, boy. You stick, uh, it to old Benny boy, boy."

He hiccupped violently. "I 'member I told you once I had so-ome good advice for you, 'member?"

I nodded.

"We-ell, here it is, short and brief. Two words: Get out. 'Cause, Davy, you're too fine for this business, boy. 'Specially you're too fine to work for Ben, uh, Day, Davy, 'cause . . ."

His grip on my arm tightened.

" 'Cause they perform a p'culiar operation on you when you work too long in the *Sun.*" He laughed hoarsely. "Too long in the sun—get it?" He grew suddenly deadly serious. "P'culiar operation, Davy boy. They remove the spine without the knowledge of the patient."

When I had poured Prall into his bed, I took a stroll to clear the tobacco smoke and liquor fumes out of my head. I don't believe I consciously walked toward Quinncannon's, but in a few minutes I was on Broadway within a block of his rooms. It was a cloudless, breezy night, one of the first warm evenings New York had had after a particularly brutal winter. My spirits rose with each step as I drew closer to the Irishman's lodgings, anticipating good conversation and excellent brandy.

An empty hansom stood at the curb near a streetlight. As I neared Quinncannon's door, it opened suddenly and a tall, angular figure stepped out, shot a stealthy look about him, and climbed into the cab. For a moment his face was silhouetted against the light. There was no mistaking that incredible nose. It was James Gordon Bennett.

In that second it became abruptly and painfully clear why Bennett had changed his editorial position so swiftly. He had been bribed with Joe Hoxie's money by my friend and mentor, Lon Quinncannon! This was what Quinncannon had in mind when he said that if one would eat with pigs one must get in the trough. This was what Attree meant when he called Quinncannon a parasite of the rich and a dealer in perjury.

I turned away from the Irishman's door, feeling sick to my stomach, and crossed the street to the American Hotel, where I hailed a cab. I spent the next few hours at Mother Gallagher's in Duane Street with a girl named Rose about whom I can recall absolutely nothing except that she giggled incessantly and got the hiccups whenever she took a swallow of wine. Some time after midnight I left the house and made my way on foot to the Five Points.

I don't know how many taverns I crawled out of during that endless night, or by what miracle I managed to hold on to my wallet. I remember my overwhelming feelings of self-pity and betrayal, betrayal by Ben Day and above all by Quinncannon. I vaguely recall weaving into a saloon where I ordered a beer, gulped at the foam, and then lowered my head to rest on my folded arms—just for a minute—just until my head cleared. God knows how long it was after that that someone removed my cap, seized me by the hair, and pushed my face so near the candle that it was almost burned by the flame.

A low Irish voice behind me said, "Is this the lad?"

"It is," said a youthful voice from the other side of the table.

Through the flame and the whiskey haze I could make out the vengefully grinning features of the street tough Michael. "It's him, Uncle Colum," the boy repeated. "There was four of 'em that jumped me and beat me when I was alone."

"That's a lie," I managed to say, putting out one hand and shoving the candle away from my eyes. "You had your whole gang with you."

Uncle Colum hauled me up by my lapels. He was a great grizzly of a man with an ugly, whiskey-flushed face. "You'll not be calling the boy a liar, young fellow," he growled. "It's not Delmonico's you're in now, you fancy whelp. I've a mind to destroy you here in front of the company."

"Here now, Colum!" the bartender bellowed. "There'll be no fighting in my place of business!"

"Shut your gullet, Eamon," the big man shouted. "Don't you know who this lad is?" He shoved me against the bar. "This lad is a friend of the murderer Robinson, who killed that girl over in Thomas Street."

An angry murmur rumbled through the crowd of men. They elbowed their way into a circle around me, scowling at the friend of "the murderer Robinson." I shook my head furiously, trying to clear it. Drunk as I still was, I was fully aware of the danger I was in. Flight was my best hope, but flight was out of the question. There were sixty feet between me and the door, and a dozen men ready to stop me if I made the dash. Stone-cold sober and carrying a club, I was no match for the mammoth B'hoy before me, and it was he, not I, who was among friends.

"Murderer or no, Colum," the publican insisted, "I'll not stand for a customer of mine being stretched in my establishment. Take him out in the street and destroy him there."

"Wait a minute!" I cried. "Listen to me!"

"There'll be no orations made by you," Michael yelled. "The young master has a honey tongue, I'm telling you. Don't be listening to him."

"Enough!" said Uncle Colum between clenched teeth. "I've something must be done."

He pushed me toward the door, the mob melting away before us and offering blood-curdling shouts of encouragement to the great Gaelic ape. "Hold the door open, lads!" he cried, pitching me over the wooden sidewalk and into the street, where I rolled up against the wheel of a hansom.

I sat with my back to the wheel and watched him lumber out of the tavern toward me, with the crowd pouring out of the door behind him. I struggled to get to my feet and raise my fists, and he stopped and waited for me, then threw his head back and roared with laughter.

"You're a game little bantam! I'll give you that. Another lad would have tried to run."

"I'm a stupid little bantam," I shouted back at him. "Another lad would have thought to run!"

The big man grinned. "I'm developing a fondness for you, lad," he said, "and to prove it I'll only break one of your arms."

"Put your fists down, Colum Pheety."

This last command came from behind me, from someone seated in the hansom. Without turning I recognized the voice.

"Is that someone else looking to spend some time in splints?" Uncle Colum inquired pleasantly. "Just step down from your fine carriage and I'll be proud to oblige you."

I heard the cab door open and a pair of boots drop softly to the street. "Stop exercising your jaw, you brawling Irish lout," said a thick brogue. "By God, Colum Pheety Ryan, you're still the biggest, ugliest lummox in the Western Hemisphere!"

The big man's face broke into a broad, toothless grin. "Mr. Quinn-cannon! By all the martyred saints!"

Quinncannon stepped up beside me and put a hand on my shoulder. "Any bones broken?" he asked in an aside.

"Damn it," I said. "Is there anybody in this town you don't know?"

He patted my shoulder. "You can put your fists down too, little bantam."

I lowered my hands a bit foolishly.

Colum Pheety was pumping Quinncannon's hand between huge paws. "Boys, this is Mr. Quinncannon who gave the orders when we put out the great fire. As brave and fine a gentleman as I've ever served under! By God, this calls for a round of drinks. Eamon, set them up!"

The barkeep was shaking his head. "I've told you, Colum, no more drinks on the cuff!"

Colum took a gentle hold on the publican's shirtfront. "This ain't on the cuff, Eamon," he explained quietly. "This is on the house."

When the crowd had flowed back to the bar, I spotted Michael sulking beside the door. I walked toward him slowly, smiling, keeping my hands clenched but at my sides. He watched me defiantly, putting up his own fists, but as I got nearer he began to back away, moving ever faster to maintain a safe distance from me until he hooked his heel on the edge of the sidewalk and toppled backward into the horse trough.


In Quinncannon's hansom we trotted down Pearl Street and turned south into Broadway. "How did you happen to find me?" I asked.

"Were your whereabouts supposed to be a secret? You blazed quite a trail across this island last night. By the way, how is Rose?"

"When I left her? Drunk and hiccupping."

He nodded. "Always had a weakness for champagne."

"How did you happen to go looking for me?"

"Beach came to see me about midnight. He's worried about you."

"He's worried about his damn newspaper. I'm twenty years old, you know, Lon. I'm a big boy now. I can take care of myself."

"Keep your back to the back of a friend, Davy," he answered. "A man is never too old for that."

I sat for a while in silence, listening to the sounds of the street and the gentle clopping of the horse's hooves on the pavement. At last I brought it out. "Look, Lon, I want you to know I saw Bennett leaving your place last night."

"I know," he said. "The housekeeper spied you in the street when she let him out. I didn't get home until later."

"Then you didn't meet with him!" How stupid I had been! "Lon, I'm sorry. I thought you had bribed Bennett to accuse the women in the house of the murder."

"Davy, Davy," he said slowly. "Last night you leaped to one conclusion, and this morning you leap to the opposite conclusion." He looked at me steadily. "What, if anything, is between James Gordon Bennett and myself is, for the moment, none of your business. While you maintain loyalties to the *Sun* that's the way it has to be. If you accept that, we can lay the matter to rest."

I met his gaze. "I can accept that," I said.

"Good." He rapped on the roof of the cab with his cane and we stopped before his lodgings. He jumped down. "Well," he said, "come on."

"Oh no! I'm going home and get some sleep."

"The hell you are," he said. "We've got a full day, my friend. This morning we visit the murder room."

"And this afternoon?"

"This afternoon we have an appointment with a gentleman named Richard P. Robinson."

## 23 The Murder Room

We changed into clean linen in Quinncannon's rooms, divided a pot of his housekeeper's coffee and some sweet rolls, and were again in a cab headed for 41 Thomas Street. The watchman, McCraw, was on duty and led us up the narrow stairs to the second floor, where he unlocked the door to Helen Jewett's room.

"It's just as we found it the night of the murder, Mr. Quinncannon, except that the corpse has been removed and her trunks and papers are down at the Police Office."

The murder room was the right-hand one of two at the rear of the house, occupying the southwest corner. The left-hand room had belonged to the girl calling herself Maria Stevens, "Sweet William" Prall's acquaintance from the Park Theater. The doors of these two rooms were immediately adjacent. One entered the murder room at its east end, pushing the door in and around to the right until it stood flush against the wall.

The bed was just to the right of the door, standing against the same wall with its foot closest to the door. It was an elegant, high, four-poster double bed of French design with a canopy, but without curtains. The door was slightly over three feet wide, and the bed measured about four by six. I estimated the room to be fourteen feet long and approximately ten feet across.

Directly opposite the door a curtain hung by rings from a curved rod.

This had served as a wardrobe. Beside it, a window overlooked the rear yard. A second window beside the head of the bed opened onto the roof of the piazza below, which I had first noticed on Sunday. Beneath this window was a small, square night table, on which stood a brass candlestick about a foot tall.

The chimney stood at the southwest corner of the house with the hearth in the rear wall directly opposite the bed. Between the mantel and the rear window was a chest of drawers, and a small, cluttered writing desk sat before the window so that Helen might enjoy the view of the yard while conducting her correspondence. A dressing table and mirror were on the left wall. A little cushioned rocker of Colonial design was drawn near the fireplace. An oil lamp was placed on the writing table, and a basin and a pitcher on the dressing table. The walls were decorated with theatrical posters and a copy of a portrait of Lord Byron. There was considerable smoke damage.

"This is interesting," Quinncannon said, gazing at the hearth. "Take a look and tell me what you see."

"Very little. The remains of a fairly large fire which burned itself out after they ran out of wood."

"Notice the splinters and small chips such as would be struck off by a hatchet trimming firewood."

"That's not surprising," I said. "Robinson killed her with the hatchet and then carried it off."

"That," said the Irishman, "is the prevailing theory."

He examined the bed closely. It had been fired by holding a flame, presumably the candle, since it was found standing beneath the bed, to the underside of the mattress, which was seventeen or eighteen inches above the floor. Most of the mattress and bedclothes had been reduced to ash except for that directly beneath the victim, which had burned poorly because it was saturated with her blood. Blood had also spurted from the fatal wound and splattered in tiny droplets on the floor beside the bed. The fire had been confined to the bed, however, and had smoldered without flame, smothered by the smoke. This was due in large part to the closeness of the room, and it had been proven in evidence at the inquest that when the fire was first discovered the door and both windows had been shut.

Quinncannon took the brass candleholder from the night table and inspected it and the stub of candle which remained in it. He lit the candle and stretched out full on his back on the floor, edging under the bed and examining the underside of the mattress. At last he stood, extinguished the candle, and replaced the holder on the table.

"After the girl was murdered," he said, "this candle was lit and held under the bed until the mattress began to burn. What do you make of that, Davy?"

"It seems rather obvious."

"Nevertheless."

I shrugged. "The killer tried to cover his crime by setting fire to the house. Isn't that the police theory?"

"It is," he answered, watching me closely.

"Which, I suppose, means that it's wrong. Now wait a minute, Lon Let me think. If the bed wasn't fired to burn down the house, then it must have been fired *not* to burn down the house." I had spoken sarcastically, but it occurred to me suddenly that this made perfectly good sense. "Of course! Because if he'd wanted to burn the house, he had *two lamps full of oil* right here to do it with."

He smiled slightly and kept his eyes on mine. "Go on," he said.

"Then the purpose wasn't to cover the murder at all, Lon, but to call attention to it. The candle was used instead of an oil lamp because it would set the mattress smoldering and give the killer time to get away before the smoke roused any of the inmates."

"Think, Davy. If the killer wanted time to get away, why set the fire at all?"

"Then the fire was set by someone other than the killer?"

"For what purpose?"

I tried to imagine. "To cover another crime?"

"What other crime?"

"Theft perhaps. Isn't it said that she owned much more jewelry than was found here after the murder?"

"And yet," he said, "a few valuable pieces *were* found here after her death. Why would a thief leave them behind?"

"Maybe the intent was to disfigure the corpse?" I ventured. "That would make sense, especially if the killer was a jealous rival, as Bennett keeps braying."

"Possibly, though if that was the motive, a much more efficient means of mutilation was at hand."

"Meaning the hatchet?"

He nodded grimly.

I threw up my hands. "I give up, Lon. I've run out of guesses."

"You're not guessing, Davy," he said quietly. "You're thinking, my friend. You're reasoning." He put his hand on my shoulder. "Now I want you to test one of your theories about this case."

I eyed him warily. "Absolutely no more fences."

"Didn't you tell me that the killer could have escaped through the window by dropping from the piazza roof into the alley?"

"Yes," I groaned.

"Try it," he suggested.

I climbed through the window, leaving him standing in the doorway squinting thoughtfully at the bed. The roof of the piazza sloped slightly, but I found it a simple matter to gain my feet and inch down to where the roof abutted the adjoining house. I walked toward Thomas Street until I reached the edge. The roof was between eight and nine feet above the alley. I swung off and lowered myself slowly until I was hanging by my hands—then let go and dropped easily to the ground. It was not much more difficult than jumping off a chair.

I enjoyed the look on McCraw's face when I presented myself for readmission to the house. Quinncannon's face was another matter. He was frowning gloomily, and alternately dragging and gnawing on the stem of his pipe.

"At the inquest," he said, "Rosina testified that when she brought the wine up that night she stood in the doorway and did not enter the room. Still she claims to have been able to see the man who was lying in bed well enough to identify him positively as Robinson. I'm saddened to report that she might be telling the truth. If there was a man in bed, she could have seen him clearly. The room was darker, but there was a candle right beside his face. Either she's lying or . . ."

"Or Robinson is."

"Yes, damn it!"

"Then it really doesn't matter whether Rosina recognized Robinson when she first let him in," I said.

"You're wrong, Davy. If anything, the question of her identification of him as arriving at nine-thirty is even more crucial now."

"I don't see why. If she can place him in this room at eleven, what difference does it make if she can place him in the entry at nine-thirty? Helen wasn't killed until *after* eleven."

"Rosina let somebody in at nine-thirty, somebody who asked for Helen and came to this room. If it wasn't Robinson, who was it?"

"And if Robinson didn't come until eleven, how did he get in?"

"And how did the first visitor get out?" said Quinncannon. *"If* he left at all."

"But Helen called the first man 'Frank.' Could there be *two* 'Frank Riverses'?"

"At least two. James Teer, Robinson's roommate, also used that alias, and Teer admits to having been in this house on the night the girl was killed."

"With Helen?"

"No," he said. "Not with any of the women, as a matter of fact. He claims to have stayed in the entry and to have left before ten, and he has witnesses to that effect; still it's interesting, isn't it?"

I dropped into the rocker. "Good God. Two identical lamps. Two men using the name Frank Rivers. Two visitors to the victim on the night she was murdered. It's strange, Lon."

"What is?"

"That this should be a double house. It's as if there were only one house and some god or demon were holding up a mirror to it. Every clue, every suspect has its double. The oil lamp found burning downstairs, for example, has an identical twin in Maria Stevens' room, and that room is the mirror image of this one."

"Except," he said, "that there's no piazza and no alley on the other side. From the fact that you walked back in here through the door, I gather that a man could escape over the roof."

I nodded, absently, because the mention of the lamps had raised another question. "Rosina found it lit. Why, Lon? Why would he leave it lit?"

Quinncannon said, "Go on."

"Well, I mean, the point of taking the lamp is to light himself through the dark house. Once he reached the rear door he'd turn the lamp off, wouldn't he? That door can be seen from the upper floors of several other houses. If I'd just committed a murder, I doubt I'd stand at the back door waving a lamp around."

"It's interesting that the lamp and the fire should serve the same purpose," he observed. "Intentionally or not, both attracted attention *to* the murder."

"To what end?"

Quinncannon lit his pipe. "I think we've found everything here we're going to find. I suggest we investigate a couple of broiled lobsters at Delmonico's."

# 24  The Prisoner

As Robinson had not yet been indicted, he continued to be confined in the Death House until the grand jury could be convened. After his indictment, against which no sane man in New York would have wagered a nickel, he would be transferred to Bellevue to await trial. Meanwhile, he remained behind the splendid façade of the new building under the sleepless eyes of the Argo of the place, the mammoth Pappy Lowends.

The Dead House had been erected literally around the old debtor's prison so that, brilliantly as its marble shell shown on the law-abiding strollers on Chambers Street, its interior was as grimly foreboding as in the days when hollow-eyed bankrupts and bearded pirates haunted its dank, narrow cells.

We were ushered to a small room deep in the bowels of the building where the only light blinked down from a tiny window which, although set at ground level, was several feet higher than our heads. This dungeon contained only a rough oak table and three chairs, all of which had one leg shorter than the others and creaked eerily against the flagstone floor at the slightest touch.

After several minutes the heavy door swung back on its iron hinges and a slender young man was thrust inside. The door immediately clanged shut and we could hear the massive bar being set in place and the ancient key turning in the rusted lock. I felt what must be the sensation of being entombed alive.

Quinncannon lit a candle which stood on the table. By its glow I could make out the soft, boyish features of the prisoner, framed in delicate ringlets of light-brown hair, with unshaven down on his cheeks and eyes opened wide in seeming innocence, yet gleaming in the semi-darkness like a cat's.

"Come, gentlemen! No rack? No boot? Surely there must be thumb-screws at least!"

His lips pursed into a mock pout and then drew back into a dimpled smile. He threw one leg over a chair and sat down, resting his folded arms on its back and his chin on his arms.

"May I smoke, sir?" He took out a seegar. "The ladies, bless them, keep me well supplied."

He lit the seegar with the candle and cradled his chin again on his arms. "Good afternoon, Mr. Cordor, sir. May I say you appear to have become my evil angel? I find you present at all my moments of greatest shame, sir." He touched his nose with his finger as if it were still tender and smiled.

"You, sir, must be Mr. Quinncannon. It is an honor, sir. My other attorneys have told me you were coming, sir, and that I must be completely honest with you, and so I shall be. Though I beg you to understand that I know nothing of my poor Helen's murder. How could anyone think I would have caused her death in that horrible manner? I know nothing of the cloak, sir, though they say it is mine. I never owned any cloak but an old camblet one, which I showed Mr. Brink in my room. And the hatchet too, sir—I never took it from Mr. Hoxie's. I swear it! I'm a young man of tremendous prospects, barely nineteen, sir! Why would I cast away my whole future in this horrible fashion? I did not set foot in Thomas Street on that night. Why would I? Helen and I had parted amicably. I had sworn to change my evil habits, sir, to throw off the deceitful mask I had worn before the world. I was—did you know it, sir—I was to have been married. A poor, gentle, honest girl who loved me for myself, whose tender affection would have made a man of me. Oh, I've been such a young fool! It's piteous, piteous. I'm caught in a web of my own spinning, sir, but how good it is for a helpless boy to have friends like you and Mr. Hoxie and Mr. Hoffman and . . ."

Robinson buried his face in his arms. I heard what I thought was a sob.

Quinncannon took out his pipe and lit it slowly. His chair scraped along the stone floor as he pushed it back and rose. He came around the table and stood beside Robinson.

"If, by some miracle, you escape the rope, Mr. Robinson, I suggest you become an actor and tour the country as George Barnwell in *The London Merchant.*"

The Irishman went to the door and rapped loudly with the head of his cane. Robinson remained motionless save for his shoulders, which heaved up and down as though he were weeping. The bar outside was withdrawn and the key turned in the lock. I got to my feet. The door screeched open.

Then from the prisoner came a low, guttural, moaning sound which I could hardly recognize as human. Without raising his head, Robinson spoke in a harsh, rasping, anguished voice which did not seem his own but, to my imagination, the tormented cry of a possessing demon deep within his soul.

"For the love of God, Quinncannon, *help me!*"

Quinncannon seized the door and slammed it shut. "Do you know, Robinson, what it is to be hanged?" he asked quietly. "The brain, the power of thought, dies at once, but the sensations linger through agonized seconds of eternity. The head feels at first merely congested, and then bloated; and keen, exquisite pulsations of pain scream from the temples through the body into the extremities. It is like being burned alive. The brain seems about to ooze out of the ears and nostrils. The entire muscular system lapses into mechanical spasms, uncontrolled and hideous."

"I am innocent of the murder," Robinson groaned. "I have told you the truth."

"You have told me lies. It was *your* cloak they found, Robinson. *You* were with Helen Jewett at eleven that night in her room."

Gradually the youth raised his head from his arms. Real tears rolled down his pale cheeks. He gaped at Quinncannon.

"Now, Richard, you are going to tell me the truth. You're going to tell me about Emma Chancellor and William Gray. You're going to tell me about Robert Douglass and Elizabeth Stewart."

"My God," Robinson gasped. "You know everything!"

Quinncannon sat down opposite him. He put his elbow on the table and held his hand out, palm up. "I want you to understand, Richard, that at this moment your life depends entirely on me. In a manner of speaking, I hold it here in my hand. If you tell me a lie, one single lie, I will know it, and . . ."

He slowly spread his fingers.

"Do you understand?"

The boy lowered his head. Barely audible, he answered, "Yes."

"Look me in the eye like a man, damn you!"

Robinson looked up. For a few seconds he met Quinncannon's gaze steadily. Then he drew in a deep breath and managed a smile. "Yes, sir!" he said firmly.

There were many questions to which I wanted answers at once, but Quinncannon led Robinson back almost three years to his arrival in New York from Connecticut. Through a cousin, B. F. Robinson, the boy's father had obtained a clerking position for him with a dry-goods firm on William Street. The cousin was supposed to keep watch over Richard, but he proved a poor guardian.

"I was scarcely more than sixteen years old, Mr. Quinncannon. I was ardent, tender, and rather handsome—well dressed, with money at my command. I suppose I attracted a bit of attention."

"From Emma Chancellor?"

"Among others, yes, sir. She was then eighteen and I thought her the most beautiful girl I had ever seen. She was poor, vain, and selfish, and she fancied me a gentleman's son of high expectations and hoped to entangle me in a secret marriage. Long before we were actually introduced I began to notice that we often passed each other casually in the street or chanced to be in the same shop, by accident I thought then. At last we began to meet every evening. I escorted her to the theater and the public gardens, and lavished gifts of trinkets and money on her. At my expense she enrolled us both in a dancing school in Tammany Hall, where we regularly attended the winter balls. She became increasingly flirtatious and coquettish on these occasions, and I would react with uncontrollable jealousy. There were violent quarrels, always ending the same way, with me crawling back to her on my knees and tremblingly presenting an expensive peace offering."

Quinncannon coughed. "You're not on the witness stand, Richard. Spare us the theatrics. I'm having a difficult time visualizing you as the seduced innocent even at sixteen. Get on with it. The girl became pregnant."

Robinson looked as though he would deny it. Then he said meekly, "Yes, sir."

"And you matriculated her for a semester at Madam Restell's finishing school for young ladies."

Madam Restell's mansion on Greenwich Street was the most infamous abortion hospital in the city. The penny press called it "The House Built on Baby Skulls."

"Yes, sir," Robinson said. "You must understand, sir, this is not easy for me."

"I'm aware of that. Suppose I continue the story for a while and you nod or grunt or something. Emma Chancellor had been living with her family until she became pregnant, but afterward you boarded her in a private house kept by a woman named Elizabeth Stewart—the sort of house where only young ladies with special male friends to support them are received. What was the board there?"

Robinson sighed. "Ten dollars a week, exclusive of her other expenses, which were extravagant."

"In order to meet these expenses you began to defraud your employers."

"I had to! She threatened to instigate her family to prosecute me for her seduction. Then she said she would betray me to my employers. I didn't dare to refuse her demands."

"Who was Robert Douglass?"

Robinson hung his head. "I was Robert Douglass."

"That was the *nom de guerre* you were using at the time?"

"Yes, sir. Emma also took the name Douglass, so her connections couldn't find her."

Quinncannon leaned back in his chair and dragged on his pipe. "All right. Now, there was another girl living at Mrs. Stewart's, a girl whose rent was being paid by a wealthy Kentucky businessman to assure her availability during his trips to New York. Between those visits time hung heavily on her hands and she began making advances to you, advances which were not altogether unwelcome. What was her name, Richard?"

"Helen Jewett."

"Helen Jewett," the Irishman echoed. "Shortly after you met Helen, your problems with Emma were resolved, weren't they?"

"Yes, sir. Emma's people learned somehow where she was and sent her to relatives in South Carolina. They refused to prosecute me, and I was able to leave my employer without being suspected of theft. I applied to my cousin, who arranged a position for me with Mr. Hoxie, with whom he was then a partner."

Quinncannon lifted one eyebrow. "You have no idea how Emma's family discovered her whereabouts?"

"No, sir, except that I thought it a wonderful piece of luck for me at the time."

"Who is William Gray?"

"Gray . . . he and I shared a room for a time before his marriage. He was an agent for me in certain pecuniary transactions."

"That's an interesting way to put it," Quinncannon said. "As a matter of fact, Gray was your accomplice in a scheme to systematically defraud your second employer, Joseph Hoxie, was he not?"

There was no response.

"Answer the question," the Irishman said evenly.

"Yes, damn it!" Robinson shouted. "Do you want to hear me say it? All right! Yes! Yes! It's nothing I'm proud of. I had no choice. Helen was making demands on me, don't you see? I had to have money or I would have lost her!"

"Were you in love with Helen Jewett?"

"Yes!" The youth stood and began to pace the narrow cell. At last he stopped, his palms behind his back, pressing against the wall. "I thought I was," he said slowly. "What did I know about love? I was seventeen. I wanted her. I was afraid of her. She had the power to ruin my reputation and she held it over me. Mr. Quinncannon, Helen was a truly remarkable woman. She had a powerful mind and a noble, generous spirit. She detested the . . . the mode of life into which she had been seduced. She was so much finer than the other girls. She had educated herself. You've seen her room. She had volumes of Shakespeare, Byron, Scott. She taught me . . . many things."

"How did you meet Sophia Willett?"

Robinson reddened. "I want her kept out of this! I told Hoffman that. I don't want her name dragged into this, Quinncannon. I'm warning you!"

"Sit down," Quinncannon commanded. "You're in no position to issue warnings, Richard. You became acquainted with Miss Willett at the dancing balls last winter. Her family is an old and reputable one of moderate fortune, roughly the social equal of your own. You paid court to her. Naturally neither the girl nor her relatives knew anything of the nefarious side of your character. The Willetts encouraged the relationship. In February you told Helen you were engaged. How did she receive the news of your impending marriage?"

"She agreed to let me go."

"That's a stupid lie," Quinncannon said quietly. "I've read the letters which passed between you, and so have the police."

Again the prisoner was on his feet and pacing. "If you've read the correspondence, sir, you know how fond Helen was of quarreling by mail. The man who she claimed had originally seduced her, for example, is now married in New England with a family. She frequently wrote him threatening letters, vowing vengeance against him. She wrote, I believe, to almost all her suitors in a similar vein. From the outset of our acquaintance I received letters from her accusing me of infidelity and endeavoring to intimidate me into submission by threatening to expose my thefts. At first I was cowed and groveled before her, but gradually I became better acquainted with her disposition and acquired the courage to brave her anger. Her temper was capricious, veering from one extreme of passion to another. I found that my best defense against her moods was her own style of defiance."

"Suppose we return to my question, Richard. How did Helen react to your engagement to Sophia Willett?"

"She suspected that something was wrong from the first, sir. For Sophia's sake I sought to—I suppose the term is 'reform myself.' I broke off with Gray, using his marriage as an excuse, and ceased my defrauding of Mr. Hoxie. Helen was then living with Mrs. Berry in Theater Alley and I attempted to cut off our intercourse by pleading that my visits to her house were suspected at the store. She changed her residence to Mrs Townsend's, but I objected to the house as too public. Finally she accused me of desertion, and I did not deny the charge. I demanded she return my letters to her and my miniature, which had been painted for Emma. How Helen got it I have no idea, but she refused me and several letters passed between us. She threatened me and I retaliated. Two weeks to the night before her death we met at the theater and struck a truce. I told her about my love for Sophia and begged her to release me and give me my chance to extricate myself from my crimes. She was in a generous humor, and she agreed. She even wept for my happiness."

"But she changed her mind again," Quinncannon prompted.

"Yes, sir. She was like quicksilver in her moods. She sent letters stating that if I tried to marry she would expose me to the Willetts. This, however, I knew she would not dare, because it would destroy the hold she had over me. I would lose Sophia, but Helen would lose me and she knew it."

"Was she in love with you?"

"I believe she was, sir, in some manner peculiar to herself. But I was no longer in love with her. My deep affection for Sophia had taught me that I had never felt anything for Helen but a sort of passion, a shallow infatuation. When I understood that, Helen's only real power over me vanished, and I think she realized it. On April 4, the Monday before she was killed, she sent for me and we exchanged forgivenesses. She was very tender and confirmed me in my resolution of changing my life. At the end of the evening I promised to come again on April 6 and bring the hatchet with me."

At the word "hatchet" I leaned forward in my chair. Quinncannon leaned back in his. I could see the yellow glow of his pipe.

"Helen asked me," Robinson said, "for a little hatchet she could use to break her wood small and make the fire burn quick. If she sent a servant to buy one, she said, the other girls would borrow it and she should be plagued to keep it, but if I brought it the others would not know she had one. On Wednesday I bought one and took it to her."

"You didn't bring the hatchet from Hoxie's store?" Quinncannon asked.

"No, sir! I swear it."

Quinncannon's mouth tightened at the corner. "Go on," he said.

"When Mrs. Townsend admitted me on Wednesday, I was carrying the hatchet under my cloak so the girls would not see it. I was disguised, but I heard Eliza Salters say that she knew I was Frank Rivers by my air and step. Helen again was in a gentle humor and promised that if I called on Saturday night at eleven she would return the miniature and all my letters."

"When you brought the hatchet," Quinncannon asked, "did you attach it to the tassel of your cloak?"

The youth shook his head. "There would be no need, sir. It was a simple matter to conceal it in the folds of the cloak."

"Very well," the Irishman said. "Now, Richard, I want you to proceed methodically, step by step, through your actions on Saturday night."

Robinson resumed his seat and sucked in a deep breath. "I thought that night would be the beginning of a new life for me." He looked about the cell grimly. "I suppose in a sense I was right. That afternoon I took tea with some of the other boarders in my rooming house and we formed plans to ride horseback the following morning. After tea I put on the cloth cloak and left with another young man."

"Let's stay with that cloak for a minute," Quinncannon interrupted. "Why did you lie about it to the police?"

The prisoner grinned. "It was not exactly a lie. Mr. Brink asked me if

I owned such a cloak and I said I did not."

The Irishman frowned. "It wasn't very clever. By whom was the cloak technically owned?"

"By William Gray. He left it with me as security for some money he owed me."

"Go on," Quinncannon said, but there was a hint of skepticism in his voice.

"I parted from my companion and walked on alone toward Clinton Hall, but not wishing to be recognized in the cloak, which I used only for masquerading, I went into an oyster cellar near the Park. I ate and remained there until the clock struck nine. Helen had informed me by note that she expected a rich new admirer shortly after nine who was to take my fictitious name. I confess to curiosity as to his appearance and whether I knew him. I went on foot to Thomas Street, arriving about nine-fifteen. While I watched the house a man, closely muffled, knocked and entered, but I could tell nothing about him except that he wore a dark cloak similar to mine.

"My understanding with Helen was that she would let her first visitor out at eleven with her key, and that I was to enter at that time. Near the hour I passed through the hall of a house on Chapel Street from which I could see the light in Helen's window and discern the shadows on the wall through the curtains. There were two persons moving about—Helen was one, and the other was apparently her visitor, preparing to leave. I sprinted out and around the block and gained Mrs. Townsend's porch just as the door opened. Helen's figure concealed me from observation and I glided behind her and lightly passed in unseen. When we reached her room Helen laughed at my harlequin-like agility, saying, 'Frank, you would do to steal an heiress.'"

"You saw the face of Helen's visitor as he passed you?" Quinncannon asked.

"No, sir. He kept it hidden and it was dark. Helen did say something strange to him. She thanked him for bringing her her boot."

"Her boot?" My friend thought that over. "All right, Richard. You're in her room."

"Yes, sir. We then spoke of the cause of my visit. She gave me the miniature and I returned her letters to me, but she refused me mine, saying that I must come for them again. When I objected to this her face became clouded. To soothe her and prevent high words, I asked her to get a bottle of champagne, took up a book that lay on the toilet table, and tried to conceal my face by lying on the bed with my back to the door.

"Helen returned without the wine, which Mrs. Townsend brought up, impelled by curiosity to see who Helen had there. But Helen took the wine from her before she could enter the room and abruptly shut the door."

Quinncannon stirred. "Do you mean Helen did not ask Rosina to step in for a drink?"

"Certainly not."

A wave of the Irishman's hand bade Robinson continue.

"Helen and I drank a glass of wine between us—then sat down by the fire, which was nearly out. I wrapped my cloak around her. We sat conversing in whispers till after twelve, when Helen lit a candle and held it at the top of the stairs to light me down. At Mrs. Townsend's door I knocked and demanded my liberty but received a refusal. I then slipped through the parlor into the yard, climbed over three fences, and passed through the hall, which I knew to be open into Chapel Street. The Clinton Hall clock struck one just as I entered my boardinghouse."

"You did not go into the Hudson Street yard?"

"No, sir, I scaled the fence on the eastern side. It's high, but the fences beyond are much lower."

"And you are a young man," the Irishman said with an eye on me, "nimble and reasonably athletic. Was the eastern fence whitewashed?"

The boy shook his head. "My clothes were stained but that was from the paint at the store. I explained that to Mr. Brink."

"Did you take the cloak with you?"

"*No*, sir!" Robinson answered emphatically. "Helen's fire had gone out and there was no more wood. I left the cloak to warm her during the night."

"All right," Quinncannon said. "You have remarked to Mr. Hoffman that you saw what Helen's 'game' was."

"Yes, sir. What I meant was that I realized she had never intended to return all my things at once. Each letter I had written her could be used to induce a separate visit from me. But I was resolved to play the game for as long as was necessary to retrieve those papers by which she might substantiate charges against me. I was resolved, too, to go to my kind employer and throw myself on his mercy, pledging to return every cent I had cheated him of if it took the rest of my life."

It would hardly have taken that long, I thought, if he used the Willetts' money.

"Never in my life," Robinson continued, "have I been so filled with good resolutions or with hope. I could see the way out of my troubles for the first time in three years. My God, sir, do you think if I had murdered Helen I would have stolen the miniature and left the incriminating letters behind?"

"That is a point in your favor," Quinncannon said. "There are still a few questions that need clearing up, Richard."

"Ask me anything, sir," the youth replied. "I have told you the worst. Of the rest I am innocent."

"Why didn't Helen let you out of the house, since she had a key and you both knew Rosina habitually retired at midnight?"

"The truth, sir, is that Helen and I parted on a bitter note. I asked when I might return for my letters and she refused to name a time. That is all."

"When the police woke you on Sunday morning, what were your thoughts?"

"The worst idea that occurred to me was that my theft had been discovered by Mr. Hoxie and that Helen had betrayed me to the punishment of the civil law. Terrified as I was by actual guilt, I became passive and obeyed all orders silently until I heard the charges brought against me. Then I received hope from the calm knowledge of my innocence."

"You were pleased to be charged with murder?" I asked in astonishment.

"I was relieved not to be charged with crimes of which I was guilty, Mr. Cordor," he answered.

"You have accounted for your time on the night of the murder," Quinncannon said, "with the exception of the hours between nine-thirty and eleven. Where were you then?"

For an instant Robinson appeared shaken, but he recovered quickly. "I walked about a good deal, I believe. I really don't recall precisely where, sir."

"Just walked around?"

"Yes, sir."

"No particular place."

"No, sir."

The sun had apparently set, for there was no more light from the narrow little window. The candle flickered valiantly on the rickety wooden table between them, casting huge spectral shadows up against the high stone walls of the dungeon. I could hear the prisoner breathing heavily.

"On the eighth of April, the day before the murder," Quinncannon said, "a young woman checked into the Clinton Hotel in this city, signing herself Miss Carrie Norris of South Carolina. She was accompanied by a young man who identified himself as her cousin, Mr. John C. Riker, of the same state. They occupied adjoining rooms. The following morning Mr. Riker checked out, but Miss Norris remained lodged at the Clinton for several days."

Robinson had covered his face with his hands. His elbows rested on the table. He began to run his hands through his hair. I noticed that his hair seemed to come out of his head in tufts.

"I am going to ask you just four questions, Richard," Quinncannon said. "And if you lie to me you are a dead man! Who was John C. Riker?"

"I was," the youth murmured.

"Who," said Quinncannon, "was Miss Carrie Norris?"

"Carrie Norris was . . . was Emma Chancellor."

"Where were you on April 9 between nine-thirty and eleven?"

"I was at the Clinton Hotel with Emma Chancellor."

"All right," Quinncannon snapped. "Think carefully before you answer this. Has Emma Chancellor been murdered?"

"No! No!" the prisoner cried. "She can't be dead! My God, my God, *she* can't be dead!"

# 25  Four Ladies

## The Fawn

"Thank the Lord you've come, sir. I had no notion of what to do with her."

"With whom?"

"With the lady, sir."

Quinncannon's housekeeper stood in the doorway wringing her reddened hands and peering anxiously at me.

"It would have been different if she'd come in the evening, sir. I know what to do with them when they come in the evening. But when they come at the crack of dawn, sir, I don't know what to do with them. Lord bless me, sir, I don't even know what *he* does with them."

I stepped inside and removed my gloves. "I gather Mr. Quinncannon is not here."

"Gone before sunrise again, sir," she said. "Gone without breakfast again. And after being up half the night with those gentlemen."

"Gentlemen?"

"Yes, sir. Two of them. One is tall and dresses like a dandy. The sort of fellow that loiters about in front of the tobacco shops." She sucked in her stomach, protruded her behind, puffed out her cheeks, drew up to her full height, and pranced about the hall on her toes, dabbing at the corner of her mouth with her handkerchief.

I laughed out loud. "Whitlaw Price!" I cried. "He would not appreciate the impersonation, but his friends would recognize him at once."

"The other," the housekeeper said, "is a stout, bearded man with a booming voice and a great red nose. He smells of Scotch whiskey, sir, and he has one habit that endears him to me whenever he comes."

"By all means," I said, "let's have a demonstration." I had already deduced that this must be Ogden Hoffman.

She threw back her shoulders, stuck out her stomach, cleared her throat loudly, and strutted before me, the personification of the former district attorney. She slipped behind me suddenly and I felt a sharp pinch—

" 'I want to do that every time I see you . . .' "

I spun around and dropped my hands defensively.

". . . Mr. Hoffman always says to me," she finished.

"Uh, yes, ma'am." My cheeks were burning. "A little dignity is required, ma'am. We were speaking of the most distinguished lawyers in New York."

"That Mr. Hoffman is the very devil, sir," she said, moving toward me.

"The lady, ma'am," I said, backing away.

"Lady, sir?"

"Who came to see Mr. Quinncannon," I said. I felt like an utter fool. Then, abruptly, I wondered why.

"Is she still in the house?" I asked, moving toward the housekeeper.

"I put her in Mr. Quinncannon's rooms," she replied, backing away.

"Give me half an hour to get rid of her," I said. "Then come upstairs and bring a ballpeen hammer and a loaf of pumpernickel bread!" I lunged for her.

She threw her apron over her head and fled screaming to the kitchen.

I climbed the stairs slowly, wondering which of Rosina Townsend's girls I would find waiting behind Quinncannon's door. That it would be one of them I knew, for the Irishman had told me on the preceding evening, as we walked from the Dead House, of his arrangement with the authorities to interview three of the women from the murder house.

Quinncannon's door was unlocked. The young lady who rose from a wingback chair as I entered was fashionably dressed and delicately pretty, with rich, reddish-brown hair worn in an upswept style and a milk-white complexion. Her figure was small but perfectly proportioned, and her waist was so tiny that I found myself wondering whether my hands might not fit around it snugly enough for my fingers to touch. She could not have been over seventeen. It seemed a pity that she should already have fallen into the clutches of Rosina and the sisterhood.

"You must think this dreadfully forward of me," she said, "to have come alone to a single gentleman's lodgings."

"Not at all," I replied. "You were expected, you know."

"I?" She seemed quite staggered.

"Yes, of course. It was all quite carefully arranged."

"Then you know who I am?"

"Let us say that I know the place from which you came."

"But," she said, "this is most remarkable! I have heard, naturally, of your brilliant reputation, but to have known that I would come here when I myself did not decide to do so until an hour ago! Perhaps you also know the reason for my visit?"

"I believe I do. Please be seated."

She perched gracefully on the edge of the wingback. I took a seat in the opposite chair and folded my legs. "You have come," I said, "to speak of the unfortunate murder and the young man who is accused of it."

She clapped her hands. "This is nothing less than a miracle! I believe, sir, that you can read my mind." For an instant the cloud of concern passed from her face and she laughed brightly. Her laugh was clear and her green eyes crinkled slightly at the corners.

"You are, you know, much younger and more handsome than I imagined you."

"Oh?" I said.

"Oh, yes," she avowed. "I expected you to be quite old, I'm afraid—thirty-five at least. With a bushy moustache and a smelly old pipe."

About to remove my pipe for a smoke, I thrust it back into my coat pocket.

"Whereas," she continued, "you can't be older than twenty-six."

I smiled on her paternally.

"And you have," she concluded, "such a kind face that you have laid to rest all my foolish anxieties in coming here. I know I shall be able to open my heart to you, sir."

I leaned forward, taking her tiny hand in mine and squeezing it gently. "You must," I said, "place all your faith and trust in me. I am your devoted servant, dear lady."

She withdrew her hand, smiling. "I do believe, sir, you are flirting with me."

"I?" Nothing could have been further from my mind. "Look here," I said impulsively, "you really must not remain another night in that horrible house under the influence of that dreadful woman."

"Oh," she replied lightly, "it is not so horrible or so dreadful as you may imagine. Though I was unhappy there at first, I have quite grown accustomed to it now. As for my being under her influence, I rather think the opposite is true. She's really an old dear, you know."

I had heard many descriptions of Rosina Townsend, but never as an "old dear." "But surely you have a father," I persisted, "who would forgive you and offer you the protection of his home if he knew where you were."

She smiled sadly. "I'm afraid he may never forgive me. I seem to have permanently disgraced the family name. And of course he knows where I am. It was he who forced me to go there."

"Your *father* placed you in that house?" I was thunderstruck.

"Why, yes, naturally."

"Forgive me," I said fervently, "but there appears to me nothing natural about it. On the contrary, I cannot imagine a more unnatural action or a more unnatural father."

She reddened. "Really! My father and I have had our differences, but I will not permit you to speak so of him in my presence. He has done only what he thought was best for me."

"Best for you?" I cried. "To drive you from his own roof and compel you to reside with a woman like Rosina Townsend?"

She stood abruptly and frowned down on me in regal high temper. "You think me one of those—*those* women? I find I must revise my first impression of you, sir. You are a fool, and I was a greater fool for coming here. My name, sir, is Sophia Willett."

"You're Robinson's sweetheart?"

"Hardly, sir," she answered haughtily, "though Richard may have so deceived himself. When he was arrested my father thought it wise to send me to stay at the house of my maiden aunt in Greenwich Village until after the trial. I came here this morning over my aunt's protests to offer whatever help I could to you in your efforts on Richard's behalf. It may seem strange to you, sir, but I *do* retain a shred of pity for him in a corner of my heart."

"It does you great credit, Miss Willett," I murmured, completely crestfallen.

"Please don't flatter me," the lady snapped. "I can only pray that Richard's other attorneys are more astute than you have proven to be, Mr. Quinncannon."

I stared up at her and the ludicrousness of the comic scene we had just played burst full upon me. I'm sorry to say I broke into laughter. This did nothing to improve Miss Willett's humor.

"I apologize humbly and profoundly," I said, wiping my eyes. "I am not Mr. Quinncannon. My name is David Cordor."

"But," she said, "these are Mr. Quinncannon's rooms, are they not? Then naturally I assumed . . ."

"Ah, but you see, dear lady, I came here this morning to interview three women from Rosina's house, and finding you here, naturally *I* assumed . . ." I began again to laugh.

She glared at me. Then gradually the corners of her eyes started to crinkle and her lips unpursed and drew up. She smiled. She laughed.

"My poor Mr. Cordor, I'm afraid I have abused you unjustly."

"Not at all, Miss Willett," I protested. "You have served me most fairly. I can offer in my defense only that you are so young and so beautiful that I was horrified at the thought of your having been betrayed into such company as Mrs. Townsend's."

"Now, Mr. Cordor," she said, offering me her hand, "I am positive you are flirting with me."

"Now, Miss Willett," I responded, taking her hand, "perhaps I am."

"If I'm intruding, I can come back in an hour," said a brogue at the door. The damned Celt's sense of timing was, as always, unerring.

*"This* gentleman, Miss Willett, is Mr. Lon Quinncannon. But then you might have recognized him by his advancing years and dark moustache, and by the smelly old pipe between his teeth."

Quinncannon regarded me quizzically.

"Lon, may I present Miss Sophia Willett."

The lady smiled. "How do you do, Mr. Quinncannon?"

His sharp eyes shot quickly, just once, from my face to hers. He did not smile exactly, but his lips relaxed. I wondered what he was thinking.

"Your servant, Miss Willett," he said, taking her hand and motioning her to the wingback I had just vacated. He settled in the chair opposite. "You were, I understand, Mr. Robinson's fiancée."

She shook her head sadly. "That was never true, sir, although I fear Richard thought of me in that way. My father and my aunt rather encouraged him to. They were quite impressed with him."

He was studying her with more intensity than I suspect she was aware of. "And you," he said, "were not quite so impressed."

"Oh, Richard was charming and attentive and very handsome, and he was a young man with prospects." She paused. "He *did* go on about his prospects." She looked up at him. "But he always seemed to me, well, something of a Montraville."

"And you had no intention of playing Charlotte Temple to his Montraville."

She brightened. "You are familiar with the novels of Mrs. Rowson, sir?"

Quinncannon smiled. "I have a preference for Fielding," he said.

"Strange," she said, "but that was the way I always thought of Richard. He's graceful and amusing but not at all the sort of boy a girl would want to— You see, Mr. Quinncannon, Richard really lives in a kind of dream in which he is always the hero. He imagines himself"–

she fought for the phrase—"in *control,* but he never is. Circumstances, people—*everything* manipulates him."

She leaned forward, her eyes on his, her words coming faster and yet faster. "Richard overestimates himself in every way—his cleverness, his charm, his intelligence, his prospects. He wanted me to see him as he saw himself, but I couldn't, Mr. Quinncannon, I just couldn't. And he didn't mind that at all. He simply *pretended* that I did." She threw up her hands in a gesture of frustration. "He's so awfully weak—he's like a little boy. He never acts. He only reacts." Her voice became suddenly softer and even more persuasive. "He *couldn't* have murdered that woman. It isn't just that he's too weak. It isn't even that, in his own way, he's too decent. I know all the evidence is against him, and I know that defending him is your job and you're paid to do it, but I want to say this to you because there's one thing about Richard that only I know, one thing above all that makes me fear for him."

She drew a deep breath. "Mr. Quinncannon. Somewhere, deep in his soul, Richard *wants* people to believe he was capable of that murder."

Quinncannon regarded her for a long minute and a warm smile slowly creased his face. "Miss Willett," he said at last, with rare but genuine admiration, "you are a remarkable young woman."

He was only echoing my own conclusion, but I was pleased to have it confirmed by so reliable a source.

Miss Willett blushed at the compliment and, to my surprise, cast her lovely green eyes up at me briefly. She turned back to the Irishman. "Then you *do* understand, Mr. Quinncannon."

He nodded thoughtfully. "I believe I do, Miss Willett, and I am most appreciative of your visit. You have put your finger on the soul of my client in a manner that I could never have done."

She stood and offered him her hand. "I have such pity for Richard," she said, "but I have great faith in you, sir. I know now that you would not have undertaken his defense if you had not believed him innocent."

He took her hand and smiled. "No, Miss Willett," he responded. "I would have accepted the case regardless of my private opinion. However, if I had any doubts, you have gone far toward removing them."

"Then I am satisfied, sir." She turned to me. "Mr. Cordor."

"Miss Willett, your obedient servant. May I see you to your carriage?"

"Oh, no, thank you," she replied lightly. "It's waiting just outside. I imagine I can negotiate the stairs."

I accompanied her to the landing and closed the door. "You're his friend," she said. "He *is* a good man?"

"He?"

"Mr. Quinncannon," she answered.

The devil take Quinncannon, I thought. "Yes, he's the best there is." *And,* I thought, old enough to be your—

"I knew it!" she cried. "He so reminds me of my father!"

I smiled at her. Dashing young journalist: 1, I thought. Aging Irishman: 0.

When I re-entered the room I was in excellent spirits, but Quinncannon looked to me, at that moment, a bit older and more tired than usual. I wasn't going to say anything, but I found I couldn't help it. "She is remarkable, isn't she?"

"Yes," he said, intent on his notes. "To have learned so much of human nature at so tender an age, in spite of reading the sentimental sludge of Susannah Haswell Rowson, is an extraordinary achievement." He looked up at me beneath knotted brows and smiled.

I returned his smile. "I suppose," I said, "there are some questions you'd like to ask me."

"There is one," he said, "but it's not on the topic you imagine. I *would* like to know what the hell my housekeeper was doing, ten minutes ago, lurking outside my door with a ballpeen hammer and a loaf of pumpernickel bread."

# The Heifer

Eliza Salters, at twenty-five, was a well-scarred veteran of a decade of hand-to-hand combat in the silk trenches of her profession. Deep lines were already etched in her forehead and at the corners of her mouth and eyes. Those eyes, narrow and yellow, darted constantly around Quinn-cannon's sitting room, expressing both trepidation and a simmering defiance. It was evident that, even at fifteen, it was Eliza's body, not her face, which had been her fortune, or misfortune. After ten years, na-ture's endowments were commencing to sag. Her face, never attractive, was puffed and jowled. In five years she would be bloated and hideous.

Quinncannon won her confidence simply by treating her as a lady. All solicitation and Gaelic charm, he escorted her to a wingback chair and offered her a glass of sherry. She expressed a preference for gin. It was obvious that Eliza was used to being dealt with in a very different manner by the police. Under the influence of blarney and gin she positively began to glow.

"It was a horrifying experience, sir, horrifying. If my visitor hadn't come when he done, why all of us would have been broiled in our beds!"

"Then," Quinncannon said, "the man that Rosina let into the house just before she discovered the fire was your friend?"

She nodded. "No use to ask me his name. The police have got it, though God knows how. It wasn't from my peaching."

"I know his name, Eliza, not that it matters." He glanced over at me. "None of the men in the house that night was called to give evidence at the inquest, Davy; therefore, none of them can be forced to testify at the trial. A quirk in the law. The coroner has subpoena powers which are denied to the district attorney unless the coroner has first exercised them."

"Do you mean that important witnesses need not give evidence if their identity is unknown until after the inquest? Has the prosecution no recourse?"

Quinncannon shrugged. "None beyond ordering fines for non-attendance and embarrassing them by publishing their names."

"That is ridiculous," I exclaimed. "What happened to justice?"

"We were speaking," he replied dryly, "of the law."

"I heard Frank come in that night," Eliza Salters interrupted in an effort to regain Quinncannon's attention. "It was after nine–closer to nine-thirty. I was in the parlor with Helen and some of the other girls when we heard Mrs. Townsend opening the street door. I heard Helen say her 'dear Frank' was come to see her."

This was spoken with such intense bitterness that I looked up from my notebook. Her lips were drawn back in a thin hard line and her yellow eyes were glowing.

"Was Frank Rivers in the habit of visiting the house before Helen came there?" Quinncannon inquired mildly.

"He was."

"And on those occasions, whom did he come to see?"

"Me."

"Never one of the other girls, Eliza?"

"Never!" She gulped at her gin. "Only me."

"How long was it that Frank Rivers called on you?"

"Seven weeks. Until *she* came."

"Now," he said, "Helen came to Mrs. Townsend's house about three weeks before she was murdered. After that did Frank Rivers visit you again?"

She finished her gin and stared down into the empty glass. At last she said, "No."

"But he did continue to come to the house?"

"Yes–to see *her.*"

"And this made you angry, didn't it, Eliza? Did you argue with Helen over Frank?"

"Helen and me," she said, "we never talked about him."

"Did you know that Frank had called on Helen at other houses, before she came to Thomas Street?"

"I heard it, after she moved in."

He brought the bottle of gin over and refilled her glass. When he resumed his seat he put the bottle on the table beside his chair. "Was Frank Rivers a special friend of yours?"

"Not special," she said. "He was . . . regular. You know what I mean? He was what I call occasional-steady. Look! What does a fine gentleman like yourself know about the likes of me? I been in houses since I was fifteen. A girl has to produce, see? She has to earn her keep or she's out in the street. I ain't pretty—never was. I can't talk about Shakespeare or the stock market. No man ever wanted me to dress up in green satin and go to the theater. But I got talents, mister. I know my business. There was things I could do for Frank, things he said no other girl could do, like—"

"Needlework?" Quinncannon asked quietly.

"What?"

"Didn't you sew one of the tassels back on his cloak after it was torn off on a sleigh ride?"

"Yes," she said, growing increasingly defensive. "That was about two weeks before—"

"Before Frank stopped visiting you. It was by that tassel that you identified Frank's cloak on the morning after the murder, wasn't it, Eliza?"

She nodded and took a swig of gin.

Quinncannon lit his pipe. "Let's go back to the night Helen died, Eliza. What time did you go to bed?"

"About ten-thirty. But I was still awake at eleven. I heard Helen calling down for champagne. After a few minutes I heard Mrs. Townsend come up with the wine and hand it in at the door."

"Where was your room in relation to Helen's?"

"Directly opposite, in the next building."

"In other words you were diagonally across the landing, on the opposite side of the double house. Your window overlooks Thomas Street. Was your bedroom door open?"

"No," she answered, "but I could hear her all right. She was standing in the middle of the hall yelling."

"Did you get out of bed?"

"I wasn't spying on them, if that's what you mean."

"Now, Eliza, did you have any other visitors before your gentleman arrived at three the next morning?"

"No."

"You were alone in your room from ten-thirty p.m. until three a.m.?"

"That's right."

Earlier I had jotted in my notebook: MOTIVE—jealousy; revenge. Against *both* Helen and Robinson.

Now I made another note: OPPORTUNITY—excellent.

"As far as you know," Quinncannon said, "did Helen keep any jewelry or money in her room?"

Eliza shook her head. "I don't know nothing about any money. She had a few ornaments—a watch and chain and two or three rings."

"Some of those things were not found in her room. Have you any idea what happened to them?"

Her eyes flashed with sudden suspicion. "Here now, you can't pin anything like that on me! If anybody knows what become of those trinkets, it's Rosina Townsend. Just you ask her if she didn't have Helen's watch in her hand on Sunday morning after the coroner came."

"All right, Eliza, I'll ask her. Just a few more questions and we'll be finished. You knew a second young man who called himself Frank Rivers, didn't you?"

"Yes. They said they was cousins."

"Did the second Frank Rivers ever visit you in your room?"

"Sometimes."

"In fact, he came to see you on the evening of the murder, didn't he?"

"Yes," she said warily, "but only to talk for a few minutes. We stayed in the entry. He had another boy with him."

"What did he want to talk about, Eliza?"

"I don't see how that's anybody's business."

"He didn't happen to mention his cousin, Eliza? He didn't happen to say that his cousin was coming that night to see Helen, did he?"

She sat facing him, nervously fingering the empty gin glass.

"Did he tell you that?" No answer. Then . . .

"Well," she cried suddenly, "what if he did?"

"Miss Salters," Quinncannon said sternly. "I'm going to read you part of a letter written by Helen Jewett to Frank Rivers on the Monday before her death. 'I shall not live long, Frank! I feel a presentiment that my life will be short. Eliza S. hates me with a deadly hatred, and, like the snake when charming the bird, smiles on me and openly professes the warmest friendship for me; the others envy and dislike me, but her hatred is deadly.' "

He put down the letter and looked at her. "Why would Helen Jewett have feared for her life, Eliza? Why was she so afraid of you?"

She sat in silence, sullenly staring up at him.

"Eliza," he said evenly, "did you murder Helen Jewett?"

Eliza Salters threw back her shoulders. Her yellow eyes blazed. "Mr. Quinncannon," she said firmly, "I wouldn't have dirtied my hands on her."

# The Lynx

Maria Stevens was a trollop of the type connoisseurs classify as saucy. Scarlet dresses were her trademark, and like any successful mercantile firm, she believed in the value of advertising. Her blond hair was deliberately styled in long, dangling curls after the fashion of a dozen virginal stage heroines.

I have not made a study of the matter, but it does seem that not all the girls are betrayed into the sisterhood by their own deprivations and desires, abetted by the seductive wiles of tobacco-shop Romeos, as the moralists of the penny press would have us believe. A few, and Maria Stevens was one, appear to have been fashioned for their trade by their maker, and find their way to it regardless of heredity or circumstance. The ancient Athenians distinguished three roles for women: as courtesans, concubines, and wives, and warned that men must keep these roles distinct and avoid love, which could end only in disaster.

The Boeotian sage Hesiod wrote: "Do not let any sweet-talking woman beguile your good sense with the fascinations of her shape. It's your barn she's after."

St. Thomas Aquinas accepted the view of Aristotle: that woman was the result of defective procreation, since "active power in the male seed tends to the production of a perfect likeness according to the masculine sex." Even the divine Plato was uncertain whether to place woman in the category of reasoning beings or of brutes.

Small wonder, then, that our modern Platos and Hesiods, the newspaper editors, have portrayed the sisterhood as frail, helpless creatures, seduced and abandoned, "slaves" (as the Duchesse du Berri would have it) "to the whimsies and tuggings of their hearts." Still, there are girls to be found in the pleasure palaces of Thomas and Duane Streets and Theater Alley who serve to remind all but the most callow young rakes that for every Pamela there was a Marwood, for every Magdalene a Jezebel.

To adopt the Athenian definitions, Eliza Salters was a mere concubine, but Maria Stevens, and Helen Jewett as well, were courtesans, the royalty of the profession. In the house, as in the hive, there is room for only one queen, and Maria and Helen had shared more than one hive, and, as it transpired, more than one drone.

Scarlet silks rustling, blond curls tossing, Maria Stevens sat daintily in one of Quinncannon's chairs and accepted a glass of wine. She took a sip and smiled sweetly at the Irishman. "Let's not waste each other's time, Mr. Quinncannon. You suspect me of murdering poor dear Helen. Shall we get on with it?"

Quinncannon returned the smile and settled back comfortably with a snifter of brandy. "Why don't you tell us about Boston?" he suggested.

"Ah, the Little Belt. I had almost forgotten her. There was a brilliant woman of business."

"The Little Belt, Davy," Quinncannon explained to me, "was better known to the Boston police as Mrs. Susan Bryant. She took her nickname from a British man-of-war whose entire crew she once entertained in such a brief time that she instantly became a legend."

"I remember her very fondly," Maria Stevens said. "She was more of a mother than a madam to her girls. Hers were my first lodgings."

"And Helen Jewett's second," Quinncannon added.

"Yes. She called herself Helen Mar then. I used the name Maria Livingston. Of course, Mr. Quinncannon, you obviously know all this."

The Irishman waved his hand. "Just tell the story in your own way, Maria."

"Well," she said pertly, "there isn't much to tell. You're referring, I suppose, to the Radcliffes, *père et fils*. Papa was one of the richest merchants in Boston, and Junior was fresh out of Harvard, and I mean fresh. He took a fancy to Helen—well, the truth is, he was insane over her. He bought a cottage for her in Cambridge and even proposed marriage to her. The only problem was that Papa Radcliffe found out about dear Helen's, uh, background, about the same time he caught sonny boy with his paws in the company till. Unhappy ending. The old man packed Junior off out West someplace and Helen had to come back to living among us peasants."

"You've left out the most interesting part," Quinncannon said. "Exactly how did Mr. Radcliffe learn about dear Helen's, uh, background?"

"Why, I told him of course. Did I forget to mention that? It was Mrs. Bryant's idea actually. Helen had been—I suppose you would call it—the premier attraction at Mrs. Bryant's hotel. She was more experienced than I was at the time, and much, *much* older."

"Without Helen business sagged at the Bryant bagnio," Quinncannon said. "The Little Belt schemed to get her back by breaking up her romance, using you as an informer, and it worked . . . up to a point. Helen returned, but within a few weeks she had left for New York. Why do you imagine she went over the wall, Maria?"

Maria appeared thoughtful. "I would imagine someone must have told her how Papa Radcliffe discovered what sort of girl Junior was fixing to bring to the altar."

"And right after Helen left Boston you followed her. In fact, you were thrown out of Mrs. Bryant's. Would you imagine that Susan Bryant learned how Helen learned how Mr. Radcliffe learned?"

The perpetual sweet smile played about her ruby lips. "I would imagine," she purred.

"Which brings us to New York and Richard Robinson. Tell us about that evening at Mother Gallagher's."

"You don't miss much, do you?" she said sharply.

He reached for his pipe. "As I recall, you were ensconced at Gallagher's and Helen was presiding at Mrs. Berry's—not a little like rival queens. Robinson—Frank Rivers—was calling regularly on Helen at the time, and you were determined to lure him to your own lair."

"That is nonsense!" she blurted. "Frank followed me around like a little puppy dog. Everyone knew that Helen was wildly jealous."

Quinncannon raised an eyebrow. "My dear lady, it was whispered in every bordello from here to Brooklyn that you were on the boy's trail like a hound tracking a rabbit. Caught him too, one night at the Bowery Theater, during the third act of *'Tis Pity She's a Whore,* I believe."

She looked as if she were planning his murder.

"A few nights later—this was about eight months before Helen was killed—she dressed herself as a man and shadowed you and Frank from the theater to Mother Gallagher's. And there she found you at a most inopportune moment and laid about you with a convenient blunt instrument." He paused and sipped his brandy. "In the ensuing confusion Robinson managed to slip away, but that was your last tryst, wasn't it, Maria?"

By a supreme effort she controlled her anger, sank back in the chair, and forced a smile. "You shouldn't listen to vicious gossip, Mr. Quinncannon."

"I know, I know," he sighed. "It's one of my worst habits. Still, it must have been awkward, Maria, when Helen moved into Rosina's, where you had already established yourself as—what was your phrase?— the 'premier attraction.' Right in the room next door, too. Cheek to jowl, so to speak. That wall between your rooms is pretty flimsy, nothing but lath and plaster. You must have been able to hear everything that went on in her room."

"Perhaps, if I had listened," she answered sweetly. "But, you see, I was always occupied with entertaining friends of my own."

"Always?"

"Always," she cooed.

"On the night of the murder?"

She hesitated. "Yes."

"His name is known to the police, Maria," Quinncannon said.

"And to you?"

"And to me."

"I don't believe you."

"Thomas Cushing," he said gently.

"Don't hurt him," she whispered. She put down her wineglass and folded gloved hands in her lap. "Don't let the police hurt him. Please, Mr. Quinncannon, you're a man with influence. Tom is such a timid, kind little man. He only comes to talk. He's lonely, you see."

"What time did he come on the murder night?"

"About ten-thirty."

"What time did he leave?"

"In the confusion, after the fire alarm was given."

"After three?"

"Yes."

"And he came only to talk?"

"He fell asleep. We talked for a while and he fell asleep." Again she raised her eyes. "He always does. He's really harmless. He doesn't know anything. He was asleep! He's only a little bookkeeper someplace downtown. If his name is dragged into this he'll lose his job. He'll lose his mind, Mr. Quinncannon. I know him. He's not . . . strong."

"All right," Quinncannon soothed. "I can't prevent the police from talking to Cushing. Brink and I are on opposing sides. But I can give you my word Cushing will not have to testify at the trial if . . . *if* you will answer the rest of my questions, Maria."

She nodded gratefully. It occurred to me that since Cushing, like the other men in the house that night, had not testified at the inquest, he would not have to give evidence at the trial whether Maria answered Quinncannon's questions or not.

"I want to know," Quinncannon said, "what happened on the night of the murder as you remember it. I want to know minute by minute."

"I went to my room about eight," she began. "Tom came up about ten-thirty—I've told you that. A little after eleven I heard Helen calling for champagne from the landing, and then Rosina bringing it up. After that the house was quiet. Rosina always locks up about midnight. Tom had fallen asleep in the chair in my room. I . . . I went to bed."

"You heard nothing from Helen's room? No voices? An argument perhaps?"

She shook her head. "Only my own shutters banging during the night. I got up once to close them. I don't know what time it was."

"Go on."

"I went back to bed until I was awakened by Rosina. She was pounding on one of the girl's doors across the landing. Mr. Cushing was still in my room, just awakened and terrified of being caught by the watch. I told him to watch his chance and slip out the front door."

"Wasn't the street door locked?"

"Rosina had an arrangement, whenever the house was raided, to leave her key in the front door so the men could get out."

"And did she do so that night?"

Maria nodded. "I unlocked my bedroom door and went out on the landing. All the girls were there, milling about, and a couple of men in their shirttails. Smoke was pouring out of Helen's room. I went in and tried to reach Helen's bed, but at first the smoke prevented me."

"But a few seconds later you *were* able to reach the bed," he prompted.

Again she nodded. "The bedclothes were all consumed. They seemed to be burnt without blazing. I remember I took up a handful of the ashes to show to Rosina."

"And Helen?"

"She was lying nearly on her back, with her left side very much burnt and a large gash on the side of her head."

Quinncannon rubbed thoughtfully at a corner of his moustache. "How do you suppose the police got Richard Robinson's real name and address?"

"Any of the girls might have told them."

"No," he said slowly. "The others knew him only as Rivers and they had no idea where he boarded. Perhaps it would refresh your memory if I read part of the evidence given before the coroner. Peter Collyer, a watchman, swore: 'One person present, it was Miss Stevens, who occupied a room adjoining Helen Jewett, stated that she knew him. Miss Stevens stated that he attended a dry-goods store at Pearl and Maiden Lane, and that if it was a weekday she could find him in a few minutes.' Thomas Garland, the first watchman to enter the house, deposed: 'Maria Stevens told me she knew who the murderer was and would tell at the proper time and place.' "

Quinncannon looked up and she returned his gaze. "When you found Helen," he asked, "did you try to do anything for her—waken her perhaps—pull her from the bed?"

Again there was the sweet smile. "But there would have been no reason," she mewed. "It was easy to see dear Helen was dead."

"It's no wonder," I observed when Maria Stevens had gone, "that Robinson protested when Helen moved into Townsend's. On top of his other troubles with her, he certainly didn't need two ex-girlfriends rooming on the same floor."

I'm not certain Quinncannon heard me. He sat deep in thought, his dead pipe dangling from the corner of his mouth.

"Still," I continued, "the girl's concern for Cushing seems genuine and, if you ask me, even poignant."

"Keeping in mind, of course, that Cushing represents the closest thing Stevens has to an alibi."

"Do you know you are a carper and a cynic?"

He smiled and said, "Shall we have the next one up?"

## The Barracuda

Rosina Townsend was thirty-nine, going on fifty. She had managed to keep her figure, however, and her face, or what I could see of it behind a heavy veil of mourning, still showed signs of the ravishing beauty she must have had in her youth. She was dressed entirely in black except for the white lace at her throat and wrists. Her hair was a striking silvery gray, swept back and up beneath a black bonnet, and her black-gloved hands held a white lace handkerchief with which she occasionally dabbed at her eyes behind her black veil.

"I have buried the unfortunate girl just this morning," she said. "I had a funeral service performed over her in the Methodist church. The Episcopalians are too nice people."

For Rosina, Quinncannon selected Remy Martin. As the afternoon was growing overcast and chilly, he lit the fire. I thought I detected a shudder in Mrs. Townsend when the flames began to crackle, but perhaps it was only my imagination.

"It must have been a terrible experience for you," Quinncannon offered sympathetically.

"Mr. Quinncannon, it has been a nightmare. It *is* a nightmare. There was no one else at the funeral, you know, except myself and someone from the police. My poor, poor Helen. She said once to me, 'I shall die, Rosina, in youth, and leave all my soul-condemning gains to those who will treat my name with contempt.' " She dabbed at her eyes. "But that shall not happen, sir. Not while I have a breath left in me."

"You will not treat her name with contempt?" One Irish eyebrow was arched, but his voice was soothing.

Still, she was sensitive to his meaning. "I have taken no more of her jewelry than was necessary to inter her decently, sir. I must say that I deeply resent the accusations of certain of the newspapers that I have stolen, in a manner of speaking, the coins from the poor murdered girl's eyes. If Helen's few miserable trinkets be missing, the press would perhaps do well to inquire of the officers and the watch for their whereabouts." Her eyes shot suspiciously at me. "May I ask who this young gentleman is? I understood our interview was to be private."

"Tell the lady who you are, Davy."

"David Cordor, ma'am," I said. "I'm a newspaper reporter for the *Sun.*"

Her shoulders, which had tensed visibly, relaxed at the word *"Sun."*

"Very well," she said. "As long as you don't work for that damned vermin at the *Herald.*"

She turned back to Quinncannon, and when she spoke, her deep voice was icy. "I am here, sir, because I have been ordered by the authorities to cooperate with you, and to answer all questions truthfully. I understand that others of my girls have been given the same orders, and I understand, too, that we have been put in this position only because you are a close personal friend of the high constable. I am willing to speak with you because I have been advised to do so if I have nothing to hide, and because, sir, I *have* nothing to hide. You must understand, however, that in the past week I have had my house almost burned down around me, my girls scattered, my business ruined, and myself accused in the public press of theft, arson, and murder. If, then, I appear at times waspish and in bad humor, I must ask you to excuse it."

Quinncannon stretched in his chair and propped his boots on the ottoman. He touched a match to his pipe, puffing methodically and exhaling great clouds of white smoke into the darkening room. The corner of his mouth twisted up when he finally spoke.

"You are here, Mrs. Townsend, because you are being held by the police as a material witness in a murder case, and because your alternative to cooperating with the authorities is to be prosecuted for prostitution, keeping an illicit house, and sodomy. You are at liberty only because you are a close personal friend of Officer Brink, and of a justice or six who shall, for the moment, go unnamed. You are under suspicion of theft because a great deal of Helen Jewett's jewelry and all her cash are reported missing, and by your own admission, you were the first person to reach her room. You are under suspicion of arson because you recently tripled your fire-insurance policy. You are under suspicion of murder because you were in deep debt to Jewett and because you quarreled with her violently over the affections of a gentleman whose nocturnal sobriquet is 'English Charley.' "

Rosina Townsend stood abruptly. "I wish to leave at once," she announced.

"Meaning," Quinncannon said, "that you have just remembered you have something to hide."

She drew herself up to her full height and clenched her hands into little gloved fists at her sides. The lace handkerchief fluttered to the carpet. "You," she hissed at Quinncannon, "are the devil himself!"

The Irishman regarded her calmly. "Sit down, Mrs. Townsend, and let's get this over with."

A long minute passed, during which Quinncannon's grandfather clock ticked thunderously.

Then the lady sat down. "I can tell you no more than I've told the police."

"That," he said, "will do nicely."

"Very well. At about the hour of nine on Saturday, April 9, I was called to my front door by a knock, and on inquiring 'Who's there?' the reply was 'Frank Rivers.' I did not, however, open the door at once, because Helen had said that under no circumstances did she want a man named Bill Easy admitted that night."

"Was Bill Easy expected?"

"Saturday was his regular night with her."

"Did he show up on the murder night?"

"No," she said. "I asked a second time who was there, to be sure that the voice was not Bill Easy's, before I unbolted the door."

"So you were certain it was not Bill Easy. Did you recognize the voice as that of Frank Rivers?"

"No—only that it was not Bill Easy's."

"And when the man entered, did you recognize his face?"

She eyed him. "I have been instructed not to discuss that."

"By Officer Brink?"

She merely repeated the statement.

Quinncannon smiled. "What occurred after you opened the door?"

"He passed me and went up the right staircase. I went into the parlor and told Helen Frank was there. Helen left the parlor and went out saying, 'My dear Frank, I am glad to see you.' They both went to her room and nothing more was heard from them until about eleven, when Helen came partly down the stairs and asked me to bring her a bottle of champagne. On looking into the closet I found that there was no bottle there. I told Helen this and told her, as she was in her loose dress, to return to her room and I would bring up a bottle, as I should be under the necessity of going into the cellar and opening a basket. I went downstairs and got a bottle, knocked off the rosin, and took it to Helen's door. I rapped and Helen said, 'Come in.' I opened the door and entered and saw Frank lying on the bed."

This entire speech was delivered in a weary monotone, as if rehearsed over and over for presentation at a school recital.

"What was Frank doing?" Quinncannon asked.

"He was lying on his left side, with his head resting on his arm in the bed, the sheet thrown over him, and something in his other hand."

"What was that?"

"I can't say."

"Was it a book?"

"I think it was—either a book or a paper. I saw his face."

"Clearly?"

"Yes—his profile."

"Don't you think it rather odd that a man who had brought a hatchet with him for the purpose of murder should allow you to see him in the room with his victim?"

She looked at him steadily. "I think a great many things are odd."

"And so do I, madam. So do I. Did Frank speak?"

"No. Helen said to me, 'Rosina, as you have not been well today, will you take a glass of champagne with us?' I replied, 'No, I am much obliged to you, I had rather not.' I then left the room, as some of the other girls called me from below. I neither saw nor heard anything more from that time. The house was locked up at a few minutes after midnight and I went to bed. About three I heard a noise at the street door and found that it was a young man who was in the habit of visiting Eliza Salters. I let him in and then found a lamp burning in the parlor and the back door unbarred and opened. I called out but got no answer. I returned to my room, but having heard no one go up the stairs, I went back to the parlor and called again into the yard. There was no reply and I locked the door—then went upstairs to Maria Stevens' room."

"Because of the lamp?"

"Yes—there were but two lamps like it in the house, one in Maria's room and the other in Helen's. I tried Maria's door and found it fast. I then found that Helen's was on the latch, and on my opening it, the smoke rushed out and nearly suffocated me. I raised the alarm of fire. Maria Stevens went into Helen's room but could not reach her. She returned to her own room and then tried again to reach Helen and brought out a handful of ashes from the bed. She said the bedclothes were all burnt up but there was no flame. Then I called for the watch. The watchman went into the room and then found that Helen had been murdered and the bed set on fire."

Again this was spoken in the tired singsong of a tediously memorized school piece. Rosina appeared completely bored, but Quinncannon brought her to indignant attention with his next question.

"Who told the police who Frank Rivers was and where he resided?"

"Not I! I am aware that the papers have accused me of it, but I did not know his right name or where he boarded. It was Maria Stevens who said she knew him. That louse Bennett has tried to make it look as if I set Brink on his trail, but I couldn't have done so. I knew him only as Frank Rivers. I am prepared to swear to it."

"I hope so," Quinncannon said, "for I expect you'll have to. Had you ever seen him before that night?"

"Only once, close up. He was sitting in a room with me and some other girls—Helen was present—and on Frank's rising to go out, Helen remarked, 'Rosina, don't you think my Frank very handsome?' I replied yes."

"How many girls lived with you at the time of the murder?"

"Ten, including myself."

"And how many men were in the house?"

"Six," she answered. "I admitted them all myself. I knew all but two who came together and appeared by their accent to be from the South."

"Six," Quinncannon repeated, "including Frank Rivers?"

"Including Richard Robinson," she said firmly.

"And you admitted them all. How many did you let out again?"

"Why, none. They all escaped in the uproar after the alarm."

"But—" He appeared perplexed. "Wasn't there one who knocked on your bedroom door during the night and asked you to unlock the street door?"

"Yes—I've told the police that. I told him to get his woman to let him out. That was sometime before three. I don't know exactly when."

"What time did your own gentleman friend arrive?"

"About eleven."

"Did you go into your room with him at that time?"

"For a few minutes. We did not retire until I had locked the house."

"And he was with you until the alarm was given?"

"He was," she said defiantly. I could see from her manner that she was bracing for an accusation of murder, but it was not forthcoming. Instead, he settled back into a voluminous cloud of tobacco smoke and fell silent, leaving me to usher our last guest out to a waiting paddy wagon. When I returned he was slouched in the chair with his eyes closed.

"Do you want some brandy?" I asked.

"Please."

I poured two. "Do you want to talk?"

He gradually opened his eyes. "Not tonight, Davy. Tonight, if you don't mind, I prefer to meditate and get drunk."

"Just one question, then."

He closed his eyes. "Just one, then."

"Who was the man with Rosina that night?"

"Well, Bennett knows. You might as well know. It was Thomas Hamblin."

"The manager of the Bowery?" I recalled Hamblin as the nervous Iago on the night Junius Brutus Booth staged his inebriated walkout in the first act of *Othello*.

"The same," Quinncannon said.

"Does he corroborate Rosina's story?"

"Just two questions, then," he said. "Yes, Davy, to the extent that he can."

A log cracked in the fireplace. I finished my brandy and rose to leave, but at the door I turned back.

"Lon, how *did* Brink learn Robinson's real name?"

He opened one eye. "Just three, then. At the inquest Rosina testified that, on the Tuesday before the murder, Jewett told her that Rivers was going to be married, that he had returned to her the letters she had written and asked her to return all his letters. When the police searched her room Sunday morning, they found both packets of letters. Jewett's all opened 'Dear Frank,' but the envelopes were addressed to Robinson."

"At his boardinghouse or Hoxie's store?"

"Both, Davy."

I asked another question, but there was no reply. Though I knew he was not, Quinncannon appeared to be asleep. I went out and the door clicked shut behind me.

# 26  The Scavengers

Every new issue of the *Herald* hammered at the thesis of Robinson's innocence, despite the fact that the whole city appeared already to have convicted and condemned the boy. Over and over Bennett proclaimed that the guilt lay with one or more of the inmates of 41 Thomas Street:

> Who is the murderer? It cannot be possible that Robinson is the person. How could a young man perpetrate so brutal an act? Is it not more like the work of a woman? Are not the whole train of circumstances within the ingenuity of a female, abandoned and desperate?

The *Herald* coupled its defense of Robinson with a steady stream of accusations against the authorities. At the very least, Bennett charged, the police were incompetent. At worst, they might actually be suppressing evidence against Rosina and her girls from the same pecuniary motives, he hinted vaguely but darkly, which led them to permit the open operation of bawdy houses and gambling dens throughout the city.

> Look at the state of society and morals—look at the hells and gambling houses permitted by this very police—look at those houses of abandonment, protected by some of the very officers of justice. The Police have been remiss. We say it boldly and deliberately. Why are all these

women in that house now at large and out of custody? Why is Rosina Townsend out of custody? Why should her solemn assertion be taken rather than Robinson's? There is a juggle and a mystery yet unrevealed. Conscious of virtue, we shall probe it to the bottom.

The *Herald*'s reporting was so aggressive that the *Sun* and the *Transcript* held back, content to assert periodically their faith in the police and their belief in Robinson's guilt. Bennett, meanwhile, puffed himself up with moral outrage and, with the fury of an Old Testament prophet, attacked the world's oldest profession, the dissipation of the city's youth, and the general condition of New York's morals, while the other journals prepared to attack Bennett.

It was my old friend Bill Attree, at the *Transcript,* who fired the first salvo:

The excitement in the public mind in reference to this monstrous affair, continues to be unabated; and, notwithstanding the puny and purchased efforts of a rickety, tottering print—notorious only for its easy access to petit bribery, and as being the most corrupt, profligate, and contemptible concern that was ever yet palmed upon any community—to produce an impression that other persons than Robinson have been the perpetrators of the foul assassination: yet the general conviction, from the evidence already before the public, is, (and we record it with regret,) that he alone is the guilty individual, and that his hands only are stained with the blood of Helen Jewett. We are constrained to say thus much in respect to truth, and we do it without any intention to wound the feelings of the accused, or to add to the keen distress of his numerous relatives and friends.

This remarkable paragraph appeared on Monday, April 18, and that afternoon, during a lull at the Police Office, Attree invited me out for coffee. He had a copy of his paper under his arm and he was obviously terribly pleased with himself.

"Do you know, Davy," he said when we had ordered, "I believe that, aside from Bennett of course, you're the only journalist in the city who hasn't congratulated me on my item on Robinson?"

"Is that so?" I took out my pipe and began to fill it.

"Frankly," he continued, "I expected Ben Day to have gone for Bennett's jugular before this. Since he hasn't, I considered it my duty."

I merely blew out a billow of tobacco smoke.

"I gather," said Attree, "you do not agree."

"I'm trying to reconcile your paragraph with your well-known aversion to journalists throwing libels at one another."

"A statement is not libelous when it is the truth, Davy," he replied in a patronizing tone, as if he were patiently instructing a schoolboy.

"Truth?" I repeated. "Oh, yes, I'd forgotten your respect for truth. You mention it in your paragraph, as I recall."

"Is it possible . . . ?" He waited while the coffee was set down and then began again. "Is it possible that you are the only reporter in New York who doesn't know why Bennett is crusading for Robinson? Is it possible that, green as you are, Davy, you are truly that naïve?"

I endeavored to smile at him through taut lips. "Why don't you just say it, Bill?"

He regarded me with infinite pity. "The *Herald* is for sale, Davy. For God's sake, Bennett has been bought with Joe Hoxie's money! He's nothing but a puppet of the defense, Davy, a puppet on a string, and Lon Quinncannon pulls the string. Didn't you know?"

Didn't I know? I had known since I saw Bennett stealing out of Quinncannon's lodgings like a detected thief. I didn't want to believe it—perhaps I didn't believe it—but I knew.

"Or is it," Attree said, "that you *approve?* Are you so loyal to your Irish friend that you've sold out every decent journalistic instinct you have?"

Dull anger ached in me. It was anger at Day and at Bennett and at Quinncannon and, I suppose, at myself as well, but it was also anger at Attree, and Attree was in the vicinity and practicably assailable. If I'd had a gun I believe I could have shot him.

"Possibly you could define what you mean by 'decent journalistic instinct,' Bill? You know how young and inexperienced I am, and how much I rely on you for guidance and advice."

The poor ass positively beamed. So closely had I hit on his perception of our relationship that my sarcasm eluded him completely.

"It is my experience, Davy, that the true journalist is born, not made," Attree intoned. "Any moron can be trained to spell, or to cross his *t*'s, but the true journalist has the proper instincts—for what is humane and moral and, above all, for the truth. These instincts are innate. You have them, Davy. I think that's why I liked you from the moment we first met."

I nodded with what I trust was the proper air of humble appreciation. "Do you mean that the born journalist instinctively recognizes truth?"

"That has been my experience," he replied modestly.

"Then," I said, "the true journalist doesn't need to reason to his conclusions."

"Oh, of course he uses reason, Davy, but he uses reason to arrive logically at the truths he already has sensed intuitively."

"I see." I sipped my coffee, watching him over the rim of the cup. "But I imagine the true journalist wouldn't require facts to reason from, would he?"

He looked at me sharply. "On the contrary, it is essential to uncover those facts which will support the logic which leads to the conclusion."

"Now I'm confused, Bill. I really am." Attree relaxed somewhat at this confession. "If one senses the truth instinctively at the outset, why does one need logic or facts?"

He sighed deeply. "Because, lad," he said patiently, "one must convince others of the truth. That is the role of the journalist in a free society. The average man does not have an instinct for truth. To be convinced he requires at least the appearance of fact and logic."

I shook my head. "It's amazing how thoroughly you and Ben Day agree on the role of a journalist."

"Day!" he snorted. "That reactionary idiot!"

"Look, Bill, suppose you're right and Bennett has been bribed. How does it follow that Robinson is guilty?"

He leaned back and folded his arms. "Robinson is guilty because Bennett has been bribed to write lies," he asserted firmly.

"But isn't it possible that Bennett had to be bribed to write the truth?" My impassioned tone surprised me. Until that moment the thought had not occurred to me.

Attree frowned. "I almost suspect you're being deliberately dense, Davy. It's not becoming, you know. It really isn't."

"Come on, Attree!" I was tempted to punch him. "Tell me how you *know* that Robinson is guilty, that—how did you phrase it?—'his hands only are stained with the blood of Helen Jewett'? Did that truth come to you in a vision? Was it written by a flaming finger on a tablet of stone?"

He stared at me for a long minute. "Little boy," he said finally. "Little boy, I thought you had promise—I truly did. I thought you were beginning to understand that this country will never be a true democracy until the aristocracy and their satellites are overthrown. Can't you comprehend, even now, that it is the wild spawn of aristocratic drones like Robinson, and the cheaters and deceivers of the poor like the merchant Hoxie, and the parasites of the rich like Quinncannon and Hoffman, and the little bloodsuckers like Bennett, who are the real whores of this whorehouse society?"

"But suppose that Richard Robinson didn't kill Helen Jewett," I said.

"Robinson is guilty, Cordor," he answered, "whether he held the ax or not. He is the very *symbol* of this oppressive society—respectable, Protestant, Anglo-Saxon, and male."

"I suppose," I said, "it is foolish to point out that if those were capital crimes, you and I would be in a fair way to hang."

He fixed his eyes on mine. "I know my guilt," he said solemnly, "and I do my utmost to atone."

I met his stare and relit my pipe. "So this," I said, "is the 'truth' which you felt 'constrained' to state in your paragraph."

"I noted, I believe, that I expressed it with regret."

"To bloody hell with your regret," I said. I rose from the table. "And to bloody hell with your truth."

It was the last time Attree and I had coffee together.

The *Herald* answered Attree with a letter purported to be from a newspaperman in the city to Helen Jewett and signed "Wandering Willie." It was clear to the entire journalistic fraternity that the writer was supposed to be Attree, and the joke lay in Attree's renowned prudery:

> Dearest Helen.–Most lovely and enchanting creature! I shall never forget the moment I saw your fair form in the Police Office. You are fit to be a princess–a very queen. What a prize the villain had who first seduced you! How I should like to have been in his place! Yet you are as sweet a companion now as ever. Oh! lovely creature, what a form! what a figure! what a fine bust! Your lineaments *********** rich lips ******** full bust ***** Your mind, too, is of the first order.

The fourth estate laughed to Attree's face for a week and behind his back for months. The last laugh, however, was on Bennett. I wrote the following during an idle moment, and for one whole morning I was back in Ben Day's graces.

> A LEAF FROM THE DIARY OF HELEN JEWETT.–The following *morceau* from the diary of this unfortunate young creature, was probably overlooked by a certain gentleman of the press in his search for curiosities among her cast-off clothing.
>
> Jan 6.–Had a strange visit today, from a queer looking, cross-eyed man who represented himself to be the editor, proprietor and publisher of a penny paper printed in Nassau Street. Said he was smitten with my beauty yesterday as he met me walking in Broadway–represented his paper as in a flourishing condition, and himself the very paragon of editors–full of wit, humor, sentiment, and all that is requisite to give piquancy to a daily publication; and abruptly concluded by offering his hand to me in marriage. I am tired of my present mode of existence, and had I a tolerable offer, might be induced to accept it. But then to pin one's existence to the skirts of a cross-eyed, meager looking Scotchman! He stood before me, and the picture he presented forbid it. He strove hard to win me over, but finding all his eloquence in vain, he changed his ground and appealed to my generosity for a loan of money. From the bottom of my heart I pitied him, and gave him a ten dollar bill, glad to get rid of him.

Jan 7.—Received a letter this morning from the same strange personage. I transfer it to my Journal—returning the original to him who sent it.

### THE LETTER

*My adorable Angel Helen*—It was my intention last evening to have paid you a visit and thanked you in person for the kindness you conferred on me yesterday. Accordingly I made the best of my way to the mansion that contains "all that my soul holds dear." With a trembling hand I essayed to knock, and brought to the window the mistress of the house. "Who is there," asked she with the tone and look of the Witch of Endor.—"It is me," said I, "the editor, proprietor, printer, and publisher of the saucy little H_____, on a visit to the magnet of my heart, the charming Helen." "Begone! you lazy, begging, dirty vagabond," said she, and, with a heavy heart, I made my way to my miserable, solitary pallet. Helen! you have set my heart on fire! Unfortunate that I am, I never yet knew what it was to possess the affections of a woman; and as I am now falling into the "sere and yellow leaf," I fear I never shall unless yours are bestowed upon me. Farewell, my sweet; you shall see me again soon.

Thine till death,          J_____G_____B_____.

# 27　The Crying Clerk

"Ah! Mr. Cordor."

Dennis Brink almost bounded across the Police Office, waving two sheets of foolscap. "Here's a piece of news for your friend Quinn-cannon. You know I try to keep him informed of our progress in the Robinson case. Do you know who William Gray is?"

Gray was Robinson's former associate in the swindle of Joe Hoxie.

"Did you know that Gray is now in prison on a charge of fraud?" Brink asked.

"No, I didn't know."

"Here," Brink announced in triumph, "is a letter written by Robinson to Gray when both were in the Dead House, and intercepted by the keeper, Pappy Lowends. Read it."

> My dear Gray,
>
> I have said the cloak is yours. You must back me up and say that you had lost it, you know not where. I know that you are in want, and so soon as I am free, I shall be able to provide for your needs. A word to the wise, as they say.
>
> After my liberation I shall seduce your wife into your betrayal, as we discussed, and then stand evidence of our mutual guilt, which should enable you to take proceedings against her for a divorce. My word is my bond. Destroy this note.
>
> Richie

I whistled softly. Brink was beaming. "Lovely, lovely. The little rat admits the cloak is his. And we can prove the hatchet as well. By the way, Cordor, the other morning in Thomas Street the Irishman seemed sinfully curious about motive. It develops that Robinson had got himself affianced—nice little girl, good family. His whore was threatening to break it up. We found this epistle in Jewett's room."

*Dearest Helen,*

*My entire future, my very life, are in your hands. One word, one whispered syllable from your fragrant lips, and I lie mortally wounded. Oh! could you be so cruel as to betray me? Will you expose me to the world, to become the despised of men and abhorred by all the fairer sex, the shameful burden of my parents' age, and miserably cast away by my trusting employer?*

*Say no, dearest Helen, for if you persist in what you threaten I know my course—it will be short and sweet. No, not sweet, bitter, bitter, dearest Helen.*

*Your beloved Frank*

"What say, eh? Sounds like a death threat to me." Brink was fairly dancing, his swine lips smacking. "Oh, we've got the little bastard cold, Cordor. You can bet the rent on it!"

I was there the evening that Richard Robinson was escorted from his cell in the Dead House to the grand-jury room, where he underwent examination before the coroner, William Schureman, Police Justice Oliver Lowends, and the grand jury. The assistant district attorney, Robert H. Morris, handled the prosecution. Ogden Hoffman and Whitlaw Price appeared for the defense, although Hoffman allowed Price to cross-examine all witnesses, rising only to speak for the prisoner when it was asked if he had anything to say in his own defense. Accused, said Hoffman, would, on advice of counsel, avail himself of the privilege granted him under the law and refuse to answer any questions at this time. No defense was presented, and Robinson was routinely indicted for murder and conducted back to his cell.

The following evening I visited Quinncannon in his rooms to inform him that Robinson's note to Gray had been intercepted and the police knew the cloak was not Gray's. He nodded grimly.

"The cloak," he said, "was made for Robinson at Oateman's shop on Broadway. Mr. Oateman has the record of the order and the charge against Robinson in his day book. One of his journeyman tailors identifies it particularly, because the cape was accidentally cut a wrong way with the nape."

"Then," I said, "Robinson lied when he told you the cloak was not his."

He smiled wearily. "Not exactly, Davy. The cloak is Mr. Oateman's. It seems Robinson never paid him for it."

"Do the police know about Oateman?"

"Good God, I hope not!"

"But isn't it Oateman's duty to come forward with the information?"

"It is Mr. Oateman's duty not to suppress any information which is particularly inquired for."

"That's a nice distinction," I said tartly. "There are rumors that the hatchet has been proven to belong to Hoxie's store."

His mouth tightened at the corners. "It has been positively identified by James Wells, the porter in Hoxie's shop. He can't recall seeing it after the Wednesday preceding the murder, although he did not actually look for it until the Monday after the crime."

"That means that Robinson lied when he claimed to have purchased the hatchet he took to Helen's on Wednesday night."

"He might have." Quinncannon stroked his moustache. "Or the ax might have been carried away from Hoxie's by anyone at any time between Wednesday and Sunday morning, when it was found. But unless the police are correct and Robinson brought the hatchet to the house on Saturday night, there can be no explanation for . . ."

"For the string found tied round the handle," I finished.

"Yes," he said darkly. "That is just one of the extraordinary puzzles of this case. That string strikes me as too neat, too pat. Then there is the matter of the lamp and the open rear door. And the miniature—why, if Robinson killed her, did he take the miniature and leave the letters?"

"The fire is odd, too," I added. "Was it set to cover the murder or to call attention to it? Did the killer set it, or did someone else in the house?"

"Then there is the matter of the crying clerk," he said.

"The crying clerk?"

Quinncannon paused to light his pipe. "According to Rosina there were six men in the house on the murder night. Two were strangers with Southern accents. Rosina herself spent the evening with Thomas Hamblin, who arrived about eleven and left after the fire alarm was sounded. A fourth was the man let in between nine and nine-thirty, and identified by Rosina as Frank Rivers."

"That's the fellow Robinson told us was to visit Helen and use his alias," I said. "You'll pardon me for observing that story sounds a bit fishy."

"Yet, if Robinson was at the Clinton Hotel with Emma Chancellor at nine-thirty, it must be true."

"Have you found Emma Chancellor?"

He shook his head.

"Is she really dead, Lon?"

"The police think so," he answered. "They think Robinson poisoned her."

"Robinson! But—if he did, it had to be before Helen was murdered. Robinson was arrested almost immediately."

Quinncannon shrugged. "The police theorize that Chancellor was killed weeks before Jewett. They believe that Jewett knew about the murder and that the boy had to kill her too to silence her. On the other hand, Robinson swears that the girl who registered at the Clinton as Carrie Norris on April 8 and remained there for several days after Jewett's death was Emma Chancellor. If I can locate her alive, obviously it would clear Robinson of her murder and confirm at least a partial alibi for the murder night."

"At all events," I said, "if the man who visited Helen at nine-thirty was not Robinson, he could not be the killer, since, according to Robinson's own story, he left the house at eleven when she was still alive."

"Granted," he acknowledged, "but if Robinson is telling the truth, there were at least *seven* men in the house on Saturday night, including one not admitted by Rosina. I refer to Robinson himself."

He puffed on his pipe. "Now we have accounted for five of those seven men. The sixth was a young merchant from the lower part of the city who visited Eliza Salters, and whom Rosina admitted at three in the morning. He has stated that he saw the burning lamp in the parlor when he arrived. The authorities consider his evidence crucial, but they can't compel him to testify because he was not called at the inquest. He has since fled the city bound for Rochester. The district attorney has sent an officer after him, but it is unlikely he will be unearthed."

"And the seventh man?"

"The seventh is a clerk who told the prosecutor he knew nothing beyond being awakened by the cries of fire and murder and escaping from the house half dressed and in terror. He burst into tears and begged not to be put on the stand."

"The crying clerk," I said. "Obviously this is Thomas Cushing, the fellow who visited Maria Stevens."

Quinncannon smiled sourly. "I'm going out of town for a few days, Davy. I'd like you to stay here in my rooms while I'm gone in case anyone attempts to contact me."

"Where can I reach you?"

"At the moment I can't be certain," he said. "I'll keep in touch with you by post."

"But," I protested, "if there's an urgent matter here?"

"I rely on your discretion," he answered.

It must be admitted I was extremely flattered by his trust. Whether it was well and wisely placed, however, is another question.

## 28  The Surprise Witness

"**M**r. Quinncannon, you must see me or I'm a dead man."
I had descended from a hansom to Quinncannon's door near
midnight in mid-May and was applying the key to the lock when I heard
these words behind me, spoken in a high, whining whisper which was
almost a sob. Turning, I caught a glimpse in the dim gaslight of the
street lamp of a small, fashionably dressed man, albeit somewhat disheveled, and so nervous that he trembled violently although it was a very
mild night. He wore rimless spectacles and his receding hair was
combed straight back without part. He was clean-shaven and appeared
to be in his late twenties. Beyond that I could tell little, for he caught
sight of my face and retreated rapidly into the shadows of St. Paul's,
from which he had stepped.

"You're not Quinncannon!" he rasped out of the darkness.

"Mr. Quinncannon is away," I said. "My name is Cordor. He's asked
me to—"

"No! No!" he said quickly. "I must talk to Quinncannon! Oh, my
God!"

This last exclamation escaped him in a groan like a death rattle, and
he, or rather his shadow, turned and rushed up Broadway. Behind him
another shadow, huge and hulking, seemed to emerge from the graveyard beside the cathedral and followed him up the street.

I stood for a moment in the doorway and then unlocked the door and went up the stairs, haunted even then by the strange little man's frightened face. It would haunt me again, less than a week later, when I saw him for the second and last time, lying on a hardwood floor with his throat cut.


Five days later a note was delivered by messenger from Whitlaw Price asking me—as "Quinncannon's surrogate"—to meet him at Bellevue. I ordered a cab and rode uptown that afternoon.

I had not visited Bellevue since Robinson's transfer there from the Dead House, nor in fact since my first day in New York, when I had witnessed the execution of Manuel Fernandez. The massive prison seemed even more dismal than before, its grim stone towers stretching up bleakly against the iron-gray sky across which bitter gusts of wind whipped the heavy black clouds of an approaching storm.

We trotted through the rusted iron gates and across the cobblestone yard to the great iron doors, nearly two stories high, which guarded the entrance to the main building. As it had every day since Robinson's transfer, a crowd of perhaps two hundred had gathered outside the prison, craning for a glimpse of one of the principals in the case while entering or leaving, or of the "notorious murderer" himself lounging behind one of the barred windows on the third story, where he was supposed to be incarcerated. The crowd was in an ugly mood, for it was rumored that one of "Rosina's girls" was at that moment visiting Robinson. The hansom thought to have brought her stood near the door, the hackman glancing about in skittish apprehension.

I instructed my driver to wait and met Price in a small, spartanly furnished interrogation room off the office of the head keeper, Mr. Lyons. The man with Price, perched tentatively on a straight-backed chair in a corner of the room, was a stranger. I judged him to be in his early fifties, red-faced and completely bald save for a narrow fringe circling his head behind his ears. He wore bushy side-whiskers, but his lip and chin were clean-shaven. His clothes were conservative and well-fitting, if drab and a bit threadbare, and I sized him up correctly to be a minor merchant or shopkeeper.

"Mr. David Cordor," Price said, "may I present Mr. Robert Furlong. Mr. Furlong has brought us information most vital to young Robinson's case. It appears that he can prove an alibi for Robinson on the evening of the murder between nine-thirty and ten-fifteen. You will note that is precisely the time when Rosina Townsend claims to have admitted the young man to her house and recognized him."

I looked quickly at Furlong, who returned my look briefly and then averted his eyes from mine in what then seemed to me a decidedly furtive manner.

"Mr. Cordor," Price continued to Furlong, "is associated with Lon Quinncannon, and therefore, after a fashion, with the defense in the trial. I'd like you to repeat for him the events which occurred in your shop on the evening of April 9, exactly as you described them to me."

The red-faced man shifted his gaze from Price to me and back again. "Yes, well, uh, you must understand, gentlemen, I had no idea that my testimony was so important."

"Well, you may take my word, sir, it is extremely important," Price said. "How is justice to be done unless honest citizens such as yourself come forth to tell what they know in open court? Pray proceed, sir, proceed."

I leaned against the wall, my arms folded. Furlong began uncertainly but soon warmed to his tale. "I keep a grocery store, Mr. Cordor, at the corner of Nassau and Liberty Streets. I've been in business there for twenty-six years. I knew Mr. Robinson by sight but not by name. He often came into my store to buy seegars and sometimes stayed to have a glass of gin and pass the time. He was in on the evening of Saturday, April 9, at nine-thirty, and purchased a bundle of seegars containing twenty-five. He then lighted one and took a grocer's seat on a barrel, and sat smoking and talking with me until the clock in Clinton Hall struck ten."

"Was there anyone else in your store during that time?" I asked.

"Yes, my porter, but he was asleep when the boy came in, and remained dozing, with his head laid back and his mouth wide open, until Robinson, in a jocular manner, knocked the ashes off his second seegar upon his face, which awoke him just before the clock struck ten."

That, at least, had a ring of truth to it. It sounded in character for the "jocular" Robinson. "What," I inquired, "makes you so certain of the time?"

"When the clock struck," Furlong answered, "my porter said, 'There is ten o'clock, and it is time to shut up.' Robinson remarked that he thought the Clinton Hall clock was before times, and he took out his watch—a small silver Lepine—to compare it with mine. We discovered it was one minute past ten."

"You would recognize this watch if you saw it again?"

"Oh, yes," exclaimed the grocer. "I knew it the minute Mr. Price showed it to me."

I glanced at Price. His ferret's mouth was smiling slightly. Methodically, he knocked the ash off his seegar, perhaps into the face of an imaginary porter.

"Go on," I said to Furlong.

"Well, Robinson remained smoking until the porter got the store shut up. After the store was closed the young man said to me that he was afraid he was encroaching on my time, but I said, 'Oh, no, not at all.' Before he went away he stood with me a short time on the steps and then said, 'I believe I will go home, I am tired,' and he bade me good night. This, I would estimate, was about ten-fifteen."

"I see," I said without much conviction. "At the time you saw him, what was Robinson wearing?"

"A dark frock coat and mixed drab pantaloons with a cap," Furlong answered, rather too quickly to suit me.

"No cloak?" I asked.

"No cloak," he said.

"Please explain to Mr. Cordor how you happened to come forward with your evidence," Price said.

"Well, on Monday—that would have been the eleventh—I read about the murder in the papers and that a young clerk from Mr. Hoxie's store had been arrested. I had always thought that Robinson was a clerk somewhere in the neighborhood, but at first, of course, I made no connection between him and the accused because I'd never learned his name. At last, not having seen the young man in my store as I was accustomed, I had the curiosity to come here to Bellevue to see if I recognized the prisoner. I did recognize him at once as the boy who had been in my store that Saturday night, and was myself recognized by the prisoner. Robinson requested me to communicate immediately with his attorneys."

Price jumped to his feet. "Thank you, Mr. Furlong. I'd like just a moment alone with Mr. Cordor, if you would not mind waiting in Mr. Lyons' office." He opened a door and ushered the grocer out.

When the lawyer turned back to me I said, "He's lying, you know."

"The jury will love him," Price said, smacking his fat lips.

"Does Hoffman know about him?"

"He does."

"Where *is* Hoffman?"

"Indisposed," Price replied, and I nodded. In his later years Ogden Hoffman was fighting an increasingly losing battle with first-rate Scotch whiskey. Sober, he was still the finest courtroom orator in the country. Even Daniel Webster was not his equal. But, sadly, his "unfortunate weakness," as his friends termed it, was gradually getting the best of him, and many of us suspected that, win or lose, the Robinson case was to be his last.

"Where is Quinncannon?" Price asked sharply, as though I were on the witness stand.

"God knows. I haven't heard a word from him. But he won't be pleased when he learns about Furlong."

Price attempted a snort. "What pleases or displeases Mr. Quinncannon does not concern me."

"Perhaps not, Whit," I said. "Still, if that's true, I can't help wondering why you brought me here to parade your witness in front of me like a trained dog."

He showed his teeth. "I merely thought Mr. Furlong's testimony might be worth a line or two in the *Sun* newspaper, lad," he said. "That's all. That's all."

## 29  The Rescue

The storm which had been gathering when I arrived at the prison was about to break as I left. The crowd had dwindled only slightly, and when I emerged they pressed forward and then fell back in angry disappointment. They had expected to see the girl from Rosina Townsend's whom they still imagined to be closeted inside with the prisoner.

The two hansoms stood together at the rear of the crowd, the hackmen at the heads of their horses and engaged in agitated conversation. When he saw me, my driver sprang up to his box with evident relief. "Glad you've come, sir," he shouted down. "We're in for a hell of a storm, and that mob's getting mighty restless, if you was to ask me."

Lightning flashed through the ebony sky, followed by low, ominous rumblings of thunder, and then a roar went up from the mob and I turned in the act of mounting to the cab to see a young woman appear from the grim prison and stand alone on the steps before the iron doors, which now swung shut with clanging finality behind her. Shouting and waving their arms, the crowd surged toward her as her driver leaped to his seat, and she began to run down the steps and across the treacherous cobblestones toward him. In another instant, huge raindrops were splashing into the yard and she suddenly lost her footing and sprawled forward to the ground. There was a brilliant flash of light and an immense clap of thunder, and both horses reared in terror. Both hackmen shouted and cracked their whips, and then, as I clung to my own cab to keep from being thrown off, I saw the other hansom dash madly for the gates, leaving the girl struggling to regain her feet while the mob moved ponderously toward her.

I bellowed to my driver to hold his horse on penalty of his life, dropped to the pavement, and sprinted toward the fallen girl, gathering her up in my arms and racing back to the hansom. I managed to hoist her up into the cab, leaped to the dashboard, yelled to the driver, and the vehicle lurched forward, tore through the gates, and veered down Second Avenue with sparks flying from the horse's hooves.

I swung in beside the girl as the rain began to pound down on the roof of the hansom, loosened the ribbons of her bonnet beneath her chin, and removed it and the heavy veil attached to it. At that second another bolt of lightning flashed above us and I looked down into the ashen, unconscious, and delicately beautiful face of Sophia Willett. Her rich reddish-brown hair fell over my arm and touched my hand.

For one horrible moment I dwelled on the thought of what might have happened to her in the yard of Bellevue prison. Then, as the cab careened wildly into Broadway and the thunder crashed and the skies emptied their deluge over us, I pressed her as tightly as I could against my breast.

I brought Miss Willett, still unconscious, to Quinncannon's door and carried her up to his rooms after sending the housekeeper for a doctor. I waited downstairs while the physician was with her, but jumped to my feet when I heard steps descending the stairs.

"She's going to be fine, son," the doctor said, "but she needs rest and quiet at the moment."

"Do you wish to see her, sir?" the little housemaid asked.

I took an eager step forward, then caught myself. "Only if the lady asks for me," I said.

The doctor held up his hand. "Out of the question, at least until tomorrow. I've given her a sedative, which should allow her to sleep straight through the night."

I nodded. "I'll take a room at the American tonight," I said. "I'd appreciate it, Doctor, if you would write a message which I could have delivered to her aunt in Greenwich Village. The old lady is probably frantic by now."

While he wrote the note and I engaged a cab to deliver it, Aggie, the housemaid, slipped out the street door and came up behind me. When I turned back to the house I almost tripped over the girl.

"Oh, sir," she cried, "she's *beautiful!*"

"Yes, Aggie, I've noticed."

"And, sir," she said, "she *did,* you know."

"Did what?"

"Why, ask to see you!"

"Did she?" I smiled. "Now, Aggie, that's very kind of you to tell me."

I said nothing else of importance to anyone, but when I had entered my room at the hotel and closed the door I found myself whistling for no reason in particular.

# 30 A Digression

In order that I might make clear many of the events which follow, some mention should be made of the evolution of police work, both in America and in Europe, prior to the Jewett case. Modern police methods, as they are now understood in the nineteenth century, began in 1810 in Paris with the creation of the Sûreté under the command of M. Eugène François Vidocq. Vidocq, who has become something of a legend, did not resign his post until 1833, and has since established an agency of private detectives. I have often heard it said, especially by William Attree, that Quinncannon was a particular protégé of Vidocq and spent time as an investigator in the Sûreté. It is further rumored that Quinncannon left Paris in 1832, shortly before Vidocq was relieved, and arrived in Boston in time to be consulted by the Methodist Church fathers of that city in the matter of Ephraim K. Avery.

Such stories, however, are clearly slanderous, since it is well known that Vidocq employed only convicted criminals in the Sûreté. A believer in the ancient adage that it takes a thief, Vidocq was, himself, an ex-convict who had served his time beside the most vicious criminals in France, among them the Cornu family, which instructed their children in homicide and accustomed the tots to cadavers by permitting them to play with the severed heads of their victims.

Whether or not Quinncannon ever worked for the Sûreté, he had, so far as I could tell, little use for Vidocq's methods. The Frenchman was fond of disguises, made wide use of a vast network of underground informers and *agents provocateur,* and maintained extensive files detailing the appearance of known criminals and their methods of operation. By contrast the Irishman never went out in disguise, thoroughly distrusted informers, and kept no criminal archives of any kind. "I can recollect all I need of the human capacity for crime," he once told me, "by glancing through the morning paper."

The uniqueness of Vidocq's Sûreté lay ultimately in their political independence. Their function was not, as the function of virtually all police had been before Vidocq's time, to unearth "enemies of the state" but to arrest apolitical felons—thieves, embezzlers, burglars, and murderers—criminals who posed a danger to society regardless of what faction was in power at the moment. In this alone, perhaps, lies Vidocq's greatest contribution to the modern role of the police in civilized society.

In one way the English were almost a century in advance of the French in the development of police work. Certainly the Bow Street Runners anticipated M. Vidocq's minions in both character and method. But, in a more profound sense, London was almost two decades behind Paris, for it was not until December of 1829 that Sir Robert Peel was able to found the London Metropolitan Police.

It is generally acknowledged that it was the English concept of individual civil liberty which so long led that nation to regard any suggestion of a police force with the deepest suspicion. The English frankly feared that the police, once established, would divide their time between illegal collusion with criminal elements and obnoxious harassment of decent citizens. By contrast the United States, a country with at least as much pretension to concern over individual liberties, had created police forces in most of its major cities nearly thirty years before Peel's Police Bill was passed.

Ironically, British fears of the consequences of an official police have proven far more justified in America.

But I anticipate myself.

"The ancestors of the police in every nation of the world were criminals," Quinncannon once observed to me. "It is not surprising, Davy, that blood will tell."

In England, by 1700, crime had become so rampant that justices of the peace found themselves increasingly reliant on informers, self-styled law enforcers, reward seekers, bounty hunters, or, as they all came to be dignified, thief-takers.

The most infamous of these, Jonathan Wild, headed an organization of these vigilantes and called himself "Thief-Taker General of Great Britain and Ireland" before he was hung for robbery at Tyburn in 1725.

In 1750 the English novelist Henry Fielding, who was also justice of the peace for Middlesex and Westminster, with his chambers in Bow Street, wheedled enough money from the British Secret Service to establish a small force of a dozen men, the originals of the Bow Street Runners. The Runners continued after Fielding's death in 1754 under his successor, his blind half brother, Sir John. It is said that by his own death in 1780 John Fielding could distinguish three thousand outlaws by their voices.

But the Bow Street Runners gained a reputation every bit as unsavory as the thief-takers of a century ago. Crime prevention became a bunco game with a hundred variations. Youngsters were seduced into felonies and then betrayed for the prices on their heads. Stolen goods were returned for rewards which were then divided with the burglars. Innocent men were incriminated for a fee from the guilty, or for a reward, or both.

By 1828 in England it was estimated that there was one professional criminal for every 822 citizens—a total of 30,000 men and women who lived habitually outside the law—and still it was necessary for Peel to risk his political career by, in effect, ramming his "Bobbies" down his countrymen's throats. As I write this, there is still no detective force as such in London, no English equivalent to the Sûreté, except about fifteen Bow Street Runners; for the "Bobbies," jeeringly nicknamed for Bobby Peel, are uniformed officers whose efforts are largely directed at minor crimes.

In New York, Jacob Hays had been appointed high constable in 1802, only three years after the murder of Elma Sands, and had recruited such a tough gang of enforcers and hooligans that only Hays' personal reputation for total honesty held his staff together for almost thirty-five years. By the time of the Jewett murder, "Old Hays," as he was now known to all segments of society on both sides of the law, had become an institution.

The New York police are separated into a day force and a night force, the former called roundsmen and the latter watchmen, also known to the populace as "leatherheads," since 1827, when they began wearing leather helmets. The watch are required to varnish these helmets twice a year, and for many of them, this is the most exhausting of their duties. Their nights are whiled away drinking in the taverns or catching up on their sleep in one of the watchboxes, where more than once they may be ambushed by the gangs of young toughs who prowl through the slumbering city. If they are lucky their helmets are stolen. If they are not, a rope is looped around the box and the whole affair, leatherhead and all, dragged triumphantly through the streets.

The roundsmen are plainclothesmen but, with very few exceptions, scarcely detectives. No training is required in criminal investigation or, for that matter, in anything else. No physical or written examinations are given and few of these men are particularly imposing or athletic. They are enlisted, primarily, from the ranks of unemployed stevedores, porters, and laborers. They are political appointees and their jobs are generally just as safe as the next election. Here lies a major weakness of the system, for while in Britain and France the police are kept largely clear of political influence, in our country they have become part of the unscrupulous patronage game so recently dignified by the approval of no less a personage than General Jackson himself.

No regular salary is paid. The roundsmen would have to subsist on what they receive for serving warrants and on puny dollar-a-day witness fees, but for the rewards collected, primarily for the return of stolen goods, and for the fees received for hiring out their services to private citizens. These same evils pervaded the Bow Street Runners, with the same pernicious results: bribery, blackmail, and blood money.

# 31 *The Liberty Street Horror*

The event which I must now describe matched for sheer horror anything that occurred in connection with the Jewett case. On the evening of May 21, I retired early to my room in the American Hotel, glowing with pleasure, it must be admitted, over the fate which had presented me the opportunity to do heroic service for Sophia Willett, and filled with anticipation for the morning when that lovely lady should again ask to see me. It was not yet six o'clock when I was awakened by someone vigorously shaking my shoulder and calling my name. With a heavy groan I rolled over and squinted up at the leathery face of Colum Pheety Ryan.

"They told me at Mr. Quinncannon's where to find you." His breath would have felled an ox. "I think he's dead!"

I was instantly awake. "Quinncannon?"

He shook his great head. "No, laddie. 'Twas himself told me to shadow him and report to you if something smelled wrong." He took a pull on a bottle of gin and offered it to me, but I declined. My rule is never before sunrise.

"Who?" I demanded. "Who did Quinncannon tell you to shadow?"

"Cushing," Ryan rumbled. "Thomas Cushing. Only I don't like the look of it. Him locked in his rooms all night and the curtains drawn on all the windows. He don't answer when you rap on his door, but I know the man's got to be inside." He stared at me without blinking. "I tell you, he ain't among the living."

I was still buttoning my coat while our cab rushed down Broadway and into Liberty. The dreary rooming house was in dire need of paint and repair. As I jumped to the pavement the street door opened and a portly man of about thirty appeared on the steps, obviously distraught and glancing hastily in all directions. "That's Meeks," Colum Ryan said. "Cushing's roommate."

Mr. Meeks puffed toward us, sweating and wringing his pudgy hands. He eyed the huge Gaelic gorilla with some terror, but decided to address me. "A watchman is required, sir. We are in urgent exigency for a watchman."

"Is it Mr. Cushing?" I asked.

"It is indeed." He peered up at me, his swine jowls quivering. "May I query, are you coadjutive with the police?"

"I am conducting a private inquiry," I said.

By this I intended to convey the impression that I was an officer but involved in an unofficial investigation, and I succeeded, for Meeks immediately took me into his confidence.

"My name is Meeks, sir, Obadiah Meeks. Mr. Cushing and myself share rooms and have both been employed for an extensive tenure as bookkeepers in the house of Bailey, Keeler, and Remsen. For the past week, sir, Mr. Cushing has been sufficiently indisposed to prevent him from attending to his business; however, last evening he appeared to be quite convalescent. His demeanor was almost salubrious when I left him at seven. But when I returned between eleven and twelve I discovered our door locked and bolted from inside, and when I solicited admittance, Mr. Cushing responded through the door, 'Mr. Meeks, I would rather you don't come in tonight.' Those, sir, were the very words."

"And what did you do then, Mr. Meeks?"

"Why," the little fat man replied, "I went away. The door, you see, was locked, sir."

"Have you your key now?" I asked.

He nodded. "But the door is still locked from inside."

"And bolted also?"

"Why, naturally, sir, I *assumed* . . ."

The others followed me into the house. I tried the door which Meeks pointed out and found it fast. I knocked and called Cushing's name.

"That is nugatory, sir," Mr. Meeks said. "Mr. Cushing does not answer."

"I could put my fist right through that door," Colum Ryan observed. He could have, too.

"Your key, Mr. Meeks," I said, and he surrendered it. I inserted it in the lock and turned it, and the door clicked open and slowly gave way on creaking hinges. Meeks seemed astounded. "But," he sputtered, "that is *most* prodigious."

Again I spoke Cushing's name without response. I stepped into a dingy sitting room, shabbily furnished and dimly illuminated by the few shafts of gray light permitted by the tightly drawn draperies. The air was close and musty and smelled slightly of roses. There was a bolt lock on the inside of the door, but the bolt had been drawn back. Two doors appeared in the rear wall of the room, one leading to Meeks' bedroom, the other to Cushing's.

On a dressing table in the outer room lay a volume of the writings of Seneca open to the heading "Anger." Beside the book lay an open razor. It was covered with blood. Blood had dripped onto the small rug beneath the table, and a trail of drops of dried blood led away, across the hardwood floor, toward Cushing's bedroom.

"Jesus, Mary, and Joseph!" Colum Ryan said under his breath.

Thomas Cushing lay on his back on the floor, halfway into his bedroom, with his head toward the sitting room. His eyes were wide open and gaped sightlessly up into my own. He was fully dressed except for his coat, vest, and boots. His throat had been cut in a single gash from ear to ear, nearly slicing his head from his body. The neck muscles were cut down to the spinal column, so that his backbone was visible. The large blood vessels transporting blood to and from the brain were severed and he lay weltering in a hugh pool of blood. His windpipe and gullet were slit through.

I turned toward a choking sound behind me. Mr. Meeks shook himself all over like a fat, wet pug dog. But it was Colum Pheety Ryan who commenced to vomit.

The police were summoned, and Mr. Schureman, the coroner, held an inquest at the house on the body of the man I now recognized as the same who had mistaken me for Quinncannon on Broadway less than a week before. Cushing was a native of Richmond, Virginia, age twenty-seven, for the last five years resident in New York.

It developed from Meeks' testimony that Cushing had been something of a hermit. "His general habits were moody and retired, and he was occasionally subject to fits of melancholy." Even Meeks, who worked beside him and shared his quarters, and who was Cushing's only friend, knew little about him. The two had never addressed each other by their first names.

The jury declared the razor, which was identified as Cushing's, to be the weapon used, and they accepted the police theory that the dead man "cut his throat in the sitting room where the razor was found, and, in attempting to get to his own room, fell on the floor, where he expired." Relying heavily on the evidence of Meeks, their verdict was "suicide, committed while laboring under a temporary insanity."

While the jury deliberated, I had returned to the death room, where the officer on guard, a friend of Quinncannon's, unlocked the door with Mr. Meeks' key. The body still lay where I'd found it, covered with a shroud of oilcloth. I rolled back the cloth until only the head and throat were concealed and forced myself to go through the pockets. Then I stepped over the corpse into the bedroom and checked Cushing's coat and vest. I rifled the drawers in all three rooms, probed under the dead man, peered behind drapes, poked beneath cushions, and was at last reduced to crawling about on all fours, rummaging through the dust wads under the furniture, but it was *not* there.

"Hilliker," I said to the officer who was staring at me as if I were mad, "did the police find a door key in here?"

"No, sir," he replied. "Did you lose one?"

"No, Hilliker."

"Oh," he said, eyeing me cautiously. "Well, then, that explains it."

"Yes, Hilliker."

I twice paced off the distance from Cushing's feet to the dressing table where the razor had been found. Then I dusted myself off. "Just one more question, Hilliker."

Warily he said, "Yes, sir?"

I spoke confidentially. "Where would I find the privy?"

He brightened. "Oh. It's just down the hall, sir, in the rear yard. But the door is locked. I'll have to open it for you."

"Is it always kept locked?"

"Night and day, sir. But it's no problem for the boarders. All the room keys open it."

From the doorway I could see that the fences in the surrounding yards were low and contained gates. Abruptly nodding to Hilliker, I left him in a state of considerable confusion.


When the verdict was in, I found Colum Pheety Ryan on the front stoop looking pale and sheepish and obviously out of gin. "You won't say nothing to the boys at the Points about it, will you, lad? Or to himself? I'd never hear the finish of it!"

I pitied the big man's embarrassment and swore an oath of secrecy.

"I saw a fellow was killed like that once," he insisted on explaining. " 'Twas my first berth—Mate Beamer on the *Mary Deere*—the whole crew hated his vitals—and one night three weeks out of Liverpool somebody with a knife caught him alone on watch. I was only a lad and I saw it. Cushing in there, he brought it all back."

I was thinking. "Colum, when the mate's throat was cut, how many steps did he take before he fell?"

"Why, none at all, Davy. He dropped like a rock!"

"And so would any reasonable, God-fearing man," I said, "but Tom Cushing took five."

"Now," said Ryan, "that's damn queer!"

"Isn't it? And there's something else. Cushing locked himself in with his key and now the key has vanished."

"Well, what do you make of that, Davy?"

"Colum Pheety, I don't know what I make of it."

"I don't know what you make of it either, lad. But himself will know," he added with conviction. "Himself will know what it means."

# 32  Mr. Cordor Meets the Family

The desk clerk at the American handed me a message when I returned. I eagerly assailed the envelope, having guessed whose graceful hand had addressed it. The contents brought me both disappointment and hope.

> *Sunday, May 22   10 a.m.*
>
> *My dear Mr. Cordor,*
>
> *Having learned from Dr. Bond something of your heroic action yesterday on my behalf, I desired to express my obligation to you in person, but I find you were called away suddenly from your hotel. I regret that I must return at once to the home of my dear aunt who, in spite of your kind note to her, must be beside herself with worry.*
>
> *As I am already so deeply obliged to you, I must shamelessly request one more favor of you. Would you be so kind as to attend a small supper party at my aunt's home, number 1, Gansevoort Street, this Thursday evening at 8:00? I so look forward to showing you off.*
>
> *Yours in gratitude,*
> *Sophia Willett*

I purchased a new frock coat in honor of the event. On Thursday evening I stood before the full-length mirror in Quinncannon's rooms flicking tiny specks of lint from the lapels, carefully smoothing my hair across my forehead, and occasionally dabbing with some concern at a nick I had opened on my chin with my razor. The housemaid knocked and stuck her head into the room. "There's a coachman downstairs asking for you, sir."

To the coachman's confusion I insisted on riding up on the box beside him, which was permitted after I had promised to take a seat in the carriage before we reached our destination. At my direction we drove west on Fulton and took the scenic route up West Street beside the river.

A slight breeze was blowing and the cool air tasted of salt. The setting sun, visible over the rim of the Jersey Palisades, crowned each ripple on the water with silver. To the south two great packet ships were docked, one just arrived from Le Havre, the other loaded and ready to depart. The North River was dotted with the white and yellow sails of small boats leisurely tacking toward their moorings off Hoboken before darkness set in. Great crowds prepared to board the *Nimrod* at the foot of Liberty Street for the overnight voyage to Albany. Smaller groups gathered at Barclay Street for the steamer to Newark or ran for the last ferry of the evening for Hoboken.

It was dark when we reached the foot of Troy Street and I yielded to the coachman's pleas that I ride the last three blocks inside the carriage. We rolled through the stone gateposts and down a gravel path between rows of towering poplars, stopping before the front door, where small black boys seized the horses' heads and a liveried footman with a lantern lighted my way up the steps of the magnificent three-story house.

Just within the brilliantly lit entrance hall I was greeted by a handsome, elderly woman, stylishly dressed and with bright, pale-blue, smiling eyes which made me welcome before she herself had.

"Mr. Cordor? I am Abigail Willett," she said, offering me her hand. When she saw me looking past her to the splendid staircase which rose at the left of the hall, the lady smiled. "She has not come down yet, Mr. Cordor. I believe she was waiting for your arrival to make her grand entrance." She took my arm and steered me to the drawing room. "Won't you come in and meet the boys?"

"The boys" were Miss Sophia's brothers. Marinus, the elder, had been named for his grandfather, who had held office as mayor of New York in 1807–8. He was about twenty-four, tall, stoop-shouldered, and balding. He was clerking law for Livingstone and Hicks. He drank sherry, had an evident sinus condition, and spoke with a slight lisp.

Philip, the younger brother, was the namesake of his great-grandfather, who had fought heroically (I was informed by Aunt Abigail, the family historian) during the Revolution. Philip was eighteen and in his second year at Columbia College. The family resemblance to his sister was strong—he was slender with wavy, reddish-brown hair and an easy smile—and I liked him at once. On the snuffling, posturing Marinus, I charitably decided to reserve judgment.

"I should say to you, Mr. Cordor [he pronounced it *Cawdaw*]," said Marinus, "what my father [he pronounced it *fawther*] would say, were he present. The family is deeply appreciative of your successfully protective action toward my sister."

"I was fortunate enough to be able to be of service, Mr. Willett," I responded, accepting a Scotch from Philip.

"Although what my sister was doing at Bellevue," Marinus continued, "I must confess remains a mystery to me. Surely she cannot retain any feeling for that Robinson creature. Yet she has always had the most abominable taste in young men."

Aunt Abigail glanced at me. "Really, Marinus!"

"Awww," he said, "Aunty!" (He pronounced it *Awntee*.)

Philip sat with his ankles crossed and his drink clutched in both hands on the very edge of the ottoman belonging to my chair. "Is it true, Mr. Cordor, that you actually work with Lon Quinncannon?"

"Nonsense, Philip," said Aunt Abigail. "Mr. Cordor is a journalist."

"I am," I said, "but, Philip, I am also associated with Mr. Quinncannon."

"Dear me," exclaimed Aunt Abigail. "That dreadful man!"

"How exciting!" Philip cried. "Have you been investigating the murder, then? Do you really think that Robinson will hang?"

"Philip!" said Marinus sternly, "you know Awntee has forbidden his name in her house."

"Do you think," Philip rephrased, "that the prisoner will hang?"

"I think it most likely," I replied.

"Dear me," said the old lady again. "I hope not. Of all the uses to which a handsome young man may be put, hanging does seem the least satisfactory."

Since my arrival I had kept my eyes on the foot of the hall staircase, which I could just see through the door of the room. At last Miss Sophia descended the stairs. She wore an elegant, light-blue ball gown with a single strand of pearls at her throat, and her rich russet hair fell in lustrous waves over her white shoulders. Extravagant similes struggling to convey her spirit and beauty as I felt them at that moment would be foolish and futile. She walked toward me, smiling warmly and holding out her hand, and I rose to take it in my own. It was not a conscious thought then, but I believe it was at that instant I determined to make Sophia Willett my wife.

I recall a little of the conversation at supper. Marinus droned on at some length regarding his preference for Mr. Webster over Mr. Van Buren in the coming election. Finding that no one was listening (except Aunt Abigail, who remarked that in *her* opinion neither candidate was a match for "that noble gentleman," Mr. Quincy Adams), Marinus eventually lapsed into moody silence. His place as chief interlocutor was eagerly filled by Philip, who proceeded to regale us with his impressions of his college professors, cheerfully unconcerned over whether anyone was interested or not.

"McVickar is all right, and Anthon too, though the old fellow's a bit stodgy, but 'Dr. Blowpipe,' alias Professor Renwick!—*there* is a pedagogue to warm the heart of the late Diedrich Knickerbocker! The chemical room is the greatest of all farces. We had a grand crash in Renwick's a week ago. Some worthies tied one end of a string to the knob of the door, carried it out through the laboratory window, and tied it to a large box containing nearly a bushel of glass bottles, cracked retorts, and so on. When the door opened, crash it went like a volley of artillery! Renwick was in fidgets to find who did it." He felt his aunt's disapproving eye and quickly added, "I had no hand in it."

"I should hope not!" said the lady.

Philip caught my knowing look and smiled. I was recalling that dead cow in the tutor's room at Princeton.

"All that was merely an hors d'oeuvre," the boy continued merrily, "compared to the main course they served poor Jemmy this afternoon. The 'gunpowder plot' was carried into effect finely! A tremendous howling was begun around Renwick's door when the class came in, and the moment his back was turned to find out the authors of it, the slow matches were fired and a general *feu de joie* commenced—double headers—squibs and spiders—in sublime confusion. Renwick attempted to put them out, but some must have been left, and they kept popping off during the whole hour at the rate of one every five minutes. When the class went out, the grand finale was played, consisting of a larger box containing perhaps thirty pounds of glass retorts and all sorts of articles, which was hauled down from the top of the highest shelves by a string through one of the windows. Poor Jemmy! They'll tease him out of his senses!"

The boy laughed happily while his aunt shook her head and clucked her tongue. "Really, Philip, if your father could hear you."

"Ah, but he can't," Philip said playfully, "unless, of course, old brother Marinus goes running to tell him."

"Your juvenile pranks are of no particular consequence to me." Marinus sniffed. "Though it does seem a pity to waste Fawther's good money sending you to the college if that is a sample of the way you deport yourself there."

"Now, now, Marinus," said Aunt Abigail mildly.

"Well, it's true," the law clerk protested, "and you know it, Awntee. Philip with his childish escapades and Sophia becoming involved with that—that notorious *person*—and slipping off behind your back to go to that prison! Ever since Mother died, both you and Fawther have continuously winked at their indiscretions. You well know that if it were up to me I should shackle them both to their beds until they were twenty-one."

"Really, Marinus," the old lady responded. "You should sympathize with your brother and sister. I have your father's word for it that you were young once yourself. Besides, we have a guest at the table."

"It's all right, Aunty." Sophia laughed lightly, like the sound of a silver teaspoon tinkling against crystal. "Everyone knows that Philip is a disorderly scamp, badly in need of discipline, and as for my own hopeless incorrigibility . . ." She placed her hand over mine. "No one is a better witness of that than Mr. Cordor."

I'm afraid I blushed deeply, not at her words, but at the touch of her hand. I suspect her aunt noticed, but neither of her brothers did. Marinus glowered at the chandelier, while Philip said, "Sophia's quite right, you know. Never mind, Marinus. We're all aware that you were born at the age of fifty and we make allowances."

The boy shifted the conversation easily into a more pleasant direction. "Did I mention that Chittenden and Templeton-Strong are after me to join that mysterious fraternity, the ΦBK? As no information about the society can be gained before you are tied fast to it, it is something like a leap in the dark, or a Turkish marriage, but still I'd like to join, though it is so exclusive I can't imagine I have much chance of succeeding . . ."

The meal was excellent, though I have now no recollection of the menu. Afterward I passed up an invitation from Marinus to retire to the library for brandy and seegars in favor of a tour of the grounds by moonlight conducted by Sophia. It was a beautiful, cloudless night. The lawns of the estate swept down to the river, where the beams of the nearly full moon glanced off the water with shimmering grace. On the opposite bank the Palisades loomed in shadowy majesty against the deep, placid blue of the western sky. For a few moments we saw the North River much as it must have appeared to the captain of the *Half Moon* as he glided quietly up its gentle waters. Then the blazing decks of a steamboat came into view, probably the *Nimrod* on her way to Albany. The darkness hid the massive, ugly clouds of smoke which belched from her stacks. Gay music and gayer laughter drifted from her decks across the water. I had the sudden, bittersweet sense that this was a moment in time which would never come again and which I must reach out for and seize and hold fast. I took my arm from hers, groped for her hand, found it, and squeezed it tightly.

"I do love this place," she said. "It's so beautiful and tranquil—so different from Father's house, where there are always carriages in the drive and mud on the carpets and the odor of seegars in the sitting room. Yet, I must confess, Mr. Cordor, that in the past several weeks I have, at times, been terribly nostalgic for a little mud and the smell of tobacco." She looked up at me. "Does that seem awful?"

"Not at all, Miss Willett," I said; "in fact, I find it encouraging. I have a confession or two of my own to make. My landlady, with the sharp eye of an Indian, can reconstruct all my movements from my tracks on the carpet, and I am, I'm sorry to say, rather addicted to tobacco."

"Seegars?"

"No, a pipe, I'm afraid."

"Why, that's wonderful," she cried. "Father has always smoked a pipe. Aunty, too, though she'd never admit it. I've always loved to fill Father's pipe and light it for him, ever since I was a little girl. Won't you let me light yours?"

We found a bench and sat down, and I gave her my pipe and tobacco pouch. She skillfully filled the bowl and tamped down the mixture, then lit a match and sucked in her cheeks until the pipe glowed orange in the darkness. She handed it to me and folded her shawl more tightly against the cool river breeze, and I put my arm around her shoulders. She rested her head against my breast. "How do you like them?" she said.

"I think your aunt is charming," I answered, "and I like your brothers very much."

"Marinus *is* a terrible stuffed shirt," she said, as if I had expressed that opinion, "but he's really a dear, and completely devoted to Philip and me. I think if I was really in trouble, Marinus is the first person I would turn to. He's an awful bore and he does make a rotten first impression, but he's just like a rock in a crisis. He was marvelous when Mother died. The rest of us were quite helpless—even Father." She paused. *"Especially* Father. You must meet him. He's such a gruff old bear. Father will like you. Marinus, you know, was sent tonight to spy on you and report back to Father. And Marinus liked you—I could tell."

I was glad she could tell. I'd had no hint of it.

"You *do* like Philip," she said. "Everyone likes Philip. Isn't he handsome? There are at least a dozen girls quite dotty over him. He's studying to be a surgeon when he grows up." She smiled. "Even though he's a year older than I am, we all think of Philip as the baby of the family."

The night was perfectly still except for the constant chirping of the crickets. The steamboat had passed and the river was so quiet that once in a while I imagined I'd heard a fish jump. A small black spider struggled to crawl over the folds of her dress. "Don't move," I said, and flicked it onto the lawn.

"What was it?"

"Spider, I think. A very little one."

"Oh, I'm not afraid of spiders. Just now I don't feel as if I could be afraid of anything."

She moved nearer to me. I could smell the scent of her hair. "Did I tell you that the driver of the hansom came to see me the morning after you rescued me? A very nice man named Sheridan—he brought me some flowers. He told me all about how you stood between me and those dreadful men, and how you carried me to the cab. He said that he was frightened to death but you were as cool as ice. It was a very brave thing you did, Mr. Cordor."

"It was a very foolish thing you did, Miss Willett," I replied gently.

"Yes," she said, "I can see that now. It accomplished nothing, you know. Oh, he consented to see me, but he really didn't listen to a word I said."

"Are you speaking," I asked, "of Robinson?"

She laughed. "Good heavens, why should I want to visit Richard? I went to talk to the district attorney—to convince him, as I convinced Mr. Quinncannon, that Richard is simply incapable of that terrible crime." For a moment I felt her shoulders tense. "It just seems so *obvious!*" She relaxed against my arm. "But Mr. Phenix didn't believe me. I'm afraid it was rather a foolish impulse."

I held her more tightly. "It was a very generous impulse," I said, "but extremely dangerous. Perhaps your brother Marinus is right. You should be locked up until you're twenty-one."

"Oh," she said, "Marinus is almost always right. It's an abominable trait. He gets it from Father, who is *absolutely* always right. They inherited it from Grandfather, the one who was mayor. I rather suspect Philip and I are throwbacks to Great-grandfather Philip, the pirate."

"I thought he was a hero in the Revolution."

She laughed again. "That's Aunty's version of the story. He was a privateer during the war. According to the family history, he offered his services to the Continental Congress and was commissioned by John Paul Jones himself. But there is a legend that originally he was a 'London Trader' who made a fortune smuggling provisions and ammunition from Sandy Hook to the British in Manhattan. When he was captured, he simply proposed to General Washington that he switch sides. But I seem to be doing all the talking."

I puffed on my pipe and drew her closer to me. "I enjoy hearing you talk."

"Tell me about your family," she said.

"Very little to tell. Most of them were hung. A few managed to die in bed, and seldom was it their own bed they died in."

"But are you all alone, then?"

I nodded.

"How awful!"

"I'm used to it," I said. "I've been on my own for some time and I find I prefer it."

"I've always believed," she said, moving very close to me, "that independence matures a man so much earlier. Truthfully, Mr. Cordor, you seem to be remarkably self-sufficient. I feel terribly safe when I'm with you."

"Perhaps, Miss Willett, you shouldn't feel quite so safe."

She rolled her head over on my breast and gazed up at me. "Really, Mr. Cordor?"

"Really, Miss Willett," I said, "because when you sit as near to me as you are at this moment, I find I have a compulsion to take you in my arms and make love to you."

"Dear me," she said. "A compulsion! That's virtually irresistible, isn't it?" She held her face next to mine and shut her eyes. "Well, I shall probably scream, Mr. Cordor, but I suppose it can't be helped."

I held her tenderly at first and then harder and harder against me, as I had in the hansom. She seemed to me then so fragile and warm and spirited and helpless and, above all, so beautiful. She yielded to me and I pressed my lips against hers, and then I cradled her head on my shoulder while I touched my lips gently to her hair. "Sophia, Sophia, I seem to have fallen in love with you." There were tears in my eyes.

"Oh, God, Davy," she whispered, "I think I loved you the first minute I saw you." She looked up at me. "Those gray eyes of yours seem to see to the bottom of my soul. I'm frightened, Davy. No one but you knows it, but I'm really always frightened. Hold me, Davy. Promise me you'll always hold me tight—you'll never let me go."

I held her, and I promised.

# 33  Mr. Quinncannon Explains Some Fine Points of Law

At last on Tuesday, May 31, there was word from Quinncannon, a letter dated the previous Saturday from Charleston, South Carolina:

> My dear Cordor,
>
> The elusive Miss Emma Chancellor is alive and in tow. She can, as I suspected, provide an alibi for Robinson between 9:00 and 10:30 on the night of the murder.
>
> The Charleston papers carried a reprint of the Cushing inquest by which I see you were the one to discover the body. If the evidence was accurately published here, it is obvious, doubtless to you as well, that the jury's verdict was incorrect and Cushing was brutally murdered.
>
> La Chancellor and I leave at once for New York, and will arrive in time for the trial.
>
> Q.

The letter arrived on Tuesday morning, but I did not find it until I returned that evening. I thought immediately of Robert Furlong and was relieved I had not taken Price's suggestion and published the grocer's testimony. It seemed essential, now that Chancellor had been found alive, that I communicate with Hoffman before Furlong's perjury became known.

I took a cab to Hoffman's offices in Reade Street. The door was locked and the blinds drawn, but there was a light inside and I kept rapping on the glass until the door was opened. To my immense relief Quinncannon stood before me in his shirt-sleeves, with his pipe in his teeth and a whiskey in his hand.

"I got in this morning," he said in response to my question, "and came here almost at once. There's a mountain of work, Davy. We go to trial in two days. I'm afraid I can only give you a few minutes."

He poured me a drink and I asked after Hoffman.

"At home preparing his summation for the jury, Davy. It keeps the good old fellow off the streets and off the bottle. It's to be the crowning glory of his career, I understand."

"Lon, have you seen Whitlaw Price?"

He smiled. "That popinjay! He drove me crazy for a couple of hours until I casually inquired whether he'd ever considered changing tailors. That sent him scurrying out to be fitted for a new suit for the trial. Tomorrow I'll set him to rooting out good-character witnesses for Robinson, if he can find any."

"Then," I said, "you plan to call such witnesses?"

"Good Lord, no, Davy. If we present evidence of the boy's good character, we open the way for the state to call witnesses to his *bad* character. The trial could last for weeks."

I lit my pipe. "Are you going to put Robinson on the stand?"

He shook his head.

So he *did* think his client was guilty. "Why not, Lon? Are you afraid of what he'd say under cross-examination?"

He looked up from his desk. "Davy, under the laws of this state the prisoner is not permitted to testify in his own defense."

This struck me as ridiculous and I said so.

"Oh," he said lightly, "it's sometimes advantageous."

"At least you located Emma Chancellor," I said.

"Yes, I've got her safely stashed at Madam Stewart's home for wayward girls, where Robinson used to keep her. It was a touching homecoming. Not a dry eye in the house. That should quash any attempt by the prosecution to accuse the boy of her murder."

"And," I added, "provide him with a partial alibi for the murder night."

He looked me in the eye, and the corners of his mouth tightened. "Davy," he said evenly, "I intend to use Furlong."

This required a full minute to sink in. I took a deep breath and accepted his offer of another whiskey. I sat down again and stared at him. "I just don't understand your reasoning, Lon. Chancellor is obviously telling the truth—Furlong is lying—yet you prefer to put a perjurer on the stand. For God's sake, why?"

Quinncannon leaned back, stretched, and began to massage his temples with the heels of his hands. "Davy, the district attorney is prepared to offer the testimony of three witnesses that young Robinson arrived at the murder house between nine and nine-thirty. Evidently it is in the best interests of the defense to impeach that testimony. Now, who are these three prosecution witnesses? They are harlots, procuresses, the scum of society, but, Davy"—he leaned forward—"but there are *three* of them. And who will the defense call in rebuttal? Emma Chancellor? But Emma Chancellor is herself a whore, an erstwhile resident of Elizabeth Stewart's establishment, and a lady whose presence on the stand could permit the state to raise any number of issues embarrassing to our client. And even then, Davy, they would still have *three* whores, and we would only have *one* whore to refute them. And whom do you imagine the jury would believe?"

He downed his Irish and poured another. "However, Davy, if our witness was a respectable businessman—say a grocer—a family man, middle-class, middle-aged, middle America. And this 'right-minded' fellow were to come forward, oh . . . so . . . reluctantly, out of a sense of civic duty, and give evidence that on the night of the murder, at the very moment Richard P. Robinson was supposed to be entering the house on Thomas Street with lethal intent, said Richard P. Robinson was actually perched on a pickle barrel smoking a seegar in a greengrocer's over a mile away—now, *that* is a story a jury can believe."

I sat for a while in silence, nursing my drink. Every vile accusation

Attree had ever made against Quinncannon was ringing in my head. At last I said, "What about Cushing?"

"What about him?"

"He was all but decapitated, yet he was found five steps from the bloody razor. He couldn't have killed himself. Someone slit his throat from behind as he entered his bedroom, and placed the razor on the dressing table—the trail of blood which seemed to lead from the razor to the body actually led the other way. Then the killer opened the Seneca book in a clumsy effort to simulate a suicide message. That same person locked the corpse in the room and escaped through the rear door, carrying away the key. The murderer was waiting inside, in the entry, for Cushing when Colum Ryan followed him home. That's why the big lout didn't see anyone except Meeks enter or leave the house."

Quinncannon was watching me and smiling. "Very good, lad, excellent."

"You know Cushing was murdered," I pressed. "Suppose his death is connected with Jewett's. Robinson couldn't have killed him because Robinson is in jail. Couldn't you use that somehow?"

He shook his head. "At the moment I don't see how. Poor Cushing. The unfortunate fellow even wrote asking to see me, but I didn't find the note until I returned this morning. His death is inadmissible unless the prosecution inadvertently lets it slip in on direct examination. And even then an inquest has already ruled it suicide. It would probably only confuse the jury. One murder at a time is an excellent rule with juries."

"What is this," I asked, "about the state having *three* witnesses to place Robinson in the murder house? I count only two—Rosina and Emma French."

"Don't worry," he said. "I promise you there will be three."

I finished my drink and stood. "Well, at least I'm not eligible to serve on the jury."

"Wouldn't have you if you were. Married men only."

"You're just full of surprises," I said grimly. "I should have thought you'd want young single men. They seem to be Robinson's strongest supporters."

"I want each juror to have a nice, respectable, right-minded wife waiting at home to whom, should he vote for conviction, he will have to explain why he believed the testimony of three whores."

"Mr. Quinncannon—good night." If I sounded surly, I felt surly.

Behind me he said quietly, "Davy, how did you think murder trials were won? Prayer and fasting?"

# BOOK III

## The Trial

## 34  Rosina Townsend Takes the Stand

The weather was wet and boisterous on Thursday, June 2. Promptly at ten a.m. the doors of the large courtroom in the City Hall were thrown open to the equally wet and boisterous mob which poured in dripping, tumbling, elbowing, shouting, and almost instantaneously filling every seat, nook, and corner outside the bar. Fortunately on this morning, as throughout the trial, crowd control was in the indefatigable hands of High Constable Hays and a battalion of hand-picked deputies. The spectators, of course, were entirely male, mostly young, with an ill-concealed interest in the prisoner's cause. They had already begun to affect the dark cap with a glazed visor which, with the controversial cape, had formed Robinson's nocturnal uniform. Not even stern warnings from the bench and the strong-arm tactics of the officers could completely suppress the clapping and whistling which invariably greeted every fragment of evidence elicited in Robinson's behalf.

Within the bar, benches were arranged for the more than twenty reporters attending. Every major daily in New York was represented, and newsmen were there, not only from Newark and Philadelphia, but from as far away as Boston, Baltimore, and Washington City.

Mr. James Phenix, the grim, haggard district attorney, and his first assistant, a youthful, intense man named Robert Morris, were in attendance, though the defense table was empty, when Judge Henry P. Edwards and his court of four aldermen filed in. The court crier, Mr.

Bedell, glanced from the defense table to the judge as if uncertain whether to open the session in the absence of the prisoner.

A reporter hissed, "Where's Robinson?"

"Quinncannon's sense of the dramatic," I whispered. "The star of the show must make an entrance."

At that moment the side door flew open and the accused, escorted by Mr. Lyons, the Bellevue keeper, entered. He was followed by his counsel—a prancing Price, a beaming and apparently supremely confident Hoffman, and a smiling Quinncannon. A sudden silence ensued. Two elderly, white-haired gentlemen, whom I recognized as Mr. Hoxie and Robinson's father, also took seats at the defense table. Judge Edwards nodded to the crier. "Hear ye," bellowed Bedell. "Hear ye, hear ye . . . !"

Robinson wore the same blue suit he had worn at his indictment. In his hands was a cap of matching blue cloth. While in prison his head had been completely shaved and he now sported a light-brown, curly wig closely approximating his own hair. His complexion, while hardly ruddy, seemed to me much healthier, and his deportment far freer of embarrassment and anxiety, than at his earlier court appearance.

All eyes were on him, James Gordon Bennett's in particular. The *Herald* would later speak of his "face as fair, as soft, as graceful as a young girl," and of his "soft, liquid, melting eye that would provoke the adoration of any woman." "An invariable girlish melancholy continually hangs over his features," said Bennett, marked by "a slight soft quivering that went over his fair lips, that put me in mind of a young sensitive girl going to cry because her mother said, 'Sally, you must not go to the ball—your health is delicate.' "

Well . . . maybe, but Bennett had not seen this soft, sensitive, delicate youth in action at the Five Points.

Phenix announced they were ready for the state, and Hoffman declared the same for the defense. At Hoffman's request Henry Meigs, the court clerk, called out the names of the prosecution witnesses. All were present except the women of Rosina's establishment, Mr. Phenix explaining that because of the abuse they might suffer from the crowd he had not brought them to court. They were, he asserted, readily accessible. Without rising Hoffman nodded assent, the judge nodded at Meigs, and Meigs said, "Richard P. Robinson, stand up!"

The boy had to remain standing through the arraignment, the empaneling of the jury, and the reading of the indictment, all of which occupied the better part of the next five hours. This ordeal he endured without blanching, square-shouldered and erect, his cap in his hands, never twisting it, though occasionally he dangled it or spun it nervously on his finger.

A panel of fifty-nine jurors had been called, of whom only twenty-one were present. A fine of twenty-five dollars was imposed on each defaulting juror and those attending were closely questioned. Each side had twenty peremptory challenges, plus an unlimited number for cause. One was excused as a Quaker, another as a distant relative of the prisoner by marriage, a third as a friend of Mrs. Townsend. Only one literate soul admitted his mind had been made up by the newspapers. At last seven of the twenty-one were sworn: Isaac Winslow, merchant; Burtis Skidmore, coal dealer; Daniel Comstock, grocer; Joseph Imlay, merchant; Perry Jewell, grocer; Edward Boker, clothier; and James Schermerhorn, Secretary to the Ocean Insurance Company. As each stepped up to the bar to be sworn, he was ordered by Meigs to "look upon the prisoner" while Robinson was commanded to return the gaze.

The district attorney made a motion for a *tales,* which was ordered by the court for an additional panel of jurors, Phenix insisting that the panel be recruited from outside the courtroom lest someone be accepted who had come expressly to serve on the jury. Sheriff Hillyer and his chief deputy were dispatched to ensnare unsuspecting freemen, who were literally dragged in off the streets, until at last, despite frequent challenges by Price, five additional talesmen were sworn: Iziah Bull, merchant; James Field, merchant; James Parcelles, fancy-store keeper; Caleb Waterbury, shoemaker; and John Mattrass, druggist. I noted that each and every juror was married.

With the jury finally seated, Robinson remained standing while the indictment was read by Meigs. It contained only one count, charging the boy with the willful, premeditated murder of Helen Jewett on the tenth of April last. I watched the defendant's face carefully. Not a feature faltered, not a muscle twitched. When the clerk was finished and the plea requested, Robinson visibly straightened and replied in a firm voice, "Not guilty!"

It was nearing three p.m. Judge Edwards appointed eight officers to take charge of the jury for the duration of the trial and recessed for half an hour.

In the corridor a Boston journalist said, "I don't understand. Why didn't Phenix charge him with arson as well?"

"Probably hasn't got enough evidence," a Baltimore reporter speculated.

"Or else," said the Newark correspondent, "he doesn't want to clutter up his case for murder with extraneous counts."

I shook my head slowly.

"What do you think, Davy?" someone asked.

"I think," I answered, "that if Phenix can't nail him for murder, he figures he can try him for arson."

It took some time for Jacob Hays to restore order following the recess. At length Phenix opened for the state. His address was brief, but both impressive and elegant. He dwelt for a short time on the "heinous" nature of the crime and the facts which he intended to prove, upon which he relied for the conviction of the prisoner. The charge was the "most atrocious and diabolical that had ever been presented to a jury in this or any other country, not only in reference to the murder itself, but also in relation to the aggravated crime of arson which was connected with it." By eyewitnesses he would place the accused in the victim's room from nine-thirty until well after eleven on the murder night. The murder weapon had been found in the rear yard of the fatal house: he would prove that it came from the shop of the prisoner's employer, and that it had been fastened to a tassel of the prisoner's cloak by a length of twine. The cloak itself would be proven to be the prisoner's, and shown to have been abandoned in a yard adjoining that of the murder house. A motive would be proven, and a painted miniature of the accused, proven to be in the possession of the victim on the night of the crime, would be shown to be in the room of the prisoner on the following day. Letters passing between the accused and the victim would be introduced. Phenix admitted that the evidence against the prisoner was "almost exclusively circumstantial, yet it is of so strong, clear, and conclusive a character as to render the situation of the unfortunate accused a most perilous and awful one."

Defense chose to defer its remarks until the opening of its case, and Phenix called his first witness.

Fully conscious of the sensation her name and appearance were causing in the packed courtroom, Rosina Townsend swept regally to the stand. She wore the same mourning dress she had affected since the murder and the inevitable black veil hung from her bonnet. Beneath the veil her rouged lips were firmly set. For the moment she was the leading character in the great melodrama and she was determined to make the most of it.

Phenix led her through essentially the same story she had told Quinncannon and myself in his rooms. She positively identified the prisoner as the "Frank Rivers" whom she had admitted between nine and nine-thirty on the night in question, and whom she later saw in Helen's room when she carried up the champagne shortly after eleven. She now claimed that on the second occasion she had noticed "something about his head which peculiarly struck my attention. His hair was extremely thin on the back part of his head, where it was parted. It was on the upper part of his head directly in the back."

"Since that time," Phenix asked, "have you had any other opportunity to observe that fact?"

"No, sir."

"Have you mentioned this circumstance to anyone since that night?"

"Once or twice," she said. "I believe I mentioned it once to Mrs. Gallagher and once to Mr. Brink. I cannot recollect just when, but I think it was on the nineteenth of April, when my furniture was sold."

Robinson's head, of course, had been shaved at Bellevue and he was now wearing a wig. Obviously the prosecution was preparing to suggest that this was a ploy to hide the telltale bald spot.

Nothing else in Rosina's direct testimony was new. She recounted again how she shut up her house and retired—was awakened by a man demanding to be let out whom she told to "get your woman"—was awakened again at three a.m. by a man demanding entrance, and then noticed the lamp burning in the parlor and the door open to the yard. Her discovery of the fire and the murder, her attempts with Maria Stevens to reach the body, her summoning of the watch, all were as described to Quinncannon. She denied that there had been any quarrel between Helen and herself, or anyone else at all.

Phenix thanked her and bowed slightly toward the defense table. "Your witness," he said. The defendant, who had been resting his left cheek in his hand and staring at the ceiling through most of her testimony, now stirred and sat up straight. After shuffling through some papers Quinncannon stood.

The entire press section strained forward, pencils poised. Quinncannon's reputation as a sharp cross-examiner was legendary, and he was now facing, at the outset of the trial, the prosecution's most formidable witness. Rosina had placed Robinson in the Thomas Street house at nine-thirty and the murder room at eleven. Though the defense had a secret alibi witness under wraps, the grocer's story accounted for the boy's whereabouts only until ten-fifteen. The inferences intended by Phenix to be drawn from Rosina's evidence were that Robinson had remained in Helen's room until he killed her—that he had fired the bed and then lighted his way downstairs with her lamp and, finding the front door locked, had rapped at Rosina's room—that, on being told to get his woman to let him out but fearful of returning upstairs to search for her key, he had escaped through the French doors and the rear yards. If the jury believed her story, then it, with the cloak, the twine, and the hatchet, would doom Robinson to the scaffold. It was essential that the defense discredit the witness.

Quinncannon leaned back against the table, arms folded, smiling slightly. The redoubtable Rosina squared her shoulders and stiffened her spine. "Now, madam," the Irishman began pleasantly, "let us learn a little of your history. You first came to this city in September 1825, did you not?"

"Yes, sir. I lived in Duane Street and took in sewing until December, when my head became so affected that my sight was injured. I applied to Dr. David L. Rogers, who operated on me."

"The same Dr. Rogers who performed the examination of the body of Miss Jewett?"

"Yes, sir."

"And you recovered. Where did you next reside?"

"At the house of a woman named Maria Pierce. I remained there, I think, until April of 1826."

"And this house, madam. Was it not what is commonly called a house of assignation?"

Her lips compressed. "I believe it is called so, Mr. Quinncannon."

He strolled to the jury box and put his hands on the rail, looking from one to another of the twelve respectable gentlemen seated there. "And from that time up to the present moment, madam, you have been either a boarder at, or the keeper of, a house of prostitution?"

"Yes, sir," she answered with quiet defiance.

"Are you aware, madam, that boarding at or keeping such a house is a violation of the law?"

"Objection!" snapped Mr. Phenix.

"Sustained," said the judge, but the point had been made.

Quinncannon turned back to the witness. "Prior to Helen Jewett's living with you in March of this year, had she ever boarded with you before?"

"Yes, sir. It was for nine or ten months beginning, to the best of my recollection, in the spring of 1833."

"Do you recall having an argument with her during that time?"

"Not as I recollect, Mr. Quinncannon."

"Well, then, did you have an argument with someone else regarding her?"

"Not as I recollect."

"Do you think," he asked, "that if you had such a quarrel you should now recall it?"

A little smile for the first time played on her lips. "I should think so," she answered.

"Would you say you had a good memory, madam?"

"Beg pardon?"

"Do you remember the question?"

"Oh," Robert Morris groaned. "Objection!"

"Withdrawn." The Irishman waved his hand. "Now, madam, on direct examination you spoke of Mr. Robinson's having visited Helen at your house on six or seven occasions. Did any of those occur during 1833?"

"No, sir. All those visits were during the three weeks Helen boarded with me before her death. He usually came at night, but once he came on a Saturday afternoon."

"During those six or seven visits, did he ever enter your parlor?"

"No, sir, but once he entered my room." She smiled. "Helen was there, of course, with two other girls."

"Did you see him in the week prior to the murder?"

"I believe he was there on Wednesday or Thursday."

"And on each of these visits he used the name Frank Rivers?"

"He did."

"Did any other person use the alias Frank Rivers when visiting your house, madam?"

Rosina sucked in her breath but failed to respond.

"Please answer the question, Mrs. Townsend. Did anyone besides the prisoner use the name Frank Rivers?"

"There were," she said at last, "two visitors at my house who called themselves Frank Rivers."

Immediately a hissing and clapping commenced among the defendant's partisans, which did not cease until Judge Edwards instructed the officers to drag all demonstrators before the bar. Then, however, order was quickly enough restored. The judge issued a sharp rebuke to the spectators and Quinncannon resumed.

"If there were *two* Frank Riverses, how can you be certain that it was Mr. Robinson you saw on the murder night?"

But Rosina was not cowed by the demonstration. "I have testified that, on one occasion, Helen Jewett asked me to take particular notice of Robinson. She wished me to say whether he or Bill Easy was the handsomest. This required me to observe Mr. Robinson closely."

"And which young man did you decide was the more handsome?"

"In my opinion, the prisoner. His skin is as smooth as a baby's. Bill Easy," she added, "has pimples."

'And Bill Easy used the name Frank Rivers?"

"No, Mr. Quinncannon, he used the name Bill Easy."

"Then which of the two Frank Riverses is the more handsome?"

"I can't give an opinion," she said patiently. "I never paid much attention to the other Frank Rivers."

Quinncannon seemed perplexed. "Then how do you know which Frank Rivers came to your house on the night of the crime?"

Rosina smiled. "I believe you are confusing the jury, sir."

Quinncannon returned her smile. "I believe one of us is, madam."

He changed the subject. "You testified that you could not recognize the voice of the man outside your door on the murder night as that of the prisoner?"

"I have said I could not."

"Tell the jury again—why did you open the door?"

"Because I was certain it was not Bill Easy's voice."

"And Helen had left specific instructions not to admit Bill Easy?"

"Yes, sir."

"Do you recall, madam, testifying during the inquest that you recognized the voice as that of the prisoner?"

"I have no such recollection."

"Do you recall, madam, testifying before the grand jury that you recognized the voice of the prisoner?"

"No, Mr. Quinncannon."

"Do you recall mentioning the name of Bill Easy before either the coroner's jury or the grand jury?"

"I have no recollection."

"You have *no* recollection at all?"

"Objection," drawled Phenix. "The witness has answered that."

"Sustained," said the judge.

Quinncannon turned to the jury and shrugged his shoulders. I noticed that several of them shrugged back in sympathy. "Let's return, madam, to the night of the murder. You testified that when you opened the street door to Helen's caller at nine-thirty the light from your entry lamp shown on his face. Now that lamp was six or seven feet above and behind you, near the right staircase. You were obviously standing between the lamp and the face of the caller. How large a shadow did you cast across his face, madam?"

"I don't think I cast any shadow."

"You don't think so. Do you think that because you were between the lamp and the caller that would prevent the light from shining on his face at all?"

"I don't think so."

*"Think!"* Quinncannon thundered. "Madam, don't you *know* whether or not you could see his face?"

"Objection!" shouted Mr. Morris. " 'Think' is Mr. Quinncannon's word, not Mrs. Townsend's."

" 'Think' is the witness's word, as the record will show," Quinncannon responded.

"Why don't you ask the witness if she *knows* that the light illuminated Robinson's face?" Morris said.

Rosina took the hint. "I do know that I could see him plain. The lamp is a globe that hangs very high near the ceiling, and when I opened the door I stepped a little aside."

Quinncannon sighed. "If Mr. Morris wishes to put a question to the witness, I'm sure the bench will grant him that opportunity when the defense is finished."

"The witness is instructed not to answer questions put by the prosecution." The judge yawned.

"When I said I only thought so, I didn't mean it," said Rosina a bit sullenly.

"When you said you only thought you could see the prisoner's face, you didn't mean it," said the Irishman.

"No, sir."

"And now when you say you know you could see him you *do* mean it."

"Yes, sir."

Quinncannon turned his back to her and faced the jury. "From now on, madam, to accommodate myself and these twelve gentlemen, will you kindly preface your answers by telling us whether you do or do not mean them?"

"Oh, your honor!" Morris wailed.

"I withdraw the question," said Quinncannon lightly. He turned again to the witness. "Now, madam, this caller pulled up the collar of his cloak to conceal his face, did he not?"

"When he came into the entry he did."

"Did that fact excite your suspicion?"

"No, as Mr. Robinson was in the habit of hiding his face in his cloak when he called on Helen."

"For fear that you would recognize him, madam?"

It was a clever question. If the caller hid his face from Rosina it would cast further doubt on her identification. Yet, if he had come to kill Helen, why would he let Rosina see his face?

"Oh, not from any fear of me, but, I should imagine, lest someone else should recognize him."

Quinncannon was smiling at the prosecution table. "Then it is your testimony that Frank Rivers made no effort to conceal his face from you?"

"None whatever," she exclaimed in imaginary triumph.

"Did anyone else observe him when he arrived?"

"A girl named Emma French, who lives with me, was standing in the passageway at the door to her room. Her door is at the left side of the house, directly opposite mine. She, I have no doubt, saw him as plainly and as well as I did."

"No doubt," Quinncannon echoed dryly. "What occupied your time between the admission of Helen's visitor and her call for champagne?"

"I was in and out of my room, admitting persons and letting persons out of my house. No person was admitted to my house after eight that I did not admit myself."

"And who attended your door prior to eight?"

"Others of my boarders, sir. I was not feeling well that evening and did not dress until almost eight."

"Then," said Quinncannon, "is it not possible that some persons might have been in your house on the night of April 9 whom you did not admit and of whose presence you were unaware?"

"It is possible," she conceded.

"On that night were you alone in your room?"

"I had a person with me."

"Did you know him?"

"I did. I admitted him about eleven."

"Was he in your room when Helen called for the champagne?"

"He was."

"Was he then in bed, or were you, or had either of you been?"

"No, no, and no!"

"How long did he remain in your room?"

"Until the fire alarm was sounded."

"How many beds are there in your room?"

"One."

"One . . . bed," Quinncannon said to the jury, as if pondering this remarkable fact. "May I assume that neither of you slept on the floor, madam?"

"You may."

"Or in a chair?" he said. "Or dangling from the ceiling?"

"Objection," said Phenix.

"Sustained," said the judge.

"When you saw the man you say was Robinson in Helen Jewett's room that evening, what was he doing?"

"He was lying on his stomach covered with the bedclothes nearly up to his shoulders and reading."

"What was he reading?"

"I cannot say."

"And where was the candle?"

"Either on the pillow or on the table beside the bed."

"But you cannot say which."

"I cannot say."

"But you *can* say that the man you saw was the prisoner, knowing that his young life may depend on your testimony?"

"I can," she said with assurance.

"How long did you remain in the doorway, madam?"

"Perhaps two minutes."

"Do you recall stating before the grand jury that you handed the wine to Helen and immediately went away?"

"Not to my recollection."

Quinncannon grimaced. "Again, not to your recollection." He walked slowly to the jury box and put his hands on the rail, his back to Rosina. "When you observed the man in the bed, madam, did you see his full face?"

"No, only his side face."

"Only his profile?"

"I have said so."

"While you remained at the door, for however long a time, did he shift his position?"

"I don't think that he did."

"Yet you claim to have seen a bald spot *at the back of his head?*"

"It was very thin," she said, "or nearly bare. I noticed it because I thought I would mention it to Helen the following morning."

He wheeled around. *"Did* you mention it to anyone the following morning?"

"No."

"Did you mention it to anyone at the Police Office?"

"No. I was so much agitated by the murder that I forgot many things that did not occur to me till afterward."

"How many men were in your house when the murder took place?"

"Six."

"Six that you admitted. And when the fire alarm was given, how did they escape?"

"Through the front door, I believe."

"But," he said with mock surprise, "wasn't the street door kept locked?"

"I left my key in the door, sir, when I let in the party of watchmen."

"Who was the first watchman to enter your house?"

"As I recall, it was Mr. John Palmer."

"Do you recollect Mr. Palmer telling you to lock the door and allow no one to leave the premises?"

"I have no—"

He cut her off savagely. "Of course! I forgot. You have no such recollection! Was it your wish that no person should leave your house until an examination had been conducted into the murder?"

"It was. When the gentlemen were about going and had collected on the stairs, I said, 'Gentlemen, don't go.' "

"You pleaded with them," Quinncannon said bitterly. "You said, 'Gentlemen, don't go.' And all the time the key was in the door! You wished no one to leave until the murder had been investigated. Yet you have testified, madam, that up to that moment you did not know that a murder had been committed!"

Morris was on his feet. "If Mr. Quinncannon wishes to put a question to the witness, let him put it."

"Very well," Quinncannon growled. "Do you remember, madam, that when the watch first came into your house there were two men in their shirt-sleeves standing near your door?"

"I do not."

"Or that the watchmen, on going up the stairs, found a man partially dressed near the door of Helen Jewett's room?"

"No, sir."

"In the course of a week, madam, how many men would you say visit your house?"

"Between eighty and a hundred." There was a hint of professional pride in her answer.

"And how many of these eighty to a hundred do you know well enough, say, to identify positively in a court of law?"

"The majority—" Rosina began.

"Objection!" Morris shouted.

". . . are complete strangers to me," she concluded.

Quinncannon nodded. "Mrs. Townsend, did you see the prisoner at the coroner's inquest or at the Police Office, and if you did, had he his hat on when you saw him?"

"I saw him when he was brought to my house by the officers," she replied, "but he then had his hat on. I don't remember whether he had his hat on or off at the Police Office."

The Irishman elevated his eyebrow. "Now, don't you remember that when you were before the grand jury, you sat near Robinson, who then had his hat off, and that you had then an opportunity of seeing the bald place on his head?"

"Now I recollect," said Rosina, "I think that I did."

"I thought so, madam." Quinncannon leaned against the table. "Did you ever think before that time of mentioning anything in reference to this remarkable discovery of yours?"

"Yes, I think that several days previous to that I mentioned it to Mr. Brink."

"Have you not seen an account of Robinson wearing a wig in one of the papers, and did not this fact lead you to make the statements to Mrs. Gallagher and Mr. Brink that you say you have done?"

"I did," she answered, "see some account in the *Transcript* or *Sun*—I forget which. But that did .not lead me to mention the fact I have related. I had mentioned it before."

Quinncannon gave her a slight smile. "On the night of the murder, which of the Frank Riverses was at your house?"

"Why, both of them," Rosina replied.

"Both of them," he repeated grimly. He looked at the bench. "Your honor, I'm finished with this witness, for the present. Defense wishes to reserve the right to recall her at a later time."

Edwards rapped his gavel once. "Granted," he said.

## 35 *The Problem of the Twine*

Dr. Daniel L. Rogers was the second prosecution witness. He deposed that he was the surgeon called to examine the body of Helen Jewett on the morning of April 10. She was, he said, lying in her bed, partially on her back, partially on her left side, very much burned on her legs, arms, and torso. Her limbs had become very rigid. She had sustained three wounds on the right side of her forehead. The largest was attended with a fracture of the skull. This wound was about three and a half inches in length. The bone of the skull was driven in upon the brain, which was thus wounded. The two smaller wounds were simple contusions, not attended with fracture, and had been delivered while she was still alive.

The large wound, he believed, was the cause of death, and death had been instantaneous. He deduced this "from the position of the body, and rigidity of the body, and there having been no distortion of the countenance." Had she died by burning or suffocation, her countenance would have been distorted, and the burn was not extensive enough to produce death. He had seen persons burned much worse who had lived for several days. Not only were the burns too slight to be fatal but, had she died of suffocation, the face would be discolored and other parts of the system affected which a postmortem found unaffected. "There can be," he concluded, "no reasonable doubt that she died from the blow on the head."

He judged she had been struck with a dull instrument such as the edge of the back of a hatchet. The fatal wound appeared to have been dealt with the blade. The hatchet found by the watch in Rosina's yard was here shown to Dr. Rogers and he agreed it was "a very likely instrument to make such wounds." He had been shown this weapon by the coroner at the inquest and it then had "considerable blood upon it, and a string around the handle as it has now."

The cross-examination by Whitlaw Price was brief. The defense, apparently, did not intend to challenge the surgeon's opinion as to cause of death. Rogers stated that "there was but a small quantity of blood on the body" when he viewed it, though blood had spurted from the lethal wound and "the bedding immediately beneath the corpse was blood-soaked." He added that "when death is instantaneous the circulation ceases at once, and consequently the blood does not flow so copiously." The doctor was excused.

By the time the third and final witness of the session was called, there was considerable yawning among the spectators, the press, and especially the jury. But we were all soon awake again. For Richard Eldridge, a watchman, was about to prove the star witness of the day.

Eldridge, a tall, athletic man in his early thirties, deposed to Phenix that on the morning of April 10 he heard the alarm sounded in Thomas Street; however, as that was not part of his beat, he did not go to the house until he had completed his tour, arriving between four and four-fifteen. He had viewed the body and spoken with Mrs. Townsend, "who told me what had happened and how it happened." He took a candle into the rear yard to search for clues, but, being unable to keep the candle lit, he returned to the house and sat in the parlor with some other watchmen, Mrs. Townsend, and a few of the girls until sunrise. Mrs. Townsend "then made a remark, that as it was light, we might go out into the yard and perhaps discover something."

At this there was a great commotion of stamping and clapping among Robinson's supporters in the crowd, not the last such outburst during Eldridge's testimony. After Judge Edwards had gaveled for order for several minutes Old Hays stood and glowered at the spectators. This immediately had the desired effect.

Eldridge resumed. With another watchman, John Palmer, he had gone out into the yard. Palmer scaled the fence and discovered a cloak lying in the adjacent yard of a house fronting on Hudson Street. Eldridge got up on the fence and saw the cloak in the center of the yard. He told Palmer to retrieve it. Asked if he recalled seeing the privy, the witness said he did not.

The hatchet which had earlier been identified by Dr. Rogers was here shown to Eldridge, who also identified it as the one he had found in Rosina's yard. It lay about six inches to a foot from the fence, in the southwest corner of the yard. He caused another sensation by stating that he observed no marks to indicate that another person had climbed the fence.

Eldridge had the hatchet in his possession for "about half an hour" after he found it. He acknowledged that the blade was wet and discolored, but refused to swear that this was from blood. The dampness might have resulted from a heavy dew and the discoloration might have been rust. A harried Phenix at last asked if he could swear the stains on the blade were *not* blood and the witness said he could not so swear. With this answer the district attorney had to be satisfied.

Along with the ax, Eldridge had also had possession of the cloak until he locked both in a room to the right of the parlor, the room under the piazza roof outside Helen Jewett's window. He had closed and barred the shutters of the room's one window (which faced the rear yard) and locked the door, keeping the key until the inquest jury was convened, at which time he gave the key to the coroner.

While in possession of the cloak and hatchet, Mr. Phenix suggested, he had of course noticed the twine on the handle of the weapon and the tassel of the garment? No, answered the witness, he had not.

Now a real tumult erupted in the courtroom and even Old Hays had trouble restoring order. Even when the bench had threatened eviction of all disorderly persons and the deputies had offered to pass among the spectators with clubs, there remained a low but ominous hum of voices and the shuffling of feet, which did not cease until the unnerved Phenix had nodded to the defense table and a positively radiant Lon Quinn-cannon had commenced the cross-examination.

"Now, Mr. Eldridge, you have testified that you arrived at Mrs. Townsend's house before daylight. Was it your idea to take a candle into the yard before sunrise to search for evidence?"

"No, sir. That was Mrs. Townsend's suggestion."

"And when you went into the yard, did you go alone?"

"No, sir. Mrs. Townsend and some of her girls went out with me."

"And during that initial search, did you examine the southwest corner of the yard, where you eventually found the hatchet now in evidence?"

"Yes, sir. I must have passed within six inches of it."

"Yet at that time you failed to notice it."

"Well," Eldridge explained, "the candle kept blowing out."

"So you said, sir. How high would you estimate the fence between Mrs. Townsend's yard and the yard where the cloak was discovered?"

"About nine feet, I should say."

"I see. Now, you testified that you climbed to the top of the nine-foot fence. Of course there were steps to assist you in getting up?"

"No, sir."

"No?" Quinncannon seemed surprised. "Then how did you get up?"

"I made a spring and caught the top board."

"And where was the cloak when you first saw it?"

"Spread out on the ground at least fifteen feet from the fence."

"In your opinion, could it have been dropped there by a person situated on the fence as you were?"

"No, sir."

"In your opinion, could it have been thrown there by a man from Mrs. Townsend's side of the fence?"

"In my opinion, it could not. The cloak lay nearer to the rear of the house in Hudson Street than to Mrs. Townsend's house."

"Did you examine the Hudson Street yard, sir, and if so, would you say that a man could have escaped over one of its fences?"

"I did, Mr. Quinncannon, and in my opinion a man could not."

With a smile Quinncannon turned to face the prosecution table. "Mr. Eldridge, please remind the jury, when was the first occasion on which you noticed the twine on the handle of the hatchet?"

"When it was handed to me by the coroner during the inquest."

"Before you locked it up, how long was the hatchet in your hands?"

"About thirty minutes."

"During that time did you examine it closely?"

"I looked at it repeatedly, sir."

"And you *never, once,* noticed a string tied round its handle?"

Said the witness, "No, sir, I did not."

"What did you notice about the hatchet?" Quinncannon asked.

"The blade was wet, sir, on both sides, and rusted the same as sheet iron rusts. There was, as I have said, a heavy dew that particular morning."

"While handling the hatchet, did you discover any blood on the blade or the handle?"

"None, sir."

"Or any blood on your hands?" Quinncannon pressed.

"None. There was a collection of rust on the edge of the blade which I do not see now. And . . ."

"And?"

"And there is now an appearance of blood near the edge which I do not remember seeing before."

Quinncannon strolled to the jury box. "Please describe again the measures you took to secure the hatchet and the cloak."

"Yes, well, I put them in a room at the rear of the house at the southwest corner of the ground floor. There are two doors to that room, one opening on Mrs. Townsend's room, which I locked from inside, leaving the key in the lock. The other door, leading to the parlor in the rear, I locked from outside and kept the key. I also bolted the shutters from the inside."

"And you kept this key until the inquest was convened?"

"Yes, sir, when I gave it to the coroner."

"Once again, Mr. Eldridge, could anyone, in your opinion, have escaped from the yard of the house in Hudson Street?"

"Not in my opinion, sir."

The Irishman glanced at the prosecution table. "I assume, gentlemen, you wish redirect."

Phenix rose. "Mr. Eldridge, is it not true that there are a number of alleys leading to Duane and Thomas Streets through which a person might escape from the rear yard of Mrs. Townsend's house?"

"If he were to climb over several fences, yes, sir."

Phenix picked up the hatchet. "I believe I understood you to say that you now recognize the stain on this blade as blood?"

"No, sir, I could not swear to it."

Phenix put down the hatchet. "How many people saw you lock up the cloak and the hatchet, Mr. Eldridge?"

"To the best of my knowlege, sir, only Mrs. Townsend."

Phenix drew a very deep breath. "After you locked up this evidence, sir, how long a period elapsed before you surrendered the key to the coroner?"

"About two hours."

"During that time did you remain in the house?"

"Yes, sir."

"Then you would have noticed if anyone attempted to enter the room where the ax and the cloak were concealed?"

"No, sir, as I moved about the house and was away from the door a good deal."

"When you put these articles in this room, Mr. Eldridge, how did you place them?"

The watchman shrugged. "I don't know. I just chucked them down."

Phenix threw up his hands and returned to the table. Immediately Assistant District Attorney Morris was on his feet. "When you saw the hatchet for the second time, by whom were you given it?"

"By the coroner."

"And you identified it as the one you had found in the yard, did you not?"

"Yes, sir, to the best of my recollection."

"At that time, didn't the coroner point out a spot on the blade, and didn't he ask you if you thought it was blood?"

"As I remember, Mr. Morris, I expressed the opinion that it was rust."

"You recall, do you not, seeing the twine on both the hatchet and the cloak?"

"Yes, sir, but only after they were pointed out to me by the coroner at the inquest."

Quinncannon stood. "Just one or two more questions, Mr. Eldridge. Is it not true that when you found the hatchet some of Mrs. Townsend's girls were leaning out of the rear windows watching you?"

"Yes, sir."

"Were there any other persons in the yard besides yourself?"

"Only me and Palmer."

"In your opinion, could someone have thrown the hatchet from one of the windows to the place where you found it?"

"Objection," Morris said.

"Not from the second story," Eldridge answered. "Maybe from the first story."

"Objection!" Morris shouted again. "Mr. Eldridge, will you please not answer questions until the court has ruled on my objection?"

"Never mind." Quinncannon smiled. "I withdraw the question."

An exasperated Morris barked, "Mr. Eldridge, don't you suppose if someone had flung that hatchet from the house into the yard you would have heard it when it hit the ground?"

The witness speculated. "Yes, sir, I suppose I would have . . ."

"No further questions," said Morris.

". . . if it was thrown out while I was in the yard," Eldridge concluded.


It was the consensus of the journalists who gathered for a late supper at the American that the day's honors had been carried off by the defense. Quinncannon had reaped an unexpected windfall in the testimony of Eldridge. The obvious inference of the watchman's evidence was that the hatchet, and the cloak as well, had been tampered with between the time they were deposited in the piazza room and the time they were produced for the inquest jury. The possibility of a frame-up of Robinson had been introduced into the case.

## 36  The Coroner and the Captain

It is with deep shame for the citizens of my adopted city that I record their behavior on the morning of the trial's second day. Though the doors of the courtroom were not scheduled to open until ten and the weather continued stormy and miserable, vast crowds began to assemble outside the City Hall as early as seven. By a little past eight, when Old Hays arrived with his posse of officers, the mob had swelled to between five and six thousand. When the doors were opened this dense mass flooded the auditorium, packing the seats, swarming the aisles, climbing onto the sills of the windows. Some literally lashed themselves to the columns with ropes apparently brought for that purpose. The pressure against the bar rail was so great that it threatened to splinter. It is terrifying to imagine the consequences had any substantial portion of the mob been hostile to the prisoner.

To his credit Judge Edwards acted swiftly. He ordered the defendant, counsel, and jury removed at once, sent for the mayor, retired with his fellow judges into the Common Council chamber, and refused to convene until not merely the room but the entire west wing had been cleared. The undersheriff arrived with fifty additional marshals, and a few of the crowd left grudgingly. The majority held fast until Jacob Hays emerged from the outer chamber to address them.

The mayor, he said, was mobilizing the entire police corps and was prepared to call out the militia. The trial would not resume until the room was cleared, and he suggested they retire peaceably and without requiring the use of force as *go they must.*

At last the auditorium was emptied, and spectators were then passed in single file through a gauntlet of deputies into the chamber again until the seats were filled. The doors were slammed shut, the jury recalled, and the court seated. The judge ordered fifty marshals armed with clubs to be stationed about the room to keep order, with another fifty outside to keep the west wing clear. With proper decorum finally restored, shortly after twelve noon, the trial continued, with Mr. Phenix calling as his fourth witness William Schureman, coroner for the city and county of New York.

Schureman was a stout, well-dressed, elderly man. He seemed, considering he was not unaccustomed to giving evidence in capital trials, exceedingly nervous. Yes, he agreed, he had been called to 41 Thomas Street between three and four a.m. on April 10 to hold an inquest into the death of a female, one Helen Jewett. Yes, he had arrived before daybreak.

"Were you present," Phenix asked, "when a cloak was found in one of the yards adjoining the rear yard of the house?"

"I was."

"Did you handle the cloak?"

"Yes, sir, it was handed to me in the yard of the Thomas Street house by the watchman who found it on the other side of the fence, in a yard in the rear of Hudson Street. I saw him coming over the fence with it."

The cloak in evidence was produced and the witness made a positive identification. Phenix continued, "When you first saw the cloak, was the string which is now attached to one of its tassels then attached to it?"

"Yes, sir, it was. I was induced to notice it particularly because, when I was still in the house, one of the girls told me—"

"Objection to the witness stating what he was told," said Ogden Hoffman.

Phenix said, "As a result of some conversation you had with persons in the house, did you pay special attention to the cloak?"

"I did."

"Did you see the string attached to the cloak *before* it was taken into the house?"

"Yes, sir. I noticed it shortly after I received it from the watchman in the yard."

Phenix looked at the jury. "Very well. *After* you perceived the string on the cloak, what was your disposition of it?"

"I gave it into the hands of one of the police officers, or one of the watchmen. I cannot positively say which."

"Do you know, of your knowledge, what was then done with the cloak?"

"I have no idea, Mr. Phenix. It was not brought to me again until I had empaneled the jury."

"When you examined the cloak in the yard, how long was it in your possession?"

"I should say about five minutes."

"And you are positive the string was then attached to it?"

"I am positive," Schureman replied.

"Very well. There was also a hatchet found in the yard, was there not?"

The coroner agreed that there was, and that it had been given to him while he was in the yard, though before or after he received the cloak he could not be sure. He rather thought it was after. Shown the hatchet in evidence, he made a positive identification.

"When you examined the hatchet," Phenix asked, "what, if anything, did you observe?"

"Well, I did not really discover anything particular about it at that time. The blade was wet with dew or with rain. At that time I did not perceive a string upon the hatchet—I mean, when it was handed to me in the yard."

A murmur in the crowd was at once gaveled to silence.

For the first time Mr. Phenix appeared uncomfortable. "But you did, did you not, observe the string on the hatchet?"

"Oh, yes, when it was brought to me a second time, before the inquest jury. It was handed to me by Mr. Brink, who especially called my attention to it."

At the defense table Quinncannon glanced up at the witness. One Irish eyebrow elevated.

"Did you then examine and compare the string upon the cloak and the string upon the hatchet?"

"Yes, sir, in company with some of the jurors."

"And what, if any, were your conclusions?"

Schureman smiled as though he recognized an expected question. "The two strings," he answered, "were exactly similar in all respects." Then he added, "The string appeared to be new, and to have been recently cut apart."

I started at the word "cut." The state's theory was that the string had been *broken* during the escape. Phenix closed the direct examination before Schureman could harm his case further, but Judge Edwards had a few questions to put.

"At what time, Mr. Witness, would you say the cloak and hatchet were first handed to you?"

"I didn't consult my watch, your honor. It was shortly after daybreak."

"And how much time passed between the time you surrendered these items and the time you again saw them?"

"It was two, possibly three hours, your honor. I should say I saw them again between nine and half past."

Edwards nodded and Phenix again rose. "Are you certain, Mr. Schureman, as to which officer brought the items to you at the inquest?"

The coroner scratched his head. "I believe it was Mr. Brink," he said, "but it could have been someone else. Another officer or one of the watch."

"Then you are not certain?"

"It seems," Quinncannon observed aridly, "that the district attorney is now cross-examining his own witness."

Phenix glared at him, but withdrew the question, and Quinncannon faced the coroner. "Now, Mr. Schureman, do you know a watchman named Richard Eldridge?"

"Not that I am aware of, sir."

"Do you recall hearing that there was a watchman of that name at the murder house on the morning of April 10?"

"I remember there was someone there by that name. There were a great many officers and watchmen at that house on that morning."

"Were you in court yesterday, sir, when Mr. Eldridge testified?"

"I was not."

"Would it surprise you, sir, to learn that Mr. Eldridge testified that he found the hatchet and that he had it in his possession for thirty minutes before he handed it to anyone?"

The coroner leaned back in his chair. He seemed much more at ease under cross-examination than he had under direct. "Certainly it would surprise me. If Mr. Eldridge is the man who took up the ax, he must be mistaken if he made such a statement. I do not think the person who found it had it in his hand more than a minute before he gave it to me."

"And when you saw the hatchet, sir, was there any appearance of blood on it?"

"None that I noticed. The blade had a reddish aspect."

"The same reddish aspect that it now has?"

"Yes, sir."

"You notice no difference?" ·

"I have so stated."

"So you have," Quinncannon said. He began to pace before the bench. "When you turned over the cloak and hatchet for safekeeping, did you give any particular instructions?"

"Yes, sir, I ordered them to be kept safe, with special regard to the cloak and the string upon it, since I had been told—since I had understood from conversation that suspicion might rest on someone who had visited the house that evening wearing such a cloak."

"Did you give special instructions regarding the hatchet and its string?"

Schureman began to answer, but the Irishman interrupted him. "Ah, but I forgot. You saw no string on the hatchet when you examined it, did you?"

"Not in the yard, sir."

"Not in the yard, but *three hours later* there was a string on the hatchet!"

"My attention was called to it."

"Yes," Quinncannon growled, "by Mr. Brink! Now, sir, you stated that the string appeared to be *cut* at the ends."

"If I said so, Mr. Quinncannon, I withdraw it."

"It did not appear to be cut?"

"I cannot say what condition it was in, except that it then appeared to be clean and now it is dirty."

"The string on the cloak, sir. Does it now seem longer or shorter than when you first examined it?"

"I cannot say."

"You cannot say?" Quinncannon frowned. "Do you recollect who first suggested a search of the rear yard for clues to the murder?"

"I do not recollect, sir."

"Do you recollect a conversation on that subject with Mrs. Townsend?"

"I do not."

Quinncannon returned to his chair. "Finished with the witness," he said. Schureman started to get up, but the Irishman turned suddenly and held up his hand.

"Excuse my retaining you for a moment, Mr. Coroner. Are you certain that when you first saw the hatchet the string was not on it?"

"Reasonably certain, sir."

"Before you examined the hatchet, you *had* noticed the string on the cloak, had you not?"

"Yes, sir."

"Do you think," Quinncannon said, "upon full reflection, that under the circumstances, if the string had been on the hatchet when it was found, you would have noticed it?"

The witness attempted to simulate "full reflection." At last he said, "Yes, I believe I should have seen it."

Immediately Morris was on his feet. "When you first saw the hatchet, it was a dull, gray morning, was it not? The light was poor. Answer yes or no!"

"Yes, sir."

"It is true, is it not, that because of a conversation you had had with someone in the house, you were induced to examine *only* the cloak, and not the hatchet, for a length of string? Answer true or false!"

"That is true, sir."

Quinncannon looked up. "Tell his honor, when you were first handed this stringless hatchet, were you standing up or sitting down? Answer up or down!"

"Up, your honor," said the witness.

"Your honor," Quinncannon sighed, "I must object to this knee-jerk method of cross-examining one's own witness."

"Sustained," said the judge.

"A few more questions on redirect, your honor," said Morris. "Mr. Schureman, when your attention was focused, by this earlier conversation, on the tassels of this cloak, was there any mention of a *string,* or simply of the peculiar appearance of one of the tassels?"

"It was the latter, Mr. Morris."

"Regarding the string, you have said that, when it was shown to you during the inquest, it appeared to have been cut at the end. I ask you now if you meant 'cut' as with a knife or shears?"

"No, sir. I meant to say that it had the appearance of being jerked or broken off."

"You did not mean it had been cut with a blade."

"No, sir."

Morris sank back in his chair. He said, "Recross."

Quinncannon said, "Am I correct that you wished both the cloak and the hatchet deposited in a safe place until the inquest?"

"You are, sir."

"We understand your concern over the cloak, Mr. Schureman. Please explain your concern over the hatchet."

"From the condition of the wounds on the body," the witness answered, "and the circumstance of the hatchet being found in the yard, it was my impression that it might be the murder weapon. I ordered them to be kept together, thinking they might be jointly identified."

"You stressed that they be kept together?"

"I did."

"Then, sir, isn't it possible that some of the persons to whom you gave the cloak, having the string then attached to it, might have tied the hatchet to the string and subsequently broken it off when the exhibits were presented separately to your jury?"

The question was brilliant. It implied neither a deliberate manipulation of evidence nor the coroner's collusion. Mr. Schureman considered it while a hushed courtroom waited. Then he answered, "It is *possible.*"

Quinncannon was satisfied.

With enormous and obvious relief the coroner was finally permitted to leave the stand. The next witness was summoned, not by Phenix, but by the assistant prosecutor, Robert Morris. It was the captain of the watch, George W. Noble.

The witness deposed that he went to the house on first hearing the alarm in company with some of his men, including, he thought, Eldridge. He was in the house about one and a half hours before the cloak was found. He was in the murder room when he heard someone cry, "Here's the cloak now!" On looking out the window he saw one of his men jump down from the fence, and he immediately went down into the yard. By that time the hatchet had also been discovered, and he received them both, examining them carefully. *He was certain that the string was on both the cloak and the hatchet when he first saw them in the yard.*

"Captain," said Morris, "would you say that the string which is now upon the hatchet has the same appearance as it had when you first examined it on the morning of April 10?"

"In every respect the same, sir."

"No longer? No shorter?"

"No, sir."

"On that morning in the yard did you compare the string on the hatchet with that on the cloak?"

"No, sir, but Mr. Brink did in my presence and he concluded, as I did, that they were the same."

The ax and cloak were then given to one of the watch—Noble didn't know who—and deposited in a back room of the house. The witness did not see these articles deposited but thought the hatchet had been wrapped in the cloak. He was also unsure whether the room was locked, but "there were watchmen about the place all the time." The witness had remained at the house until past noon, when the inquest was completed, except for the time when he accompanied Brink in making the arrest of the prisoner. The arrest occurred about seven a.m.

"Your witness," Morris said.

"Captain Noble," Quinncannon began, "when you arrived at the house, had the coroner yet made his appearance?"

"No, sir. I suppose I was there full three-quarters of a hour before he came."

"When he came there, had the cloak or hatchet yet been discovered?"

"They had not."

The captain was in the yard when the coroner received both articles. They were not received at the same time, although "not more than a moment intervened." The coroner was in the yard all the time that the witness and Brink were there, and held the cloak and hatchet about five minutes before handing them to be put away. Noble didn't know if the coroner was standing nearby when he and Brink compared the two lengths of string. When they found the strings alike, the witness considered it an important fact; he thought Brink considered it an important fact. But he had not then communicated it to the coroner, nor, so far as he knew, had Brink.

"You considered it an important fact, yet you failed to mention it to Mr. Schureman?"

"That's it, sir."

Quinncannon stood near the jury box. "Now, you have testified that you heard one of your men say, 'There's *the* cloak. We've found *the* cloak.' Something of that sort?"

" 'There's the cloak' or 'There's *a* cloak.' I don't remember which."

"Don't you remember that some of the girls suggested that you might find something of importance if you searched the yards at the rear?"

"I don't recall that, sir."

"Don't you remember some of the girls suggesting that if you searched the yards you might find the killer's *cloak?*"

"I have no such recollection."

"All right, Captain. Is it just barely possible that some person or persons might have entered the room where the cloak and hatchet were deposited between the time they were first placed there and the time they were retrieved for the coroner's jury?"

"I hardly think so."

"I did not ask for your thoughts," Quinncannon said with seeming fatigue. "Is it possible?"

"I suppose it is *possible* while Brink and me were away from the house making the arrest."

"While you were away it is possible that some person might have entered the room and gotten possession of the cloak and the hatchet. Is that now your testimony?"

"Yes, sir," answered Noble.

Quinncannon returned to his seat. Just before resuming it he said, "Captain Noble, when you arrested Mr. Robinson, did he make any objections?"

"No, sir."

"He went quietly? No fuss?"

"None."

As quickly as the Irishman sat down, Robert Morris jumped up. "On redirect, your honor. Captain Noble, when you arrested the prisoner, what, if anything, did you notice about his clothes which might seem unusual?"

"Well, not when he was dressing, Mr. Morris, but later, when we got him to the house in Thomas Street, I noticed white stains on his pantaloons. There was one on the right side of the right leg below the knee, and another on the left side near the hip."

"Very good. Now, please describe the fence in the rear of Mrs. Townsend's yard."

"It's a board fence, at least nine feet high all around, and whitewashed."

"A man scaling that fence into the next yard would necessarily get white stains on his pantaloons, would he not?"

"I should imagine so, though it would depend on the manner by which he got over."

"Thank you, Captain," Morris said.

Quinncannon drummed his pencil on the defense table. "Mr. Noble, do I understand you to say that the stains you claim to have seen on the defendant's trousers were whitewash?"

"I took them to be."

"You *took* them to be? When you tested them, sir, did you taste or smell lime?"

"Well, no, sir."

"Meaning you neither tasted nor smelled lime?"

"Meaning I did not test the stains," said the witness.

"Good God!" Quinncannon groaned, his head rather inclined toward the jury. "No . . . further . . . questions!"

# 37 The Problems of the Cloak and Hatchet

Phenix called James Wells to the stand. Wells was, and had been for almost a year, the porter at Joseph Hoxie's store. He was examined for the state by Morris.

"Yes, sir, there was a hatchet belonging to the store which I chiefly used for splitting wood."

The last time Wells saw the hatchet was on the Wednesday before the murder. That would be April 6. Yes, Richard Robinson was employed at the store at that time. Wells first missed the hatchet on the Monday morning after the murder. That would be April 11. Yes, he missed it before he had heard of the murder and he looked thoroughly for it without success.

The hatchet in court was here shown to Wells and he was directed by Judge Edwards to examine it carefully. The witness had no doubt it was the same one he had used at the store. He knew it especially by a peculiar gap in the blade.

Edwards asked, "The last time you saw this hatchet, did it differ in any way from its appearance now?"

"No, your honor. It had the same general appearance of rust that it has now."

To Morris' next question, Wells said, "I have not seen this hatchet in Hoxie's store since I first missed it."

The prisoner's attorneys seemed willing to let Wells's identification of the hatchet stand. Under Quinncannon's cross-examination the porter stated that he had last seen Robinson at Hoxie's store on the murder night between five and half past. The prisoner was conversing cheerfully with both clerks and customers; in fact, Wells had always found Robinson "amiable and mild."

"Mr. Wells," said Quinncannon, "have you had occasion to observe the defendant without a cap or hat?"

"Oh, yes."

"Have you ever observed a bald place on his head?"

"No, sir. If there had been one, I think I would have seen it."

Wells also testified that on the Friday and Saturday before the murder he had painted the windows and uprights of the store with white paint and whitewashed the ceiling. Persons not particularly careful in moving about, he thought, would have been apt to get white paint on their clothes, especially from brushing against the front upright of the store. Even Mr. Hoxie had gotten some paint on himself.

The prosecution called Charles Tyrell, a bovine young man of about twenty who roomed in Robinson's boardinghouse. His primary function on the stand was to link the prisoner with the cloak. Early on the murder night Tyrell and Robinson had left the house and walked up Beekman Street to the corner of Nassau opposite Brick Church. There they had parted, the witness turning down Nassau while Robinson continued toward the Park, announcing that he was going to the Clinton Hotel. This was between eight and nine o'clock. The prisoner "then wore a dark-colored cloth cloak with a velvet collar and facings, and I think he had a cap on."

But when the cloak was shown to Tyrell he could not make a positive identification. The best Phenix could coax from him was that it was "very similar" to the cloak Robinson had worn.

Then Quinncannon went to work. Tyrell had seen Robinson put on the cloak in his room, and he got down from the stand and demonstrated how the defendant had whipped the garment around his shoulders.

"If there had been a hatchet attached to the cloak when Mr. Robinson put it on, would you say you would have seen it?"

"I certainly would have!"

"Did you have any other opportunity to observe whether or not there was a hatchet tied inside the cloak?"

"Yes, sir, twice," Tyrell said eagerly. "Once at the top of Dey Street, and again on Beekman, his cloak flew open and he threw it together again. If the hatchet had been there I should have seen it."

"What would you say was the prisoner's mood that evening?"

"Oh, very cheerful! He was laughing and joking with some of the boarders. While we were walking on Beekman he told me that on that day he was nineteen years of age."

"And he spoke of that circumstance with evident emotions of pleasure?"

"He did, yes, sir."

Phenix had some questions on redirect. "Mr. Tyrell, how often would you say you have seen the prisoner wear a cloth cloak similar to this one?"

Frequently, Tyrell answered. He had seen no such cloak in the prisoner's room since his arrest. He thought, but was not certain, that Robinson had removed the cloak from his trunk on the night of the murder. The trunk was where the garment was usually kept.

"Once again, Mr. Tyrell, tell the jury, the cloth cloak you have seen on numerous occasions in Robinson's possession, *and which he wore on the night of the murder,* is *precisely similar* in all respects to the cloak shown you here in court?"

"Yes, sir."

"In all respects the same?"

"Yes, sir."

"Cloak, cloak, cloak, cloak," Quinncannon said to the ceiling. "Your honor, I wonder if the jury is as sick of this tedious garment as I am." He went back to his papers, then, after a moment, added without looking up, "In the fervent hope that it will expedite these proceedings, defense will stipulate that the cloak in court is Mr. Robinson's."

The Irishman might have shot off a gun and gotten the same response. The courtroom thundered with stunned silence. It was Robert Morris who recovered first and leaped from his seat.

"Are we to understand that the defense now *admits* that the cloak found in the Hudson Street yard is the property of the prisoner?"

Quinncannon raised his eyes from his notes and smiled. "We do not admit it, Mr. Morris," said a slight brogue. "We insist upon it."

Eliza Salters took the stand looking even more puffy and wan than when I first saw her, despite her pitiful efforts to make herself attractive. Her answers under direct examination by Phenix paralleled her responses to her interrogation in Quinncannon's rooms.

She admitted knowing Robinson for several weeks before the murder and being visited by him in the month prior to Helen Jewett's residence in Rosina Townsend's house. Eliza knew him only as Frank Rivers, and when he came he generally wore a dark cloth cloak with long tassels of braided silk. Five weeks before the murder the witness noticed that one of the tassels had been broken off and she sewed it back on.

"Now this is very important," Phenix told her. "On the morning after the murder, at Mrs. Townsend's house, *did you mention this peculiar fact about one of the tassels on the prisoner's cloak to anyone present?*"

"Yes, sir, in conversation with—"

Phenix anticipated the defense's objection. "Never mind with whom you were conversing, Miss Salters. The point is, did you mention this peculiar fact about the tassel *before* or *after* the cloak was discovered?"

"Before, sir."

"And when the cloak had been found, was it then exhibited to you?"

"Yes, sir."

"And did you then and there observe the same peculiar fact about the tassel upon that cloak?"

"Yes, sir, I did."

"Your witness," Phenix said.

Quinncannon conducted the cross-examination from his chair. "Miss Salters, I notice the district attorney omitted asking you to identify the cloak for the jury. Perhaps the clerk would show you the exhibit."

Eliza swore to the cloak.

"Tassels and all?"

"Yes, sir."

"Miss Salters, have you had an opportunity to observe the prisoner while he was undressed?"

"Yes, sir."

"Several opportunities?"

"Yes," she answered defensively.

"On those occasions did you ever notice a bald spot on the prisoner's head?"

"No, sir. I only heard of that yesterday from Mrs. Townsend."

"From Mrs. Townsend?" Quinncannon mulled that over. "Do you think, if there had been such a bald spot, you should have seen it?"

"I should think so," she said.

"Now, the district attorney will want us to be perfectly sure of ourselves on this point, Eliza. How many times would you say you saw the defendant undressed during the seven weeks before the murder?"

"Several occasions, Mr. Quinncannon, in the first four weeks."

"That's all." The Irishman glanced at the prosecution table, where an eager Morris was pushing back his chair. "Ah, but I see that Mr. Morris is breathless to ask you a question, so I will put it for him. Did you entertain the prisoner at all during the last three weeks, Eliza?"

Morris sank back. Eliza answered, "No." There was an edge on her voice.

"He stopped coming to see you?"

"He came to see *her!*"

"Whom do you mean by 'her,' Eliza?"

"Jewett!" She spat out the name.

The jury was intent on the witness. Quinncannon asked quietly, "Eliza, did you hate Helen Jewett?"

There was a long pause. Eliza's yellow eyes smoldered. "Yes," she finally said, just as quietly. "I hated her and I'm glad she's dead."

Next to take the oath was a small, doe-eyed, frightened black girl in her late teens named Sarah Dunscomb who had been employed by Helen Jewett to clean her room each morning and return in early evening to help her dress. Sarah was called to identify the miniature of Robinson found in the boy's bureau by Brink after the murder. She made a positive identification of the miniature and swore it was in the victim's possession on the morning before the crime. At about ten a.m. she had dusted it and replaced it in Helen's bureau.

Quinncannon handled her gently. She told him she had arrived at Helen's room at five-thirty on the murder night and left at seven-thirty. She had twice been out of the room, once to bring up wood for a fire which Helen kindled and once to fetch a pitcher of water.

"Now, Miss Dunscomb, did you watch Miss Jewett while she kindled the fire?"

Sarah had.

"Did Miss Jewett use her hatchet to break up the wood?"

"Yes, sir."

Morris roared an objection and Quinncannon turned in wide-eyed amazement. "On what possible grounds, Mr. Morris?"

"Incompetent," Morris sputtered. "Irrelevant, immaterial, and dealing with matters not brought out in direct examination."

"Overruled," Judge Edwards said sternly.

The Irishman was purring. "Now, Sarah, you saw Miss Jewett with a hatchet in her room on the evening *before* her murder?"

"Yes, sir."

"How long had she had that hatchet?"

"I first noticed it on the Thursday morning before her death, sir, when I was cleaning her room."

He showed her the hatchet and asked if she could recognize it. She looked at it hard but refused to touch it. "I can't say, sir. Those things all look alike to me. Only one thing I'm sure of, sir."

"What's that, Sarah?"

"Miss Helen's ax—it didn't have no cord on it."

The final witness of the second day was a pert, pretty girl of eighteen, an inmate of 41 Thomas Street named Emma French. It was her purpose to corroborate Rosina's identification of Robinson as the man admitted to the house at nine-thirty.

Emma had boarded with Rosina for sixteen months. Though Robinson, whom she knew only as Frank Rivers, had never visited her, she had seen him there four or five times and once had spoken with him in Eliza Salter's room. Emma's own room was off the entry near the front door, directly opposite Rosina Townsend's. Between nine and ten on the evening of the murder the witness had been standing at her door when Rosina let a man in. She heard the man knock and the madam twice ask, "Who's there?" although she could not make out his responses. When he entered he pulled up his collar, but she recognized him as the prisoner. She was *positive* it was he. She watched him go up the right staircase until he disappeared and did not see him again, though she saw Helen later, around eleven, when she came down to get a boot which the shoemaker had brought.

The lamp in the entry was lighted, she said. It hung high from the ceiling opposite the stairs and gave enough light so that she could see the prisoner distinctly. About thirty minutes before the prisoner arrived she heard Helen in the parlor saying she expected "Frank" that evening.

On cross-examination Quinncannon made short work of little Emma. "Where have you spent this long day, Miss French?"

"In the building opposite this one."

"Alone?"

"No, sir. Mrs. Townsend and some of the girls were there with me."

"And how much did Mrs. Townsend tell you concerning her testimony yesterday?"

"Why, sir, she never told us nothing of the questions and answers."

"She *never* told you *nothing?*" Quinncannon rubbed his eyes as if from exhaustion. "How many Frank Riverses visited your house?"

"Two of 'em, sir. They said they was cousins."

"Did they look alike, as relations often do?"

"Lord, no, sir. The other was dark and this one, the prisoner, was fair."

"Very good, Miss French. You have answered all my questions quite smartly and honestly." The lady beamed. He seemed about to release her when suddenly he added, "Miss French, when the prisoner entered and pulled up his collar, what part of his face could you see?"

"His eyes and his forehead, sir."

"And you identified him by his eyes and forehead?"

"Yes," she said slowly.

"Come now, miss. You knew him *only* by his eyes and forehead?"

"Well, I thought it was him."

"Do you now *swear* that the man you saw that night was the prisoner, Richard Robinson?"

There was a long pause before she answered. "No, sir, I cannot swear it."

The Irishman nodded. "Now, Miss French, you testified that you saw Helen around eleven that evening when a boot was delivered to her by the shoemaker."

"Yes, sir."

"Was there anyone else in the entry at that time?"

"No, sir. I heard Helen's voice in the hall and opened my door to peep out."

"Did you see the shoemaker?"

"No, sir. When I looked out Helen had the front door open. It opens toward my room and it blocked my view. But I heard her thanking him for bringing the boot at that hour."

"You did not see Helen come downstairs to go to the door?"

"No, sir."

"Did you wait to watch her go back upstairs?"

"No, sir."

Quinncannon had his eyes on the jury. "Is it possible, Miss French, that Helen let someone *out* of the house while she had that door open?"

"Yes, sir, I suppose it is."

"Is it possible, Miss French, that Helen also let someone *into* the house through that door at that time?"

She pondered the question. "Yes, sir, I guess she could have done."

## 38  Mr. Brink Testifies

Yet another stormy day and still the mob began gathering in the Park before six a.m. Fortunately the authorities had now reduced the problem of crowd control to a science and perfect order prevailed when court convened at ten, though the marshals came close to outnumbering the spectators.

Officer Brink was called by Mr. Morris. The policeman settled his bulk in the witness chair, and from time to time consulting a grimy note pad, he deposed that he had reached 41 Thomas Street on April 10 before daylight at about four-thirty. He was there when the cloak and hatchet were found, between daylight and sunrise, and was present in the yard when Mr. Eldridge gave them to the coroner. Brink himself had handled them and he identified the court exhibits. He knew the cloak from the tassel particularly, and had seen the twine attached to it when he examined it in the yard. The string now tied to the ax handle was also there when he saw it in the yard, and he had compared the two strings, determining that they had once been a single cord which "appeared as though it had broken apart." He made this comparison "not more than two minutes after they were found." After the items were given to Mr. Eldridge to be kept safe, he did not see them again until they were brought before the coroner's jury, perhaps two or three hours later.

"And when you viewed these articles at the inquest," Morris asked, "did you see any difference in the strings from the time you examined them earlier in the yard?"

"Not a particle of difference," Brink answered with assurance.

"You went with Mr. Noble to arrest the prisoner, did you not?"

Brink had. When he and Noble first aroused Robinson, the boy came into the hall wearing his nightshirt tucked into his trousers. The witness did notice something white on the trousers but, at that time, did not pay close attention. He asked if Robinson owned or ever wore a blue cloth cloak. "His answer was no—that he had never had a cloth cloak. He then remarked that he had an old camblet cloak which was then hanging in his bedroom, at the same time pointing to it and saying, 'There it is.'"

When he returned to Thomas Street, Brink stated, he then first observed that the rear fence was recently whitewashed on the western end of the yard, and made a connection with the stains on Robinson's trousers. These stains were "partly in front and partly on the side of the right leg of his pantaloons."

"Very well," Morris said. "Now, after the inquest did you search the prisoner's room?"

"I did, on Sunday afternoon, April 10."

"And what, if anything, did you find there?"

"I discovered a miniature in a drawer of his bureau, which I believe to be Robinson's portrait."

He identified the miniature. He had come upon it while looking for letters, which he did not find.

"Cross-examine," Morris said.

Quinncannon began his questioning easily enough, but there was a wicked gleam in his eye. I leaned forward. It was going to be interesting.

"Mr. Brink, how long have you been a police officer in this city?"

The witness settled back comfortably. "Nine or ten years."

"And how long have you known Mrs. Rosina Townsend?"

"Perhaps three years."

"Were you intimate in Mrs. Townsend's house?"

"Not particularly."

"Not *particularly*. Were you particularly acquainted with the location of the premises and the surrounding lots?"

"Not particularly, until the murder."

"Previous to the murder, had you ever been on the upper floors of Mrs. Townsend's house?"

"No."

"Did you know Helen Jewett?"

"I did."

"Ever visit her professionally?"

The witness hesitated.

"I speak of your profession, Brink, not hers."

The courtroom exploded into laughter.

"I will rephrase," Quinncannon said. "Did you ever visit Helen Jewett at Mrs. Townsend's?"

"No." Anger was beginning to color Brink's jowls.

"Ever visit her elsewhere?"

"No!"

"Prior to the murder, how often had you been in Mrs. Townsend's house?"

"I would suppose several times, but always officially. I went there when I had process against someone in the house—sometimes one of the servants, sometimes against one of the girls."

"Were you ever at the Townsend house when you had no process to serve?"

"I believe I have been. Sometimes she would send for me when she had been threatened by rioters there."

"Did you ever see any rioters at her house?"

"No."

"Ever see a riot at her house?"

"No!"

Quinncannon glanced through his notes. "Have you ever received any money, goods, wares, or merchandise from Rosina Townsend?"

"No, except on one or two occasions my regular fees for process serving."

"Perhaps, Mr. Brink, your memory is faulty. Do you now remember that she paid you for attending the auction of her furniture?"

"Yes," the policeman admitted. "She did pay me, and some other officers, five dollars a day."

"Did you make any purchase at the auction?"

"I bought a clock for thirty dollars."

"Paid cash, did you?"

"No, not myself, but I believe Officer Welch paid for it when he settled with Mrs. Townsend for our services."

"How many days did you attend the sale?"

"Two days, as I recollect."

"And how much money did you pay Officer Welch?"

Brink appeared confused.

"If you were at the sale for two days," Quinncannon explained patiently, "you earned ten dollars. You owed Welch twenty more for the clock."

"Well, I paid him."

"You paid him twenty dollars?"

"Fifteen or twenty," Brink said evasively.

"Where is the clock now?"

"At my house."

Quinncannon nodded. "When she was murdered, how much money did Helen Jewett have?"

"I don't know that she had any money!" Brink snapped.

Quinncannon approached him. "Now, don't you know that she was considered remarkable in her sphere of life for possessing money, fine dresses, and expensive jewels?"

"I do not!"

Just as he seemed about to pounce, the Irishman waved his hand and returned to the defense table. Ogden Hoffman rose majestically.

"Now, Mr. Brink," said the prisoner's senior counsel, "you and I have been public officers together, and I may ask you a few questions with a little more freedom than usual. Did you ever receive any money from Mrs. Townsend for speaking to the district attorney in her favor?"

"I don't think I ever did."

Hoffman grunted. "Did you never receive any money for going to the district attorney in relation to an indictment that was pending against Mrs. Townsend to intercede with him in her behalf?"

"I never did," answered Brink, and then quickly added, "that I recall."

"Who was the district attorney at that time?"

"Mr. Hoffman was—you were, sir."

"Do you now recollect the incident?"

Brink furrowed his brows. At last he said, "I do."

Hoffman bowed and sat down. Standing at the table with his back to Brink, Quinncannon observed, "The witness's memory appears to be improving as the morning wears on."

Morris wailed, "Oh! Your honor—" But the Irishman cut in with a question.

"When you arrested Mr. Robinson, you interrogated him in the entry of his boardinghouse. What was your purpose in asking him to leave his bedroom?"

"Why," the policeman responded, "I was going to charge him directly with the murder, but I changed my mind and began questioning him about the cloak."

"Couldn't you have questioned him in his bedroom just as well?"

"I suppose so."

"Why didn't you?"

"I cannot say. I suppose it was a notion of mine at the time."

"This notion—had it anything to do with getting Robinson out of earshot of his roommate so there could be no witness to your conversation except Mr. Noble?"

"Certainly not!" snapped the officer.

"Kindly repeat your exchange with Robinson regarding the cloak."

"I asked him if he had a blue cloth cloak and he said no, he never owned one."

"He didn't tell you that he had such a cloak belonging to another person?"

"He did not."

"When you compared the strings on the cloak and the hatchet, and found them, as you say, similar, did you consider that an important fact?"

"Of course."

"Why did you fail to communicate that fact to the coroner?"

Brink looked uncomfortable. "I cannot say."

"Did you consider yourself acting under the coroner or superior to him?"

"Acting under him, naturally."

"I see. When you first saw the white mark on Robinson's trousers, did you feel it or sniff it or attempt to dust it?"

"No. I have said I did not attach much importance to it at the time."

"Did you observe the whitewash on Mrs. Townsend's west fence closely?"

"I did. It was thickly laid on."

"Yet you *still* made no effort to test the white marks on Robinson's trousers?"

"I believe I mentioned the stains before the coroner's jury."

"You did, sir, and still you made no tests." Quinncannon stood before the witness. "Mr. Brink, do you, upon your oath, solemnly avow that you did not question Robinson about those stains either at his rooming house or at Mrs. Townsend's?"

"I do!"

"And he never told you that those stains were white paint?"

"Absolutely not, sir."

"Did you notice any stains on the cloak when you examined it?"

"No," the officer acknowledged, "but in my opinion a person could have got over the fence without getting any whitewash on the cloak."

Quinncannon's eyes narrowed. "In your opinion, exactly how?"

"Well, he might have thrown the cloak over the fence first and then got over."

"Would the clerk give the cloak to the witness?" The Irishman leaned back against the defense table, folding his arms. "Would you demonstrate, Mr. Brink, how you would throw the cloak over a nine-foot fence?"

Brink wadded up the garment and flung it as high in the air as he could. It landed in a lump at Quinncannon's feet and he let it lie there.

"Mr. Brink, please estimate how far the cloak is from where you are standing."

"Six feet, maybe seven."

"And what is its present condition?"

"Why, it's all bunched up in a heap."

"Mr. Brink, are you aware that when this cloak was found in the Hudson Street yard it was fully *fifteen* feet from the fence?"

"Uh—"

"Are you aware that it was found spread out *flat* on the ground?"

The policeman's mouth worked noiselessly.

"Resume your seat," Quinncannon said. "I ask you again, sir, how do you think a person could scale that fence without staining his cloak?"

"I guess I can't imagine."

"Neither can I, Mr. Brink." Quinncannon stepped carefully over the cloak. "Neither can I."

As if on a sudden thought the Irishman asked, "You did examine the prisoner's clothes carefully for stains, didn't you?"

Brink was back on familiar ground. "Oh, yes, both at his rooming house and at the inquest."

"No chance he was wearing different clothes after his arrest than he'd worn the night before?"

"No chance! You needn't worry about that, Mr. Quinncannon."

"And how many bloodstains did you discover?"

"Objection!" Robert Morris shouted. "Not covered under direct examination!"

"Your Honor," Quinncannon said mildly, "Mr. Morris raised the question of stains on the clothing. I am merely inquiring after the nature of the stains."

"Overruled," Judge Edwards said. "The witness will answer."

Brink was baffled. "But we didn't find any blood, your honor."

"No bloodstains?" Quinncannon echoed. "None? Mr. Brink, surely you examined the corpse."

"Certainly!"

"And how, in your professional opinion, was she killed?"

"Robinson stood over her while she slept and bashed her head in!" Brink snarled.

"Did you observe the bloodstains from her wounds spattered on the floor beside her bed?"

"I did."

"Then how, in God's name, did the killer, standing where you say he stood, where he must have stood, avoid getting her blood splashed all over his clothes?"

Without waiting for an answer Quinncannon spun around to the prosecution table. "Redirect," he said.

Morris almost bounded toward the witness. "Mr. Brink, would you say that a man could have murdered Helen Jewett without getting blood on his clothes if, when he killed her, *he was not wearing any clothes?*"

"You mean buck *naked?*" The policeman contemplated this for a minute. "Yeah, it could've happened that way."

"That's all, Mr. Brink." With a triumphant look at the jury, Morris sat down.

Brink seemed uncertain what he should do next. He looked at the judge. He began to heave himself out of the chair. As he was about to leave the box, a light brogue said, "Are we keeping you from something, Mr. Witness?" Quinncannon's chin rested in his hand and his eyes were almost closed. "Are you in a hurry? Have you an auction to attend?"

Brink sank back. "I thought you were through with me," he said sullenly.

The Irishman smiled. "Oh, no." He opened his eyes. "I'm not through with you, Brink."

The huge mob in the courtroom was silent. It was coming.

"Did you search Helen Jewett's room on the morning after the murder?"

"I did," the officer answered cautiously.

"What did you find?"

"I didn't find no jewels or money," Brink barked, "if that's what you're hinting."

Quinncannon sighed. "Let me rephrase the question. What did you find?"

"Just two packets of letters."

"By whom were they written?"

"One bunch from Jewett to the prisoner, and one bunch from the prisoner to Jewett."

"Did the prisoner sign his name?"

"He signed them 'Frank.' "

"How did you know that this 'Frank' was the prisoner?"

Brink smirked. "Because the envelopes had Robinson's real name and address on 'em."

"Which address? His boardinghouse or Mr. Hoxie's store?"

"Both. Some was addressed to one place, some to the other."

"Is that how you knew the prisoner's real name and where he lived?"

"It is," Brink affirmed.

"And you went to his room and arrested him?"

The officer nodded. "Me and Noble."

"Was that before or after the cloak and hatchet were found?"

"After. When I'd inspected the hatchet and cloak in the yard, they were given to Eldridge to lock up. He kept the key until the inquest, when he gave it to the coroner, who gave it to me. Then I unlocked the room off the parlor and fetched them for the inquest."

"Then between the time they were found and the time you went to 'fetch' them, could anyone have tampered with the exhibits?"

"Not a chance!" Brink said.

Quinncannon handed the hatchet to the witness. "Will you say again, is this the same hatchet you gave to the coroner at the inquest?"

Brink examined it. "It is the same," he said.

Robert Morris smiled. "May I ask, is the defense preparing to argue the identification of the hatchet?"

Quinncannon returned the smile. "On the contrary, defense will stipulate that this is the weapon exhibited at the inquest." He took back the hatchet and weighed it in his hand. "Mr. Brink, when you went to arrest Robinson, why did you first stop at Hoxie's store?"

"Well, me and Noble thought he might be there."

"At seven a.m., on a Sunday? No, Brink, you went to Hoxie's store to steal his hatchet. You took *this* hatchet back to Thomas Street and, when the coroner gave you Eldridge's key to the room off the parlor you switched *this* hatchet for the one which was locked there. You tied *this* hatchet to a loose string from the tassel on the cloak and broke it off."

"Lies!" Brink thundered. "You're lying, damn you!"

"George Noble watched you do it, Brink."

The side door opened and Noble was thrust into the room in handcuffs. Behind him loomed the formidable Jacob Hays.

"Damn you," Brink roared at Noble. "It was your idea!"

## 39   The Third Whore

Dennis Brink was taken into custody by the high constable. It required almost an hour to restore order to the packed courtroom. I scribbled out a dispatch and sent a copyboy scurrying to the *Sun* office. Judge Edwards and the four aldermen flanking him had retired to chambers while the army of marshals and special deputies waded ponderously into the mob, brandishing their clubs and shouting for silence. The mood at the prosecution table was dark. At the defense table Richard Robinson chatted in animated fashion with his father and Hoxie and two of his attorneys. Quinncannon sat apart and alone at the core of the uproar, chewing the stem of an empty pipe, studying the notes spread before him. Then, as the marshals retreated to their posts along the walls and the court clerk cried out and the black-robed justices filed back to the bench and the district attorney rose to summon his next witness, one corner of the Irishman's mouth tugged up in a half smile.

"The state," said a haggard James Phenix, "calls Maria Stevens to the stand."

Blond curls tossing, scarlet silks rustling, the witness stepped smartly up to the box and smiled in a sultry fashion at the jury. The twelve gentlemen were not unappreciative.

Her profession notwithstanding, Maria Stevens had style. She perched demurely on the edge of the witness chair, gloved hands folded in her lap, and with the tiniest tilt of her head she flirted with every man in the hall. There was an aura of Circe, a whisper of Versailles about her

She brought a glamour to those grim and grimy proceedings that was sadly lacking in the wolfish Rosina, the frumpy Salters, or even the merely pretty Emma French. Helen Jewett's voice had been musical; Maria's was no less so. But Helen reminded you of bells in a light breeze. Wherever Maria went there was a brass band playing.

Phenix established that she had lived some months with Rosina. "Are you then thoroughly familiar with the layout of the house and the surrounding yards, Miss Stevens?"

"Oh, completely!"

Phenix produced three large sheets of cardboard and placed them on an easel. "Your honor, these diagrams represent the premises at 41 Thomas Street and we ask that they be marked for identification."

Whitlaw Price was on his feet. "Defense objects to this testimony, your honor, as not being best evidence."

The district attorney groaned. "Your honor, the state had hoped to prove these exhibits by Officer Brink, but . . ."

Quinncannon placed a restraining hand on Price's arm. In some confusion Price said, "Withdraw the objection."

Phenix took Maria on a tour of Rosina's house and grounds, using the diagrams for the benefit of the jury. He dwelled particularly on the fact that Maria's room adjoined Helen Jewett's.

"Now, Miss Stevens, prior to the murder, were you acquainted with the prisoner?"

"Oh, yes. Frank—well, I knew him as Frank—visited me many times at Mrs. Gallagher's." She smiled at Robinson. "We're old friends."

"About how many times did he call on you?"

"At least ten. He used to take me to the theater and buy me the most lavish gifts."

"Would you say you are thoroughly familiar with the prisoner's voice?"

"I surely am, Mr. Phenix."

"And when was the last time you heard his voice?"

She set her liquid eyes on Robinson. "I heard him in Helen's room, arguing with dear Helen on the night she was murdered."

I gaped at her in disbelief. She had coolly changed completely the story she'd told us in Quinncannon's rooms. I glanced at the Irishman. He did not seem the least surprised. The judge gaveled for order. Phenix said, "Please explain the circumstances, Miss Stevens."

Maria sat basking in the glow of the sensation she had caused. "I went to my room shortly before eleven that night, Mr. Phenix. In a few minutes I heard dear Helen bellowing for champagne on the landing and Mrs. Townsend bringing up a bottle. There was some conversation at the door which I couldn't understand and Mrs. Townsend left. Perhaps five minutes later I heard voices arguing in Helen's room. One was dear Helen and the other was unquestionably Frank, the prisoner."

"Now, Miss Stevens," said Phenix, "this is extremely important. Are you absolutely certain that the voice you heard was the defendant's?"

"Oh, yes," she answered with conviction. "The wall between the rooms is lath and plaster, paper-thin, and they *were* having a perfectly awful row."

"Could you hear what was said?"

"Objection to the witness stating what was said!" shouted Price.

"Not all of it," responded the lady, "but the word 'letters' was used several times."

"Your honor!" Price yelped.

"Sustained," rumbled the judge. "The witness will refrain from stating what was said."

"Yes, Judge." Maria pouted. "But I really think Helen was blackmailing him." She looked around the courtroom wide-eyed. "I mean, that's certainly what it *sounded* like."

Phenix said, "Take the witness."

Quinncannon concentrated on his notes for a moment. Then, with a sweep of his arm, he pushed them off the table into the wastebasket.

"Now." He rose and walked slowly toward her. "Miss Stevens, prior to her moving to Thomas Street, were you acquainted with Helen Jewett?"

She smiled, showing pretty dimples. "Why, of course," she answered. "I knew her back in Boston."

"In Boston, weren't you instrumental in breaking up Helen's engagement to the son of a wealthy merchant?"

"I suppose I played some small part."

"As a result, weren't you thrown out of employment and forced to leave the city?"

"Not directly, sir," she said a bit archly.

"When you entertained the prisoner at Gallagher's, wasn't he also seeing Helen Jewett?"

"Frank," she said, fluttering her eyes at the defendant, "trailed after me like a love-sick little calf."

"Whimpering piteously?" Quinncannon asked, and then, more sharply, "Pawing the turf under your window?" He wheeled on her. "Helen followed the two of you to Gallagher's, didn't she, Maria? She broke down your door and she beat you silly with a two-by-four!"

"That incident," cried the lady, "has been blown all out of proportion—"

"Miss Stevens!" he said savagely. "You hated Helen Jewett and you wanted her dead! You had motive and you had opportunity. And if you choose to invent some cock-and-bull fable about voices through the wall, there is no reason under the full moon why this jury should believe you!"

"Am I being accused of perjury?" she shouted. "Every word I've spoken was the truth!"

She leaned forward, her gloved hands gripping the arms of the chair tightly, her eyes blazing, and Quinncannon, when he turned back to her, was smiling. "Dear lady, of course you've told the truth. You must calm yourself, Maria. You do seem," he said, with an eye on the jury, "to have quite an ungovernable temper." He placed his hand on hers. "If it's any comfort to you, Maria, I believe you implicitly."

She recovered herself quickly. "Of course, Mr. Quinncannon, it is a great comfort to me." Her manner seemed to suggest that he would not do *that* to her again. She refolded her hands in her lap.

"Then," he said mildly, "perhaps you would tell us just what it was you heard."

"I heard," she said, selecting her words carefully, "a quarrel between Helen and the prisoner. It had something to do with letters which had passed between them. I gathered that Frank had determined to marry and was trying to break off with Helen, and Helen was using his letters to hold him."

"About what time did this argument occur?"

"It began shortly after Rosina brought up the wine and lasted perhaps fifteen minutes." She paused. "It really became quite heated, Mr. Quinncannon."

"They appeared to be very angry with each other?"

"Very," she replied, "especially Frank. He seemed to be losing the battle, you see."

The Irishman looked thoughtful. "From what you overheard, Maria, would you say the prisoner had a motive to murder Helen Jewett?"

Whitlaw Price went white. His mouth jerked open. At the brink of an objection he suddenly realized the question had been posed by his own colleague. Morris and Phenix were watching the witness intently.

Quinncannon said, "Shall I repeat the question?"

"It's not necessary, sir," Maria said. "I should say the prisoner had an excellent motive for murder."

"And what would you say that motive was?"

"Why, to get possession of his letters to her, naturally."

"Then, why do you think he returned her letters to him that same night, Maria?"

"I don't know that he did so, sir."

"And," said Quinncannon slowly, "why do you suppose he left both sets of letters behind for the police to find?"

She thought that over. "I really don't know, sir."

"Of course you don't, Maria," he said quietly. "Nor does anybody else."

He strolled toward the jury box. "On the night of the murder, what time did you retire to bed?"

"It was somewhat before midnight," she answered. "I should think about a quarter before the hour."

"After the quarrel subsided, did you hear any more from Helen's room?"

"No, sir."

"Did you hear Robinson—the prisoner—leave that room?"

"No, sir. I fell asleep rather quickly, I believe. At one point I arose to fasten one of my shutters, which was banging in the wind. I don't know what time it was but the house was quiet. I heard nothing else until Rosina raised the cry of fire. Then I rushed out and went immediately into dear Helen's room to try to save her."

"Then Helen's room was unlocked?"

"Oh, yes. All the girls leave their doors on the latch." She smiled. "There are no secrets in a house like ours, and one never knows when friends will call."

Quinncannon rubbed thoughtfully at a corner of his moustache. "Yet, on the murder night, your door was locked, Maria."

She seemed surprised. "Was it?"

"Rosina found it so when she came upstairs and discovered the fire."

"Did she? Well, then, I imagine it must have been." She coughed slightly.

The Irishman turned his attention to the cardboard sketches of the house and grounds of 41 Thomas Street produced by the prosecution. "Maria, did I understand you to say that this diagram of Mrs. Townsend's yard is accurate in every respect?"

"Yes, Mr. Quinncannon." She smiled at him sweetly.

He smiled at her sweetly. "Would you care to look again, Maria?"

"Oh," she exclaimed. "I see what you mean. There's no hole in the fence."

"By 'hole' do you refer to the gap in the fence behind Mrs. Townsend's privy—the fence between Mrs. Townsend's and the Hudson Street yard?"

"Yes, sir. It's all broken down there and rotted through."

"Could a person go from one yard to the other by stepping through that gap?"

She watched his face. "I would imagine so," she said.

"Regarding this floor plan of the house," he continued, "would you identify this part of the structure?"

She studied it. "That is the piazza adjoining the parlor."

"'The roof of the piazza is just outside Helen Jewett's window?'"

"Yes, sir."

He nodded. "If a person had committed a crime in Helen's room—let us say, a murder—what would you imagine to be his quickest and safest route of escape, Maria?"

Again she coughed, two or three times, holding a delicate lace handkerchief to her mouth. At length she looked at him and shrugged. "I'm sure I don't know, sir. I never thought of it."

"Well, let's think about it now." Quinncannon glanced at Morris, who was in the process of rising, and added, "You *were* brought here, Maria, as an expert on the layout of the murder house." Morris slumped back into his chair.

Maria was staring at the diagrams. "I suppose you want me to say he could have climbed out on the roof and dropped into the alley to Thomas Street."

"Now, Miss Stevens," the Irishman said, "I don't want you to say anything unless you believe it. What other means of escape might be possible for such a killer?"

"Not the street door, surely."

"And why not?"

"Because," she replied, feeling the ground firm up under her feet, "Rosina always locked that door at midnight. Thereafter the girls had to let their visitors out with their own keys."

"It is in evidence that the prisoner visited both Miss Salters and Miss Jewett many times. Don't you suppose he was aware of that custom of the house?"

"I imagine he would have been."

"But, then . . ." He turned his head and regarded the jury. "Why do you think he would not simply avail himself of Helen's key after killing her and let himself out to the street?"

She looked at him coldly. "I really don't know," she said. "It is obvious he went out through the rear doors instead."

"Is it?" Quinncannon appeared to weigh that assertion carefully. "Why is it obvious?" he asked at last, with the air of a man who really wanted to know.

"His cloak and hatchet were found in the rear yards, sir," she said curtly. "He must have escaped that way."

"Possibly," Quinncannon said, "if we assume the murderer came from outside the house. Of course, then we must also assume that he abandoned the compromising letters for which he killed, and ignored the two easiest routes of escape in favor of the most difficult and dangerous. But what if we assume that the killer was not an outsider but someone belonging to the house? In that event, Maria, what would be the simplest way of leaving the murder room?"

Her eyes shot to the prosecution table, but no objection was forthcoming from that quarter. "I don't think I understand you, sir," she said.

"Oh . . . I think you do, madam." He removed one diagram from the easel and held it in view of the witness and the jury. "As an expert on this floor plan, Miss Stevens, just give these gentlemen your opinion."

Her spine stiffened. "I should think," she said evenly, "the murderer would go out the room door and return to her own bed."

"'To her own bed,' " Quinncannon echoed. "That seems logical. You see, Maria, these questions aren't difficult." He replaced the cardboard. "Now, your room and Helen's were adjacent. Were they identical?"

She searched for the trap in the question and apparently found none. "Yes, Mr. Quinncannon. It was a double house, you know."

"And furnished identically?"

Maria managed a laugh. "Oh dear, no," she said, almost pertly. "I have wonderful taste in furnishings."

"Let's not forget the oil lamps, Maria."

"Well," she said, "there *were* two lamps that were identical. They belonged to Rosina. She gave one to me and the other to dear Helen."

"One of those lamps was found by Mrs. Townsend in her parlor just before she discovered the fire, wasn't it?"

"I believe it was," the lady responded. "Helen's lamp was burning beside the open rear doors."

His eyes narrowed. "How can we be certain it was Helen's lamp in the parlor and not yours? They were interchangeable, were they not?"

"Perhaps," she answered with confidence, "but on that point I can speak with certainty, sir. My lamp never left my room. It was Helen's lamp that Frank took to light his way through the house after he'd killed her and set the bed afire."

"Yes," Quinncannon said, "that fire, set with a candle beneath the mattress. Though Mrs. Townsend discovered it, you were the first to observe it closely. Please describe it for the jury."

"There was a great deal of smoke but almost no flame," she said. "I took up a handful of ashes from the bedclothes. They seemed to be consumed without burning."

"Why do you think the fire was set?"

"Why, to conceal the murder!" she answered smartly. "He meant to burn the house down around us."

"Did he?" he said. "The poor, blundering devil! As clumsy and fumbling an arsonist as he was a murderer. All he had to do after he killed Helen was pour the lamp oil over the corpse, set it aflame, seize the incriminating letters, and go out the window over the roof to the alley. And instead, Maria, just look what a botch he made of it."

The brogue was soft and tinged with sadness. Quinncannon had leaned back against the defense table, his arms straight, the heels of his hands resting on the table's edge, his forehead furrowed quizzically and his mouth and thin moustache twisted up at one corner and down at the other. All eyes were on him, especially Robinson's. The boy stared at his back as if he could somehow see his face through it.

Maria Stevens' shoulders gave one convulsive little shake and then squared as if by instant rigor mortis. Her rouged lips were set slightly apart, showing pearl-white teeth. Her eyes were alive with wary cunning. It was as though the rest of us were painted figures and only these two drew breath.

"Do you really believe the fire was started to destroy the house, Maria?"

"I cannot imagine another reason."

"But . . . a single candle . . . placed under a blood-soaked mattress. It burned like a smudge pot, Maria. The sort of fire which would be set by a resident of the house who had no intention of being burned in her bed."

"Nevertheless, sir, it would have destroyed the body and concealed the murder."

He shook his head slowly. "No, it would not, could not . . . and did not, Maria. It brought the murder to light hours earlier than might have been expected. That was its purpose."

She smiled, just a little. "Why would the killer wish his crime to be discovered so quickly, Mr. Quinncannon?"

"To fix suspicion more firmly on the victim's last visitor, I would imagine. Don't you think that was part of the murderer's plan from the outset, Maria?"

"His cloak was found in the next yard," she said. "Obviously he lost it while fleeing over the fence."

"No, Maria. Had he scaled the fence, the cloak would be stained with whitewash."

"Not if he threw it over first, sir."

"But it has been demonstrated to the jury, madam, that the garment could not have been tossed over a nine-foot fence and landed in the manner it was found, fifteen feet the other side and spread flat."

"Ah, sir, but you are forgetting the gap behind the privy, which you, yourself, raised here. You noted, too, that the prisoner was a regular visitor to the house. He might well have known of that gap and gone through it, and then dropped the cloak as he ran."

"Now. That is very plausible. But, if so . . ." He raised one eyebrow. "Why do you suppose he would first walk to the opposite end of the yard and drop the hatchet?"

For the first time she averted her eyes from his. He took a step toward her. "As a matter of fact, Maria, why would he bother to carry away the hatchet at all?"

"I believe the hatchet was found to belong to his employer's shop, sir. I suppose he feared it could be traced to him."

"That was a wonderful bit of luck." The Irishman took another step. "Wasn't it, Maria? The police, in their no doubt admirable zeal to solve the crime, took Mr. Hoxie's ax and swapped it for the murder weapon, and thus unwittingly aided the killer's plot to frame young Robinson. But the actual murder weapon belonged to the house. It is proven to have been in Helen's room before she was killed. I cannot think why he would want to take the hatchet, madam, unless you are prepared to suggest he desired a memento of the occasion."

There was a slight edge of sarcasm in his tone. Her hands clenched and unclenched in her lap. "You are totally ignoring the oil lamp found burning in the parlor," she said.

"What about the lamp, Maria?"

"Why," she cried, "he took it to light his way out after he killed her. It was Helen's lamp!"

"No," he said. He was now standing very near her. "No, dear lady, that was *your* lamp!"

"That's absurd! My lamp remained in my room. It was found there after the fire. It was *Helen's* lamp that was missing!"

"The lamps were identical, Maria. Another stroke of the killer's luck." He leaned against the judge's bench and folded his arms. "Would you like me to tell you how those lamps were switched? All right, then. Once upon a time . . ."

She watched him with an almost mesmeric fascination.

". . . there was a little girl named Maria who heard a quarrel through a wall between the two people she hated most in all her narrow, nasty little world. One was the rival in whose shadow she had always stood and the other was the young man who had jilted her, and she derived much pleasure from their falling out. When the argument stopped she remained listening until the young man left, parting with her rival on a final, bitter note. Little Maria opened her door and heard him asking the landlady to unlock the street door, but she would not. Away flew Maria to her window and watched him disappear over the eastern fences toward Chapel Street. Then she returned to the wall and continued listening for sounds of movement, until at last she concluded her rival was asleep. And then she had a wonderful idea.

"She lit her lamp and opened her rival's door, which she knew would be unlocked, and what a sight met her eyes. Her rival asleep and her hatchet on the hearth and the young man's cloak, left behind and still covering the sleeping girl to keep her warm. Now, what do you think little Maria did? She carefully removed the cloak and took up the hatchet, and she struck her rival a tentative blow with the heel of the blade, but her rival still breathed. So she struck a second blow, but *still* her rival lived. And Maria had gone too far to turn back. The last blow struck with the edge of the blade, so light that the wound was only three to four inches long, but it drove the bone into the brain, fracturing the skull and killing Helen instantly!"

Quinncannon's voice had become a harsh whisper. Maria snapped her eyes shut and tensed. He stepped a pace aside, and when he next spoke his tone was almost soothing.

"Murder is an acquired taste, Maria. The first time is never easy, no matter how deep your hatred. And you had the worst of it before you. You had to narrow the time in which the crime could have been committed in order to fix the blame on Robinson. You placed the lighted candle beneath the bed, knowing it would not endanger the house but would create enough smoke to rouse the inmates. Then you picked up the cloak and hatchet, and your lamp, and returned to your room.

"Helen's blood had splattered all over your night dress. You changed and burned the stained one. You waited to be certain the house was dark and quiet, and then used your lamp to light your way downstairs to the parlor. The bar to the rear doors was still down, where Robinson had left it. You put down the lamp and went outside to plant your clues. You placed the ax near the southwest corner of the yard as if dropped by Robinson while climbing the fence. Then you went to the northwest corner, behind the privy into the Hudson Street yard, and spread the cloak on the ground as if lost in flight. And then, Maria, the most terrifying thing of all happened."

Her eyes had been riveted on the folded hands in her lap. Now she stared up at him as though she were reliving the horrible moment. He put his hands on the arms of the witness chair and she seemed literally to shrivel before him.

"You heard," he said, "Rosina Townsend's voice calling from the house into the yard, Maria, and your blood must have frozen. You could not get over any of the fences—you could not escape from the yards—

and, if she replaced the bar across the rear doors, you would be trapped there, with the bloody hatchet and a fire burning in your victim's room."

She gave an involuntary shudder. That was all. Yet I think I have never witnessed a more awful gesture.

"But Rosina didn't bar the doors," he said softly. "She staggered back to her room in a sleepy stupor, Maria, and you fought a desperate struggle with panic and beat it back." His manner grew even more gentle. "There was something admirable, almost heroic, for you in that moment, Maria. You returned to the house and, I think, picked up the lamp before you realized that Rosina had seen it and could identify it as yours. But that night, Maria, your gods were with you. You remembered that Helen had a lamp identical to yours, and leaving your lamp in the parlor, you fled up the stairs to the murder room, seized her lamp, and rushed to your own room, locking the door on the shadows of horror behind you."

He released the arms of her chair and returned to the defense table. Maria remained, for a while, slumped down and shrunken. When finally she looked up at him, her face was ashen under her heavy rouge, but her eyes glowed unnaturally. "You," she hissed, "are Satan himself!"

Quinncannon regarded her quietly with an expression which contained much of pity but nothing of triumph.

"That's the only way it could have happened, Maria," he said.

By small degrees she regained her dignity. She straightened her spine and threw back her shoulders and drew a deep breath, and at last she tossed her head and smiled.

"In that event," she said, "I suppose I really ought to confess. I am nothing, Mr. Quinncannon, if not gracious."


In the tumult which greeted Robinson's release, even as I dashed off my dispatch for an eager copyboy, I recalled Quinncannon in his rooms reading to Maria the inquest testimony of Peter Collyer and Thomas Garland, the watchmen to whom she had stated on the murder night that she knew Helen's killer. I thought I understood why, that last evening in Hoffman's office, the Irishman had been certain the prosecution could produce three whores who would swear to Robinson's presence in the house that fatal night.

I scanned the melee in the courtroom. Caps with glazed visors were flung to the ceiling to the ring of frenzied cheers. Spanish capes were waved madly in the air. One had been draped over Robinson's shoulders as a mantle of triumph, and the boy, grinning broadly and raising his hands at arm's length, had been torn from the emotional grasp of his father and Hoxie by a crowd of frantic youths who now struggled with uncoordinated but grunting enthusiasm to hoist him to their shoulders.

I caught a glimpse of Maria Stevens, head held high, being led, unshackled, from the courtroom by Jacob Hays. I might have worked up some sympathy for Maria had I not remembered Thomas Cushing weltering in his blood with his throat cut to the nape. I fancied I now knew who had slaughtered that harmless little man, and why.

The door closed on Maria, and I searched the mob for the Irishman. Phenix and Morris were silently gathering their papers, oblivious to the crazed celebration encircling them. Hoffman and Price waded into the crowd, smiling and shaking seemingly disembodied hands.

There was no sign of Quinncannon. It did not surprise me.

# 40  Epilogue

Rosina Townsend and four of her girls headed for Albany and shipped up Clinton's ditch to Buffalo, where she hung out her shingle on a sumptuous seraglio rumored to rival the achievements of Rathbun, and the kings of Babylon, for that matter. Little doubt remains of the fate of Helen Jewett's jewels.

Eliza Salters fled to the Magdalene Society and now preaches on street corners.

Dennis Brink, while awaiting trial for perjury in the Dead House, was murdered by one of the Chichester gang.

Two weeks after the trial ended, Robert Furlong leaped from the deck of the Bull ferry and was drowned in the North River. I hear Quinncannon attended the services.

Emma French is now the reigning empress of Mary Gallagher's splendid new quarters at 41 Thomas Street. La Gallagher has insured her life for $30,000 with the Ocean Company. The policy was purchased through Mr. Schermerhorn, one of the jurors.

Maria Stevens caught a chill while planting the cloak in the Hudson Street yard and, after the trial, was confined to the City Hospital. On June 7 she burst a blood vessel in her throat during a coughing fit and died.

Richard Robinson swindled his father out of his savings and vanished, leaving Joseph Hoxie to meet the entire obligation to his attorneys. The unfortunate old gentleman went deeply into debt to pay

Hoffman and Price, and at last in desperation offered his store and stock to Quinncannon. He allowed me to read the Irishman's reply:

> *Hoxie, you ancient rogue—your offer has the reek of a sawdust game. I have inspected your termite-infested premises and discovered the foundation shaky, the beams rotten, the roof leaking—in short, the place is not worth the powder to blow it up and I will not have it as a gift.*
>
> *I have informed you of what I will take to settle your debt, and by God, I mean to have it!*
>
> Q.

"What could I do, Davy?" The old man looked up at me. "I had to give it to him."

"What did he want, sir?"

Hoxie was barely audible. "He wanted the hatchet."

Robinson was to be heard from one last time in a letter sent from New Orleans to me, believe it or not, as his "last sincere friend." The message was lengthy and rambling but a brief excerpt will convey the flavor:

> *I retain only a confused recollection of the circumstances so lately connected with my destiny—an imperfect dream of Brink, Bridewell, Bellevue, hatchet, Helen, Hoffman—ha! ha! Richard is himself again. I am Richard P. Robinson, Esquire—bound for New Orleans, on board the crack steamboat* Tuscarora, *which has made the quickest trip ever to that city from Louisville—am going South for my health, being of a rather consumptive habit. Left New York, it is true, partly on account of a slight misunderstanding with my lady love, "daughter" of a wealthy broker in Thomas Street, sign of the "Red Ram."*

Armed with a rifle, a cutlass, a brace of pistols, and an introduction to a Texican army officer, he shipped out of New Orleans on the *Polander* in late June, determined to "offer my precious self to the one-starred banner of the new Empire of the South West."

And perhaps he really meant to. According to my calculations, the *Polander* reached Galveston Bay two days after the war ended.

The penny press reacted in character to the trial. Bennett was jubilant: "Conscious of virtue, we will fight on for justice, decency, morality and truth!" Circulation also went up.

At the *Transcript* Attree wept over Maria Stevens, inventing out of his fertile imagination a "nefarious satyr" who had supposedly seduced her from her mother's apron strings and betrayed her into the sisterhood before the luckless child was out of puberty. Maria was "a veritable Symbol of the destitute and despairing souls whom this oppressive and wicked Society tramples daily—nay, hourly—under its well-shod heel."

As for Ben Day, on the morning following Robinson's release I was summoned to the office of the sole proprietor. I expected to find him apoplectic, but he was icy calm. He motioned me to a chair.

"Leave the wrap-up of the trial for Prall," he said. "I've got a much more important assignment for you, Cordor. You're going to write a series of articles exposing the foulness and corruption of our system of justice and public order which led to the escape of the murderer Robinson. I'm titling it 'The Great Unhung!' " Day, and his voice, rose from behind the huge desk. "The *Sun* is going to charge the defense with jury tampering, with manipulation of evidence, with suborning perjury, with bribing a public editor, with every filthy trick by which they engineered that disgusting charade. You, Cordor, were with Quinncannon every step of that twisted path. You're the man to write this story." He slammed his fist down on the desk. "You and I and this newspaper— we're going to blow the lid off this cesspool!"

I merely sat there, smiling at him. "As you say, Ben, I *am* the only man who could write that story."

" 'Stand and deliver,' eh, you young bandit?" Day scowled darkly. "All right, by God, I'll double your salary!"

"Oh, I have no interest in money, Ben," I said quietly. "There's only one thing you could offer that would tempt me. I want to sleep with your wife every other Tuesday."

He sat down. I believe he was considering it.

I stood and put on my hat.

"If you walk out of here you're finished in this business," Day snarled. "I'll see that you're blackballed in every editorial office in this city."

I said, "Go to hell," and closed the door behind me.

To escape Prall I abandoned the boardinghouse and moved into the American, which I could now ill afford. I camped in the taproom and waited for the offers to trickle in.

By midweek only Attree had approached me, an obviously unwilling emissary from his employers. I declined the offer without hearing it.

"Been thinking of throwing up the wretched business myself," Attree confided. "Become a counter-jumper or something."

"Why not a clergyman?" I suggested. "That was quite a sermon you preached on Maria Stevens."

"Journalists and preachers have much in common," he said, trying to look wise. "We both live by casting artificial pearls before genuine swine."

The ranks at the *Sun* were rapidly depleting. Wisner, whom I had liked, died suddenly of a heart seizure. Locke was uncovered as the source of Colonel Webb's knowledge of the horse-express escapade and Day rewarded his perfidy with dismissal. On Friday I entered the taproom to find Moses Beach already seated at my table.

"Davy," he said anxiously, "you've got to come back. With Wisner's death we're in desperate need of a crime reporter."

"Moses, you know damn well I'll never work for Day again."

He shook his head. "No, no, Davy, hear me out. Ben is a tired man. He's furious over the Robinson case, you walking out on him, and Bennett crowing over him—you know how he hates to lose to Bennett.

Now Webb's dragging him before the grand jury over that horse-express and Locke is the colonel's star witness. I tell you, Davy, the man feels nothing but impotent rage and it's drained him dry."

"If you're looking for sympathy, I gave at the office."

Beach waved his hand. "Ben's found a new toy, Davy. A Sunday weekly called the *Brother Jonathan*. He's decided he's conquered the world of the penny press, and he's sold the *Sun.*"

"Who bought it?"

He reached out and put his hand on my arm. "I bought it," he said with great pride.

I smiled at his obvious pleasure.

"I want you as my crime editor, Davy. I want to do a series on the tricks and methods of the criminal classes—burglars, sneak thieves, pickpockets, banco men—warning decent citizens how to spot them and protect themselves. Do you know how many varieties of confidence games alone are practiced in this city? Quinncannon was telling me about them over dinner at Delmonico's last evening." He grew confidential. "Davy! Have you ever heard of the gold-brick swindle? The panel game? The horse-car game? The eight-dice cloth? Do you know the 'skin stables' dodge? Are you aware there's a man in this city who's sold *the same horse thirty-seven times?*"

I endeavored to look appropriately awed. I wasn't going to admit that, at Princeton College, I had run an eight-dice cloth.

Again Beach seized my arm. "Davy, are you acquainted with Paper Collar Joe Bond, or English Charlie Mason, or Grand Central Pete Lake, or Hungry Joe Lewis? The Irishman knows them all!"

I did not doubt it.

"And you and I are going to expose them, Davy. I'm offering you the position of crime editor with total editorial control of your staff at a salary of . . ." And he named a figure.

But it was the phrase "total editorial control" that stuck in my mind. I heard nothing else, and I accepted.

———

That afternoon I rented a calash and a spirited bay named Caesar and went to Gansevoort Street a-courting.

With the reins in my hand, the lady at my side on the box, the top folded down, and the stupefied coachman seated where the gentry normally ride, we sprinted out of Aunt Abigail's gates and north along the river. The coachman was pacified with a shilling and a promise to retrieve him from the saloon on West Fifteenth where we deposited him. Sophia, Caesar, and I continued toward Harlem.

"Oh, Davy," she said, slipping her arm into mine, "I've been telling some monstrous lies about you. I've almost convinced Father and Marinus that you are descended from General Washington, or at least from an illegitimate son of Benjamin Franklin." She smiled. "I'm afraid Father no longer trusts my judgment in matters of the heart."

"A very wise man, your father."

"Yes, but, Davy, Father has had you investigated, you know. You received an excellent character from Colonel Stone and Mr. Hoffman."

"And Ben Day?"

"Mr. Day referred Father to Arunah S. Abell," she answered, and I laughed out loud.

She released my arm. "I really don't know what is so amusing. It's very important to Father that you stand well with the Whigs."

I reined in the horse suddenly. "Look here, Miss Willett, I'm very much aware that my antecedents are far inferior to yours, and that your family has wealth, while I have hardly two pence to strike a spark with, and I want to tell you something—I don't care! I want you to be my wife, and I want to be your husband, if you and your father will have me."

She placed her hand in mine and looked up at me, smiling. "Oh, sir, I cannot speak for myself," she said, "but Father will have you."


"So, it's after being engaged you are, laddie, or what else ails you at all?"

His slippered feet resting on an ottoman and a glass in his hand, himself sat in a leather wingback chair beside his roaring grate and regarded me with a wry twist at the corner of his mouth where the pipe hung down.

"I am that surely," I said, "for I'm riding the crest of the flood of luck and I've come, master of the house, to ask your blessing and the favor of having you stand up beside me on the glorious day itself."

"I will, then," he said, "and prop you up in the bargain, and tie your blindfold if need be, and kiss your bride while you pay the preacher."

He filled my glass and I sat in the chair opposite his own, and we drank an unspoken toast and lit our pipes and smoked.

# Acknowledgments

O! Time, Strength, Cash and Patience!
Herman Melville

My warm appreciation goes to my editors. To Cork Smith, who believed in this book and stuck with me through thin and thin. To Abby Luttinger, my "partner in crime," whose sage advice and effervescent enthusiasm I cannot repay.

My gratitude also to Raymond V. Paul, who not only offered encouragement but read the manuscript twice, which is clearly beyond the loyalty owed by a father to a son.

And finally to my friend and medical expert, Dr. Gordon Randolph Kelly, whose information was, as always, invaluable and sound.

Troy Hills, New Jersey                                                      RP